50 Miles from Anywhere

50 MILES FROM ANYWHERE

Book 1 in the North Sea Noir series

by
R.M. Cartmel

50 Miles from Anywhere © R.M. Cartmel

ISBN 978-1-912563-09-8
eISBN 978-0-9929486-7-2

Published in 2015 by Crime Scene Books
Previous ISBN: 978-0-9929486-6-5

New edition in 2018 by Crime Scene Books

Cover design by George Foster – www.fostercovers.com

Printed and bound in Great Britain by
Marston Book Services Ltd, Oxfordshire

Peterborough, this one's for you.

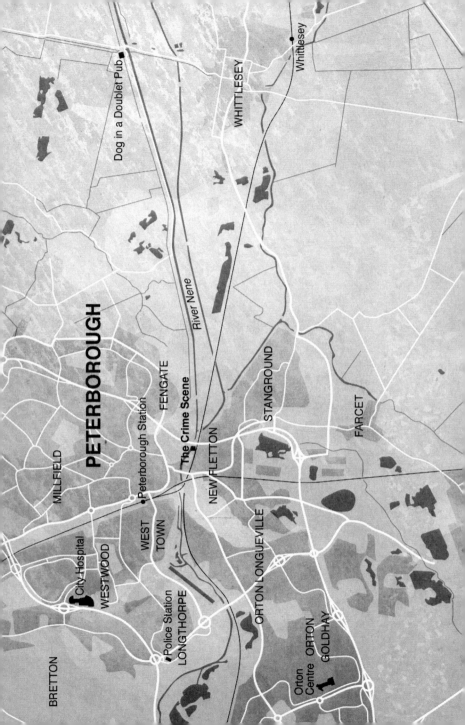

Chapter 1

Steff walked down the library steps. The threatening appearance of the sky caught her eye. It was getting blacker by the minute, she thought, and rain looked imminent. Damn, she wished she had had the foresight to take a mac with her when she had left home that morning, but at that time it had looked bright and sunny. 'Global warming,' she muttered to herself. 'In England we all talk about the weather but we never know what it's going to do from one minute to the next.' Still, if she got home all bedraggled and soggy, then perhaps her uncle might not find her so attractive for once, and she might get a night off her 'domestic duties', so it was an ill wind that brought no good.

She had got about five hundred yards down the road, and was nearly at the bus stop, when it started. Big wet drops they were, not traditional British drizzle but large, cold drops that soaked her to the bone in an instant. She couldn't help holding her folder over her head. Being a star student, she reckoned she would probably get away with, 'My essay got rained on, sir.' Especially as she could produce the sodden remains of the essay in question. She knew others who wouldn't. She broke into a run. It was no longer about avoiding her uncle's urges; it was more about not catching double pneumonia. Oh, for heaven's sake, she could cope with her uncle now. It was ten minutes of tedium, top whack, and that was that. She had tried to discuss the situation once with her aunt, and had been given a simple choice – get her uncle locked up, and go into a foster home somewhere, or lie down and take it like a woman. It had been really a very simple decision to make. It wasn't as if she was a child any more.

'Steff, Steff!' She heard a voice calling her from a minicab that was passing. 'Do you want a lift?' It was Aziz from her French class. The car was slowing to the kerb. Aziz threw open the door and leaped out. She climbed in and settled into the middle of the back seat. Aziz climbed back in after her and pulled the door to.

'You were getting soaked out there,' he said.

'Thanks, Az,' she said. 'It came on so fast.' Her breathing slowed down as she sat back. She looked round the car; there was a young man in a sharp suit on her right who looked slightly older than Az, with a razored haircut round to a very sculpted set of 'burns. There was a large lad up in the passenger seat, and a middle-aged man, slightly thinning on top, who said nothing, behind the wheel. She wondered whether these were the cousins and uncles he had talked about after class. She heard a 'pfsst' sound from her right, and the well-groomed man sitting there passed her a cola can with the ring pulled.

'Drink?' he asked.

She welcomed it eagerly. If she'd been a dog, her tongue would have been hanging out. She took a long pull from the can. It tasted slightly strange, she thought, but then cola did sometimes if it wasn't a familiar brand. Still, it hit the spot. She passed the can back, and the man put it in the cup-holder on the door beside him.

'You going all the way out to Orton Goldhay?' she asked. 'If not, can you drop me off at the bus station in the town centre, and I'll catch a bus from there.'

'Orton Goldhay it is,' said the driver. 'Any friend of Az's. Bloody weather.' Cracked it, she thought. I've managed to score a lift all the way to my aunt's gaff; result! A momentary wave of lethargy passed over her as she caught sight of Az's face. Why does he look so worried? she wondered as she closed her eyes for a moment.

When she was next aware of anything, she was feeling wet again. The rain had stopped, but then so had the car. What's more, she was no longer in it. Her right arm was above her shoulder, and ached, so she tried to straighten it, but it wouldn't move. She pulled on her left arm, and that wouldn't move either. Funny, she thought. Very, very odd. She pulled on her leg and that wouldn't move either and in another moment she was wide awake. She was spread-eagled face up, and her wrists and ankles were stretched wide apart and tied to metal stakes, each lashed down with a thick piece of rope. In the small of her back, there was what felt like a glass bottle; unbroken, but hard and distinctly uncomfortable.

'What the fuck are you doing, guys?' she said angrily. 'Untie me.'

The well-groomed young man turned and snarled at her, 'Shut up, bitch.' She wound herself up to scream, and then stopped before any sound leaked out, as she had spotted what he held in his right hand. It was an Arab dress dagger. It had a curved blade, with a very sharp edge on its concave side; designed to stab into the enemy, and then slit him open with a sharp upward movement.

They locked eyes for a moment. She had seen one of those knives before, and she knew exactly how it worked.

'No, please, no!' she pleaded, wide-eyed, thinking that he was going to cut her up.

'Well then, shut your hole,' he said. She became very quiet indeed. Her eyes hunted round for Az, but he was looking away. The dapper man took Az's raincoat and put it on the ground beside her and knelt down. Looking directly at her, forcing her to watch him, he took hold of the buckle of her belt, undid the belt and pulled it free. It unthreaded itself from the loops in her trousers and came away intact.

'Yaah!' he said, making a movement with it like cracking a whip. 'Mo, a trophy for you,' he said, tossing it towards the big lad.

'Now,' said the dapper man to the girl, 'what are we going to do next, I wonder?' Suddenly the knife was in his hand again. 'I think it has to be this.'

'No,' she sobbed, 'please don't.'

He put his hand inside the waistband of her trousers, and pulled it slightly towards him. She closed her eyes, waiting for the pain, already beginning to hope it wouldn't last very long. She felt the cold of the knife blade against her right hip. She felt the knife run all the way down her leg to the ankle. To her surprise, it didn't hurt; it just felt cold.

3

'Halfway there,' said the dapper man. She looked down at her leg. Her trousers had been slit from belt to ankle and her leg was open to the air, but it wasn't bleeding.

When he pulled on the waistband on the left side, it came easily, but he still managed to persuade the knife to slit the cloth, and the outside of her left leg was exposed to the air too. The dapper man pulled at her trousers and what was left of her panties, and they came away in his hand. He waved them as if they were a toreador's coat. 'Mo?' he asked.

The big lad they called Mo took the clothes. 'I don't know, Ruke,' he said. 'Why do we always go for skinny white girls? Why don't we get a girl with a bit of meat on her for once?'

'Az picked this one,' replied the dapper man they called Ruke. 'Blame him.'

Ruke turned back to the girl. 'Now you probably have some idea what's going to happen next,' he said. 'You damned white Kafaar bitches are all the same.' He put his hand on her vulva and started massaging her. He found her clitoris, and caressed it almost gently.

'Oh, please don't,' Steff sobbed, trying to buck away from his hand. The awful knowing intimacy of his touch was almost worse than any violence.

'See, the little tart's up for it,' said Ruke, 'all juicy and raring to go.' He moved across and pulled his trousers down to his knees, releasing his erection. He guided himself into the girl.

There was an elongated 'No-o-o', which the girl didn't think came from her, followed by a muffled thud. Ruke may have appeared stylish, but it only took him a few seconds to spend himself inside her. 'I've left some jizz in there to keep her lubricated for the next customer,' he said as he stood up. 'Next?'

'Me,' said the big one they called Mo. He tossed the girl's clothes at Ruke, dropped his jeans to his ankles, and almost collapsed on top of the spread-eagled girl. The sudden extra weight almost suffocated her, and she screamed.

'Shut the bitch up, Ruke, I can't cope with all that yelling in my ear.' Ruke took the remains of her panties, still intact at the gusset, but cut at both ends of the elastic, and fashioned a gag, which he pulled into her mouth. She struggled against the

4

gag, and the huge man pushing into her, and lost both battles. Tears were now streaming down her face. She felt a dreadful ripping sensation deep inside her. Behind her back, she could also no longer feel the milk bottle. Had he crushed that too? She lay completely still, to avoid getting glass shards in her back, wanting to get the whole filthy business over as soon as possible. Mo was more like her uncle. There was nothing subtle about him. He breathed in her face, and the smell of garlic on his breath forced its way up her nose. By now he was really hurting her, but she couldn't scream because of the gag.

'Mo, what did you do to Az?' asked Ruke over her shoulder. In between pig-like grunts, Mo told him that Az was making so much fuss that he'd hit him.

'What with?' asked Ruke.

Mo, on the point of coming, said in a howl that he'd hit him with his sap.

'Leave the jizz in there as a lube,' reminded Ruke.

Mo pulled out of the girl and examined himself.

'Oh, you bitch,' he said and punched the girl hard. 'There's blood all over my knob. Have you just started your period, you cow? She didn't bleed all over you, did she, Ruke?'

'No, she didn't, but I'm still worried about Az. He isn't moving. How hard did you hit him?'

Mo turned to the taxi driver. 'Your turn,' he said, 'she's nicely jizzed up for you.' He got up and walked away, wiping himself. 'What's this about Az?'

'Well, this is his initiation thing, and he did get us a girl, like we said…'

'Not much of a girl. Oh, come on, get up, Az, don't be a wuss. I didn't hit you that hard.'

'I think you did,' said Ruke grimly.

The driver knelt down between Steff's legs, and then looked at Ruke. 'Oh man!' he said. 'What have you done? Ruke, next time, bags I go before Mo. She's bleeding like a stuck one here. This isn't a fucking period – look, he's burst her.'

Ruke bent down and looked between the girl's legs. There was a steady flow of fresh bright red blood coming from her.

'Oh fuck, Mo, what did you do to her too? We can't take you anywhere, can we?'

They all left the spread-eagled girl, and went to look at the fallen boy.

'Oh, fuck, Mo, you've fucking killed them both. You're a fucking disaster today, aren't you?'

'Well, at least we've got a solution to the problem of what we do with her,' Mo replied, and picked Az up. 'Pull his kecks down to his knees,' he said. The driver unbuckled Az's belt and pulled his jeans down. Mo then arranged Az on top of Steff, as if they were doing the business. 'She'll bleed out, and when they find them, people will think that she killed him too and no one will be any the wiser.' He flicked his toe under the steel stake that restrained her right hand, uprooting it from the ground where she lay. Making a glove with his coat, he wiped the stake over Az's left temple, where he had previously hit him, and then he carefully put the stake in Steff's outstretched right hand. She closed her fingers round it, but she was already too weak to move her friend's dead body from on top of her, let alone swing the stake with any force.

Ruke picked up her bag, and pulled the wallet and phone out of Az's pocket. 'That'll make it a little more difficult for everybody,' he said, putting Az's things in her handbag.

'Let's go, lads,' he said, apologising to the driver for having missed his turn, and they walked down to the car park by the railway track, climbed into the minicab and drove off.

Chapter 2

The little dog was snuffling around the rubbish. Suddenly it yapped, and looked up at the old man it knew so well and wagged its tail.

'What you found there, boy?' came an old male voice. The dog yapped again, and the old man walked over to where his little friend was pointing with his little wet nose. Suddenly he realised what the dog was looking at.

'Oh my giddy fuck,' he said, looking at a pair of bare brown buttocks pointing into the air. The owner's trousers were down round his knees. The buttocks were positioned between a pair of rather paler bare legs, presumably supine, as the feet were pointing upwards; those legs were wearing socks and trainers only. They were separated and tied in that position by ropes to steel stakes. Neither moved. Motionless in the missionary position, he thought, flippantly, then called out to the dog, 'Get away from them, right now!' He approached them slowly. 'Hello there, are you all right?' he asked. He couldn't imagine why they weren't moving, considering the position they were in. It might have been the staring expression in the girl's open eyes, or it might have been the blood, that he spotted first. The memory of both never left him from that day forward. It was the girl's good fortune that he was carrying a mobile phone, and knew how to use it.

'Hello, emergency services, which service do you require?' he heard in his ear.

'Ambulance, police, oh God!' he said.

'Ambulance or police?' said the voice testily. 'We don't have a hot line to the Almighty as an emergency service.'

'Both,' he replied.

'Please describe the location and the nature of your emergency.'

'I'm by the Nene Valley railway station underneath the railway arches, off the Oundle Road, near the Green Backyard. I'm walking my dog.' Once he had explained what he was looking at, the voice told him, in the same unemotional tone, that an ambulance and a police car would be with him as soon as possible.

He looked back at the kids. That's all they were, a couple of teenagers enjoying themselves, perhaps for the first time, and it appeared to have gone horribly wrong. He had no idea what had actually happened, but he walked slightly closer and looked at them more carefully. The girl, her shortish straw-coloured hair awry, he noticed, was holding another of the steel stakes that pinned her ankles to the ground, in her right hand. She wasn't brandishing it or anything, but it looked as if she might have. Her outstretched left hand was near another stake, which was still deep in the ground.

Had the boy tied her legs down before they started playing around? he wondered. He looked more closely at the person he took to be a girl. What was that round her face? Surely she hadn't got a black beard? Maybe she was a he? But why would he dye his hair straw, or perhaps only dye his beard black? The old man was getting increasingly confused. No, hang on, that was a piece of black cloth tied round her mouth like a mask. The little bugger, he thought, he's tied her down and then gagged her before having his way with the poor little girl. No wonder she hit him with the stake: serves him right too. The old man knelt down beside the girl's head, and felt behind it for the knot. It was tight, but not too tight for his old bony fingers to work it loose. Once the piece of cloth hung in his hands, he realised what it was. It was a pair of knickers that had been cut at the outside of both leg holes. Were they hers? he wondered. She wasn't wearing any others.

He wasn't waiting very long before rotating blue lights joined him under the arches of the railway embankment. They couldn't have been busy that night, he thought.

The crew got out of the ambulance and carried their bags over to the scene. The paramedic was already kneeling by the couple when two uniformed police officers arrived in a marked car.

'I think the girl's still alive,' said the paramedic.

'And the boy?' asked the smaller of the two policewomen, in a soft southern Irish accent.

'I don't think so; I can't feel a pulse. Can I move them?'

'If the girl's still alive, then you need to get to her, so sure.' She pulled a camera out of her pocket and said, 'I'm going to try to preserve as much of the scene as we can before we have to wreck it.' She snapped away until she was satisfied she'd captured all the details she needed.

They lifted the boy off the girl. His penis dragged up across the girl's labia. It was partly stuck to her by drying blood. The ambulance driver swore and pulled the boy's trousers back up. The paramedic took out an ophthalmoscope and looked into the boy's eyes. 'Pupils fixed and dilated.' She pulled a stethoscope out of her pocket and slapped it onto his chest. 'No heart or breath sounds; this boy is dead,' she said.

The little old man with the dog thought to himself that it was rough justice, but if what he thought had happened was actually how it had gone down, then perhaps the boy deserved it.

The driver, meanwhile, had put a blood pressure cuff round the girl's arm. He had also thrown a blanket over her lower half to preserve her modesty.

'Nine gets you one, I know what was going on here,' he remarked coldly, 'and it didn't do much good to either of them.'

The paramedic ignored him, concentrating on the girl's vital signs.

'Pulse one-twenty, regular; BP eighty over fifty-five. She's cold and going into shock.' She turned to the police officer. 'Can we grab and run, please?'

'Go for it,' said the Irish police officer. 'I've got all the pictures I need.' She helped them untie the girl's ankles from the stakes, so now all her limbs were free.

Both of the ambulance crew ran to the back of the ambulance and pulled out the trolley, and a scoop. The driver split the scoop into its component halves, and slid one half under

9

the girl's left side. Under her other side they slid the other half and then snapped the two ends together. The girl wasn't particularly heavy, and they lifted her easily onto the trolley. The paramedic stabilised her neck with rubber blocks on either side of her ears, in case she had damaged her neck. The last thing she needed was to be permanently crippled by a moment of carelessness by those who were saving her life at the scene – if she survived. The trolley was then wheeled to the back of the ambulance, and loaded in. The paramedic climbed in with her, and slipped a Venflon cannula into one of the veins visible under the skin of her right arm. Within seconds, isotonic saline solution was dripping into the girl to keep her fluid volume up.

'Go for it, Reg.' She tapped on the window between her and the ambulance's cab. 'Blues and twos,' she added. As they went out under the arches back into the car park, another ambulance was pulling in. Reg waved at his colleagues as they arrived, but didn't slow down. The flashing blue lights on top of the police car would guide the second ambulance to the scene.

Chapter 3

The ambulance drew up to the doors of the Accident and Emergency department. The paramedic who had been working in the back of the ambulance on the bleeding girl announced she'd got a line in and there was a bag of saline up.

'Her BP is eighty-five over sixty, and her pulse is a bit thready,' she told the sister who came out of the department to receive the new patient. The paramedic added, 'She was assaulted, and almost certainly raped. Bleeding p.v. She's not been conscious since we collected her from the scene. No IV analgesia administered, as she wasn't complaining of pain.' Two porters appeared out of nowhere alongside the sister, and they wheeled the girl down the ramp into the department.

'Take her into resus,' said the sister, rapidly assessing the situation, 'She needs blood, a couple of bags of O neg, and then cross-match four units. Bleep the on-call gynae. *Fast.*'

The senior registrar in charge of the department that night walked into the cubicle and raised an eyebrow at the paramedic who was still handing over to the sister. He was followed by a medical student, still young enough to be recovering from teenage acne. The doctor took the girl's blood pressure, and flicked open both her eyelids, and looked in with an ophthalmoscope. 'Any history of head injury?' he asked.

'None that we know of, but there was a dead boy out there too, so we don't really know what went on. They were both naked from the waist down. It looks like a bit of teenage hanky-panky that went horribly wrong.'

'Name?'

'She didn't have any ID on her, or a phone,' said the paramedic. 'Sorry, no idea.' They took blood samples and sent them off to the lab. A bag of O Rhesus negative blood replaced the bag of saline, dribbling down the giving set into the girl. The doctor took a speculum from the instrument trolley and looked

11

into the girl's vagina. All he could see was fresh blood, still flowing, and the red was bright enough for it to be arterial.

'I think she needs to be prepped for surgery,' he said. 'I know it's not my call, but it's what I would do if I was the gynaecologist. We've got to stop that haemorrhage, and I can't see where she's bleeding from. Can we get hold of the on-call anaesthetist PDQ?'

A normal night it was, therefore, in Peterborough Casualty. This time it was an assault. On other occasions it might be a road accident or a mugging, and that was only the major trauma side of the business. There were also medical and surgical emergencies that went through there, which were not created directly by the hand of man. It was where the major cases were filtered and triaged to the appropriate departments deeper within the hospital, and the trivia were strapped up, patted on the head and booted back out into the city to find another reason to come back later.

The anaesthetist, Rena, was the first to arrive. She was a young woman who looked desperately in need of sleep. She too checked the girl's vital signs but did not examine the area that was bleeding; that would be the gynaecologist's business when he arrived. It was her job to keep the patient alive until he did. Further blood samples were taken for haematology and chemistry, including toxicology. They knew that the ambulance men hadn't given her any medication while she was in their care, but that didn't mean that she hadn't taken any drugs earlier that evening. Rena cleaned the vulva, and passed a sterile urinary catheter into the girl's bladder. There was only a small amount of urine, which the sister collected in a sterile pot, then dip-tested it. There was no sugar in it, and only minimal blood. This suggested that the blood that appeared to be everywhere had not come from the bladder.

'Can you do a simple drug screen on that too?' Rena asked. The sister poured what was left of the urine into a small pot and dip-tested it with a drug screen kit. She looked at the screen and said, 'No opiates, cocaine or methadone; positive for benzodiazepines.' So she had taken a benzo or two that day. The test strip did not tell them how much benzo there was in her system, just that there was some. This wasn't so much of a problem in the absence of the drugs, and suggested that her current state of unconsciousness was the result of the trauma she had suffered, not an overdose.

The final arrival was the gynaecology registrar. He was well-dressed and smart. He took a quick history from the Casualty team, and laid his hands on the girl's abdomen. He asked for a swab on a sponge holder, as well as a speculum to look in her vagina. Once he had cleared the clot out of her vagina, he could see more clearly. There was a trickle of fresh arterial-looking blood coming from her cervix, and severe bruising alongside it in the left fornix. It all looked swollen, and dangerous. The vagina itself looked okay.

'She's still bleeding in there,' he said. 'I think we should take her straight to theatre for a laparoscopy, with a view to full laparotomy if it turns out necessary. Can we cross-match four units?'

'Already ahead of you on that,' said the anaesthetist, 'We've got another bag of O neg waiting for her, and the cross-match should be ready by the time we're in theatre.'

'Let's get her up there, then,' said the registrar. 'Post-op she'll need to go to the ITU. Are there any beds still in there?'

'I'll check on that,' said the sister. A moment or so later, she put the phone down, announcing that there was one left, and she had booked it for their Jane Doe.

The Casualty officer looked at the medical student who was standing behind him.

'Did you get all that?' he asked.

The student replied, 'I think so. The girl who has just come in is still bleeding from the cervix, and the gynaecologist wants to take her to theatre now to look in with a telescope to see if he can see where she's bleeding from. He also wants to be prepared to do a full open operation if he can't stop it down the laparoscope. Following that, she is going to be admitted to the intensive care unit – er, you call it the intensive treatment unit here, to be monitored.'

'Well done, that lad,' said the Casualty doctor. He turned to the registrar. 'Do you have a student with you?' he asked.

13

'Not at the moment,' replied the gynaecologist.

'Would you object if mine shadowed you, to follow this case through?'

'Not at all.'

The Casualty consultant turned back to the student. 'Well, lad, you've got a choice. We've no idea what is going to come through that door for the rest of the evening, and you can take pot luck, or you can follow this case through as a potential "long case" for your exams and see what happens. Up to you.'

'May I follow the case, sir?' he asked.

'Your student, Ahmed. I'll see you later, then.'

'Cheers, Manfred,' said the gynaecologist, and turning to the student he continued, 'Follow me. Have you ever been in an operating theatre before?'

'Yes, sir,' he said, 'in my first surgical attachment and in my orthopaedic firm too.'

'In which case, you're a positive expert, and you needn't call me "sir"; you're almost up there with me. Call me Ahmed.'

'I'm John,' the student replied.

'We'll have a houseman up there as well, and I'll try to include you both; but it all depends on what we find. What I saw was arterial blood from the cervical os, and severe bruising and swelling in the left lateral fornix.'

'Sorry?' said the student.

'The pocket to the left of the cervix, where the cervix pushes through the pelvic floor. It looks like she's still bleeding in there, and we've got to see how serious it is. We may need to go in and tie off the bleeder.' The medical student was now deep in the everyday business of saving lives, and the decision-making process.

They arrived in the operating theatre's anteroom together. Here they changed into surgical scrubs, which would be used for this one operation, and then put in the bin to be thoroughly washed in the hospital laundry. The student was amazed how the surgical scrubs seemed to grow smart creases when worn by Ahmed the gynaecologist, but still looked untidy on himself. From the anteroom with its lockers, they walked through to the room where they scrubbed up. On the way through, they both drew on a face mask, so that neither of them would breathe germs into the wound – or was it to protect them from an infected wound they might be about to incise? Both consultants, in whose firms he had worked so far, had emphasised the importance of personal safety first.

'The country has spent a small fortune in training you, and the last thing it wants is for you to kill yourself before it's got its money's worth. Always bear that in mind when you're thinking about being a hero.'

They scrubbed up and then a nurse helped them into sterile gowns, and tied them round their backs, and finally dressed them in a pair of pre-packaged rubber gloves. The student already knew his size was seven and a quarter. They walked through into the operating theatre. The houseman was already there, scrubbed and dressed, talking to one of the nurses. The registrar briefed him about what they were going to do, and introduced him to the student.

From a different entrance to the theatre a porter wheeled Steff, already prepared and connected to the gas trolley, followed by the anaesthetist.

'She's ready,' she said. 'I suggest we get on with it, as she's not too well, and I want her out of here as soon as possible.'

The registrar once again got a 'swab on a stick' and dipped it in iodine cleaning fluid. He inserted it into her vagina to make everything as sterile as possible. He then took an alarming-looking pair of tongs called a vulsellum, and clipped it onto the cervix. He called the houseman down to hang on to the vulsellum, while he moved up to the abdomen. He cleaned the abdomen with iodine too, and caught Rena's eye. She nodded to him to go ahead. The sister passed him a cylindrical probe with a sharp end.

It took him a few moments to get the probe through the skin at the bottom of the umbilicus. There was very little fat on this girl. He pumped her stomach up with a little air, and slotted the laparoscope down the probe and into her stomach.

'Light,' he said. 'Suction,' and the nurse sucked the blood out of the wound. He looked at the anaesthetist. 'How's the patient?' he asked.

'Still alive,' came the dry reply.

'I need to do a formal laparotomy; she's haemorrhaging into the left broad ligament, and I can't do anything through a laparoscope; she might blow at any minute.'

'Go for it,' said the anaesthetist, as the theatre porter walked in with two more bags of blood, and told her there were another two on the way.

So the registrar opened the girl up from the pelvis nearly to the umbilicus. He needed good access as quickly as possible while causing minimal trauma to the anterior abdominal wall, so that he could then close the incision quickly and easily. Both doctors and the student could see the damage to the left broad ligament, the 'hanger' that stretched from one side of the pelvis to the other, with the uterus hanging in the middle of it. The right side of the uterus was slender and healthy-looking, while on the left it was swollen and dark and looked under pressure. Was it just his imagination, or was that broad ligament actually pulsating? He took the decision that needed to be taken to save her life.

'That uterus has certainly never carried a baby, and I'm going to have to do a hysterectomy,' said Ahmed to himself and silently apologised to all the children she was never going to have. 'Clamp,' and he stuck the curved clamp on the broad ligament as close to the pelvic wall as he could.

Ahmed was a neat and tidy surgeon, and Rena was a good anaesthetist, so the girl survived the operation. Afterwards, she was wheeled from theatre into the ITU, while the two surgeons and the medical student went back through to the anteroom, stripped off their blood-stained scrubs, and got back into their ordinary hospital gear.

'Sorry, I wasn't talking very much in there,' Ahmed said to the student. 'We had one or two quite tense moments when I thought we might lose her; and if I had dropped a blob, there would have been blood everywhere, a theatre in need of a deep clean, and a dead girl. We'll find out exactly what had blown in that broad ligament when we get the results back from histology.'

'You took the cervix out too,' said the student.

'We had to take the uterus, as its blood supply is in the broad ligament, so why leave the cervix behind? She won't need it, and it's one less piece of tissue to turn malignant on her later in life. The left ovary was also a complete mess so I took that too. We needed to be in and out as quickly as possible, and as she's only going to need one ovary from here on in, I left the right one behind as it was undamaged, so she'll still have her normal supply of hormones, until she goes through the change. I left the vagina behind, and closed the end off, where the cervix used to be, so she can still have a bit of fun. As my old tutor used to say, we took the factory, but still left her with the playground. I have to say, though, if I could find the bastard who did this to her, I would do some surgery on him too, and I wouldn't bother wasting any anaesthetist's time in the process.'

Chapter 4

As the ambulance left the scene of the crime, it started raining again. The uniformed officers huddled together waiting for the crime scene officers, the police surgeon and the first detectives to arrive. The smaller of the two sounded Irish enough, but her colouring was darker than one usually associates with those from the Emerald Isle, suggesting either a very recent Caribbean holiday, or maybe a little more likely a drop of Caribbean blood in her genetic make-up. The other girl was chunkier. Of the two, she looked as if her extremities would be the first to turn blue if they were left standing around in the rain much longer. Once again the raindrops were big, wet and cold. The paramedics were itching to get back on station, as they might be needed to collect a living patient to ship to the hospital. Little John, the huge ambulance driver at the scene, looked as if Mother Nature had been contemplating making a gorilla, and then changed her mind at the last minute, and given him a larynx. Bill, the paramedic of the team, was rather more practically constructed, which made it easier for him to move about and work on a patient in the back of an ambulance on the move. Both of them knew if there was a scramble then they would be off, and that would be that, but at the same time they knew they would probably feel guilty if they left these two uniformed girls at the site on their own with the corpse. They were well aware that there had been no witnesses to the attack, and if it hadn't been for the old boy walking his dog, the victims would still be out there. Were the perpetrators still out there as well, hiding and watching? The girl had been taken to hospital in the other ambulance, but the boy was dead, and therefore this was now a murder scene and shouldn't be disturbed any more than necessary to save a life until it had been examined and released by the forensics team. Well, the scene had been well disturbed to save that life which was now on its way to hospital. It was with some relief to all that another blue light appeared under the arches.

It was an unmarked car driven by a detective constable. Wasn't it all pretty pointless them driving an incognito car if they were going to flash blue lights from its radiator grille, thought Little John, but I'm not a plod and never did understand their logic, so there you go. From the passenger side a detective inspector climbed out. He was just under six foot tall, lean and gaunt, or putting it another way, dwarfed by the ambulance driver. His face did not look as if it smiled easily without damaging its musculature in some way.

'I'm DI Drake. Somebody tell me what's going on here then.'

The Irish uniformed PC spoke up.

'I'm Constable Flynn,' she said. 'We were called to the site by a 999 call. A bystander had discovered the scene while out walking his dog. He had also called an ambulance at the same time, which got here at the same time as us. There were two victims on the scene, a girl who was still alive, and the boy you see there.'

'Where's the girl?'

'On her way to hospital under blue lights,' said Bill.

Drake looked at the ambulance driver coldly. 'The constable was telling me her version of the story,' he said. 'If you want to change anything, you may speak after she has finished. Constable? Carry on.' He nodded at his driver, 'Take notes,' he said, and the driver pulled out a green notebook and black biro. He stood poised to write.

The ambulance men looked at each other for a moment. There was no reason why anyone should speak to them like that. Little John was about to collect their kit from the scene to put it back in the ambulance when Drake spoke to them again over the constable, who had just started speaking again.

'You're not moving anything until we've got all the pictures taken. This, gentlemen, do I have to remind you, is a crime scene. Constable, you were saying?'

'The boy over there has been moved, sir,' she said, sounding dismayed.

'Why?'

'Because he was lying on top of the girl, and the paramedics needed to get to her. She was tied to the ground by both ankles and her left arm to those stakes. And he was on top.' She pointed to the stakes, which were still where they had been placed. 'She was still alive, sir.'

'What else did you do to him when you arrived apart from move him?'

'We pulled his trousers up, sir. They were round his knees. We thought that the crime scene would be better preserved by his not getting dirt all over his bits, sir.'

'His what?'

'His bits, sir.' She struggled for a moment. 'His genitals.'

'And why were his genitals open to the air?'

'I don't know, sir, but they were in contact with hers.'

'And they too were open to the air?'

'Yes, sir.'

'Were her clothes pulled down to her knees too, then?'

'No, sir, she wasn't wearing anything below the waist, apart from ankle socks and trainers. She was wearing what was left of her knickers as a gag. They're still at the scene, marking where she was lying.'

'So the scene's a bit compromised, then?'

'Yes, sir, but on the other hand, the girl might still be alive.'

The arrival of the crime scene team in a black Ford Transit stopped all conversation for the moment. They were dressed in smocks and had cameras hanging round their necks. They looked like a convention of beekeepers on tour somewhere. The divisional surgeon got out of the passenger side and checked Aziz's vital signs. He stood up and formally declared life to be extinct.

'Any idea, off the top of your head, of the cause of death, doc?' asked DI Drake.

'Well, I wouldn't like to commit myself at the moment, but that is a very nasty blow he has to his left temple.' He turned back to the victim, while the crime scene photographers went to business with their flashing cameras.

The DI turned to the ambulance team. 'Anything you want to add to that?' he asked.

The ambulance men looked at each other, and decided that they didn't want to have any further contact with this man if they could help it. He took their reference numbers so that the police could get in touch with them as witnesses. Big John asked the crime scene officer if they could take their kit now, with an assertive 'please' tagged on to the end of the sentence. They were told they could, but carefully. It was with an unfeasibly light tread for so big a man that Little John picked up the bags from the scene, and took them back to the ambulance. Once the bags were all securely stowed, the two ambulance men climbed into the cab, and drove off.

'Are you telling me that she came here wearing only socks and knickers on a cold night like this?'

'I'm not telling you anything, sir, I'm merely observing that there was no evidence of skirt or jeans when we got here.'

'Was her top on?'

'Untouched, as far as we could see. She was wearing a sweater which was quite wet, but then it had been raining.'

'A wet sweater, eh? Did it show up her shape?'

'Not particularly, sir; there wasn't a lot of the girl, and what there was, it was mostly bone and sinew, as far as I could tell.'

'Smaller than you, then?'

'Yes.'

'So she wouldn't be much of a kissogram girl, then?'

'Would you be after implying that I am?' said Constable Flynn who, while not averse to being considered pretty if it was to her advantage, was not so sure about it at this moment. 'Would you be after being a bit of a larrikin yourself, sergeant?' she asked roguishly.

'I am an inspector,' replied Drake drily, 'and I so hope you're not disrespecting a senior officer, constable.'

'Now would I ever be after doing a 'ting like dat, inspector?' she replied, still in an exaggerated accent, emphasising his rank, but they both knew that that was the last they would hear of her Irish blarney that evening.

'So describe to me exactly how they were.'

'Well, she was lying down on her back tied to three steel stakes that pinned her to the ground. The fourth stake was in her right hand, though she wasn't gripping it, being unconscious. He was on top with his trousers round his knees, between her legs. It looked like they were having sex, but there was no movement. We got there at the same time as the first ambulance, and they found signs of life in her, so we lifted him off, and they untied her, piled her into the ambulance and set off for the hospital. We did pull his trousers back up before we laid him down in more or less the same position he was before, but without a girl underneath him.'

'And his trousers pulled up.' Drake sighed.

'And his trousers pulled up,' agreed Flynn.

'So there's absolutely nothing left of the crime scene as it was when you got here.' The sound of annoyance in his voice was inescapable.

'Not much,' said the constable. 'I did, however, take a load of pictures,' she added, and continued, 'but you know something else; the girl may still be alive.'

'You had better keep your fingers crossed that she stays so, or you will have absolutely no excuse for disturbing the scene at all, and I will be so all over you for it.' And they both knew that he was not thinking in a sexual way, not even slightly.

Chapter 5

'Morning, class,' said the teacher cheerfully, looking around the room at the kids, who looked awake and eager to learn. There was an empty desk near the front. 'There's a lesson we can all learn from this morning: if you're going to skive off school, don't do it with the person you sit next to in class. It's stupidly obvious straight away because it leaves a gap. Anyone seen Steff or Az?'

The class shuffled its collective feet. No, no one had seen them since yesterday was the general consensus.

'Well, let's get on with it now, and we'll chase them up during break if they haven't rolled in, blaming a broken-down bus or other such excuse. A broken-down bus? Anybody? Anybody?'

'*L'autobus est en panne*,' replied a bright-looking girl in the front row, waving her right arm in the air.

'*Pas mal du tout*, Julie,' he replied.

The missing kids had not appeared by break, and the teacher went down to the head teacher's office to see whether she knew that they were missing and, if so, did she have any reason or excuse from the parents. Well, not Steff's parents, because they had died in a road accident a couple of years ago, but from the aunt and uncle she now lived with.

'No, nobody's phoned in about either of them so far,' replied the head. 'I'll get in touch with the guardians straight away.' She pressed the intercom and spoke to her secretary. 'Could you get Stephanie Flack's guardians, and Aziz Shadeed's parents on the line?' she asked. After a moment the secretary came back to her.

'I've got Steff's aunt here,' she said.

'Hello, I'm Mrs Cookes, Stephanie's head teacher. We were just wondering whether Steff is all right? She's not turned up for school this morning.'

'Er,' the aunt sounded uncomfortable for a moment. 'No, she didn't come home last night. We assumed she was staying over with one of her friends.'

'Does she do that often?' asked the head.

'No, but she does from time to time.'

'Doesn't it worry you when you don't see her?'

'Not so much now she's a grown-up.'

'She is only fifteen.'

'Yes, but she's got all those GCSEs and she is now doing her A-levels, so that's grown-up, and all her friends in her class are older than she is. She's very clever, is our Steff.'

The head felt slightly uncomfortable. It was obvious that the girl had not inherited her intelligence from her aunt.

'Would you know which friend she is staying with? Everyone apart from Aziz Shadeed has come in to school this morning.'

'Oh, I wouldn't think she'd be staying over with *him*,' said the aunt, emphasising the 'him' as if Az was something stuck to the sole of her shoe. 'Her boyfriend would never allow that.'

'Would she be staying over with this boyfriend?' This was the first time the head had ever heard of Steff's boyfriend, but what did teachers know? Come to think about it, what do aunts know either? Steff and Az do sit next to each other in class, she thought.

'She doesn't usually go out on school nights,' replied the aunt, 'but I'll check for you if you like.'

'Yes, I would appreciate that, thank you.'

The aunt disconnected and the head put the phone down. She felt slightly saddened. She quite liked young Steff, and she had rather hoped that she would have stayed a child rather longer than she obviously had. Anyway, she hoped that this boyfriend was at least on the same intellectual level as Steff. She was a bright kid; the head hoped she would get into university. It worried her that Steff's boyfriend might be the sort who wouldn't 'allow' her to do things. What might he do to her to prevent her? she wondered.

The secretary came through to her a moment later. 'I've just spoken to Aziz's sister-in-law on the phone and he didn't go home last night either. She was surprised about that, but then she didn't say any more. There was obviously someone else there as well – she was talking to someone else at the same time in their own language. Not very helpful, I'm afraid.'

'Do you have the sister-in-law's name?' asked the head.

'No, I'm afraid not. I phoned the number and asked if there was anyone there who spoke English, and they put her on. I asked about Aziz and she said that she was his sister-in-law. That was as far as I got.'

'Can you get them back for me please?' Mrs Cookes asked. 'I'll hang on the line.'

'Hello?' she said when she got through, 'I'm Aziz Shadeed's head teacher.'

'Not here,' said a distinctly male voice back to her.

'Is his sister-in-law there? I understand she speaks English.'

'Not here,' replied the same male.

'She was there a moment ago,' she said.

'Not here,' replied the male again.

She realised she wasn't going to get anywhere with that, so with a cheery 'bye,' she put the phone down. And now she felt very uncomfortable. Ten minutes later she felt even more uncomfortable. She had finished the cup of tea on her desk, and Steff's aunt had phoned back and said that she'd talked to Steff's boyfriend's mum, and Steff hadn't been there at all the previous night, but her son had been there all night playing computer games.

She picked up the phone and dialled. When the phone was answered: 'Cambridgeshire Constabulary, Thorpe Road Police Station, how can I help you?' she introduced herself and explained that she'd got two students who hadn't turned up for class that morning, and that neither set of families seemed to know where the children were, or where they had been the night before either.

'Putting you through,' said the voice down the phone.

'Children's and Young Person's Officer, Sergeant Warwick speaking, how can I help you?' came a voice after an internal phone had rung a couple of times. The head explained who she was and why she was calling. She gave him all the details she had of the missing students.

'Could I take your number for when I need to call you back?' said the sergeant. 'I'll look into this for you straight away.'

Straight away? she thought. That sounded ominous. Maybe the sergeant had heard something as he came in that morning, and he was going to check the story.

Chapter 6

Before Sergeant Warwick left his own office he had phoned the constable standing watch in the ITU at the City Hospital, and confirmed that last night's Jane Doe was still alive. He told her he may have an ID for her, and was going to try and find a relative. He then wandered downstairs into the incident room to see whether there was anyone still there. There was: a rather worried – looking detective constable looking at the screen.

'I think I've got a possible ID on your vics,' said Sergeant Warwick. 'It may be coincidental, of course, but you know I don't believe in coincidence.'

'Go on.'

'There's a girl called Stephanie Flack and a boy called Aziz Shadeed who didn't turn up for school this morning, and the headmistress of their school says that both sets of parents told her that neither kid came home last night.'

'Do we have addresses for them?'

'Oh yes, the headmistress was very thorough.' He passed his notebook over to DC Odembe. The African copied the addresses down into his notebook, and passed Warwick's back to him.

'As it looks like the Flack girl is still alive, I'll take a uniformed PC with me and go and see the aunt. Let's hope they have an up-to-date photo of the girl in the house. I always hate bringing a stressed relative to see someone in hospital and they turn round and say to me, "What you brought me here for? He ain't the guy".'

Odembe grinned at Warwick, knowing he was a Dylan fan, and would take any opportunity to quote from one of his songs.

'You think you got problems? You take someone down to the mortuary to see their offspring, and you've been preparing them for what they're about to see, and they come back to you

29

and say, "No that's not my son, but I can tell you who it is if you like".'

Warwick shuddered and said, 'You win. So you're going off to see the Shadeeds, then?'

'I'll do that, as soon as the office manager gets back. I'm holding the fort while he's gone off somewhere. I'm sure he'll be back shortly. As soon as he is, I'm off to see the Shadeeds. We'll meet back here later? I'm sure Inspector Drake will be slightly happier if we have definite names attached to his vics.'

Constable Flynn was just walking through the front door of the police station, coming back on duty, when she was spotted by Sergeant Warwick. 'You were involved in that mess down by the Nene Valley railway station last night, weren't you?' he asked her.

'The city centre end? That was me, yes,' she said.

'Was there another incident on the Nene Valley railway last night?' he asked.

'Not that I know of, but if there was one, then I'm telling you which one I was involved with.'

'Right,' he said slowly and then continued, 'I think we've got an ID on those kids. Do you want to come with me? We're going to see the girl's aunt.'

'Oh yes,' she said. 'I'd much rather go with you and see a relative of someone's who's still living than get dragged off to see the relatives of someone who's dead. I think that's the part of this job I hate the most: giving bad news. It really buggers up their days. Lead on, sarge. Hang on, I'll just sign in, and then sign out again. I would hate for the paymasters to think I was skiving off this morning.' And having done that, she trotted out of the front door after Warwick.

She climbed into the passenger side of a marked police car, as he was already buckling himself into the driving seat.

'Where to, sarge?' she asked.

He grinned at her. 'Guess,' he said as he turned left out of the police car park, onto Thorpe Wood, and past the golf club. They came up to the roundabout at the end of the road and took the third exit down onto the Nene Parkway.

'One of the Ortons,' she said. 'It's got to be.'

'Ah yes,' he replied, 'but which one of them? Every year we get a new Orton. I think the council ought to start thinking about putting township contraceptives in the water supply.'

'At a guess,' she said, 'Goldhay. I'm sure it's the biggest.'

'We certainly get more punters from there anyway,' he agreed with her. They turned onto the Fletton Parkway towards the motorway, but almost immediately hung a left up and round the roundabout over the Parkway into Orton Goldhay itself. He tried to imagine the suburb in another fifty years' time when the new, modernistic houses had aged, and some of the timber facing had begun to rot. He didn't believe for a moment that the wood had been preserved the same way that the old Tudor woodwork from five hundred years ago had been. And anyway, he reckoned that a lot of the old houses built when the last Henrys were on the throne had long since fallen down, and at least two generations of new buildings had been built on top of their sites.

They pulled into one of the cul de sacs off Goldhay Way, and threaded their way down it. Warwick was amused by the way in which the picturesque names some of the streets were given belied their reality, like Goodacre or Stagsden. He didn't even want to think about Kilham, though that would have been appropriate in this case. There were one or two cars parked at the side of the road that didn't look roadworthy down there, but that wasn't his business. He might tip the traffic boys off, though.

They knocked on the door of number twenty-five, as the bell push didn't seem to work.

'Hello, who's that?' came from within.

'Sergeant Warwick, Cambridgeshire Police,' he said.

The door opened cautiously and a middle-aged woman looked out.

'We're here about Stephanie Slack,' he said. 'Mrs Slack?' he asked.

'I'm her aunt,' she said. 'Mrs Whilden. Have you found her?'

'We think we may have,' he said. 'May we come in?'

'Please don't mind the mess; I wasn't expecting anyone.' She cleared a couple of magazines off a couple of modern chairs

31

that were beginning to look in need of replacement. 'You said you've found her. Is she all right?'

'We think we've found your niece. She's in hospital,' said Constable Flynn.

'Well, why didn't you ask *her* who she was, then?' said the aunt, her voice going up a semitone in pitch.

'She's unconscious, I'm afraid. She was attacked last night, and she needed surgery. She's still not come round after the anaesthetic.'

The aunt took a deep breath and sobbed. 'Attacked?' she said. 'Have you caught the people who did this to her?'

'Not yet, but we have a fairly good idea who they are. We are working on this as we speak.'

She came up with a slightly strange question then. 'Why aren't you two looking for the culprits, then?'

'Because we were coming here to see you,' replied Flynn in her most gentle Irish brogue. 'But don't you worry, there are some very experienced officers out there who are tracking the criminals down who attacked your niece, as we speak. That is, of course, if she is your niece?'

'What, what do you mean by that?'

'Well, I can't see any photographs of her anywhere in this room.'

'No, we don't do photographs, not since her parents died. We always thought it would upset her. They died in a car accident on the A47. Poor little morsel was an orphan when she was just thirteen.'

'How come she survived?' asked Warwick.

'Oh, she was in school that day, so she wasn't in the car.' Flynn quietly shuddered, imagining coming out of double maths to that sort of news.

'I hate to ask this, but we do need to know for sure who the girl we have in the ICU is.'

This drew another sharp breath. 'The ICU?'

'She was really pretty poorly last night,' said Constable Flynn. 'She'd lost a lot of blood.'

'What had they done to her?' she wailed.

32

'I'm not at liberty to go into that at the moment,' said Flynn. 'Not until we're sure that she's your niece.'

'How are we going to do that?' she sniffed.

'We would like to take you along to the ICU to see the girl. We would like you to tell us if it's her.'

'But how am I going to get there? My husband's out in the car at work.'

'We'll take you there; that's not a problem.'

'But how will I get home again?'

'One of us will bring you back again. None of that is a problem.'

'But the neighbours! Me going off in a police car – what will they think?'

'Well, you can wave at them as you get in. That will show them you're not handcuffed or in any way under arrest,' said Flynn. 'Besides, it'll give them something to talk about. We'll try to bring you back in an unmarked car if you'd prefer, or even send you home in a taxi.'

'Oh, thank you so much, yes, that would be better.'

'Would you like to leave a note for your husband, just in case he comes home unexpectedly and wonders where you are?'

'Oh yes, good idea that,' she said. She pulled off a piece of paper from a pad that was pinned to the wall in the kitchen. The top sheet was obviously the beginnings of a shopping list, with three or four items on it. She pulled off a sheet from under the list, and pulled a pencil from a cup on the window ledge. She wrote that she'd gone into the hospital to see Steff, and that she would see him later. She didn't put any explanation for why Steff might be in hospital. Flynn exchanged glances with Sergeant Warwick, but didn't say anything.

The three of them left the house by the front door, and the police were very aware of the twitching of curtains in the front windows of the houses on either side. Constable Flynn leaped to open the back door of the car, and almost bowed as the aunt climbed into the back seat. The aunt waved at her neighbours, as Flynn had suggested she might, and then the police got into the front of their car, and they drove off.

Sergeant Warwick, once again behind the wheel, noticed that the very tatty-looking car he had spotted on the way in was no longer there. He really hoped that nobody was driving it; it looked as if it might fall apart any minute. He was annoyed that he hadn't noted down its number plate when he drove in.

Chapter 7

The medical student, John, walked on to the ITU. He was alarmed that, although he had never been on the unit before, nobody questioned his right to be there. No doubt it was the white coat with a stethoscope hanging round his neck that was his passport. He walked up to the nurses' station and said, 'Last night's Jane Doe?'

The nurse nodded towards the opposite corner of the room, where a policewoman was sitting on a chair. Beside her and around her were machines with flashing lights. In the bed was a shape he vaguely recognised. He walked over to them. The policewoman stood up and quietly, but firmly said, 'And you are?'

'I'm John Baker, the medical student who was with Ms Doe last night in theatre.'

'Do you know the patient's name?'

'Not yet,' he smiled at the policewoman, 'but I'm sure the police are working on that as we speak. Hopefully we'll know very soon.'

The policewoman wasn't giving up yet. 'And what happened to the patient?'

He looked around to make sure no one was listening who shouldn't be. 'She was attacked and raped last night, and the gynae team had to do an emergency hysterectomy to save her life.'

'And where was she attacked?'

He looked unhappily at the policewoman. 'They did tell me, but I'm not from round here, and it didn't mean anything to me. Something about arches, I seem to remember.' Fortunately, 'arches' seemed to be an adequate code word, and the policewoman smiled. 'I just came to see how she was doing. She may be my long case for my exam.'

'They may not allow you to do that, if the case is still sub judice,' she said. 'When's your exam?'

'Nearly two years away,' he replied.

'You'll probably be all right by then,' she said, 'but you may still need to disguise the girl's name and the locations in the exam, for confidentiality's sake.'

'I'll bear that in mind,' he said. 'Could I ask for your help when I come to write it up? It's not a timed written paper; it will be a thesis to hand in in advance.'

'If we're both around the place nearer the time, talk to me and we'll see what we can do. Changing the subject, we've got a child and young person's officer coming round shortly. He thinks that he's found a relative and, if so, that relative will be able to identify her.'

'A CYPO? You mean, she's just a kid?'

'It appears so,' the policewoman nodded.

'Oh dear God, what is the world coming to?'

'I think you're better off being a doctor,' said the police-woman. 'That's the sort of question I ask myself several times every day, but it does justify my reasons for doing what I'm doing.' She nodded at the nurses' station. 'And it probably justifies what they're doing too. Ah, here's Sergeant Warwick now.'

The student looked towards the nurses' station, where a tall man in civilian clothes was talking to the sister. Following him was a much shorter, middle-aged woman, her rather unkempt hair starting to turn grey. He got the impression that her hair had been various colours before she stopped bothering to dye it altogether. She was looking around the room as if she was looking for someone, which of course she was. She settled on their corner of the room, her eye drawn to the policewoman.

The sister from the station told them to follow her, and the three of them walked to the bed. The woman had already gasped by the time Warwick had finished asking her the question: 'Mrs Whilden, do you identify this girl as your niece, Stephanie Flack?'

'Yes, oh yes,' she sobbed. 'Oh Steff, what have they done to you?'

The sister took the aunt by the arm, just above the elbow. 'Would you like to come with me, and we'll try to get some details. I'll also explain what happened to her, and what we had to do. Then you can come back and spend some time with her.'

'Is she going to be all right?'

'We really hope so, though it's too early to say yet.'

'So she's still on the critical list?' asked the aunt, well aware of all the phrases they used in the news and on the telly.

'Yes, I'm afraid so. Would you like some tea or coffee?' the nurse asked, leading her into a side room that was set up with fairly comfortable chairs and a low table. Another uniformed policewoman who had been hovering by the entrance of the ITU followed them in.

'Well, we've got a name,' Sergeant Warwick said to the policewoman. 'She's Stephanie Flack and she's fifteen.'

'Oh dear God,' muttered the medical student.

Warwick looked at him. 'And you are?' he asked, in exactly the same tone as the constable had asked him the same question, not more than a few minutes before.

She stepped in and introduced them; Warwick nodded.

In the interview room the ICU sister was taking notes. Once they had got to the fact that Mrs Whilden was Steff's legal guardian and why, they then discussed things like Steff's date of birth; the name of the GP she was registered with and where; medications she might be taking; any drugs that might disagree with her; all the important things that would make it easier and safer to care for her. Her aunt told her that she was on the pill, because she had such dreadful periods, and the pill stopped all the pain she suffered for at least a week every month. Had the aunt any idea why her niece should have taken benzodiazepines?

'Benzodiazepines? What are they?' the aunt replied.

'They're tranquillisers; sometimes people take them as sleeping pills, sometimes they get stressed and the GPs prescribe them for that.'

'No, I don't know that Steff got stressed, and she certainly sleeps okay. Where would she have got them from?'

'Most people get them from their doctor.'

'Most people?'

'I understand that they're also available as street drugs.'

'Street drugs?'

'Some people buy them off the street from drug dealers.'

'You mean, like drug addicts and heroin and things?'

'Er, yes.' Even the ward sister was beginning to feel uncomfortable.

'No, no, no,' said Mrs Whilden. 'Our Steff isn't into any of that kind of stuff. She's a bright, clever girl, is our Steff.'

'I'm very glad to hear that. Does she have a boyfriend?'

'Yes, he's a nice boy called Sean James. He lives just round the corner.'

'Are we likely to see him here?'

'Oh I expect so, they're very close.'

'Well, will you make sure he comes and reports to the nurses' station before he walks into the unit? We tend only to admit the next of kin to the ITU, so if he is going to come and visit her, perhaps he ought to come with you, or wait until Steff is on an open ward.' The sister was alarmed at the thought of hormonal teenagers having emotional outbursts in her ITU.

'Of course,' said Mrs Whilden.

'Would you like to go and sit with Steff for a while now?' the sister asked as they finished their tea.

'Yes please,' replied the aunt, and was led out of the office onto the ward. She tried not to look at the other patients as they threaded their way to Steff's bed. Somehow she felt that she was invading everybody's privacy simply by being in that room.

The constable stood up as they got to Steff's bed, and offered the aunt her chair. The medical student said nothing, but his expression was sympathetic. Sergeant Warwick said, 'I'm so sorry. We'll be in touch again soon. Constable Green here will arrange your transport home when you're ready.'

'Thank you,' she said, and the medical student left them at the bedside.

Chapter 8

Sergeant Odembe turned off Thorpe Road through the switch left and right into Thorpe Park road and down into West Town. The road got steadily narrower as it turned into Mayors Walk, though he couldn't imagine any mayor taking a formal walk down there, though he supposed that one of them must have done so at some time. Odembe turned into a myriad of little streets with cars parked on both sides, and only a small amount of space between them. The steep camber in the streets was the only part of the street that wasn't completely flat. He had often wondered how vans made deliveries down there without marking cars on both sides of the road; maybe that was the reason for the camber. All the parked cars leaned well away from the centre of the road, and the tyres were surely the first thing that a van would come in contact with. There was a gap between two cars not far down from the Shadeeds' number, and Odembe slotted his car into it.

The constable with him threw open her door, and it grounded on the pavement with a noise that reminded her of fingernails grating on a chalkboard at school. However, the door released itself when Odembe got out of the car on the other side, and she hung onto the door to prevent it from going any further. She got out and shut the door. She would remember that when the time came for her to get back in again.

They looked for a bell by the door, but couldn't find one. What they did notice was a line of Arabic script above the lintel. I wonder what that says, Odembe thought. They knocked. There was movement behind the frosted glass in the front door, but it disappeared again. They knocked harder.

'Just a minute, coming,' came from within, and they heard a crash and a child's wail.

After a moment, the door opened half an inch, secured by a chain.

'Yes?' came the voice.

'Cambridgeshire Constabulary,' said Odembe, offering his warrant card through the gap. 'May we come in?'

The door was closed, the chain slid off, and then the door opened fully. Behind it was a young Asian woman in an iridescent green satin sari with a matching headscarf. Around her ankles were two small children with long black hair, both dressed similarly in satin. She looked worriedly at Odembe, but seemed to welcome the uniformed officer.

'I'm Detective Sergeant Odembe, CID, and this is Constable Green,' he announced.

'What can I do for you?' the woman asked.

'Is this where Aziz Shadeed lives?' he asked.

'No,' she said. 'He now lives next door in the men's house. He moved there when he became old enough to be a man. This is the women's and children's house.'

Odembe didn't bat an eyelid. 'But it is all the same family?'

'Yes,' the woman agreed. He wondered whether this was the sister-in-law who had given the head teacher such a problem. A much older woman in a long black dress and headscarf, with wispy white hair poking out the side of her scarf, interrupted them in a language that neither police officer recognised. The young woman in green replied, and they recognised one word: 'Aziz'. She turned back to the police.

'She is my husband and Aziz's grandmother, and she was asking what you want.'

'Please tell her we are sorry to bother her, and we are looking for Aziz.' He mentally slapped himself. That wasn't quite true; he was very afraid that they might have found Aziz.

'Won't you come in?' she said. 'Tea?'

She led them through a dark dining room into a much brighter room out the back. Under their feet was a layer of plastic sheeting that covered the carpet. It led through to the room at the back. Automatically, Odembe made sure that he only walked on the plastic. The room to which they were led was filled with large soft white leather furniture, also covered in polythene sheeting that fitted the sofas. The woman said, in explanation, that the children always make things so dirty, seeming to forget that she had offered to make tea. The same two children rushed through the room screaming at each other, and the woman, whom Odembe took to be their mother, yelled at them, but they didn't seem to take a lot of notice. There were two other women sitting in the white room, and they looked to be of an age between the old woman and the younger one who opened the door. She introduced them to Odembe and Constable Green as her mother-in-law and her sister. She then explained in their own language who the police were.

'They would like to know why you are here,' she said.

'Is one of them Aziz Shadeed's mother?' Odembe asked.

She introduced one of the middle-aged women as Saeeda Begum, and explained that she was Aziz's mother.

Aware that the women were already sitting, Odembe said that he may have some very bad news for them. He explained that a body had been found and that it might be Aziz, but that they needed someone to come and identify him to be sure. Of course, it took him considerably longer to actually say that as he was expecting a loud show of emotion, and was trying to gently prepare them. He was somewhat thrown when he got little, if any, response from any of them. The conversation passed back and forth between the women, and finally the woman in green delivered their final decision.

'Saeeda's husband must do that; he lives next door.' She screamed for one of the children, and after a moment a little girl with huge eyes like saucers and a disarming grin came in. The woman in green gave her some instructions, and she ran off through the French windows, into the garden, obviously shared by the two houses, and disappeared into the next house. In a minute or so, a large man with a long beard, but a shaved moustache and head, wearing what reminded Green of her father's pyjamas, except that the shirt was so long that it hung below the knee, stood outside the French window. The woman in green introduced him as her husband. They exchanged a further few words and then the man in pyjamas beckoned to the police, and said, 'You come,' and walked back into the garden. As Odembe and Green followed him out into the garden,

Green turned round to the women, and waved rather embarrassedly. They didn't react.

They followed the man in Asian dress through his French window, and found themselves in the presence of a man in his mid-forties in a grey suit. It was the first example of European dress they had seen since they had crossed the threshold of the first house. The man in pyjamas was talking agitatedly in his own language to the man in the suit. He turned to the police officers, and in a cut-glass accent he said in English, 'I think you chaps want me to come with you. Lead on.' He gestured them through the men's house, which had the same plastic over the carpet, out to the front door.

'I'm Mr Shadeed,' he said. 'Aziz is my son. Do you know what happened?'

Odembe explained that he wasn't at liberty to tell Mr Shadeed anything about what had happened until he had identified the boy. Mr Shadeed said he quite understood. They stepped out of the house and over to the car. Constable Green opened the passenger side front door, and Mr Shadeed climbed in, not even considering that the young woman might have been opening the door for herself. However, she made sure that the corner of the door did not jam on the pavement, and then closed it after him. She climbed into the back.

'Nice car, this,' said Mr Shadeed. 'We sell a lot of these.'

Chapter 9

Dr Clark's phone rang. He picked up the receiver.

'Mr Ahmed here, gynaecology registrar. Is it convenient to discuss a patient with you at the moment?' he asked.

'I've got someone in with me at the moment. Can I call you back in five minutes?'

'No problem, in five minutes,' replied the registrar, implying that as long as it was just five minutes.

'What number shall I call you on?' asked the GP, pen in hand. He wrote the number down on a pad on his desk. He clicked his mouse and it printed a prescription out for him. He pulled the green piece of paper out and scribbled his signature in the box just above his address and passed it across to the woman in front of him.

'Anything else I can do for you today, Mrs Borisova?' he asked.

'No thank you,' she said. 'Good day, doctor.' Politely she walked through the door and closed it behind her. He picked up the phone and dialled the number he had written down on the post-it note.

'Ahmed, Gynaecology,' the phone was answered immediately. He must have been sitting waiting for it.

'Tom Clark here. What can I do for you, Dr Ahmed?'

'Mr Ahmed,' he corrected. 'The youngest FRCOG yet from Egypt. I'm very proud of that. Sorry, you must be busy. I understand you've got a patient called Stephanie Flack on your list.'

Clark tapped his keyboard. 'So sorry, Mr Ahmed, my mistake. Well, we used to have a Stephanie Flack, certainly, I'll just check and see if she's still here,' he mumbled, imagining his computer whirring and clunking somewhere in the belly of the building. Stephanie's name came up. 'Yes, she's still registered with us. What can we do for you?'

'Well, right now, she's on the ICU at the City Hospital.'

'Oh lord,' said Clark. 'What happened?'

'She was attacked last night, and we had to do a hyster-ectomy to save her life. She was haemorrhaging into her left broad ligament.'

'I don't think I even want to know how that happened,' said the GP with a shudder. 'What do you need from me?'

'We need a list of her medications, allergies, any relevant medical history…'

'She's been on Microgynon 30 for the past two years. I know she's a little young to be on the pill, but she was having dreadful period problems just after her parents died, and they seemed to stop them in their tracks.'

'What? The periods?'

'No, just the pain. Microgynon made her cycle regular and pain-free, so she stayed on them. Last seen three months ago by the nurse practitioner. Blood pressure fine, weight stable, no problems, so repeated. Oh! That's interesting. She was seen a fortnight later by Dr Watt – he must have been a locum; we haven't got a Dr Watt, and she was apparently so stressed about her exams that he gave her some diazepam 5mg tablets.'

'I was about to ask about them,' replied Mr Ahmed. 'She had benzodiazepines in her urine when we dipped it. Do you know how many he issued her with?'

Clark changed screens on his computer, 'Oh lord, he gave her eighty-four tablets, and what's more, she's collected two scripts on repeat since then. I must stop that immediately, and hoik her back in to talk to her about them. Oh, sorry, I'm not thinking – she's in your ICU.'

'Did she ever need tranquillisers before then?'

'No, that's what surprises me. She was a rather sad, wan lit-tle thing when she first registered with us. Her parents had just died in a car accident, and her aunt, her mother's sister, who has been one of our patients since before I joined the practice, had just fostered her. She was suffering from period problems. We tried a few simple things like mefenamic acid, but they didn't help, and so we put her on the pill, and that worked a treat. I saw her from time to time for pill checks and she seemed to be fine on them. Apart from a couple of urinary tract infections, I never saw her for anything else. She doesn't smoke or anything. I can't see her being upset enough about anything to need tranquillisers; she always struck me as being a tough, independent little thing. Shows how wrong you can be.'

'Boyfriends?'

'Nothing on her records.'

'You know she is – or at least has been – sexually active. She had no remnants of her hymen left.'

'There is no record of that in her notes, but someone of her age, in the Ortons, already on the pill for something else, you know I'm not entirely surprised. There isn't much else for teen-agers to do round here; all the nightlife is in the city centre, and the buses pack up long before the clubs do. Even the little kids' playgrounds round here get vandalised.'

'She's had all her imms and vacs?'

'Yes. It appears her parents were diligent about that, and she had her teenage boosters from the school nurse. We were noti-fied by them.'

'Okay, doctor, thank you for all that. We'll be in touch again if we need.'

Clark put the phone down. Poor little thing, he thought, trying to work out why he felt so upset about the conversa-tion he had just had. Doctors don't tend to get emotional about patients, especially teenage girls they didn't see very often. He looked on the list of the patients he still had to see that morn-ing. Hmm, there were two more who had been added since he had last looked at it. He'd better get a wiggle on.

Once he had cleared the backlog an hour or so later, he walked down to reception and into the back office. There were two GPs and the nurse practitioner already sitting there, sign-ing repeat prescriptions, reading incoming letters and, more importantly, drinking coffee. Once the first stage of paperwork was done for the day, they would divide up the house calls between them. Generally the house calls to a regular house-bound would be done by the GP who knew them best. Once those had been divided up, then any emergency house calls would be done by the GP who was going to be in that particu-lar area. It usually worked out pretty well. He turned to Dr

Shivalkar. 'Your locum from a couple of months ago, Dr Watt, did you know him?'

'Never met him. I was away on that Oxford University refresher course, you know where you get saturation-bombed with information, and you just hope some of it sticks? You know something; a surprising amount of it actually does, at least for a short time. Why?'

'Well, I wasn't here, was doing an addiction clinic on that day, so I didn't meet him either.'

Dr Shivalkar and the other partner exchanged glances. They were relieved that Dr Clark saw all the druggies; it made life so much easier for the rest of them. Mind you, the druggies liked seeing Tom, so perhaps he was more generous than they would have been.

'I saw him,' said Sister Morris, from behind her sheaf of papers. 'Seemed a pleasant enough chap, although he went through the list like a dose of salts. I often wonder how people can think so fast.'

'Oh one of those, a speed merchant,' said Clark. 'I wonder if they think at all.'

'Why?'

'Well, you remember Stephanie Flack?'

'Nice little fair-haired girl, parents got killed in a car crash a couple of years back?'

'Yes – I've just been talking to the gynae senior reg. Apparently she's on ICU at the moment. She was attacked last night.'

'What did that have to do with Dr Watt? He was only here for a day a couple of months ago.'

'He was the last of us to see her, and he prescribed her a whole wodge of diazzies, and put them on repeat.'

Dr Shivalkar smiled at his partner's use of street slang. He also knew that Dr Clark objected strongly if addictive drugs were prescribed outside a consultation. But they all knew that the practice produced a heap of repeat prescriptions at least three inches thick each day, each of which needed to be signed by hand. During the process of signing them, the reception-ists and nurses bombarded the doctors with questions, each expecting an instant decision. It was not surprising that some prescriptions were signed without being read. The prescribers, being well aware of that situation, agreed never to put drugs onto automatic repeat prescription if they wanted to see the patient the next time they were issued. Dr Shivalkar was also aware that Tom would regularly trot out a dictum that ninety per cent of benzodiazepines were not taken by the patient for whom they were prescribed. The chemist down the road, for example, had told him only the previous week the story of a 'dear, sweet little old lady' who had sold her prescription to a 'young man who was more tattoo than skin' for cash before either of them had even got out of the shop.

'The question I have to ask is, did little Stephanie take all those benzodiazepines herself, or did she get them for some-one else? That's the first question, and the second question is did she take a lot of them at once last night? Could that be why she's unconscious in the ICU in the City Hospital?' Dr Clark and his colleagues looked at each other, each wearing expressions of concern. Somewhere they had lost control of something that should have been under their control.

Chapter 10

Sergeant Odembe sat down in the incident room. He hadn't enjoyed the past hour or so much. For instance, he was aware that he had given the pathology lab no more than ten minutes' notice that he was arriving with a possible next of kin to identify the body on which they were performing a post mortem. He understood that there had been a rapid and rather unseemly scrabble to cover up the work in progress, and the copious use of room spray to disguise the unmistakable smell. When they arrived, he was well aware that if he or Mr Shadeed had snagged the white polythene sheet while they were looking at Az's face, there would have been a most distressing display of giblets. Fortunately, this did not happen.

During the viewing, Mr Shadeed had tried hard not to betray any emotion, but on the way home his feelings had got the better of him, and by the time he had reached his front door in West Town, he had been through the whole gamut of emotion.

'Why?' he had asked. 'He was such a good boy, such a clever boy. He had got into that big school, and had done so well in his GCSEs. He was going to get lots of A-levels and go to university. He was going to be a lawyer or a doctor, or maybe even a pharmacist, and own his own shop. Why did someone do this to my boy?'

To add to his distress, there was a whole crowd of people milling about outside his house, waiting for news. He didn't need to say anything; his red-rimmed eyes gave them all the answer they didn't want to hear.

'Do you want me to call your doctor?' Odembe asked.

'No, no, just go, my family will take care of me.' Mr Shadeed let himself out of the car and shut the door behind him. Odembe drove back towards Thorpe Wood police station, leaving a community united in grief.

Inspector Drake was perusing the board, talking to the office manager. Standing to one side was the Detective Chief

Inspector, who usually headed up murder cases in Peterborough, but, as he already had three open cases on his plate, and Drake had assured him that it was an open and shut case, he was just casting an eye over proceedings before he left Drake to get on with it. Peterborough's manpower was far from optimal; as one of the city councillors had recently explained in the *Peterborough Telegraph*. There had been so many budget cuts by the Home Office, he had explained, that maintaining an adequate police presence in Peterborough was simply not feasible, the cuts were made despite the city's growing population.

'She was unconscious, lying there with the murder weapon in her hand,' he said to himself. 'That's an open and shut case if ever I saw one.' Much more loudly, he announced that they would have to interview Steff as soon as she came round – if she came round.

Odembe felt uncomfortable. If Az was such an oik, as Drake suggested, he couldn't help wondering why he had just witnessed such a public outpouring of grief at his demise. Surely a close community would smell a bad egg if it was sitting in their nest. He didn't feel that everything was quite as simple as his superior seemed to think. Maybe he was just sympathising with the father too much.

His phone rang.

'Sergeant Odembe, I've got Dr Waterhouse on the phone for you.'

Waterhouse was the pathologist who was performing the autopsy on Aziz Shadeed, and had been so tactful earlier that day.

'Morning, John. Odembe here. Thank you so much for helping us out this morning.'

'Well, quite,' came the gruff voice of the pathologist. 'One of these days an incident like that will catch us out; we need to have something in place to make sure that doesn't happen in future. Anyway, I think I've got a cause of death for you.'

'Go on,' he replied, contemplating passing him over to Inspector Drake, and then deciding against it. Drake would surely never tell Odembe the pathologist's findings, and he was often left waiting for his typed-up report before he fully understood what happened in a case.

'He died of a tear to his left middle meningeal artery,' Waterhouse said. 'He had a fracture of the parietal bone, which tore the blood vessel underneath it, and it filled the subarachnoid space with blood, compressing the brain till it didn't work any more. The blow to the head that caused it presumably rendered him unconscious, and when he came to again, so to speak, he was dead.'

'Do you know the cause of the blow to the head?'

'Blunt force trauma. There were some metal filings in his hair, that looked as if they came from Exhibit Five, the spike, but we'll check that to be sure. My immediate thought, looking at the state of the cranial vault, was that he had been hit with something larger, more like a traditional policeman's truncheon, but that spike left fragments all over the victim's skin and hair.'

'Could a girl have delivered the blow?'

'Powered by enough desperation? Oh yes, I think so.'

'Thank you so much for letting me know.'

'I'll get my report typed and sent across to the incident room as soon as I can.'

Odembe put the phone down and said, 'That was the pathologist.'

Drake looked up from what he was doing. 'And?' he said.

'Cause of death was due to,' Odembe checked his notes, 'a ruptured left middle meningeal artery due to blunt force trauma to the head.'

'So the girl killed him,' affirmed the inspector.

'In self-defence,' said Odembe firmly.

'Oh, I'm sure her defence counsel will put that case. It will be our job to get the prosecution to persuade the twelve good men and true that, in fact, they were both thoroughly enjoying themselves, and just got carried away in the excitement. Any signs of any drugs?' he added.

'Nothing like that is back yet; all we have so far is the gross physical report.'

'The presence of drugs will be helpful, especially if both the little buggers were full of the same drug.'

'Then all we need is the music to complete the set,' Odembe muttered to himself. Unfortunately Drake heard him, and didn't understand what he had said.

'What was that you said?' he asked sharply.

'All we need now is the music. You know, the rock and roll.' He paused. Drake's face was still fierce and glaring straight through him. 'As in "sex and drugs and rock and roll".'

'I suppose you think that's funny?' said Drake caustically.

'No, not really,' replied Odembe sheepishly.

'Well, when you think you're going to say something witty, just don't. It won't actually be funny, but it will succeed in pissing me off royally, okay?'

Once again silence fell on the room. He noticed that the super had already left. He looked at his fingernails for a moment. I don't know, he thought. Even if it is an open and shut case, as the DI seems to think, you have to lift up a few stones to see what crawls out from underneath just to prove the point.

He looked at the investigation board. There were only two pictures on it: a picture of the dead boy, taken in the mortuary before the autopsy, and a picture of the girl in the intensive care unit, with nasal spectacles blowing oxygen up her nostrils and her eyes taped shut with paper tape. You could almost hear the *meep, meep* of the life support machine attached to her when you looked at it. Surely, now they knew who these kids were, the office manager could have got her hands on photos taken when they were alive and well?

On the other hand, he thought, Drake wanted – and probably needed – a quickie. A swift resolution to this case wouldn't hurt his promotion to DCI. And it probably wouldn't do any harm to his own future prospects either, come to that. Start asking too many questions, and you start getting answers you can do without. What was the point? A couple of kids from Peterborough's underbelly doing each other in; done and dusted. Chances are, the girl will pop her clogs too, and there won't even be the expense of a trial. A quick inquest for the pair of them and Bob's your uncle. Yes, much as he didn't like the man, he could see the reasoning behind Inspector Drake's approach.

Chapter 11

Ruke pushed open the door to the café. He walked over to a table near the back. The two men occupying a table near the door stood up. One flipped the 'open' sign over to 'closed', and the other pulled the blind down over the door. They then both sat down again and continued to nurse their cups. One of them lit a cigarette. Nobody objected.

'Ruke, my boy,' said a male with an Eastern European accent from a table near the counter, 'come in and sit down. Would you like a cup of tea or coffee? I know you're a good Muslim boy and wouldn't dream of letting anything stronger touch those lips.'

'Coffee, please,' he said.

The man called over to the counter, 'Ruke would like some coffee, and I'll have a vodka, very cold.' A head appeared from beneath the counter, and went to the coffee machine and turned it on. A bottle appeared from nowhere, and some of its oily contents were poured into a glass.

Ruke took a breath and was about to speak when the big man put his hand up, his palm facing Ruke.

'Don't say a thing until we have our drinks in front of us,' he said. Ruke let his breath out again. His eyes wandered round the café for a moment, noticing the tables with their plastic-coated tablecloths, and the light fittings that looked old and worn.

The coffee machine finished making its noise and he watched, from the ground upwards, the elfin waitress who was carrying the tray. He watched the brown bootees that just covered her ankles. He watched the slender legs, covered in tan tights, that disappeared into the colourful dirndl, only just long enough to avoid breaking the 'decency in a public place' regulations without a licence. He wondered whether the café held such a licence. Above the low-cut dirndl, skin appeared again with the impression of the swell of a young bosom, leading to a swan-like neck. A heart-shaped face was framed by a fine cut of dark hair that didn't quite reach her shoulders, and her face was dominated by her huge dark eyes, made to seem even larger by a touch of mascara, that seemed to invite him to dive into them and disappear into infinity. She had a small straight nose and a little petal of a mouth drawn into an ironic smile. She looked very young, too young for such a get-up, or even to wear such an expression. No café in the land would get a licence to show her off.

'I see you're checking out my waitress,' said Lev. 'I shouldn't bother; she's way out of your pocket money range.' He nodded at the girl. 'Aren't you, Adelina?'

'If you say so, Uncle Lev,' she replied, without losing her enigmatic smile. She put the tray down on the table and then stepped back a pace. 'Do you want me to stay?' she asked.

'I would vanish out the back for a little while,' he said. 'I'll call you if we need further service.' She trotted out through the door. 'She was sent to me by a family in Slovakia, who asked if I could find her a job in a shop. I liked her so much, I found her a job in my own shop.'

'Does she provide other services to your customers?' asked Ruke.

'As I said already, if she does, you can't afford them. Now, let's get down to business. Where is my present?' Lev's voice took on a more business-like tone.

'There was a problem,' said Ruke, shuffling in his seat.

'We thought there might be, as you came here alone. Where is that Mo of yours? What is that short for? Is it a name from your religion, or is it just short for Moose, perhaps?'

'Monster,' Ruke replied. 'But yes, he was part of the problem, and at the moment he's in disgrace.'

'Go on,' said Lev. 'I'm all ears.'

'There was an accident, and my apprentice and the girl did not survive it.'

'Don't tell me – the accident went by the name of Mo, perhaps?'

'Exactly.'

54

'Tell me what happened.'

'Well, my apprentice brought us the girl as part of his initiation ceremony. It appears that, during the ceremony, he became a little sentimental about the girl in question. He started to object to us all giving the girl a test run, just to be sure she was up to snuff, so Mo hit him. Well, that was only the first problem Mo gave us last night. The girl – well, she was designed a little like Adelina there,' he waved a hand towards the back of the shop, 'and when he was test-driving her, Mo crashed her, badly. There was blood everywhere; it was a mess. So in the end we had to pack it all up as a bad job.'

'So what did you do then?'

'We arranged the bodies as if they had both got carried away with things and had killed each other in the process. It seemed the best idea at the time.'

'So you've got no present for me?'

'Not at the moment, no. But there are plenty more out there.'

'I know there are plenty more out there! I am out there, and I know there are plenty more. What you need to do is get me one.'

'Yes, Uncle Lev.'

'And another thing – there is no one out there who is like Adelina. Whatever your girl was like, she was not like Adelina. Do you understand that?'

'No, all I meant was that she was little, just like Adelina's little.'

'You do not even *think* about Adelina. You cannot afford Adelina, and if your performance last night was anything to go by, it's doubtful that you'll ever be able to afford Adelina.'

'Yes, Uncle Lev.'

'So what are you going to do next, hmm?'

'Well, I'm going to find you some more merchandise, and bring it to you.'

'Good boy,' said Lev. 'And don't let that monster of yours break it this time before you get it to me, or I'll arrange for your monster to be broken in return. And perhaps you too – it depends how amusingly you tell the story. So, Ruke, you are going to have to learn how to become like Scheherazade, and tell me stories so entertaining that I cannot bear to kill you till you have finished telling them. Mm?'

'Yes, Uncle Lev.'

'Good. You can go now.' Ruke looked at his coffee, still untouched on the table. 'I said go. Yuri,' he called to the man smoking by the door, 'Ruke was just leaving – can you let him out?'

Ruke stood up and walked towards the door. Yuri stood up just as he got there and opened the door for him. He threw the spent cigarette out in the street after him, and closed the door again. He flipped the sign back to 'open' and released the blind on the door. He then picked up the saucer he had been using as an ashtray and took it through to the kitchen behind the counter.

Lev walked through the door, following Yuri into the kitchen behind the counter, and through into the back room. A tall dark man in a very expensive suit looked up from the desk.

'Nicely done, Levvy boy,' he said. 'Do you think he'll come up with the goods?'

Lev shrugged. 'I'm not convinced,' he replied.

'But he knows what will happen if he fails,' replied the man in the suit.

'Oh yes, Signore, he knows what happens if he fails.' Lev smiled, touched his forelock, and made his way back out to the front of the shop. There were three new young men sitting at a table, and he noted that the blind on the front door was down again and Yuri had lit another cigarette.

Lev picked up his drink from the tray, and took it to join the new arrivals. 'Gentlemen,' he said. 'Can I offer you anything: tea, coffee, or something stronger perhaps?'

One of the men translated to the other men, who both nodded happily and accepted something stronger. Lev called out to Adelina again and ordered three vodkas, which she drew this time from an optic behind the counter.

Adelina deposited the tray on the table, drawing much less attention from the men, who knew that their future depended on Lev's approval.

'I have jobs for these boys,' he said. 'There's a gang master called Sid who will collect them at six o'clock tomorrow morning from the house and take them to work.' He waited until he had been translated and then added, 'So now, boys, as you'll have an early start, get to bed nice and early.' He swallowed the contents of his glass and shouted, 'Nastrovia!' The others round the table followed suit.

'Yuri,' he called, standing up. 'These gentlemen have jobs to go to.'

The men stood up, and Yuri showed them out, once again rearranging the blind on the door. Lev picked up the bulging envelope they had left on the table, and called for Adelina to tidy up the glasses. Meanwhile he wandered over to the telephone behind the bar and dialled.

'Pozlowicz, mortuary technician,' he heard.

'Hello, Jerzy,' he replied. 'How are you doing?'

Jerzy recognised his voice; everyone who knew Uncle Lev recognised his voice immediately. It would have been more than their life was worth not to.

'So-so, mustn't complain,' he replied.

'Or they shoot you,' Lev added and both men laughed.

'What can I do for you, Uncle Lev?' Jerzy asked after a polite pause.

'Are you busy? Anything in last night?'

'A couple of customers from the same nursing home... and it's *always* the same nursing home. If I were the owner I would be looking over my shoulder – somebody's bound to notice.'

'Not mine, I hope?'

'Not yours, Uncle Lev: people wouldn't dare die in your home, it would be more than their life was worth.' More polite laughter.

'Anything else?'

'A car crash, a boy who was apparently killed by blunt force trauma and a drug overdose. A usual night. Why?'

'Any girls?'

'No, they were all male. Why do you ask?'

'Nothing, just curious. Look after yourself, Jerzy.'

'Look after yourself too, Uncle Lev.'

Very interesting, he thought after he put the phone down. That Ruke lied to me. I wonder how he thinks he'll get away with that.

'Adelina, I'll have another of my vodkas, if you would be so kind.'

Chapter 12

Sean adjusted his clothing. 'Got somewhere I can put this?' he asked, waving a spent condom.

'No! No! No! You can't leave that here – my husband will go ballistic if he finds it. He'll know someone in this house is getting something he isn't any more.' She fished around in her bedside drawer and pulled out a small plastic bag. 'Put it in that, and bung it in someone's bin while you're walking past.' The woman giggled, and said, 'That was nice, though; you're a very nice boy, you know.'

Yeah, yeah, I know, and I'm so-o-o pretty. Yawn.

'Have you got a reward for me?' he asked. And again the woman went rummaging. She brought out two boxes from her drawer. 'Just as you asked, two boxes of prime Yellows. Oh, and here's something else you can have. My husband got some more of these from his doctor. Don't know why he gets them; he never uses them, thank God!' She tossed two small boxes at the boy. 'You can still find a use for them too, can't you? I know you don't need them yourself,' she giggled; a singularly inappropriate sound from a woman of her age. He looked at the two little boxes marked 'Viagra', and grinned at the woman. 'That,' he said, 'gets you a free visit in a fortnight.'

The woman clapped her hands, and said, 'I'll see if I can find you anything else while I'm around, my lovely Micky. I know my old dear's on all sorts of things from her doctor, and she hardly takes any of them.'

'Well, Yellows and Blues always go down well, and, as you can see, Vees, though I can't see why her doctor would prescribe her any Vees – it's not the sort of thing that packs up on a woman. There's another drug that's getting popular at the moment, and that's Gabapentin. If you can get any of that, it might get you an extra service too.'

'Do you take any of these things yourself?' she asked.

'Nah, course not. I trade them in for my stuff. My stuff doesn't come on a prescription.'

'Ooh, you're a right little devil, you are.' She nudged him in the ribs. He stuffed the Viagra in his trouser pocket and put the boxes of Yellows into a jacket pocket. 'Well,' he said cheerily, 'I'll see you in a fortnight. I'll let myself out.'

'Remember to go out the back way,' she shouted after him.

He went down the staircase through the kitchen into the small paved back yard. There were a couple of kids' bicycles and a ball lying around. On the other side of the four-foot wooden fence there was a very large Alsatian cross, almost the size of a small cow, all penis and teeth, tethered with a chain to a large kennel bolted down in the neighbour's yard. It barked throatily at him, but no one took any notice, so it soon stopped and lay down again. He activated the dog for a few more barks when he flipped open the top of the neighbour's wheelie-bin and dropped the telltale package with the condom inside, and let the top bang down again.

'Looks like someone has fun next door, eh Fido?' he said. Letting himself out of the gate, he wandered out into the car park and, emptying his pockets into the car boot, he got in, whistling to himself. 'One more house call to do,' he said to himself, 'then lunch.'

He had always been impressed by his lack of need for a recovery period before he could perform again. Maybe it was because most of his clients lived in Hampton, he joked to himself. He wondered whether the area's radioactivity had anything to do with it. The Hampton estates was the most recent township built onto the edge of the city, and had been built on the brickfields where the old London Brick Company had sourced its clay. The radon gas that pervaded the area was a noble gas that didn't react chemically with anything, like argon or krypton, but was slightly radioactive, and half of it would have decayed by the time the Sun went supernova in several squillion years' time. The presence of this inert gas was therefore not deemed to be a safety problem by the planners, but he wondered whether it was the reason why Mister Wiggly was able to stand to attention so often at his command.

He could handle giving sexual pleasure to any of these women, most of whose husbands had either left them, or certainly didn't want sex with them any more. It was just a job, after all. He received his payment in barter, and his next 'client' produced another box of Yellows, and some sleepers as well. This particular old dear was quite happy to have a spent condom in her bin. He shuddered slightly at the thought that she might open the bin and look at it with pride from time to time, muttering toothlessly, 'Mickey and I did that.'

He let himself out of the front door of the flat and made his way down the staircase to the entrance. He tossed his booty in the boot. He climbed into the driver's seat and headed off to his lunchtime business meeting.

Meanwhile, Yuri had left the coffee shop by the back door, and had grabbed a set of car keys from the bowl on the desk. He pressed the button on the key fob, and a slightly grubby Toyota Avensis flashed its headlights at him. It was a minicab, as most of the cars in the car park were. He wondered where the keys to that beautiful Maserati were. Not in the bowl, that's for sure, or he would have got it by now. He knew three different ways to get from Millfield to the Ortons, and he couldn't be bothered to battle with the sleeping policemen on Taverners Road. They always said that the bumps weren't half so bad if you put your inside tyre just by the kerb. The problem was that some idiot always seemed to park his car on that very spot, so he would have to drive over the highest point of the sleeping policeman. It claimed to be a 20 mph zone, but if you hit one of those sleeping policemen at more than 5 mph, your eyes bounced around inside your skull like ping-pong balls. Today he felt like pretending he was in the Maserati, and headed out to the Boongate roundabout onto the Frank Perkins Parkway, down by the Pizza Hut and the multiplex cinema. He pulled up onto the Frank Perkins Parkway heading south. The traffic wasn't bad, and for once lorries weren't trying to overtake each other. He had got up to a comfortable seventy when he spotted a police car pootling along in the slow lane, so he didn't push the speed any higher. As he overtook the police car, he looked over at the car. Yes he knew them, and they probably knew him, but they weren't friendly bunnies, so it was a good call. Shortly after the Frank Perkins Parkway morphed into the Fletton Parkway there was a turning to the left. There was no sign that the Frank Perkins was now the Fletton Parkway; you just knew. Maybe it was a question in the exam that Uncle Lev was forever banging on about: 'Are you a real Peterborean?' As if anyone would actually want to have a diploma that said they were.

He pulled up and over the Fletton Parkway round the flyover roundabout and into Orton Goldhay. He drove down one of the little tributary roads, never failing to be amused by how they narrowed in places to the width of a car. As if anyone would steam down one of those at a rate of knots. You were bound to get somebody's pooch, or even a rug rat, caught up in the radiator grille, he thought. He spotted the car he was expecting to meet, parked next to it, and rang the bell.

Sean opened the door, and took him round to the boot of his car. They emptied the contents of Sean's boot into Yuri's, and then Sean said, 'Lunch?'

Yuri asked, 'Is your mum in?'

'She's out at work all day,' he replied.

'In which case I would not be averse to a spot of lunch.' They walked through the door and slammed it shut. Yuri lay back on the sofa while Sean knelt down beside him and opened his trousers, freeing his impressive erection. He took a deep breath and wrapped his mouth round it. He worked the urethra hard with his tongue and, pulling back, he flicked the tip of the glans with his tongue to get the taste of the first part of the ejaculate. This was a real man's lunch, he thought, the taste of raw fresh spicy semen; you just couldn't beat it. And Yuri's was extra-specially fine; there must be some secret ingredient in his diet.

'Now,' said Yuri, collecting himself after his moments of ecstasy, while Sean was still swallowing, 'there were a couple of boxes missing. Anything you need to tell me?'

'You'll notice there were a couple of boxes of Vees in there to make up the shortfall,' he spluttered, the semen still clinging to his teeth.

'Very nice,' Yuri said. 'Very nice, but it's the Yellows and the Blues that pay your wages.' Yuri stood and zipped up his trousers, and Sean lay down on the sofa in his place. 'I've got some new pink Ecstasy for you, but I can't give you all I had hoped I could, as you haven't quite delivered.'

'Pink Ecstasy? What's that?'

'Well, they say that it's stronger than ordinary Mitsubishis.'

'They say?'

'Christ, I don't know. I never take anything stronger than nicotine, you know that.' He pulled down Sean's zip lazily. 'Hello little fellow,' he said, 'who's been a busy boy today then?'

'Supply?' he asked, pulling back Sean's foreskin.

'Well, my girlfriend, who usually gets me a box from her GP, didn't come home last night, so I haven't got my usual stash from her.'

'Your girlfriend,' said Yuri, pumping gently. 'I thought we were an item.'

'We don't do anything like that. She's very young and she doesn't do sex, but she is quite funny, and we sit around and play video games and stuff.'

'But she didn't turn up last night?'

'No.'

'Doesn't sound very faithful to me, does she?' He slowed down the wrist action a little.

'No,' he said. 'I suppose not.'

Yuri dug into his pocket with his left hand and pulled out a paper bag. He stopped working Sean's erection with his right hand, counted out nineteen pink tablets, and put them on the saucer on the table. He flicked the tip of Sean's expectant penis with his finger, and said, 'Must dash. People to see, business to do,' and walked out of the room. The next thing Sean heard was the crash of the front door.

He looked down at his unfulfilled Mr Wiggly. He was left with the decision to finish the job himself, or to leave it for work that afternoon. He chose the latter option, picked up one of the pink pills and popped it into his mouth. As he was going to have to sell the things in the club, he might as well know what they did. He would pack the rest into plastic baggies before his mum got home. Half an hour later, he felt absolutely nothing. He wondered whether the spunk lining his stomach was preventing the stuff being absorbed properly, then popped three more into his mouth just to see what would happen.

Chapter 13

Tom Clark opened his box and took out a practice letterhead with the practice address in the top right corner, and the list of partners on the left. He checked the time and wrote on the letterhead: 'Called round to see you at 12.25 as requested. Disappointed to find nobody here. If you still need to see a doctor, perhaps you might consider making an appointment for a consultation at the surgery.' He signed it and dated it. He then folded it and stuck it in an envelope, which he posted through the letterbox in the front door of the flat, turned on his heel and went back down the stairs to the main entrance. His car was parked on the rough ground on the other side of the road. That rough ground wouldn't be rough ground much longer, he thought; someone was bound to build something on it. At that moment his stomach joined in the conversation. *A delicatessen perhaps; oh please, oh please, make it a deli.*

Lunch, he thought, that was what he needed, and climbed into the car, thinking slightly jealously of Sam Shivalkar's packed lunches, so lovingly prepared by his wife. He had occasionally shared them with Tom, and those crispy-coated lamb samosas were among the best things he had ever eaten.

'You get a wife, then you too can have lamb samosas for lunch,' Sam had said.

He got on well enough with Sam to know he could get away with replying, 'That would only work if I married your wife.' And even a lifetime supply of samosas to die for would not be enough incentive to get married again, he thought wryly. He pulled into the McDonald's drive-through, hoping that he would forget samosas by the time he had finished his burger. He had eaten burgers in the States when he had taken a music holiday to Memphis and New Orleans. He had hired a little blue Chevrolet Avenger. Driving down the interstate in a Chevy listening to southern fried rock 'n' roll was just about what life was all about. He just *had* to stop somewhere outside Jackson, Mississippi, at a diner to have a burger to complete the picture. The basic burger was considerably bigger than the biggest quarter-pounder he had ever found in a burger joint in England, and the standard burgers in the UK were positively bijou by comparison.

Moving back to reality and the present, this little car had a CD player and electric windows, so when he spoke into the ordering machine, the person at the other end of it got Lynyrd Skynyrd full in the face. He turned the music down and then gave her his order. He then drove round the corner and came face to face with the windswept face of the girl he had just spoken to. She said, 'That was loud,' took his money and pointed him to the 'collect' window. He kept his fingers crossed that he wouldn't be sent on to wait in the car park while they caught whatever he had ordered, diced it and then cooked it. It was that palaver that had stopped him ordering filet-o-fish from the drive-through. He had twice been scrambled by phone to an emergency while parked in the wait-while-we-find-it park, and he had had to leave the food behind. He hoped that one of the pescatarian kids at McDonald's had eaten it; after all, it had been paid for.

The food and coffee were waiting for him when he got to the window, and he had only had to queue behind one car. He put the cup into the cup-holder in his car, and put the bag of lunch on top of his case on the passenger seat. He then drove round to Tesco and parked. Somehow he felt awkward eating a McDonald's in their own car park, and he couldn't quite face going in and eating inside. First, he felt too old, and what if his phone rang? He would have to talk really loudly on it to be heard, and that would be a breach of confidentiality.

He took the burger out of the box. It looked as if it had been standing in the rack for a little while, but at least it filled a hole. The coffee was what he really wanted, and, he had to say, it was better than any cup of coffee he had had in America. That was one thing that had thrown him: he had expected great coffee in the States but lousy beer, but actually it had been the other way round, provided you drank beer from local micros.

He couldn't remember the name of the beer he had drunk from a jam jar in BB King's saloon on Beale Street in Memphis, but it had been a real night to remember. But, no, he hadn't forgotten about Sam's samosas.

When he had finished his coffee, he drove out of the Tesco car park, and asked the car to decide where it wanted to go next. The little Peugeot set off north onto the Nene Parkway, the stretch of bypass on the west side of town. He had probably cottoned on to what the car had in mind when it reached the far end of the Nene Parkway, and got caught in the traffic lights on the roundabout at the end of the Parkway. Peterborough was the only town he knew that cluttered its roundabouts with traffic lights. He thought that was the whole point of round-abouts: with them the traffic would flow, so you didn't need traffic lights. Of course, there might be a city councillor who owned a firm that supplied and maintained traffic lights. That would explain it. He turned onto the Soke Parkway, which ran along the north side of the city centre, with various townships on its left. The Soke was named after the Soke of Peterborough, the part of Peterborough north of the River Nene which, since the Middle Ages, had technically been part of the county of Northamptonshire. It had also held quarterly assizes in the sessions house that abutted the old District Hospital. The Soke was abolished in 1965, but the Parkway was named in its memory. He had been in the sessions house when it was a res-taurant, and he had been a junior doctor in the District when he had been 'entertained' by a drug rep. This was a habit he had long since kicked as he understood now the whole country was following suit.

The first exit off the Soke was a roundabout over the Park-way itself. Long before the new City Hospital had been opened, that roundabout had grown no less than three different sets of traffic lights to turn the two hundred and seventy degrees towards the centre of the city. As usual, the traffic lights were not in sync, and he had to stop at each one. Once through the chicane, he pottered the two hundred yards to the next set of lights and turned right into the hospital. He had never been into the 'extensive scare unit' of the new hospital before, though he had been in its predecessor in the old District often enough during his days as a GP trainee.

He walked in through the main entrance of the hospital and thought how silly he had been wasting his time at McDonald's; there were several eateries in the main foyer. He found his way through to the back of the concourse to the lifts and staircases, and made his way up to the ITU. He looked through the glass window in the unit, checking he wasn't about to be flattened by a turbocharged porter pushing a trolley. He wasn't, but instead he saw a familiar face. The woman sitting at the desk with a sister's epaulettes on her shoulder had been a newly qualified intensive care staff nurse when he was a senior house officer. He walked in, and her face lit up when she saw him.

'Tom!' she said softly, but none the less excitedly, 'Long time no see. What are you doing here?'

He explained that she'd got one of his patients on the unit, and he had taken the opportunity to look at the new place for the first time to see what it looked like.

'Oh, who do we have?' she asked, and he told her.

'Oh, little Steff,' she said. 'So horrid, that.'

'How is she?' he asked.

'Well, she's breathing on her own all right, but she hasn't come round yet. That's probably not a bad thing.' She pointed to the bed at the corner of the room, which had a young police-woman and a middle-aged woman sitting on either side of her. There was a half-collapsed bag of blood above the bed.

'We're topping her up with packed cells,' she said, 'They nearly lost her, you know. That's her aunt sitting with her.' Packed cells was the opposite of skimmed milk; it was just the good bits. They had separated off the plasma proteins for other uses, like clotting factors for haemophiliacs.

The name came back to him in the nick of time. He always liked to have patients' names on the tip of his tongue; it looked professional. 'Yes, I know Mrs Whilden,' he said. 'May I?'

'Sure,' she replied, and walked over to Steff's bed.

Mrs Whilden recognised him immediately. 'Dr Clark, how kind of you to come,' she said, standing up. The policewoman looked at him with interest, but didn't stand. 'They've had to take out her womb,' Steff's aunt said, stifling a sob. 'She'll never have babies of her own now.'

Tom mentally riffled through a few platitudes in his mind. 'She was always such a nice kid, though; she'll be able to adopt some unfortunate child who wouldn't have had a chance without her,' he tried, and it seemed to work.

'Oh yes,' said the aunt. 'I hadn't thought of that.'

He looked at the sleeping figure on the bed. The tape over her eyes looked a little oppressive – as if the ITU staff didn't expect her to wake up any time soon. Otherwise she looked very much at peace, and there was no evidence of the butchery that had taken place in her pelvis, apart from the slow drip of the packed cells in the viewing chamber as they flowed slowly into the vein in her arm. The ECG above her bed showed a steady rhythm.

He became aware of his phone vibrating in his pocket, and pulled it out, mentally giving thanks, as there wasn't a lot more he could say to the grieving aunt. 'Must answer this,' he said, waving it at the aunt and the sister at the nurses' station. He left the room.

It was the receptionist at the surgery. 'I wondered if you were coming back any time soon. There are a number of letters that need signing, and the courier will be with us in about half an hour.'

'I'll be with you in about ten minutes,' he replied. 'Have them all ready for me.'

He put his head back through the ITU door. 'Gotta go,' he said to the sister, knowing she would let Mrs Whilden know.

Chapter 14

'Settle down, everybody, settle down.' If the office manager had a hammer and a gavel, she would have used them. Everyone in the incident room did indeed settle down, partly due to the steely gaze of DI Drake, and partly because the superintendent had walked into the room, and had made his way through to the back, where he had sat down.

'Right,' said Drake. 'This is probably quite a simple case and shouldn't take much of our time, but,' he caught the super's eye, 'just because it's not going to take a lot of time or effort, that doesn't mean you're going to be sloppy, is that clear?' He cleared his throat and continued. 'The victim is Aziz Shadeed, age sixteen,' he said, poking Az's picture on the incident board with the snooker cue he held in his left hand. 'We believe he was killed by Stephanie Flack, fifteen. They were indulging in a little rather excessive S and M when things got out of hand. She had allowed herself to be tied down, and gagged, on waste ground south of the city, while he entered her with his very large erect penis. It damaged her internally,' he checked his notes. 'It tore her left broad ligament, causing an internal haemorrhage, and in her desperation she managed to uproot the stake that her right hand was tied to, and she delivered a severe blow to the right side of Mr Shadeed's head, fracturing his skull, and rendering him unconscious. Unfortunately for Mr Shadeed, the fracture also tore the,' again he checked his notes, 'middle meningeal artery inside his skull. This caused an intracranial bleed that killed him.

'The first person on the scene was Mr Arthur Snape, aged seventy-three.' He tapped the board, but there was no picture of the old man on it. He turned to the office manager. 'Can we get a picture of Mr Snape, please? You never know: as the person who found the body, he might also have had a role in the affair.' The office manager made a note on her laptop.

Inspector Drake continued. 'Mr Arthur Snape, or to be totally correct, his dog Doggo discovered the scene, and Mr Snape alerted the emergency services. First on the scene was Constable Flynn,' he pointed vaguely in her direction, 'and an ambulance paramedic team. Very quick for an ambulance paramedic team to get there before I did. They made sure that Miss Flack was still alive and in need of immediate medical attention, so she was released from her tethers and the pressure of Mr Shadeed, and taken immediately to the City Hospital where she underwent emergency surgery, and where she remains on the intensive care unit. Meanwhile, I arrived with DC Rivers and took over command of the scene from PC Flynn. Dr Walsh, the divisional surgeon, declared that life was extinct in Mr Shadeed, although the first paramedic on the scene had already made that diagnosis. We released the other paramedic ambulance which was still on the scene, as there was nothing further to be done for Mr Shadeed, and scene of crime team, who had followed me in, took over. Once the scene had been surveyed, Mr Shadeed's remains were transferred to the mortuary. Anybody got anything they would like to add to that? Any questions so far?'

There was some foot shuffling and a few polite coughs, but nobody said anything so Drake continued. 'One interesting finding about this case is that neither of the kids concerned carried money, ID or mobile phones. Can you imagine kids not having a mobile phone on them? One suggestion has already been made that Mr Snape did not in fact find the scene first, but it was discovered by a person or persons unknown who looted the bodies of their money and mobile phones. They also appeared to have stolen Miss Flack's trousers, or skirt, as the clothing that covered her lower half was missing when the crime scene investigating team surveyed the area. Is that still correct, sergeant?' he asked the burly sergeant in the front row.

'It is, inspector, yes: no trousers or skirt.'

Drake shook his head in disbelief for a moment. He could understand someone taking the money and the phones, but the girl's clothing? He continued, 'So at that time we were unaware of the identity of the victims. That came to light the following morning. Apparently they usually sat together in class, and their teacher noted that they were not present in his class the following morning, so he reported it to the head. The head phoned the parents, and were informed that neither of them had returned home last night, so she contacted Sergeant Warwick of the Children's and Young Persons' unit. Miss Flynn's aunt – who now is also her legal guardian, following the death of her parents in an RTA two years ago – and Mr Shadeed's father formally identified both kids this morning.'

He took a breath and paused. 'Well, that's how it stands at the moment. What we now need to do is to allocate some jobs, so any questions?'

'How do we know his penis was very large when erect?' asked PC Flynn, with a smile. 'It was fairly unimpressive in its floppy state when we found him.'

'It must have been absolutely huge when erect; look at the damage it did to the girl's insides,' he replied. 'I have no idea whether they can re-inflate a dead man's penis in the path lab; but I'll find out, and if they can and it's the sort of thing that makes you happy, I'll arrange for a demonstration. Changing the subject for a moment; Flynn, you accompanied Sergeant Warwick when he went to talk to Mrs Whilden, the girl's aunt, didn't you?'

'Yes, sir,' she replied.

'Will you do the family support worker job on the Whildens? A touch of the Irish Blarney often calms people down in these circumstances. Find out all you can about Miss Flack – friends, other boyfriends, someone who might be jealous that she had taken up with Mr Shadeed, schooling – you know the stuff.'

'Yes, sir.'

'PC Singh, you speak Punjabi, don't you? Will you do the same job on the Shadeeds? Take PC Green with you; you'll need a chaperone. Where is PC Green anyway?'

'She's at the bedside in the ICU at the moment,' replied someone from the middle of the room.

'Well, Flynn, when you leave here, take someone to relieve her in the ITU, and PC Singh will pick her up. Meanwhile, you can link up with Mrs Whilden, who I understand is still there.'

'A moment, sir?' Virender was waving his hand.

'Yes, PC Singh, what is it?'

'The Shadeeds are Muslims. I am Sikh.'

'And?' replied Drake testily.

'There is a long history of disharmony between the Kashmiri Muslims and the Sikhs.'

'Are you telling me that you are prejudiced against the Shadeeds?'

'No, sir. Of course not, personally, sir!'

'Well, what's the problem, then? Do your job. Sergeant Odembe?'

'Sir?'

'Are you anal enough to be the exhibits officer?'

'What do you mean by that, sir?'

'Are you the nit-picky sort of person who can ensure all the exhibits are correctly bagged up and labelled so that I don't get ambushed in court by some wiseass of a defence counsel who thinks he's funny? Do you think you can do that, Odembe?'

'Yes, sir.'

'Good.' Drake thought about the good old days in the eighties when he was just a junior DC. His DCI, DCI Jones, had been a man, and that was for sure. They would have had jokes up on the board too. He remembered a similar incident where some joker had written at the bottom of the incident board: 'England 1, Pakistan 0'. DCI Jones had asked him whether he had written it, which he had denied hotly. Not just because he hadn't written it.

'Didn't think so,' Jones had come back at him. 'It was quite funny. Of course, it's also impossible. Anybody care to tell me why such a score is impossible?'

Jones had looked round the room to see if anyone was going to have the temerity to provide a punch line for the joke he was telegraphing.

'Because if the Pakis ever get a corner, they'll stop and build a shop on it.' Drake still remembered a ripple of laughter. Now Jones had been a proper policeman, he thought. He had treated punks and scrotes like they deserved to be treated: like punks and scrotes. He wore two heavy size eleven boots, one

74

on the right foot, which he used for delivering a good kicking to punks, where you kicked punks if you wanted to get information, or – better still – a confession out of them; in the head. The one on the left foot was for delivering a good kicking to scrotes, in the obvious place you would kick scrotes, and for any reason he pleased. Nowadays you weren't allowed to do any of that, because of all this nancy poofter political correctness. Kick a scrote in the nadgers nowadays and you're out on your ear. Bring back the eighties, he thought, and then you'll see some real policing.

The office manager continued to glare at him like a bulldog who'd swallowed a wasp. It was as if she could read his mind, he thought. It wasn't as if he was imagining her with nothing on; now there was an image that made him shudder.

'So, Odembe: exhibits officer?'

'Yes, sir.'

'Does anyone want to add anything that I haven't already said?'

Sergeant Molinari spoke for the first time. 'There are a few tyre tracks at the scene that they're still looking into. One set of tracks matches those on your car, sir. There are a couple of double-axle tracks, one of which matches the crime scene van, and the other is probably an ambulance. There's one other very recent set of tyre tracks, which we'll check against the car PC Flynn was driving last night when it gets back in. It's out on a call at the moment. There was fresh blood at the site, which we'll check against the victim—'

'Suspect,' interjected Drake.

'I stand corrected,' said Molinari. 'Suspect. Of course, if we take any blood off her now, it will be a real mish-mash of stuff, as she's had several blood transfusions, and it won't be genetically pure. Let's hope the lab has kept enough of her own blood to test the findings against.'

'Any semen?'

'Not that we found. Let's hope the hospital took forensic swabs when the vic – er, suspect – arrived in Casualty. We've not checked that yet.'

'Put a man on it straight away, as soon as possible, before some keen student nurse trying to impress someone has tidied it all away.'

'Will do.'

'Any feedback from the house to house team?'

A uniformed PC stood up. 'So far nobody claims to have seen anything at all, sir. We've been to every flat in the new block that overlooks the area, up on Cubitt Way, and everybody appears to have been either out or blind. No one saw a thing, and nobody saw the kids arrive at the scene either. At least, that's the state of play so far.'

'Oh well, it's probably not important,' said Drake. 'Pretty simple case, as I said. Right. Everybody knows what they've got to do; I suggest they go and do it.'

Chapter 15

Shannen McGinley sat on the step outside the house in Dog-sthorpe, where, for the time being, anyway, she lived. It wasn't particularly cold or wet, but there were times when she was cross that she wasn't trusted with a key to get in.

'When you're twenty-one, you get the key to the door, but until then you wait till a key holder comes home.' Well, the key holders were her foster mother, her foster mother's husband; was that her foster father, she wondered? And then there was their lug of a son, surely he wasn't her foster brother? She supposed that Jervis was over twenty-one,. He had a labouring job, and the gang master brought him home with his money, which he gave to his mother. She hid it somewhere in the kitchen. Problem was, Shannen was never alone in the house to look for it. Anyway, maybe she just put it somewhere temporarily before taking it and putting it in the bank and declaring it as income and paying tax on it – as if that would ever happen! But where is she, anyway? It's not as if she's got a job or anything, except looking after me.

Shannen had got out of school early – actually, she'd left earlier than school had got out. She couldn't be arsed with school that day. But she didn't have any close enough friends who wanted to bunk off with her, so it had all been a bit pointless really. She hadn't got any money, but she had nipped into the newsagents and boosted a couple of chocolate bars and a magazine, which told her all the things she could buy if she had money, which was equally pointless. She had thought of going down to Queensgate and hanging round down there, but what was the point? Queensgate was just a shopping arcade, and shops needed money. Queensgate also had security guards who were watching for young people on the pilfer, and they would almost certainly be watching her as soon as she walked through the doors. And they would be watching her for all the wrong reasons – to see if she was still a light-fingered lily – and not for the reasons she would have liked. Anyway, she had been caught nicking before, and she reckoned she would get in real trouble with the man if she got nicked again. So she sat on the step watching the world go by, hoping her foster mother wouldn't take too long.

Shannen wished she was pretty. There were girls at school who got noticed 'cos they were pretty, and not only with boys. It must be nice having boys look at you. She didn't know much about boys, but they smelled different. She reckoned boys didn't know much about her, either. If you were pretty, you got noticed by the girls too, and if you were *really* pretty, you could become an It girl, and run with the gang, or even form your own gang. Now that would be cool, having your own gang, and having boys gawp at you.

She picked at the scab on her knee, which poked through a hole in her jeans. Where had that come from? Oh that's right; she had been knocked over during break a couple of days ago in the rush to get to lunch. Why do people rush to lunch? The food sucks and it's expensive. That was one way she got money: she saved the lunch money she was given by her foster mother. And her foster mother had got that from the council to give to her. Sometimes the class bully spotted she hadn't been in to lunch and relieved her of her lunch money – either that or she'd punch Shannen – and she still didn't get to keep the money; so that sucked, because then she was hungry and she hadn't got any money. But that day she'd still got her lunch money when she bunked off.

She wasn't a bad old stick, her foster mother, and her husband and her foster brother didn't abuse her either. In fact, none of them took much notice of her. She had her supper in front of the telly with them; they usually watched football. There were times when she was amazed how much football you could find on the telly. People she knew at school had seen other things on the telly, and sometimes they even talked about them, like EastEnders, Corrie and Towie.

'Did you see Towie last night?' they asked her, and she hadn't. But she had seen Bayern Leverkusen playing some other team whose name she couldn't remember.

'Why did you watch that?' she was asked, and she replied simply enough, 'Because it was on.'

The people who knew her at school couldn't quite get their heads round the fact that she hadn't got a telly in her room, or a laptop, or a tablet or anything like that.

'Why are you so twentieth century, girl?' they would ask her.

Why should she want to take tablets anyway? she wondered.

Ow, she thought as a bit too much of her scab came loose and started to bleed.

Yes, she wished she had money too. If she had money she could get all those things that her friends had, like laptops and a phone that did more than make calls. Her phone was a homing device, pure and simple. She did have a few magazines and a couple of old paperback books, but she had read them so often that she knew every page off by heart.

With money she could also buy clothes, like she saw in the magazines she'd boosted. Maybe with some decent clothes, and some make-up, she could look pretty, and if she looked pretty, she might be popular. But she wasn't, so she wasn't. And anyway, she didn't know anything about make-up. Maybe she could boost some from the local chemist – she hadn't been caught nicking there before. Then she could try it out. That would be her plan for the rest of the day.

She was suddenly aware of a shadow falling over her. She looked up, and there was a boy standing there, looking at her and smiling.

'Hello,' he said. 'My name's Ruke, what's yours?'

'I'm Shannen,' she replied.

'Hello, Shannen, are you busy?' He was still smiling at her, and still looking too.

'Not specially,' she said, pretending to sound bored.

'Do you want to go for a walk then?'

Chapter 16

DC Danny Rivers got out of the car.

'It was here we stopped,' he said. 'Strewth, the place has all dried out already. It was raining when we got down here last night. You would have thought that the tyre tracks we left would still be here, but they've all gone, despite the marker cones and police tape.'

'Just fill me in,' Lou Molinari asked him. 'What exactly was here when you got here, again?'

'Well, the body was there,' he said, pointing to the little mound. Just behind it and above was the girder of the railway bridge, carrying the branch line to Whittlesey and March. It followed a gentle turn under the main line archway and headed towards the east. With its camber tilting the train into the curve, you wouldn't have seen anything going on if you were sitting in a train up there on the line.

The car park for the Nene Valley railway station itself was formed of impacted earth, hard as concrete, thought Molinari.

There were one or two places that double-axle tyre marks actually showed up, but not many. Access to the Nene Valley car park was either under the arches, or from the new Cubitt Way. At the end of Cubitt Way there was just wasteland. And every addict knew only too well that Peterborough Station was the first stop after King's Cross on the main express line, and was where you got thrown out if you were found travelling without either a ticket or the wherewithal to pay for one. Peterborough had a good many residents who owed their being in Peterborough to that!

They got out and walked around the site. They were lucky that the old man had even spotted the teenagers, Molinari thought. Mr Snape had been walking his dog along the towpath by the river, and the little dog had turned left past the railway and had trotted up the slight incline and found them.

Molinari doubted that anyone would have noticed them from the towpath, as it was considerably lower than the car park. The view from the Cubitt Way flats was partly hidden by the bushes surrounding the car park. Someone might have seen them if they had been looking through the bushes with a telescope, he supposed.

They had chosen a secluded site for their tryst, Molinari thought, and they would have been completely invisible if someone had parked a car directly in front of them.

He looked at the tyre marks. Now, suppose that double-axle tyre mark was from a big Transit, he thought. That would have blocked any eye line.

'What?' asked Rivers.

'Just trying to work out if there were any other vehicles here last night,' he replied.

'It's an open and shut case, that's what Inspector Drake said,' said the young DC.

'I know what Inspector Drake said, but I'm just trying to work out if he could have been wrong. It won't be the first time, you know. To make his case stick, we have to prove that his theory's right.'

'You don't like him much, do you, Lou?' asked Danny, after a moment's pause.

'Not a lot; but that isn't what this is all about. One kid's been killed, and another one badly hurt. Yes, it would be very easy to believe that they did it to each other. It's my job as the crime scene officer to prove that one way or the other.'

'I think I have an idea why there wasn't any semen found,' said Rivers.

'Go on, Danny; I'm all ears.'

'Well, maybe he hadn't actually ejaculated by the time she hit him? Of course, once she hit him, that was that as far as the sex was concerned.'

'Smart thinking, Danny, and we can get that checked out by the post mortem team. Was there fresh semen in the urethra?' He picked up his phone and dialled, asking that question when the phone was answered. He then disconnected and said, 'That's another bit of proof of the inspector's open and shut case, if there was. I suppose the other thing we should be doing is checking with Casualty about what happened to the forensic swabs they took from the girl when she arrived last night.' He turned and told the policeman at the scene that they would be off now, but if he found anything else, be sure to bag it.

They drove round the Bourges Boulevard inner ring road, until they got to the Taverners Road roundabout, when they turned left into Westfield Road and drove over the railway bridge. Their route meandered through the top end of West Town and through the edge of Netherton, until they reached the City Hospital. They parked in the disabled bay by the entrance to the Emergency department – one of the advantages of being in a marked police car. Nobody asks questions about things like that. Danny Rivers had never heard of a police car being given a parking ticket by a traffic warden, even when it was parked on a double yellow line.

A policeman in uniform drew attention everywhere they went, and Sergeant Molinari was an imposing man anyway. The receptionist took him aside and asked what she could do for him, wondering whether he had in some way damaged the rather unprepossessing man in jeans and a slightly grubby pullover he was with.

'No, no, no,' he chuckled. 'He's not a crook, he's a detective. We wondered if there were any samples taken last night when Stephanie Flack was brought in.'

The receptionist tapped her keyboard. 'Steph … a … nie Flack. Hmm, we don't seem to have anyone by that name here.'

'She hadn't been identified when she came in, and wasn't named till this morning, so she would have been a Jane Doe last night,' Rivers explained.

'Oh right,' she said, and tapped again at the keyboard. 'Yes, got her. Samples were taken for cross-match, and toxicology, chemistry and haematology. Urine tested for drugs and with multistix here in Casualty. She was bounced to gynaecology and up to theatre. It looks like she was very ill.'

'Were there any swabs taken with a rape kit?' Molinari asked.

'Nothing here says there were,' she replied. 'If you want, I'll ask Sister.'

'Yes, please do,' he said. He walked around in circles while they were waiting, hands behind his back, twiddling his fingers. She was back fairly quickly, her shoulders set to shrug.

'Sister's busy at the moment, but she says that whatever's on the screen was what was taken, and if it's not on the screen, then it wouldn't have been. Was she brought in by the police? Wouldn't they have checked?'

'She was brought in by a paramedic. The policewoman at the scene stayed with the other victim.'

'Oh well, maybe the swabs will be appended to that one, then. Name?' she tapped the keyboard again.

'No, he never got to Casualty; first stop mortuary for him,' Molinari replied drily.

The receptionist's hand flew to her mouth as she said a little, 'Oh!'

'It wasn't a pretty scene last night,' said Danny Rivers. 'They shipped Ms Flack here PDQ, but as the other kid was already dead, there didn't appear to be any immediate hurry.'

'I'm sorry we can't be of more help to you. They may have taken some swabs up on the gynae ward.' She tapped her keyboard. 'No, no, on second thoughts they won't. She apparently never got anywhere near the gynae ward; she went from here straight to theatre and from there to the ITU, which is where she is at present.' More shoulder shrugging ensued, as she said an embarrassed, 'Sorry.'

'Damn,' said Molinari.

'Reading between the lines on this screen, she was a very poorly girl last night. They were concentrating one hundred per cent on saving her life.'

'Thank you,' said Molinari, trying to make it sound like he meant it. 'Come on, Danny, we've got things to do, and an illegally parked car to shift.' He shepherded the DC out of the department.

Chapter 17

PC Susie Green always felt she was the unlucky one. Take last night, for instance. When this case cropped up, she was first on scene, but who was she with? Yes, that's right, she was with Shuv Flynn, and who got the attention? Got it in one: Shuv Flynn, the pretty one, the perky one. She wondered if anyone had even spotted she was there. I'm taller than Shuv, she thought. Really, she felt she should hate Shuv, but actually she didn't. Shuv made her laugh far too much for that. Come to think of it, she probably wouldn't like getting all the attention Shuv got, and would she really like to have her work monitored that closely? Probably not.

Today her 'unlucky' took an altogether different tack. Today she was out with Virender Singh, as one of the Shadeed family's support workers. Don't the powers that be understand? she wondered. Virender was Sikh, and the Shadeeds were Muslim. There had been years of unpleasantness between the Sikhs and the Muslims in Kashmir. Now, she accepted that they weren't in Kashmir right now, but fifty years ago, all these people's families had been glaring at each other across their garden fences and growling. Virender had never been to Kashmir in his life – in fact, he'd probably never been further away from Peterborough than London – but he still wore the name. If he'd changed his name to Joe Smith, people would then be asking why this Asian-looking man had such an English name, what was he ashamed of? He probably couldn't win. There was a very sharp intake of breath as they arrived. Susie would have no problem, as she was shepherded into the women's and children's house, but she wasn't jealous of Singh being in the men's house. She doubted he would get a word out of any of them. He knew that DI Drake was throwing him into the lion's den, and he knew there wasn't a lot he could do about it.

One of the women in the women's house, who wore an iridescent green sari, spoke good English. She made Susie feel welcome, and offered her a cup of tea.

Susie smiled, and said, 'I can make tea. One of the first things they teach you to do when you're training to be a family support worker is to make a half-decent cup of tea.'

'So you're trained to do this,' the woman said.

'Oh yes,' she said. 'I'm Constable Susan Green, by the way, but please call me Susie.'

'Yasmin Bi,' the elegant-looking woman replied. 'Aziz was my husband's half-brother.'

'I'm so sorry for your loss,' Susie said.

'Do they know who did this terrible thing?' Yasmin asked.

'Oh, we think so, yes.'

'Is he under arrest?'

'She is, in a manner of speaking,' she said emphasising the 'she'. 'She is in protective custody.'

'Sorry – what does that mean?'

'She is currently with the police, but she hasn't formally been charged yet, I understand.' Susie was wriggling. She was being asked questions that she really shouldn't be answering, but at the same time, her role was to engage the trust of the family of the victim. Whatever else he had been, Aziz was certainly the victim of this incident. Her explanation of Steff's position was technically correct: she was in ITU with a police officer at the end of her bed. She had been there that morning. Now, her job was also to find out what led the unfortunate Aziz Shadeed to be having sex with Stephanie Flack near the Nene Valley railway station.

'You said Aziz was your husband's *half*-brother?' she asked.

'Yes, Mr Shadeed, my father-in-law, is their father, but they have different mothers. Saeeda Begum, in the living room, is Aziz's mother.' A middle-aged woman in the living room looked up, and smiled faintly at the mention of her name, but didn't get up.

'How did that all work out?' she asked.

'Well, in Pakistan, Mr Shadeed had two wives. You know Muslim men are allowed four wives. But he knew that people in Britain don't like people having lots of wives, so when he came to Britain, he brought just his new wife, Saeeda, with him. She didn't have any children yet.'

'So your husband grew up in Pakistan?'

'With his mother, yes. His father did visit regularly, and took money back to them that he had earned in England. He works very hard, my father-in-law.'

'So when did your husband come here?'

'Three years ago, when he married me. His mother died in Pakistan four years ago, and his sisters were all married in Pakistan, so there was just him. He married me and came here to work with his father.'

'Had you met him before you married him?' Susie asked, instantly wishing she could take back her words, as it was none of her business, but Yasmin took no offence.

'No, it was an arranged marriage between his father and mine.'

'And you love him?' She couldn't resist asking that one – not that she knew much about love herself.

'Of course; he is my husband.'

'And you have two children?' she said, watching the two little ones running around, just like they had when she visited in the morning. Though they weren't so boisterous this afternoon; perhaps they were getting tired.

'So your father-in law came over eighteen years ago, then?'

'Yes, about that.'

'Bit of a gamble for him, coming over just with Saeeda. Suppose she couldn't have any children?'

'If she didn't, she would have been sent back to Pakistan, and his other wife would have been brought over, but that would have been more of a problem, because she already had three little ones. Anyway, that never happened because Saeeda had Aziz here in Peterborough.'

'So Aziz was born in this country?'

'Yes, and so were his sisters.'

'He has sisters?'

'Three, and a baby brother.'

'How old is the brother?'

'Six, and the girls are eight, eleven and fourteen. They're all at school today.'

'Do any of them know about Aziz yet?'

'Not yet, as far as I know, but they will as soon as they get home in about an hour.'

'I can help you talk to them if you like – that's part of my job.'

'Thank you. You know, this is the first time I have ever met a policewoman to talk to, and you have been most kind. Why did you come back with that Asian man, instead of the African man you came here this morning with?'

'Sergeant Odembe, you mean? He's a very senior policeman, compared with us, and has a very important job in the incident room itself. They send us uniformed police out as family support workers.'

'The other policeman is Sikh, isn't he?' The two women exchanged sad expressions that had nothing to do with the recent bereavement.

'Don't they understand?' asked Yasmin. 'Why didn't they send a Muslim man?'

'Do you know any Muslim men who've joined the police in Peterborough?'

'Well, no.'

'I think our chief did the best he could, and found someone who spoke Punjabi.'

'And what do you speak?'

'Like most English people, English and that's your lot. I learned a bit of French at school, but dump me in the middle of France, and I'd be lost.' She thought for a moment, and then said, 'Sorry.'

'It's not your fault. I think you're doing all right. I hope your friend is too.' They both looked at the wall that separated the two houses. Susie changed the subject.

'Did you know Stephanie Flack at all?' she asked.

'Who?'

'We understand that she and Aziz sat together in class at school.'

'She doesn't sound very Muslim.'

'She isn't. She's white, and fair. I don't know what religion she has, if any.'

'That sounds like one of the problems the family should have realised it was going to get when they sent him to that school,' she said sadly. 'Aziz and I did talk about arranged marriage,' she said, opening up a conversation that Susie knew she was going to have a problem with if she hadn't been helped by it being mentioned already. 'He did talk to me a lot. Apart from his father, and the little ones, he is the only other person in the house who speaks English, so he used to talk to me. My husband doesn't mind; after all, Aziz was his little brother.'

'And what did he feel?'

'He wasn't sure that he wanted an arranged marriage, unless he really, really liked the girl, and he wanted to get to know the girl first. He didn't want to be told to go out to Pakistan and marry some stranger, like I did. He thought I was very brave. But I wasn't, not really. It was my duty, and I knew I was going to have to do this one day for my family. Maybe I was lucky: my husband is a good man, and he works hard, and he has a nice family, so they don't make life difficult for me. Perhaps it would have been more difficult if my husband's mother was still alive and frail, because then I would have had to look after her, but Saeeda's only about fifteen years older than me.'

'How old are you, if you don't mind me asking?' asked Susie gently.

'I'm nearly twenty-one,' she replied.

'And you were at school until you got married?'

'Yes – one day I was at lessons, and then in the summer holiday, I became a bride. It must sound very strange to you, but I am happy with my life.'

'I think,' said Susie, carefully this time, 'I think I am going to learn a lot from you over the time we're together.'

'You didn't know many Muslim girls where you were at school?'

'No, I grew up in Harpenden, in the stockbroker belt.'

'So you're from a rich family, then?'

Susie chuckled. 'No, my dad was a policeman too, and that's what I wanted to do too.'

'Have you got brothers and sisters?'

'One of each, both in the police. My brother's in the Met in London, and my sister's still in Harpenden.'

There was the sound of the front door opening. They looked at each other. Yasmin said, 'That'll be Aziz's brother and sisters.'

'Do you—' Susie began.

'Let me talk to them to start with,' Yasmin said, 'but don't go anywhere, I may need you. Don't worry, the kids all speak English. My father-in-law insisted that they really learned how to be British.'

Chapter 18

'Sister, I think Ms Flack's drip's tissued.' The staff nurse was watching the chamber in the line through which Steff was receiving her blood transfusion. The drips in the chamber had stopped.

The sister walked over from behind her desk, undid the bandage, and ran her hands over the slender arm. She could feel the vein beneath her fingers, and if she could feel it, it had gone solid. Steff had another unit and a half of packed cells to go in, so she would need another drip.

'Can I do anything?' asked the constable beside the bedside.

'No,' replied the sister. 'This is entirely routine; we have to re-site drips every day. When her aunt comes back with your colleague, do explain that there isn't a problem.'

'Why does it happen?' the constable asked, while the staff nurse had gone off to get another drip pack.

'It's nature fighting back, I guess. She probably won't need a drip once we've got the last of the blood into her, unless she doesn't wake up by this evening.'

'Then?'

'It's off to the gynae ward with her, so we can use this bed for someone else. At least, I assume she'll be going to gynae, rather than paediatric surgery. She's in between the age brackets. I can't see the paediatric surgical nurses ever having nursed someone who's had a hysterectomy before, though.' The staff nurse arrived with her tray of equipment.

The first thing to do was take down the old drip. She pulled the cannula out and taped a cotton wool ball over the hole, to avoid leaving a bruise. She then rolled Steff's sleeve down, walked round the bed to her right arm and pushed the sleeve of the hospital smock up.

'Oh!' she said.

Across Steff's arm there were numerous healed cuts, faintly scarring the skin of the inner arm.

'She did that, did she? We're going to need to look into that, but first let's set up the blood.'

She set up a drip set and put a bag of normal saline up and ran it through so that it appeared at the end of the giving set. Then she put a tourniquet around Steff's arm and pulled it tight – not so tight that it occluded the arterial flow into the arm, but tight enough to stop the venous flow flowing out again. The veins obligingly stood up. There is a vein over the top of the radius further up the arm from the thumb, where two veins come together if you're lucky, and Steff had one of those. The sister slid the Venflon cannula up the arm into the vee the vein formed at that junction, and obligingly the cannula slipped straight into the vein. A trace of blood appeared in the chamber in the Venflon. She pulled out the steel trochar from the Venflon and eased the plastic cannula round the trochar further into the vein. She then pushed the end of the drip onto the business end of the plastic cannula, simultaneously releasing the tourniquet. She turned the flow of saline up full, and the drips rapidly flew through the viewing chamber. There was no telltale swelling of the tissue round the end of the cannula. The fluid was in the vein and was flowing. She taped the cannula in place, and tied a crepe bandage round it, but didn't need to bother with a splint. She then slowed the drips down, and swapped the saline bag for the rest of the blood bag, and let it continue to drip. The saline in the giving set slowly and obligingly turned pink. The process had taken about two minutes, and the girl hadn't moved at all.

'Does that hurt?' asked the young constable.

'Not really, even when you're fully awake. What hurts is all the messing about, so if ever you need to have a drip put up, make sure you've got someone doing it who's done it hundreds of times before, and knows exactly what they're doing.'

'But surely everyone who's going to be doing the job has to practise?'

'That's as may be,' the sister replied and winked, 'but they don't need to do their first one on you. I'll see you later. You understand what that was all about? Just in case Auntie comes back and spots the drip is going into Steff's other arm?'

'Yes,' said the constable. 'Got it.'

Meanwhile, the sister went back to her desk and got out Steff's medical notes. First she wrote her own entry about re-siting the drip and when and why it was done, and then she flicked through the rest of the notes. The scars on Steff's arm were evidence of self-harming. Did she have any psychiatric notes? There was nothing in the hospital notes, but that didn't mean anything. If she'd only been seen in Outpatients, then that information wouldn't appear in her general notes. Her scars were superficial, but they wouldn't have been any less painful for that. She picked up the phone and called her opposite number in the adolescent psychiatric clinic.

'Hi there, Sister Bartram on ITU here. We've got a girl up here on the unit at the moment called Stephanie Flack. She's fifteen, and we think she might be known to your department.'

'What happened?' came back a tired reply. 'Overdose?'

Sarah Bartram felt that probably wasn't an unreasonable question.

'No, actually she was attacked, and has undergone some fairly serious surgery to pull her back from the brink. It's just she's got some old self-harm cuts on her right arm, and I thought we ought to know what we're dealing with when she wakes up.'

'Right,' said the voice on the other end of the line. 'Can I have the details again?'

'You didn't jot them down the first time, did you?' Sarah teased.

'No, I have to confess, I didn't. This desk is a complete pig-sty, and none of the pens I found worked. Can I call you back? I do know your number.' The two nurses laughed, each wondering how the other coped with their working lives.

Steff's aunt had reappeared while Sister Bartram was on the phone, and when she put the phone down she walked over to her.

'Mrs Whilden, may I have a word?' and led her off to the side room.

'What?' asked Mrs Whilden in alarm. 'What's happened to Steff now? What have you found? What more can go wrong?'

'No, no, nothing's gone wrong, we just had to re-site her drip. Drips do sometimes stop working from time to time, that's all. You will notice that the blood transfusion is now going into her right arm.'

'Oh yes, I did notice that,' said Mrs Whilden uncertainly. Sarah thought, you hadn't noticed any such thing, but she let it go, because she wanted to know her answer to the next question. 'When we were re-siting the drip in her right arm, we noticed she had healed cuts on that arm. It looks like she had been harming herself. Did you know about this?'

'Our Steff, hurting herself?' the aunt asked, wide-eyed in dismay.

'Yes, did you know she did this?'

'No,' wailed the aunt. 'Why should she want to do a thing like that?'

'That's just the question I was going to ask you.'

'You mean she was trying to kill herself?'

'No, it doesn't usually mean that.'

'So what are you saying, then?'

'Well, it appears she cut her arm—'

'To cut the veins, you mean?'

'No, people who do this specifically make sure they avoid the major blood vessels. They're not trying to kill themselves. It's like, somehow, they're trying to punish themselves in a ritualistic sort of way.'

'But what would Steff be punishing herself for? She was always such a good girl.'

'I was rather hoping you might be able to tell me that. Or was she really stressed about something, perhaps?'

'How do you mean?'

'Well, often self-cutting is rather like releasing the valve off a pressure cooker. When someone who does this gets wound up, the stress builds and builds until they can't cope with it any more, and they cut themselves, and it seems to let all that stuff out. I was just asking if Steff got stressed.'

Mrs Whilden looked Sister Bartram directly in the eye, and said, 'Not that I can think of. She's naturally bright, she got all her GCSEs last summer, and she's now in an A-Level class and she's still only fifteen. Could it have been after her parents died in that car crash?' she asked.

'It's possible. Tell me about it,' Sister Bartram said gently.

'Well, my sister, Jessica, met this bloke called Richard Flack. And they fell in love, got married, then Steff came along. Anyway, Richard got this beast of a car – an Aston Martin or a Maserati I think it was – and one day, when Steff was at school, they went out to lunch in it, and on the way home, he wrapped it round a tree. Killed them both instantly. Could she have started to cut herself then? When her mum didn't turn up to pick her up from school?'

'That's how she found out, then?'

'Yes, she was waiting at the school, and her mum didn't turn up, so the school phoned her home, and they got no reply. It was only then that Richard's car was discovered, still burning, on a back road somewhere. The first Steff knew about it was when the police arrived at school.'

'Oh how horrible,' said the sister, 'the poor little sausage.'

'And the first we knew about it was the police arriving at our front door with Steff. I'd only just got in five minutes before. Hadn't even put the shopping away or anything. That was a very bad day for everyone.'

'Did you ever have any kids of your own?'

'No, we couldn't.'

'Any reason why?'

'Well, it just never happened.'

'You could get these things checked out, you know.'

'Yes, I suppose so, and we did start to think about getting tests done and things, and then that horrible crash happened, and we had Steff, and that was suddenly our family, ready-made. Oh, poor little Steff, Fate has been most unkind to her.' A large tear trickled out of the corner of her left eye. 'So I didn't know she had been cutting herself, but that might have been a reason why, if you know what I mean. She has had plenty of stress in her life that she has had no control over.'

'Quite,' said the sister, looking across at the silent figure in the corner with the young constable sitting next to her. And her stress isn't over yet, is it? she thought.

Chapter 19

Constable Flynn put her head round the ITU office door and met Sister Bartram's eyes.

'Oh – hi. I just wondered where Mrs Whilden had got to,' she said. And to Mrs Whilden, she added, 'I'm back.'

'Hello, constable,' Steff's aunt replied. 'I'll be with you in a minute.'

Siobhan Flynn walked over to the girl's bed where her colleague sat. 'How's she doing?' she asked.

'No real change,' her colleague replied. 'The nurses seem happy enough and they're suggesting it should only be a matter of time before she wakes up.'

And then you can read her her rights, Siobhan thought drily, but didn't actually say it. She had already looked closely at Steff's face, and she had been far from convinced that it was the face of a killer. She was certainly no more convinced now that she was looking at a mask of evil. She was looking forward to getting Mrs Whilden on her own and getting to know Steff the person, to see whether she could still trust her judgement. Siobhan – or Shuv, as many of her colleagues called her – hadn't often been wrong about these things, though she hadn't been a copper long.

Mrs Whilden appeared from the sister's office and walked over to Steff's bed. She looked first at Steff for a moment, silently, and then at Siobhan.

'It's soon going to be time for me to prepare my Craig's supper, and to tell him what's happened today. Is that offer of a lift home still open?'

'It certainly is,' replied PC Flynn, silently thanking her guardian angels. Things were all falling out exactly how she had hoped. She was up and running, playing the family support worker right from the start.

'I'm ready when you are.'

'Shall we go?' asked the aunt, casting one final wistful look at her unconscious niece, and then walking out of the ITU, the policewoman following.

Siobhan was good with geography, and didn't need redirecting back to the house.

'There won't be a problem with my parking this car outside your house?' she asked.

'Not at all,' the aunt replied. 'It will give Craig advance warning that all is not as good as it might be, before he gets in. I think you will be a little less of a surprise.'

She opened the front door and asked, 'Won't you come in?'

Siobhan stepped in.

'Tea?' asked Mrs Whilden.

'Thank you very much.'

'Milk and sugar?'

'Just milk, please.'

Once they were sitting in the living room, and they had sipped their tea, Siobhan started gently.

'Tell me about Steff,' she said in a chatty tone. 'How come she ended up here?'

'She came and stayed with me when my sister was killed in a road accident.'

'Did Steff blame herself for the accident?'

'I don't think so.' The aunt thought for a while and then repeated herself. 'No, I don't think so. One day, though, I am pretty sure that our Steff is going to be quite a wealthy girl, though I don't think she understands that at the moment.'

'You mean there was a lot of money, and they left it all to her?'

'One way or another, yes. Her school fees have all been paid by the trust. And if she goes to university, I understand her fees there will all be taken care of too. I don't quite know what happens to the money if she drops out of school or university. I haven't asked. The trust left some maintenance money for her carers, which is us, of course, but I have a feeling that there is a lot more. For a start, the house in Sutton is still there, though their trustees have let it out. Funny place, Sutton; we've only been there once. We were invited to my sister's for tea. I think we both felt that the curtains of the houses nearby were twitching. I don't really think that Jess ever felt really comfortable there. There were times I think she felt she had moved too far up the ladder, and she wasn't quite sure how far down it was, if she ever fell off. Do you know what I mean? My Craig's tatty old Ford stood out like a sore thumb surrounded by all those Jags and Range Rovers. I think my sister was sensitive about that too, so when we got together after that, she always came round here.'

'Are you one of the trustees?'

'Oh lord, no, I wouldn't understand any of that stuff.'

'Who is, then?'

'Oh, I don't know, some London friends of Jessica and Richard's…'

'Jessica and Richard?'

'My sister and her husband.'

'Oh, right. And your husband is?' She felt she should get to know a little bit about Mr Whilden before he arrived home.

'Craig, he's a painter and decorator. Very good at it he is, and keeps in work, despite these uncertain times, but never makes as much money as a stockbroker. Richard would make as much in a day as our Craig does in a year, and we're not poor, not like some people. You know what I mean?'

Siobhan nodded.

'I must get the potatoes into the oven,' Mrs Whilden said. 'It takes a good hour to get them done right, and my Craig does like them done right. Are you staying for supper?' she added.

'Oh, lord, no, I don't think so. I'm rather hoping there will be tea waiting for me when I get home too.' She was, however, very touched that Mrs Whilden had even considered inviting her.

Mrs Whilden turned up the cooker to two hundred degrees, and took two large potatoes out of a sack. She washed them, taking care not to damage the skin. She then popped them in the oven; Siobhan noticed that she hadn't waited for the oven to get up to temperature. She then set the timer for three-quarters of an hour, explaining that, when it went off, that would be the time to put the sausages in. She pulled a packet of sausages out of the fridge, pricked them on both sides, and then put them in a Pyrex dish on the worktop. She looked around, and then said, 'Shall we go back to the sitting room?'

Siobhan followed her through thoughtfully. There didn't seem to be much of the browbeaten little woman about Mrs Whilden, but she was certainly making sure that her husband's needs were met.

'Doris?' came a voice from the front door. 'What... have... you... done? There's a plod car parked right outside our house.'

So that was her name, Siobhan thought. How unkind: their parents had called one girl Jessica and the other Doris. You could bet on which would get the stockbroker, and which would get the painter and decorator.

Craig, a big, plethoric man covered in paint splatters, walked into the room. He dumped his work bag down on the table, and announced that he would get himself a beer from the fridge, and then she could tell him all about it. Two seconds later he was back, pouring a pint of the local Jeffrey Hudson Bitter from a bottle into a plain pint glass which looked as if it had been through a dishwasher very many times.

'That would be me in the police car,' said Siobhan. She paused, and then completed the sentence, 'parked out front.'

'Okay, so what's the silly cow done now?' Oh, Siobhan thought, perhaps 'browbeaten' was appropriate after all.

'Who are you referring to as a silly cow?' asked Siobhan drily.

'Her,' he replied, jerking a thumb at Doris.

'Your wife has done absolutely nothing to interest the police,' she said frostily. 'I'm here because of your niece.'

'Steff? Butter wouldn't melt in her mouth. Go on, giss a laugh: what do you think she's done?'

'She was involved in a disturbance last night, and is currently unconscious in hospital. When she wakes up she is likely to be arrested for homicide.'

He didn't deserve the soft soap version.

'She's in hospital? So what am I supposed to do—' He stopped, and looked at Doris, who said nothing. 'Poor little bugger,' he said, his voice softening markedly, making the conversation not all about him. 'What happened?'

Doris piled in brutally. 'She was apparently screwing some Paki boy on a piece of wasteland, and he tore her insides out, so she hit him with an iron bar and killed him.' *Well,* Siobhan thought, *that's one way of putting the official story of what appears to have happened, in a nutshell. It's not quite how I would have put it myself, but there you go.*

'What do you mean, "tore her insides out"?'

'She had to have a hysterectomy to save her life, sir,' Siobhan chipped in, to save the conversation from getting any messier.

'You mean she ain't going to be able to do sex any more?' he asked, thunderstruck.

'I don't know about that, sir, but she won't be able to have children of her own naturally.'

'Oh fuck! But doesn't that make it self-defence?' he added.

'It's too early to say what the prosecution will come up with, but that's likely to be the defence's point of view, yes.'

'You're a pretty little thing,' Craig suddenly threw in from nowhere, giving Siobhan the once-over. 'You got a boyfriend?'

Siobhan looked at him, stunned at the sudden change of direction the conversation had taken. 'Well, I have no idea what that has to do with the price of cheese, but yes, I have. And, no, I'm not going to ask why you asked, because my private life is none of your fecking business.' She threw the expletive out with a great deal of venom. 'I am your family liaison officer, and don't you forget that, boyo. I'm the copper you've got on your side, when everyone else is descending from a great height, squawking, "Kill, kill, exterminate".' And she made the last word sound exactly like an Irish female Dalek. 'Just remember that, and ye'd be ill advised to lose me as an ally.'

She could tell he wasn't going to apologise, but at least he looked a little crestfallen at having triggered a lecture on how to behave.

'Well, I'd best be leaving you two to it. You've got your tea, and I've got to be getting off home.' Siobhan's voice was stiff with warning. 'I will see you both tomorrow, and let's hope that Steff has woken up in the morning, okay?'

'Good night, constable,' said Doris, with a big grin. It had been some time since she had heard someone tell Craig where to get off. As Siobhan left the house, on her way out, in the background, she heard the timer go *ping*.

Chapter 20

Tom clicked his drugs box shut and wandered down to reception. Sam Shivalkar and Judy Cross were in the back office, already signing things that the receptionists were sticking under their noses. The secretary had left for the day, and had left a list of things for the receptionists to made sure the doctors got done before they too went home.

'Anything I need to be aware of, Tom?' asked Sam. 'I'm doing the early evening shift for the co-op tonight.' The GPs of Peterborough had set up a co-operative to cover the evenings, night shifts and the weekends. They had also invested in a couple of cars and drivers to cover those shifts. Tom's personal opinion was that the drivers probably knew more about where to find obscure addresses in the back streets of Peterborough than local taxi drivers. The drivers were also supposedly there to protect the doctors, and also to provide a second pair of hands.

Tom was aware that he had a graveyard shift coming up in the next few days, and while he had never felt particularly threatened when doing a night shift himself, he was also aware that the local louts might consider women GPs, and their drugs boxes, fair game. No, that wasn't entirely true; he did remember a house call that had shaken him up somewhat. He had been called out mid-afternoon during a weekend the previous year to what sounded like a domestic incident in a house belonging to a patient from a different practice. He could hear crying in the background, and the request was couched in the terms: 'And if you don't get your arse out here pretty damn quick, I'm going to kill the bitch.' On his way to the house, he had called the police. When he arrived at the house, there wasn't a police car in sight, so he said to the driver that he was going in anyway, and left his phone on in his pocket. Once he had got into the house the issue appeared totally different. Whoever had made the call had gone out, and the woman in question was fairly poorly, with what looked like acute appendicitis. He pulled the live phone to his car and asked the driver to call an ambulance, while he phoned the hospital admissions unit to brief them about the patient they would be getting shortly.

'Why did your dad sound so threatening and angry?' he asked one of the children sitting on the side of the woman's bed.

'Oh, Dad's always like that,' said a girl of some twelve or thirteen years, holding the patient's hand.

'Yeah,' said a teenaged boy, a little older than the girl, from the door behind him. 'He's all wind and piss.'

'Does he hit you?' Tom asked, suddenly alarmed by the potential undercurrent.

'Nah; like I said, he's all wind and piss. He wouldn't dare. I'd hit him back. We don't take any notice of him, but you'll notice one thing – *you* did.'

Tom had nodded. Yes, he had. 'We'd have been here just as quickly if he'd just explained what was actually going on,' Tom had replied carefully.

The boy looked at him quizzically. 'Would you?' he asked. 'Our regular doctor wouldn't, and that's for certain. He doesn't do home visits, not unless you grease his palm.' Now there was a telephone call Tom realised he was going to have to make in the morning. The problem with that sort of conversation was that there were two sides to every story, and one person's view of the truth was another man's fantasy. After that incident, the GP in question had agreed he had never visited that household, but had never actually been asked to do so. After another similar incident, he had been rather less convinced by the GP's response, so he had passed the comment on to the management committee, which was made up of other GPs from the area, and as far as he was concerned that case was then shut. Because the GP involved in that case was how he was, Tom never got any feedback concerning the diagnosis he had made either. There weren't any complaints flying around from anywhere, so presumably he had got it right on the night.

Tom thought through the people he had seen in the last few days. He trotted out the names of a few patients who had an imminent appointment with the afterlife. Sam knew all of them, as did the other staff in the practice. He couldn't think of anyone else who would be likely to bother a doctor out of hours, apart from the occasional 'heartsink' patient, who might phone a doctor for attention at any hour of the day or night. The problem with patients who made doctors' hearts sink, as far as the doctors were concerned, was the fear that one day a stone would be erected over their last resting place which read, 'See? I told you I was ill.'

'What happened to that girl of yours who was in the ICU?' Sam asked.

'Still in the ICU as far as I know,' Tom replied. 'She hadn't woken up yet the last time I heard. I saw her at lunchtime, you know,' he added. 'It's the first time I've been in the new ICU.'

'Oh, how is it?'

'Very high-tech. I wouldn't know where to start,' he grinned. 'The sister in charge used to be a newly qualified staff nurse when I was an SHO just after I first got here.'

'That sounds like somebody who's grabbed success by the scruff of the neck.'

'She was always very bright. That's what an SHO always needs; a nurse who knows what she's doing.' He took a breath. 'So you won't be needed to go and visit Steff Flack during your shift this evening, unless she's woken up and escaped, and then she probably won't need a visit anyway.'

Sam grinned, and Judy smiled. Judy Cross was the senior partner in the practice, a laconic Scot from Dundee, the home of rich fruitcake and smoked fish. She couldn't think of anyone who was causing her concern either.

'But then, ye ken, we're always wrong, aren't we? I'm no' going out, so if ye need to talk to me, give me a call.' She wasn't actually offering to visit a patient instead of Sam, but everything that didn't require movement was on offer.

Tom added, 'I'm out this evening, but I'll have my phone in my pocket, so if you do need to call, feel free.' But they all knew that the patient who would cause a concern would be one that none of them had ever heard of, and whose GP was nowhere to be found, and had not briefed the co-operative either. Those patients would end up in hospital, almost certainly.

Tom and Judy walked out to the car park together, and wished each other good night. Sam followed them and climbed into his car. The drive round from their surgery in Orton to the on-call centre wouldn't take him very long. It would have been even quicker if it wasn't for that speed camera on the Oundle Road. It was at a very silly location, he thought, just after the traffic lights, where the road was quite narrow and had bicycle lanes on either side. Sam's solution to the problem was to set his cruise control to thirty miles per hour before he hit the traffic lights. He would almost certainly have to stop at the lights, but the speed was already set. Once he had cleared the lights he would restart the cruise control, which would take him to no higher than thirty, and he could steer clear of the wobbling cyclists, earphones in their ears, without worrying about being caught by the speed camera, as had so many people he had known. He wondered whether that speed camera paid for the annual policemen's ball.

The on-call centre was on the way into town just before the remains of the old District Hospital, which still stood proud, but very empty, surrounded by fencing and signs saying 'Keep Out' in an assortment of languages. He wondered how many people squatted in there now. The on-call centre was a complete new build on the site of the old geriatric hospital known as Fenland Wing. It was certainly an architecturally interesting creation, if you looked at it from the outside. Inside, the waiting area was very small for the number of clients it had to hold, waiting to see a doctor, paramedic or nurse.

Sam parked his car outside the path lab. Most of the spaces were empty at this time of day, and those that were filled were almost certainly either his colleagues or a duty technician in the lab itself. He put a note on the windscreen of his car explaining who he was, and where he might be found, if anyone in the lab wondered who it was who was sleeping in their bed. He walked over to the centre and announced himself to the receptionist, who pressed the button under her desk and let him in to the back.

'Evening, Dr Sam,' said a cheery voice behind him as he walked into the space behind the office. 'Fancy a trip back to Orton?' It was Ron, one of the co-op's drivers, who was waving a piece of paper with a name and address printed along the top. 'Don't worry, it isn't one of yours waiting till you got here before they called. Actually, he sounded pretty sick when his mum called.'

'Let's go then,' he said. He usually enjoyed pottering about in the car of an evening. He got to see parts of the city he would never see during his working day, and sometimes he found himself at somebody's idea of architecture and wondering, *why*? He opened the back door of the car and slung his bag onto the floor, and then climbed into the passenger side and strapped himself in.

The driver was already at the wheel and waiting.

'Greens?' he suggested. Doctors are not allowed to use the 'blues and twos' of the emergency services. A green flashing light on the top of a doctor's car has no legal significance whatever, and entitles them to do absolutely nothing that having no light entitles them to do. It does say, however, that there is a doctor on an emergency call in the car. It also reminds people who are in the way that one day they might need the services of a doctor in a car with a flashing green light on the roof, thus encouraging them to get out of the way and let them through.

The house they were heading to may not have belonged to a client from his practice, but a number of his patients did live on that street, and he saw one or two curtains move as they pulled up. He hoped they were able to distinguish the green from a blue light, as the car did look quite like a police car, with its day-glo stripes. It did have 'Doctor' written backwards on the bonnet, so that it would read correctly in the car in front's rear-view mirror, but the curtain-twitchers probably wouldn't recognise that.

Sam pressed the doorbell, and a very distressed middle-aged woman opened the door for him.

'He's in here, doctor,' she said, leading him into the front room. Sprawled over the table, face down, was a young man – or even a boy, perhaps – and scattered on the table under him were a number of pink pills. Sam glanced at the piece of paper he was holding. It told him the boy's name was Sean.

'Sean?' he asked. The lad didn't move.

The woman nodded. 'Yes, that's his name,' she replied.

'Sean?' he said in a much louder voice, and still the lad didn't react.

Sam leaned forward and touched Sean's shoulder, and when he pulled it even just slightly, he realised why he hadn't responded. The boy had been dead long enough for rigor mortis to start setting in. For his mother's sake, Sam took the boy's pulse. His wrist was cooling and becoming clammy too. There was no pulse.

Sam helped the mother to a chair, and said gently, 'I'm afraid your son is dead, Mrs James, and he has been so for a little while.'

The mother looked up at Sam, wide-eyed and aghast.

'No, no, no,' she wailed. 'That can't be right! Can't you do something like they do on telly? You know, lean on his chest and blow air into his lungs? What do they call it, CPR?'

'Not at this stage, Mrs James, that only works at the very moment the heart stops. Poor Sean here has been dead for at least four hours. Was he ill?' Sam asked more in hope than anything else.

'Like what sort of illness?' the woman asked.

'Anything serious, like a cancer or cystic fibrosis or something?' Sam shuffled through his memory bank for diseases that took teenagers. The most common cause of death among kids of this age was an accident.

'No, nothing like that.'

'I'm afraid I'm going to have to report this to the police,' he said.

'Can't we tidy all this up first?' she said, making to sweep the pink tablets into the palm of her hand.

'No, I'm afraid not, we mustn't touch anything.' He first dialled his car to let the driver know that they weren't going anywhere for a while, and then dialled 999, and asked for the police.

Chapter 21

'Where is that girl? Her supper's nearly ready, and she's not answering her phone.' Shannen's foster mother was becoming quite annoyed.

'Send her a text,' suggested her husband from the living room.

'Do you know how to do that?' she asked.

'Gimme,' he replied and she walked in, waving her phone at the man who sat in his chair in front of the television, watching a football game.

'Who is it today?' she asked.

'Haven't the faintest,' he said, taking the phone from her. 'Tell me if anything interesting happens.' And he looked down at the phone and texted Shannen. 'Supper's ready, where are you?' and pressed send.

'There, that's that sorted,' he said, handing the phone back to his wife. 'Hopefully she'll reply to that. It's either that or she's lost her phone.'

'That wouldn't be like her,' his wife replied. 'She never loses her phone. It's Jervis who's always losing his.'

Her husband took a long pull from the beer bottle in his left hand, and he breathed out again with a satisfied 'aah.'

'They're not a bad team, this lot,' he remarked.

'Who are?'

'The ones in blue.'

'And they are?'

'Fuck knows.'

The foster mother's phone announced the arrival of a text.

'Oh, it's from Shannen,' she said, and read the message out to her husband. 'I've got a boyfriend, and I'm staying with him for a while. Shanns.'

The foster mother and her husband looked at each other. 'Well, there's a thing,' she said. 'I didn't know she was interested in boys, let alone actually having a boyfriend. Do you know anything about this boy?'

'Do you even know where he's from?' he replied.

They weren't far enough up the food chain to ask questions like 'Do we know what his father does for a living?' but they were posh enough to be interested in the boy himself. After all, they were still actually married, and their son, old enough to be at work, had been conceived after they'd got married; so they did consider themselves classy enough to have a right to know.

The phone pinged, announcing the arrival of another text, and again the foster mother read it out.

'Don't panic about the money. I won't tell the council I'm not there, if you won't, so they'll still keep paying you. Text me if they find out, and I'll be back. See ya, Shanns.'

'Cunning little vixen,' said the foster father. 'I didn't know she had it in her.'

'Well, there's easily enough supper for the three of us now. Do you want an extra chop, our dad?'

'I wouldn't say no if there's one going begging. I could always do with a bit of pork, you know that.'

At the other end of that phone, Shannen was feeling pretty full of herself, and for the first time in her life she was feeling pretty, full stop. She looked up at Ruke and said, 'Just think, at lunchtime today I was sitting on my doorstep wondering when my life was going to start. Here we are, and the sun hasn't even set yet, and I've had my first curry, I've tasted spunk for the first time, and I've even had my first fuck. Now if that isn't a life that's taken a sudden change for the better, I don't know what is.'

Ruke sat down beside Shannen, sitting naked on the edge of the bed, proud and not shy about her nudity. He patted her chubby thigh.

'That was never your first fuck,' he said, sounding amazed.

'Yeah,' she said, 'it was.'

'But you're so good at it. Shanns, you're a natural. That was brilliant. You know something? I've got a mate who would really fancy you, you know.'

'Really?'

'Yeah, really, but we're not going to see him today, tomorrow maybe; but I want to have more fun with you myself today. Isn't that what you want too?'

'Yeah,' she said, trying to sound sexy, but not sounding very convincing.

'So what would you like to do next? Curry, spunk or another fuck? Or would you like to do something else completely? More sex?' he added hopefully.

'Can we not for a little while, please?' she said. 'I'm still a little sore down there, but once it's calmed down again, yes please.'

'Not a problem,' said Ruke. 'I'll go and get some kulfi.'

'Cool fee?' she asked. 'What's that?' She sounded a little alarmed.

'Wait and see, you'll like it. Coke?'

'Yes, please.' Shannen was polite.

Ruke walked out of the room. Shannen stood up and looked for her clothes. Those she could see were on the chair. She picked up her T-shirt and pulled it over her head. Her knickers fell off the chair, and she pulled them on too. She couldn't see her trousers anywhere, but they must be somewhere. Ruke would know. But at least she felt a little less chilly. Ruke returned with a china bowl and a spoon.

'Kulfi,' he said.

Shannen looked slightly quizzically at the orange, rather lumpy, mess in the bowl.

'Try it,' he said, encouragingly.

She dipped the spoon in it, and licked the end of it carefully. Hey! It was good. It was very cold, with a flavour of mango and nuts, with pieces of nuts mixed in.

'Asian ice cream,' he said. 'What do you think?'

'Yum.'

He put a mirror on the table and a credit card beside it. He poured a little white powder onto the mirror, and started chopping it with the credit card, forming a couple of narrow straight lines. Shannen, her mouth full of ice cream, was fascinated. She let the ice cream soften in her mouth and then swallowed. She didn't want to spit any of the delicious stuff out by accident, but once it had all gone down, she asked, 'What's that?'

'That,' Ruke replied, 'is grown-up's coke.' He drew out a twenty-pound note and rolled it into a tube. He put one end of the tube into his left nostril and, running the other end of the tube along the mirror, he sniffed the powder up into his nose. He closed his eyes for a moment, and then passed the banknote over to her, still rolled.

'Me?' she asked, wide-eyed and questioning.

'You,' he replied, passing her the mirror.

Chapter 22

Meanwhile, in a different part of town, the following conversation was taking place.

'Come in, old man, don't just stand there on the doorstep.' The sound of southern fried rock 'n' roll was coming from behind the sitting room door, though he didn't recognise the singer. He listened a little more carefully. He didn't recognise the language he was singing in, for that matter.

'Coffee, tea, or do you want to risk a beer?' the host offered.

Tom looked at his host cautiously. 'Depends what beer, and what strength?'

It didn't pay to be a fool when a policeman was playing host, especially one as senior as J. Wolfgang Schmidt.

'Kölsch, around five per cent,' came the reply.

Tom grinned. 'I'll have just the one,' he replied, and followed Wolfgang's elegant silver hair as it bounced through into the kitchen and came back with two cold bottles with red labels which read 'Früh', and two glass jackboots. They were not elegant like the traditional German glass Stiefeln, as worn by knights in britches, but solid and chunky jackboots, just like his grandfather had worn before he was captured. Well, he hadn't worn glass boots, obviously; but these held the ale better than leather ones would have, and they looked to be marginally less likely to suddenly dump half a litre of the stuff down a shirt-front than the glass riding boot.

'So you've been back to Germany recently,' Tom said, pouring from the bottle into the glass.

'Not at all, there's a wonderful dealer just south of King's Lynn who sells this by the crate. It may be a bit more expensive there than if you buy it in Cologne, but it's a lot less expensive to get to King's Lynn, so these things balance out.'

'What are we listening to?' Tom asked.

'It's a live album by BAP, called *Affrocke*.'

'BAP?'

'They're a band from Cologne and they're singing in the local dialect, which is also called Kölsch. The singer-songwriter fell out with his father back in the day, and sadly, I understand, they never fell back in again. He says in his book he always felt bad about that, so he called his band "Dad" – or, as they say in Kölsch, "BAP". Oh yes, and his name is Wolfgang too. Germans I've met say they're more interested in the lyrics he writes than the music. Me, it's all about the music, though I can usually work out what the song's all about.'

'Are your roots in Cologne? I thought your family came from further east than that.'

'My grandfather was born in Stettin, deep in east Prussia. He was ambushed and taken prisoner during the war, before he'd even fired a shot, and finished up in the prison camp at Norman Cross outside Yaxley. He wasn't over-keen on being repatriated to the Russian sector when the war was over and found himself working as a farm labourer in Holme Fen.' He chuckled. 'He was probably among the first of the local immigrant workers. It was while he was at that farm that he watched Europe sorting itself out after the war, and Stettin and Danzig, among others, became part of Poland, as the border of Poland moved sharply westwards. About the only part of Poland that always seems to remain part of Poland, no matter what, is Warsaw itself. Opa stayed here in Yaxley, and he learned English, and then like you do, he met a girl, and then Dad, or as they would call him in Cologne, Bap came along. He grew up and met my mum. But because I still had a German surname, they gave me an English Christian name and a German one, so I could decide what I wanted to be in my turn. I could have been Jimmy Smith if I had wanted, but, like my dad, I hung on to the German name, somehow, I thought Wolfgang Schmidt sounded more exclusive. Struck me there were too many Jimmy Smiths around, and anyway I like being an Englishman with a foreign name, especially in the fraud squad. It does lead to raised eyebrows.'

The guitarist tore into the solo, and conversation ceased while he played. Tom sucked the pale beer through the head

114

he had poured into it. This was what he and Volffy had in common: off-centre rock 'n' roll music and the blues. He couldn't remember where they had met, but within moments of meeting, they discovered they were kindred spirits: two divorced professionals with a taste for music that rocked. They tried to get together at least on a fortnightly basis to run through each other's record and CD collections to find another new experience to share. Every now and then one of them would find a record that hadn't been played by either of them yet, and on other occasions they would find an album that had been central to both of their lives since adolescence.

'What are you doing this weekend?' asked Volffy. 'Anything chilling?'

'I'm rehearsing a play,' replied Tom.

'You're what?'

'I'm rehearsing a play. Well, you know I've got kids, right?'

'Yes?' Volffy's voice showed interest. 'I seem to remember, a boy and a girl.'

'Well, my daughter's into thesping, and is in the local am-dram society. And you know how most plays have more male than female parts, and yet most am-drams are mainly full of women? So she got me roped into a part in a thing they're putting on this autumn. It's one of two one-act comedies they're doing as a back-to-back. Quite brave, actually: the one that I'm in is a complete piss-take of amateur dramatics. Well,' he added apologetically, 'it gives me the opportunity to spend some quality time with Jenny.'

'So what are you playing in this?'

'Well, it's a spoof Victorian melodrama called *Murder at the Grange*, and I play the part of the butler. Well, to be technically correct, I play the part of the actor playing the part of the butler.'

'I don't follow at all.'

'Well, you know in all Victorian murder stories, it was the butler who did it. Well, in this one the actor playing the butler gets utterly scuttered on stage on prop whisky, long before the murder takes place, so that he is totally incapable of killing anything apart from himself. The play goes steadily downhill from there.'

'Your daughter must be very proud of you,' said the policeman ironically. 'What part does she get to play?'

'Ah well, she gets to play a right-wing agitator boy. Well, you see, the character she plays in this play is a girl filling in for a boy, because there aren't a lot of boys in this company. She's friends with the son of the victim. Now, the actor playing the son is older than the actor playing his dad, who's the victim, and he's a bit deaf, and can't hear the prompts, and he misses a whole slew of the play. Now the part my daughter's playing, Boofy, loses her main speech in that mistaken cut, so Boofy spends a lot of time trying to get to say it anyway. It's a hoot!'

Volffy rolled his eyes, not following this at all. 'How old is this daughter of yours?'

'Jenny's sixteen. Oh, don't worry, she gets to play a straight girl part in the other play.'

'The one you're not in.'

'The one I'm not in, yes. But she really is very funny in the play that I'm in. She's brilliant at playing not-a-boy.'

'Why has she got you mixed up in all this?'

'I think she's probably trying to match me up with someone in the am-dram society.'

'Who?'

'I haven't worked that one out yet. There's no one in the company who particularly takes my fancy, if that's what you mean. But I think she worries about me. Her mother got married again, and Jenny's got a couple of stepbrothers, and the two younger boys get on like a house on fire. I don't think she's quite so sure about the elder stepbrother – he's just the wrong age, and a little oily, but he's off to university shortly, and anyway I'm sure Jenny can look after herself.'

'Do you think she's trying to find you a new wife, so she can come and live with you?'

'I hadn't thought about that. No, surely not, she wouldn't want to leave her current school. She's hoping to get into Oxford.'

'Ah, so you mean she's very clever, and she doesn't want to be anywhere near either parent if she can help it.'

'Now, Volffy, I know you're pulling my leg.'

'Would you like something to eat?' asked Volffy, changing the subject completely.

'We can order in a pizza or some Chinese a bit later if you like,' Tom replied.

'Well, if you hang on a bit, there's this new girl I met recently, and before I really knew what had happened, she moved in last week. Now, she might be able to knock something up, or maybe she'll want a takeaway too.'

'A new girl? Should I be ashamed of you?'

'A little,' grinned Volffy sheepishly. 'She is a bit young.'

'How young?'

'Late twenties,' said Volffy, pulling a face.

'You old rascal! And what does her mother have to say about all this?'

'I have no idea; I've never met her. If her daughter's anything to go by, she'd be absolutely terrifying, and rather gorgeous.'

'I can't wait to meet her. Is she into rock 'n' roll too?'

'Up to a point, yes, but she has this way of saying, "That's enough music for tonight" in a way I find impossible to resist.'

They lay back in the very comfortable La-Z-Boy chairs and waited for the track to finish. It was their tradition that the host picked the music that they should listen to. Tom was very happy to continue listening to *Affrocke*, and said so. Wolfgang took the LP off the turntable and put it back into the sleeve. From the sleeve he pulled out the other LP from the set.

'I think you'll find this one interesting. They had an English guitarist and gob-iron player on this album, and he gets the opportunity to stretch out on this one.'

At the end of the side Volffy was about to flip over the LP to play its fourth side, when they heard a voice.

'Hellooo, it's me.'

Volffy leaped up and went into the hall.

'Shuv,' he said affectionately. 'We've got company.' Tom wasn't sure whether this was a positive announcement or a warning. 'Remember Tom, the doctor I told you about?' he was saying as they walked back into the living room together.

'Oh, you mean Rock-a-Doc.' A girl in her mid to late twenties, wearing a tracksuit, a warm, recently exercised glow and a smile, stuck out a hand towards him, 'Delighted to make your acquaintance. My name's Siobhan, but everybody calls me Shuv, and that's fine by me.'

'Tom,' replied the doctor, 'but if you want to call me Rock-a-Doc, I certainly won't object.'

'We were talking about supper,' said Volffy, 'but before we made a decision, we thought we'd ask what you wanted: pizza, Chinese, curry…'

'That sounds like you're planning a delivery meal,' she said. 'I take it you haven't got anything in yourself?'

'Er, no.'

'There are times, Wolfgang Schmidt, when I wonder how the fuck you survived at all till I came along.' She turned to Tom. 'Tell me, Rock-a-Doc, have you ever eaten a real Irish stew made by a real Irishman?'

'Er, no, I haven't.'

'You're fortunate,' she replied, quick as a flash. 'It's disgustin'; but in comparison with a German *Winzertopf* made by this man, 'tis positive ambrosia. Civilising him is going to be a long, slow process, but we're getting there. Shall I order in some Chinese? I don't think I'm ready to let you cook for any of your friends yet; I think I'd still find it too embarrassing.' She picked up the phone and dialled. She ordered the food, gave Volffy's name and address, and finally turned back to the room.

'Okay, that's all ordered. You've paid, I remembered your credit card numbers,' she grinned. 'I'm going upstairs to grab a shower and scrub off all the clag from my workout.'

'Well?' said Volffy. 'What do you think?'

'Amazing,' said Tom. 'She's a veritable hurricane. You know she's going to break you in half, don't you?'

'In all probability,' replied the policeman, 'but what a way to go.' He turned down the amplifier a bit, so they could hear the delivery when it arrived. They expected that it would take half an hour, and by that time Shuv would be back down again, all scrubbed and shiny. Tom realised who had now taken over the running the house, but Volffy looked like he was rather enjoying the experience.

Chapter 23

The sun had set, and Sergeant Odembe was sitting on his own in the incident room. He was pulling together the reports that Susie and Virender had brought in from the Shadeed household. He noted that there was a lot more of Susie's report. Virender had stated that he had found it very difficult to get anything out of the men. They really didn't want to talk to him at all in any language.

Sergeant Odembe had already glanced at Siobhan's rather dry report from the Whildens' house in Orton. He felt that there was an undercurrent going on there, which, no doubt, she was going to explore further. Slightly unprofessional, he thought; should anything untoward happen to PC Flynn, then her suspicions might never come to light.

He had a preliminary autopsy report from the lab, and had requested a check on the quality and quantity of semen in Aziz Shadeed's urethra, which would answer the question whether he had ejaculated during his experience with Steff, as Molinari had requested – though quite why Molinari wanted to know that he hadn't made clear.

He was a little disappointed that no samples had been taken in the Casualty department. He wasn't sure how happy Detective Inspector Drake was going to be about that, but that was the rub of the green. He would probably blame the first officers on scene for not reminding the hospital staff to use a rape kit. But then, Odembe reminded himself, it was an open and shut case anyway, wasn't it?

**

Across town, in the car park of a café in Millfield, Yuri was unloading the boot of his car. Adelina, now dressed in jeans and a shapeless pullover, was helping him, in the hope that she could cadge a lift back to the flat in Viersen Platz where she stayed. She understood all about the problems that the young Russian would have with his sexuality in his home country. On the other hand, for that very reason, she felt completely safe with him. Inside the café Uncle Lev was counting the cards of yellow pills that Yuri had brought in, and generally looking pleased with the day's takings. He had already counted the cash with a smile.

***

A minibus had just delivered two Lithuanian men to their front door after their first day's work. They'd had their first sight of British currency. They didn't get to look at it for very long, of course, before. It had disappeared into their landlord's capacious pockets as a down payment on their room. The landlord had provided them with a hot stew when they got in. He knew that a well-fed labour force would continue to bring in the rent. They knew that, by Friday night, they would have paid off the week's deposit, and they would have a little cash in their pocket to spend on themselves. Maybe they would share a bottle of vodka, or they might even go downstairs to the bar that the landlord ran for the residents. Now, though, it was time for bed, as they knew that the minibus wouldn't wait for them if they weren't ready when it called for them before dawn tomorrow.

***

Siobhan was wearing nothing but one of Wolfgang's shirts. It reached almost down to her knees. She was putting tealeaves into a very old Teasmade that Volffy had picked up in a junk shop somewhere. She could hear Volffy on the way up with a thermos flask full of ice-cold milk. When the alarm went off in the morning, there on his side of the bed would be a pot full of tea to greet the day. She thought, with a frisson of excitement, that it had taken an age, and in the end not much subtlety, to get rid of Tom. They had one more thing to do that day that certainly didn't involve Rock-a-Doc.

***

In the City Hospital a different medical student was sitting, waiting for some excitement, in the Casualty department. Rhea had talked to John about his experience the previous night, and how it had won him a long case to write up for his final exam. Jammy bastard, she thought, now that was a case and a half. Not only did it have some physical pathology, including an emergency operation, but it also had some psychiatric pathology, and even some criminal stuff too. She was really hoping that a case like that came through the doors tonight.

***

Meanwhile, John had just gone back to his room to type some information up on his laptop. He had recently been back to the ITU, and had cast an eye over his patient, Steff. She was beginning to stir, and they said she might even be awake by the morning. If she was, then he could take a formal history from her too. He thought about that for a moment. He wondered whether she would remember what had happened to her. If she didn't, then he would be able to discuss something about retrograde amnesia in his paper as well. Somewhere, in the back of his mind, he felt just a little guilty for having those thoughts.

***

Tom Clark was turning in. It had been a fascinating evening, with some brilliant music he had not heard before, and Volffy's new girlfriend, Shuv, was a blast! That was, until she had gently explained to him what the front door was for, and would he like her to sort out a taxi if he felt he shouldn't be driving?

***

121

Shannen looked up at the ceiling. There was a gentle snore in her right ear, but she wasn't ready for sleep yet, even if she would allow it to come. She had never slept in anyone's arms before, and here she had an arm lying across her naked abdomen. She was now a woman, and she thought she should really be out celebrating her new status, but then she looked at the young man asleep beside her – who so recently had been inside her. She thought she shouldn't go anywhere to celebrate anything without him; he was the point of the whole thing. There was a whole new world out there, and it was hers for the taking.

***

Susie had just been delivered back to her digs by Danny. They had had a really nice evening together, enjoying a pie and a pint down at the pub. Somehow she needed to find out how she could entice him into her flat without obviously seeming slutty. Did inviting someone in for coffee work, even though neither of them drank coffee and they both knew it? She would have to ask Shuv the next day: if anyone knew the protocol about that sort of thing, it would be Shuv.

***

Craig snored beerily on his side of the bed, and beside him Doris lay awake, staring at the ceiling. What would happen if he woke up? she worried.

***

And Steff? She was slowly coming round. She had no idea where she was, or what was going on, but Christ, whatever was going on in her tummy really damn well hurt, and what the hell were these bandages stuck to her skin?

Chapter 24

The young Lithuanian men were waiting just inside the door, as it was drizzling. It was just before dawn. The Transit mini-bus they were waiting for pulled up outside and they were aboard in a trice. The driver drove around the wet streets, fill-ing the minibus up with men, until every seat was filled. It then set off out of the town towards the country. It was difficult to see anything once they were out in the blackness.

The two Lithuanian brothers, who were sitting side by side, spoke softly to each other, but not loudly enough to be heard by anyone else – even if they understood Lithuanian. No one else spoke much, and the dominant sound in the minibus was a mechanical rattle. It was not a brand new vehicle they were travelling in, nor had the side roads they were travelling down been recently resurfaced. The occasional pothole in the road came as an unpleasant surprise to the passengers, and the oaths that resulted told the story of where they had started their lives. The colourful Polish and Lithuanian sounds amused the driver. He had no idea what the words meant, mind you – and was that a Portuguese swear word in the back there? He didn't think he had any Portuguese on this run, but who knew?

The light was just coming up when the minibus pulled up in the farmyard. The men were greeted by a round, cheerful woman whom the Lithuanians had taken to be the farmer's wife. She led them all into the refectory. There was a row of enamel mugs on the table and an urn of sweet, milky tea at the end of it, with a white enamel bucket on the floor to catch the drips. There were also bowls of thick porridge. It was there to be eaten, and eaten quickly. She knew well that you got a better day's work out of a man who was warm and had a full stom-ach, especially in the drizzle. The other equipment she had was plastic macs for them all. They wouldn't be perfect protection, by a long chalk, but it showed the men that she cared. Well, that was the intention anyway. She probably couldn't care less if the truth be told, as long as she got the potatoes and cabbages in.

Fifteen minutes after breakfast the men were all suited and booted and out in the fields, while she was back in the warm of her parlour, cigarette in hand, with a china cup of tea in the other. She checked that she had enough cash in the safe to pay gang master Sid for that day's workforce. You paid Sid on the day, or he didn't turn up with the men the following day. She wondered what he would do if she didn't pay. She had no idea; challenging Sid was a thing she had never done.

Andrzej Lanavicius, one of the Lithuanian men, in his late twenties and fit, as he would say, was bending over, picking up the potatoes that his brother Sergei had forked up. When they had filled the barrow with potatoes they would swap jobs, and Andrzej would do the forking, while Sergei would wheel the barrow up to the farmyard, and then return with the empty barrow. They were brothers and they were a team. But it was back-breaking work, and by the time it was Andrzej's turn to take over the fork, his back was already sore and he needed to stand up straight.

What? What was that? He looked carefully between the row, of potatoes. Was that metal glinting up at him?

'Sergei, Sergei, stop a minute,' he said softly.

'What?' his brother replied.

Andrzej pulled a disc out of the ground, tossing the potato next to it into the wheelbarrow. He rubbed it and looked at it more closely. He then passed it to his brother. 'Is that gold?' he asked.

'Don't know,' his brother replied. 'Look, there's a face stamped on it, and what's this written on it? *Carolus Rex*. It's a coin of some kind. If it's a coin, it won't be worth a great deal; all the big money in Britain is in banknotes, and the biggest British banknote is only fifty quid. It's not like euros or US dollars, that go up to five hundred dollars.'

'And the rest,' agreed Andrzej. 'Well, if it's worthless, I'll pop it in my pocket as a lucky charm; the first thing I found when I was in England.'

Sergei tossed the rather rough-edged coin back to his brother, who rubbed some more dirt off it and slipped it into his pocket. He picked up another potato and tossed it into the wheelbarrow.

Sergei felt slightly guilty. While he had been forking up the potatoes, he too had found a coin and had put it straight into his pocket without telling his brother. He had decided to find out exactly what he had found when he got back to the flat that night. He thought it was fairly worthless, but you never knew in Britain.

'Okay, Sergei, that's the first barrow done, do you want to run it up to the farmhouse while I start forking the next lot?' Andrzej stood up and flexed his back. Sergei tossed him the fork and turned the barrow, heading up to the house. Andrzej started his turn at forking.

'Hey, you!' came a voice. Andrzej looked up to see an angry-looking man stamping over the field towards him. He had no idea what the angry man was saying. It could have been, 'Where is your brother?' Well, it could have been practically anything, in fact, but he took it to be asking after his brother, so he turned and pointed to the farmhouse, and mimed pushing a wheelbarrow. The man continued to talk to him, but it was still in a language he didn't understand. English, perhaps? He promised that he would start learning English as soon as he could. The man was pointing at him, and pointing at the ground, and getting louder, and redder by the minute. He'll have a stroke in a minute if he's not careful, Andrzej thought. Then he had an idea. Maybe that coin had dropped out of the other man's pocket and he was looking for it. *It isn't mine, after all*, he thought.

He dug into his pocket and pulled the coin out, and tossed it to the man.

'Is this what you're looking for?' he asked.

That stopped the man in his tracks. He looked at the coin carefully, rubbed his eyes, and then looked at it again. He rubbed it on his sleeve, and then bit it. He had stopped shouting as soon as Andrzej gave him the coin. He then looked at Andrzej, and was almost smiling when he said whatever he said next. Then he walked off, looking at the coin and intermittently rubbing it on his sleeve.

Oh well, thought Andrzej, *easy come, easy go. I hope Sergei isn't too upset about it, but it obviously was the shouty man's coin all along.*

He went back to forking up potatoes, ready for Sergei to pick up once he had got back with the barrow.

Chapter 25

Shannen woke, alarmed to find the bed next to her was empty.

Ruke, where are you?

She sat bolt upright and looked around. The door opened, and Ruke walked through, carrying a tray. Oh, bless him! This was another new experience for her. She had never had breakfast in bed before either. It was one new thing after another being with Ruke.

'I got you tea,' he said. 'I hope that's all right. I didn't put sugar in it, but there's sugar on the tray. Milk and cereal?'

She nearly burst into tears; this was all too much. She was being treated like a princess. She had always imagined, ever since she could remember, that this was how you treated princesses. He put the tray on her lap and she tucked in. He took his mug from the tray, and drank from it. It was only then that she became fully aware that he was up and had shaved, carefully, alongside his beard, maintaining his look. Meanwhile she was in bed, naked and feeling rather sticky.

'You're all dressed,' she said.

'Oh yes,' he said. 'People to see, things to do. When you've had your breakfast, you'll be getting up and dressed too. Do you want a shower or a bath?' he asked.

'You mean there's a choice?' she asked. 'At my other home, we kept the coal in the bath.'

'That doesn't sound very convenient. Having to lug the coal upstairs to store it. Where was the boiler?'

'Well, the bathroom and bog were beyond the kitchen. They were all downstairs. You mean you've got a bathroom and bog upstairs here?'

'Right next door to this room. Shall I run you a bath?'

'Ooh! Yes please.'

'I'll get you a dressing gown; we don't want to excite the others.'

'The others? You mean there are other people in the house?'

'One or two, yes, but don't worry, this is my house, they're just cousins. They do what I tell them to do, when I tell them to do it.'

She finished the bowl of cereal, and drank her tea. There were a couple of pills on the tray as well.

'What are these?' she asked.

'They're morning-after pills,' he replied.

'What are they for?'

'Well, we had sex yesterday and last night, yes?'

'Just a little,' she said with a self-satisfied smirk.

'Well, morning-after pills are just to make sure you don't get pregnant, we wouldn't want that now, would we?'

'No, I suppose not,' she said slowly, and then she added quizzically, 'Why not?'

'I think it's a little early in our relationship to start having kids,' he said.

'But if I did get pregnant, we would get married and bring it up together, wouldn't we?'

'Of course,' he replied cheerily. 'Now swallow your pills,' he added firmly. And of course she did.

He wrapped Shannen in the white towelling dressing gown, and led her round the corner to the bathroom. Once in the steam-filled room, he eased the gown off her again and led her to the bath, which smelled of something sweet and spicy as she climbed into it. She looked up at him questioningly.

'Bath salts,' he said. 'They'll make you smell nice.' Even more princess treatment, she thought.

She wallowed in the bath for a while, until Ruke reappeared with a flannel, and washed her gently all over. This time his hands didn't feel sexual, just gentle, even though they went to exactly the same places. Then he said, 'Time to get going.' She stood up and climbed out of the bath, and he rubbed her down with the softest towel she had ever felt in her life. When she was completely dry, he wrapped her hair in the towel, and put the dressing gown again around her naked body, and led her back to his room. Her clothes were laid out on his bed ready for her. When did he have time to do that? she wondered. *Ruke said there were other people in this house*, she thought, *it's just that I haven't heard hide nor hair of them yet.*

Fully dressed, they walked straight out of the house into the drizzle.

'Fortunately it wasn't like this yesterday,' he said. 'I doubt we'd have ever met. You wouldn't have bunked off, and I probably wouldn't have been out for a walk either.'

'I guess I've always been lucky,' she replied, and a little voice in her head asked her, *since when?* But she ignored it.

'Where are we going?' she asked, climbing into the passenger side of his car.

'You'll see,' he replied enigmatically.

They hadn't been driving very long when he pulled off a road and drove up to a barrier. He took a card, the size of a credit card, out of his wallet and stuck it in the mouth of the machine to which the barrier was attached. The machine spat his card out again, and when he took it, the barrier went up. Ruke drove rapidly through it. Shannen couldn't help looking over her shoulder. It didn't take long. The car was hardly through when the arm came back down. There were a number of cars and vans parked back there. Ruke seemed to know exactly where he was going. He found a place to park.

'Come on,' he said, and they were out of the car, walking towards a gap between the buildings. Ruke turned and pointed the ignition key at the car. It flashed its lights at him and bleeped a couple of times, and then all was quiet.

'What happened there?' she asked. 'Did you talk to it?'

'Yes, and that was it replying,' he smiled, and then his tone changed. 'Remote central locking. All modern cars have it. The really cool thing is, when you've parked your car, and you can't remember exactly where, you press the remote central locking on your key, and the car lights up like a Christmas tree so you can find it again.'

They walked up to a gate between the two buildings. Ruke typed a series of numbers into a keypad. Shannen didn't see what they were. The gate catch released itself, and Ruke pulled the gate open.

'Come on,' he said.

Shannen followed him through the gate, which he pulled shut behind him, and the locking mechanism re-engaged itself. Shannen's eyes were becoming more saucer-like by the minute. All this modern technology, and her boyfriend was the master of it all. Wow! They walked to the other end of the alleyway, out into a busy street, and she realised exactly where they were: Lincoln Road in Millfield. They walked past a couple of shops and walked into a café. There was a very pretty (but very skinny, thought Shannen) girl in a short pinafore dress with furry bootees standing beside the counter.

'Morning, Adelina,' Ruke said. It was always a good thing to remember the names of Uncle Lev's girls. 'Is Uncle Lev in?'

'Take a seat,' the girl replied in an Eastern European accent. 'I'll go and see if he's available. Tea or coffee?'

Ruke looked at Shannen. 'Tea?' he asked.

'Milk, two sugars,' she replied. And the girl disappeared through a door, into the back.

A moment or so later Uncle Lev appeared from the same door.

'Ruke, my boy, good morning.' He nodded at the boy sitting at a table by the door. Shannen didn't notice, but the boy stood up, walked to the front door, flipped over the 'open' sign to 'closed' and pulled down the blind. He then sat down at the table again. Ruke had seen the action many times before, but he didn't recognise the boy this time. Not important. Lev had a lot of people working for him. He was relieved to see Adelina again; he had rather liked looking at her the previous day, even if Lev was never going to let him touch her. Maybe he wasn't going to let anyone touch her. That would do.

'Well, Ruke, my boy,' said Lev, putting his fingers under Shannen's chin and lifting her face slightly, 'what do we have here, then?'

'This, Uncle Lev, is Shannen. Say hello to Uncle Lev, Shannen.'

'Hello,' she said uncertainly, not sure that she particularly wanted this old man to be holding her chin and breathing into her face. 'He doesn't look much like your uncle – he's a little pale. He looks more like my uncle,' she added.

Lev roared with laughter. 'Oh yes, Ruke, I like her; she's a feisty one, this is. She's definitely a keeper. Tell me, my dear, what do you like to do?'

She looked uncertainly at him. 'Watch telly?' she said, not having the faintest idea what sort of answer she was supposed to come up with.

'What did we do lots of last night?' Ruke prompted her.

'Fuck?' she replied uncertainly, but this was obviously the right answer as it was greeted with a very loud guffaw from Uncle Lev. Then Adelina arrived with a tray holding two steaming mugs of milky tea, a sugar bowl with wrapped lump sugar in it, and a frosted glass with a clear liquid in it, which Uncle Lev picked up and poured down his throat in one gulp, slamming the glass back down on the tray.

'I'll have another of those, Adelina,' he said patting her bottom. She picked the mugs up off the tray and put them on mats in front of Ruke and Shannen, and the sugar bowl as well. Shannen wondered why she let Uncle Lev pat her bottom like that, but then, as she looked at them both more carefully, she thought it was possible that he really was her uncle. Maybe that was how uncles and nieces behaved towards each other where they came from. Adelina walked back through the door with her tray.

'So, Shannen, you like to make the beast with two backs then,' said Lev.

Shannen mouthed 'What?' to Ruke.

'I think we can do business, young lady,' Lev said. 'We'll have to get you into some more appropriate clothing for the job, of course, but that won't be a problem.' He suddenly looked at Ruke, alarmed. 'Your friend Mo hasn't been anywhere near her, has he?'

Ruke smiled. 'Mo doesn't know that she even exists,' he replied.

'That's a relief. I would hate for this one to get broken before we had the opportunity to put her to work.'

'What?' said Shannen fairly loudly. 'What are you two talking about?'

Lev stood up. 'Why don't you come on through to the back and find out?' he said and walked towards the door behind the counter that Adelina had walked through.

She looked uncertainly at Ruke, but when he said, 'Go on,' she stood up and followed Uncle Ruke through the door to her future.

Once Shannen and Uncle Lev had disappeared into the back of the building, Ruke got up, rather sadly, and headed for the door. The young man by the table got up and unlocked the door for him. He then released the blind and flicked the sign back to 'open' before sitting down again.

Chapter 26

Sergeant Lou Molinari stirred his coffee. He had been back out to the Ortons again last night as the duty officer. A dead kid always saddened him, and that was the second young corpse he had been involved with in two days. Okay, so this one was apparently a suicide, unlike the case they were calling Operation Riverbank (which was, at the very least, manslaughter), but it still felt like a bad night.

Danny Rivers joined him at the table.

'Did you have a good night off?' the sergeant asked him, hoping that it had been better than his night working.

'So-so,' Danny replied. 'You?'

Molinari told the constable all about Sean James, and the drugs scattered on the table. 'Why do you think it was accidental rather than suicide?' Danny asked.

'Well, there was no suicide note, and there were a few tablets lying around on the table. If you were planning on killing yourself, I would imagine you'd take all the pills you'd got to kill yourself with, and most people leave a suicide note telling people why they've done it. Most suicide notes are bitter and blame someone, saying, "Look what you made me do, you nasty person, you." They almost invariably have a minimal effect on the people they are aimed at, but cause considerable distress to everyone else.'

'Do they use the phrase "nasty person"?' he asked.

'Never, but the four-letter words used are many and varied, and often have considerably more than four letters.'

'What was the drug he used?'

'That's down in the lab being tested as we speak. Sean James's autopsy is being done today. We need to find out whether there is a rogue batch of something we know about out there on the street, or whether this is a new drug that we know nothing about. We also need to work out how many of them he took and, if possible, why. The last thing we want is lots of kids showing up all over town dead by accident.'

'I can't help thinking that if these sorts of drugs were legalised, then they could enforce some sort of legal quality control over them, and make them much safer.'

Lou looked severely at the young constable. 'You may think that,' he replied, 'but I couldn't possibly comment. One thing I would add is that I wouldn't ever voice thoughts like that in DI Drake's presence, if you want to keep your giblets where they were designed to be.'

Danny shuddered. He didn't know much about the drug culture, and this was something he needed to find out more about. One thing he knew was that *junkies are bad because they're junkies* was a fairly pointless position to take, though that was just the position his father had taken on the subject. His father had been in the Met, which was one reason why Danny joined the force, but was also why he had not joined the Met itself. That was, of course, if he had been given the option in the first place. He was having trouble with his tenses here. What he had meant to think was that he wouldn't have joined the Met, even if they had asked him. At least that was what he said to anybody who actually asked. He had often thought that part of the reason why he had become a policeman was to prove to himself that you could be a copper without being a bigot at the same time. He felt that he had proven that to himself, and the sarge here was a good role model.

'So what's new with *our* case?' Danny asked, changing the subject.

'Fairly quiet overnight,' Lou replied. 'I did pop in on DS Odembe before I came here, and he was shuffling papers and drinking coffee. Steff is coming round on the ITU, so no doubt she'll be formally arrested later on today. Otherwise, not a lot has happened overnight.'

'Did you see DI Drake?'

'Nope. I expect he was around, but I haven't seen him since last night.'

Danny shrugged and stirred his coffee. 'So what time are you going to stay on till?' he asked, well aware that the DS had been on duty during the previous night and all the previous day. That made twenty-four hours so far non-stop.

'Well, Danny, provided you're doing the driving, I thought I'd stay up till lunchtime, and then no one will see hide nor hair of me till tomorrow morning. What I thought we would do is revisit the scene and the local area and take one final look to make sure we haven't missed anything obvious. During that time, I'll have worked out what I think you ought to be doing for the rest of the day, and I'll see if we can team you up with somebody to help you. Do you know Constable Green? I'll see if I can pair you up with her if you like,' he added with a twinkle.

Oh, sarge, as if for a moment you didn't know. 'Yeah, all right,' he replied, trying – and failing – to sound non-committal. He took a further mouthful of coffee. Molinari looked at the slightly sad features of the copper sitting across from him.

'Cheer up,' he said. 'It may never happen.'

'That's what I'm afraid of,' replied Danny morosely.

Molinari swallowed the rest of his coffee, and stood up, casting around for another platitude. 'Come on, things to see, people to do.'

Danny swallowed the rest of his cup, rather regretting the speed, as it was still distinctly warm, and followed the sergeant out.

There was a car waiting in the car park for them, and Molinari tossed the keys to Danny, who caught them one-handed before they landed on the car roof. Molinari looked impressed. 'We'll have you playing for England, Danny boy, if you can catch like that,' he said.

Danny Rivers looked bewildered. Cricket wasn't his game, and he didn't think it would be the second-generation Italian's either. Molinari even looked like a footballer, with his wiry frame and permanent five o'clock shadow. Shows how wrong you can be. The Hyundai started on the button and he pulled up to Thorpe Road.

'Where to first?' he asked.

'The crime scene,' Molinari suggested, so Danny turned left and headed off past the Holiday Inn to the Nene Parkway. It was a bright, sunny day and somehow Danny felt the birds should be singing. *Who knows*, he thought, *for all I know they might be. After all, I'm working with Susie this afternoon, and if the birds can't sing a concert for that...*

The Oundle Road was busy that morning, as they were competing with people going to work in the town centre.

'Do you want me to flash blues and twos?' Danny asked. It was not an emergency, and they were in no hurry, so technically it would not have been justified, but all the police did it. No doubt the ambulance men and firemen did too, to clear the traffic out of their way to get back on station.

'I shouldn't bother. We'll get there almost as quickly without, and the last thing we want to do is delay ourselves by frightening some city councillor halfway up a lamp post. We'd never hear the end of it.'

'Fair enough,' replied Danny. 'Remember I asked.'

'Duly noted.' And they stayed in the queue. Lou did make a note in his notebook after the Shrewsbury Avenue junction. The damn lights were only letting five cars through at a time if you were driving into town, as most people were at that time in the morning. Lou would have a word with the traffic boys when he got back.

When they reached the car park by the towpath there was very little evidence of police activity, past or present. Lou and Danny exchanged glances. Was it really less than thirty-six hours ago that the murder had happened, and already the site had been cleared of police tape? *Somebody probably nicked it*, said a little voice inside Danny's head. They got out of the car and went over to where the kids had been found. Where *Susie* found the kids, her and that little old man and his dog, thought Danny. There was nothing left.

'Sarge, there's a little blood here,' he said, putting on his rubber gloves and taking a swab out of his pocket. He dipped the swab in the bloodstain and then dropped it into a plastic bag. He took his camera out of his pocket and, putting an unopened swab by the bloodstain, he took a few photographs to make it obvious where he had taken it from.

'I've no idea whether anyone else has taken a sample from there as well, but if they did we've got a duplicate; if they didn't, well, we have one.'

'Oh right,' agreed Lou, 'better safe than sorry. If it is some-body else's blood, then it'll throw the case wide open. Do you want a bet? Is it (a) the girl's, (b) the boy's, or (c) did it come from somebody else altogether?'

Danny thought for a moment, and tried to picture the scene. 'Well, it was the boy who was killed, so I would guess it was his.'

'But it was the girl who was bleeding out, so more of her blood would have been outside her body,' countered Molinari.

Danny thought for a moment. 'And there really wasn't any-body else there? Can I change my mind and go for the girl?'

'You certainly can.'

Chapter 27

Sorayya Shadeed, as they knew her at school, was helping her sister-in-law tidy up after breakfast before heading back to class. The atmosphere was so claustrophobic in the house that she really didn't want to be there, and her father said it was fine if that was what she really wanted to do. He added, 'If you want to come home if it all gets too much, just tell the teacher, and come home.' The little ones were staying at home anyway, and perhaps their crying was getting to her too. Fourteen is a difficult age, and when your elder brother has just been killed, doing something unspeakable to some Q'fir girl, it is even more difficult. She wasn't a little girl anymore; she had grown six inches in the past year, and suddenly she was nearly as tall as her sister-in-law, and was the only other young woman in the house. It was her sister-in-law that she talked to about the changes happening to her body, rather than her mother. Yasmin was still young enough to remember how difficult she had found starting her periods. She wasn't that much older than Sorayya, after all, whereas Mum was positively ancient, thought Sorayya. Why, she'd probably gone through the change already. Her younger brother was seven, and Mum hadn't been pregnant since he'd been born. It was also Yasmin who remembered all the other – good and bad – things about becoming a teenager. How she had suddenly become tall, and skinny, and the hairs that had appeared on her upper lip, which looked like a moustache, and because her hair was so dark it was so obvious, and then there was the odd spot on her face that had come out of nowhere. She prayed every evening, *Insha'Allah*, that she didn't get spots like that unfortunate Q'fir boy in her class, who looked like a currant bun. She did feel rather sorry for him. Her occasional spots had hurt, so his face must be agony. The spiteful Q'fir girls, with their make-up and short skirts – no one looked too closely at their complexions, but they had teased him mercilessly.

Sorayya looked at her sister-in-law.

'So it was the white girl they found him with who killed Az?' she asked.

'That's what the police are saying,' Yasmin replied. 'Apparently, he sat next to her in class.' She looked at Sorayya sadly, wondering what sort of life lesson she was learning at the moment.

'What was she like?' asked Sorayya.

'I gather she was blonde and clever. They said she was the youngest in their class.'

'I think he talked about her,' Sorayya said. She had talked about the big school with her brother. He had encouraged her to work really hard so maybe she could get in there so she could get A-levels and go on to university too. But what was the point of her going to university? You couldn't study how to be a wife and mother at university; that was what she was learning from Yasmin. Her brother had told her that getting qualifications would give her 'options'. What options? Her life was all mapped out in front of her, or at least it had been up until yesterday. But now everyone would know that her brother had done *stuff* with a Q'fir, and moreover she had killed him for it. That sort of shame could rub off on a family, and perhaps it would rub off on her. Who would want their son to marry a girl with a taint on her family?

'I warned him,' said the skinny teenager. 'I warned him that he shouldn't trust them. They have no religion, and are all sex, make-up and drugs. It doesn't matter which school they go to; there's no difference between any of them.'

'So he talked about her?' inquired Yasmin.

'There were times when we talked. He asked me about emotions and stuff, and how to make a girl like him. He told me that there was a girl in his class that he really liked. But when he told me she was a Q'fir, then I asked him, what was the point? He wouldn't be allowed to be with her. He told me that he might be able to learn about how to make a girl happy, so that when he got married, he would know how to make his wife happy. But I explained that his wife wouldn't be anything like her.' She spat the last word out as if it were coated in spines.

'What do you mean?'

'Well, his wife is going to be a Pakistani Muslim, and *she's* a Q'fir drug injector, what is he going to learn about love from her?'

'You know, that's a very unpleasant word you keep saying. It's not the sort of word a nice Muslim girl should even know.'

'Well, they should have sent me to a nice Muslim school then, and not that dump down the road, if they wanted me to be a nice Muslim girl.'

Her sister-in-law knew better than to comment on that one, so she went back to, 'You don't *know* that she injects drugs.'

'She's Q'fir; of course she does. They all do. And if he was having to ask me how to make her happy, so that she would be interested in him, then she obviously wasn't already interested in him, so she must have been having sex with someone else. So what was the point?'

Yasmin looked at Sorayya sadly. 'You're not going to say any of this stuff when you get back to school, are you?' she asked.

'What do you mean?'

'All this hate-fuelled bile. If you come out with it in school, you're going to make things worse.'

'But it's true.'

'But you can't say it. I know Az is dead, and one of them killed him, but the only person you can blame is the girl who did it. If you start blaming everybody for his death, then you're going to cause even more trouble.'

Sorayya looked defiantly at her sister-in-law. The defiant look didn't last very long, and soon became petulant when Yasmin didn't back down. She finally looked down, and Yasmin continued, 'Look, don't you think it would be better for all concerned if you didn't go to school today, and stayed home with the rest of your family? No one at school will think the worse of you, under the circumstances, and it will give you time to let your anger calm down. I have a feeling that you will do your reputation lasting damage if you go to school behaving like a volcano.'

141

The girl's face softened on being described like a fire-breathing mountain. Yasmin knew it would take Sorayya a long time to get over this completely, if she ever did, but this was at least a start. The girl took her bag off her shoulder and hung it back on the hallstand.

'I think I'd better stay at home,' she said.

Chapter 28

John was full of breakfast, and especially full of coffee. As a result, he was alert, and according to an article in the paper that was in front of him while he was eating, less likely to contract diabetes. He walked from the staff canteen up to the ITU.

The sister looked up as he walked in. Recognising him, she went back to what she had been doing. John walked over to the desk and she stood up.

'Is Sister Bartram in?' he asked.

'She's on a late,' the nurse replied. 'I'm the best there is right now.'

John shuffled his feet and looked awkward. 'No ... No, I didn't mean that, it was just, you know, I was talking to her about Steff yesterday.'

'Yes, you're Stephanie Flack's medical student, I know.' She waited for a moment and then gave John a huge radiant smile that lit the whole room, just for a moment, and then switched it off, and went back to her paperwork.

John cleared his throat, and the sister looked up again. 'Can I help you?' she asked.

'Well, I wondered how Steff is this morning. Has she woken up yet?'

'That isn't a viral sore throat you're bringing in to the ITU, is it?'

John looked awkward. 'No,' he replied. 'I was just trying to attract your attention.'

'It worked. Now, you were asking about Miss Flack,' she continued, flicking through the papers in front of her. 'Ah yes, here she is. Well, the last of the blood finished going in at midnight, so they changed the giving set, and at the moment she's got isotonic saline running in slowly to keep the line open. She woke up in the early hours, and was in a lot of pain, so they gave her 50mg of pethidine at 0300, and she had another 50mg at 0700. She's drowsy but rousable at the moment. Are you doing anything right now?'

'No, not especially, I came in to see how she's doing before going to my ten o'clock lecture.'

'Good,' said the sister. 'And you've passed for doing phlebotomy here, haven't you?'

'Yes,' he replied uncertainly.

The sister passed him a stainless steel tray with various syringes on it, and a couple of needles. 'Her left arm hasn't got a drip site on it at the moment, so would you do us the honours?'

'Very happy to do so,' he said. 'Satisfy my curiosity: why is the site of the drip so important?'

The sister looked at him for a moment, and then she said, slowly and simply, 'One doesn't take blood from just upstream of a drip site. If you do, then you get a sample of what is going in from the drip, and not of the blood in the whole body. If you take a blood sample from the opposite arm, then it will be properly mixed,' she paused, 'by the heart and its trip through the other tissues.'

John smiled, feeling thoroughly patronised, which was probably the nurse's intention. *Train a doctor young enough, and he'll be obedient for life.* He picked up the tray and walked over to Steff's bed.

'Morning,' he said to the peaceful face on the pillow, and possibly to the policewoman on the other side of the bed. Steff had some colour back now, and he noticed she no longer had tape over her eyelids.

'I'm going to take a blood sample,' he said, taking the elastic tourniquet out of his pocket. He put it round her upper arm, and he was pleased to see a vein appear in the front of her left elbow, or as it was known among the cognoscenti, the antecubital fossa.

He put a needle on a red syringe. The red one was for haematology, and after a blood transfusion, it was surely the most important. They would need to know whether she was still leaking internally. He prepared the other syringes with a vacuum so that he could change them over once the syringe he was currently filling was full. He then pulled on a pair of thin rubber gloves.

'You'll just feel a small scratch,' he said as he pushed the needle into the vein, and with a bit of gentle traction on the handle, the syringe started to fill. Once the haematology syringe was full, he held the needle still while he twisted the syringe off it, and then twisted the first brown syringe onto the needle, and it too started to fill. While the brown syringe was filling, he turned the haematology syringe over slowly a few times to make sure it was thoroughly mixed with the EDTA. He had no idea what EDTA stood for, but he knew that that would stop the blood in the syringe from clotting.

Once he had got the various samples that the sister had requested, he took the tourniquet off her slender arm, put a patch over the site from where he had taken the sample, and withdrew the needle.

'All done,' he said, 'I'll be back later.'

'Thank you,' came from the motionless girl on the bed. Her eyes were not open, but she was aware. The policewoman's eyes suddenly became more alert, though she said nothing. Steff might be half awake, but she still wasn't going anywhere.

John took the tray back to the sister's desk, and looked for the yellow plastic burn bin. The sister got one from another tray behind her, and John put the needle and prep pads into it. The gloves he dropped into a different bag by the desk. He asked for some of Steff's sticky labels from her notes. He stuck one on every sample bottle, and made sure they were properly identifiable both with her name and her hospital number. He wouldn't want the lab refusing to do her tests because they couldn't identify the patient. Finally he passed the whole tray back to the sister.

She looked up at him.

'Not bad,' she said. 'You wouldn't care to do the rest of the ward's bloods while you're here?'

John grinned, hoping that she was pulling his leg, but just to be sure he said, 'Love to, but there's this ten o'clock lecture that I've got to be at.'

The sister smiled back. 'You can't blame me for asking, though, can you?'

'I'll see you and Steff later.' He paused. 'You know she's sort of half awake?' and left the ITU, hoping he would remember how to get to the lecture hall without getting lost in all the identical passages in the hospital.

Chapter 29

Shannen's foster mother was concerned. Shannen had told her that everything was fine, and she was staying with a boyfriend. Well, even that wasn't fine. Shannen had never had a boyfriend before; in fact, she had hardly ever had a friend before. She had certainly never had a sleepover with a girl before, so suddenly having one with a boy just didn't feel right. Her husband may not be bothered, but she was distinctly uncertain. The questions that she couldn't keep out of her mind were: *How old is this boy?* and *What are they doing together right now?*

She had texted Shannen back later last night, but Shannen hadn't responded. When she texted her again the following morning, and then actually called her and still got no reply after that, she began to hear social workers' voices in the back of her head. Shannen had said that she would be back before a social worker came round, but that wasn't the point, was it? As a foster mother, she was supposed to be responsible for the kid, and that didn't just mean getting cheques and cashing them, it meant looking after her. So where was she?

She rang her husband. 'I think you're going to have to come home.'

'Why?' came the surly reply.

'Well, I can't raise Shannen on the phone, and I think I'm going to have to report this to social services.'

'So? What's that to do with me? If you feel you've got to report the girl to the social services, then go ahead and report her.'

'But social services will send a social worker round, and then the shit will hit the fan.'

'Well, they'll reallocate Shannen to someone else, but then we'll get another kid – we always do. Maybe this one will be easier than Shannen.'

'We won't get another kid if we don't sort that damn bath-room out.'

'What do you mean?'

'We've got a bath full of coal, haven't we? If we don't clear that out before the social worker comes, we won't get allocated another kid ever, and without a kid, we won't get money.'

'Oh, fuck that little bitch, I knew she was fucking trouble the moment I clapped my eyes on her. Don't call the SS yet. I'll be with you as soon as I can, and I'll see if I can find something to put the coal in out the back. Start tipping the coal out the window. Let's see if we can get the bathroom sorted PDQ. Anything else you think we ought to get sorted before we call them?' He didn't wait for her answer, and disconnected.

She walked through the kitchen into the bathroom, and looked at the bath. It was half-full of coal, shiny and black. At the end of the bath stood a hod, which she picked up and slid into the coal. Two pulls though the coal, and it was full and heavy. She put it down for a moment, walked back into the kitchen and opened the back door. Beside the steps would be convenient enough to put some sort of container in which to put the coal. Therefore that was not the place to put the coal at the moment. On the other side of the steps was a space that just held an empty milk bottle. She went down the steps and picked the milk bottle up and brought it back and put it in the kitchen sink. Then she picked up the hod, and poured it out against the wall where the milk bottle had stood. The air filled with coal dust, but at least there was a hodful that was no longer in the bath. She returned to the bathroom with the empty hod.

It didn't take her a great deal of time to empty the bath of coal. The hod was a good tool, but she knew that it would take her a great deal longer to make the bathroom clean enough to be acceptable to social services when they came round.

What she really needed was some gumption and some elbow grease. Problem was that they had stopped making Gumption, so she would need some of those magic chemicals that were advertised on telly between the bits of the games that her husband was watching. She wondered whether he would remember any of their names. She would ask him when he turned up, and they could nip round the corner to the shop to see if they had any. Meanwhile she started scrubbing.

Her husband appeared, cross and red-faced. The green plastic box on the back of his truck was easy enough for the pair of them to lift and carry down the path between their house and the next-door neighbours'. She was pleased that she had thought about where they might put it, as it fitted perfectly to the right of the back door step as you looked at it. Then she asked her husband about the cleaning stuff that was advertised on the telly. He looked at her like she had gone out.

'Why should I ever remember that?' he asked.

'Better not tell the telly people that,' she said. 'If they think you don't remember what they're advertising, then perhaps they won't advertise any more, and you'll have to pay more to watch your football.'

'When am I ever going to be talking to the telly people?' he asked, sounding even more bewildered.

'Well, you never know,' she said, as if that was the answer to everything. Then she changed the subject. 'Well, I'll just go down the shop and see what they have got. Do you want to hod the coal into the new bunker while I'm gone? And while I'm there, do you want anything for lunch?'

'It's a little early for lunch, don't you think?'

'Yes, but it won't be when we've finished, and I think it would be a good thing if the social workers found us having a nice family lunch when they arrive.'

'But Jervis won't be here,' he pointed out.

'That might not be a bad thing, but I think we should be eating the sort of lunch they'd like to see us feeding Shannen, if she hadn't bunked off.'

'But it's a school day, so she wouldn't be having lunch with us anyway.'

She rolled her eyes. There were moments when the men in this household didn't get anything. She put the hod into her husband's hands and told him she would be back in ten minutes.

She returned with two carrier bags, one containing cleaning materials, and one containing two large hunks of pork pie and two ready-prepared salads. She put the food in the fridge, and took the bag containing cleaning materials into the bathroom.

Her husband had cleared all the coal into the plastic bunker, and was now sitting in front of the telly; he was looking at it as if he expected it to go on automatically, as if by power of thought.

'A cup of tea would be nice, our girl,' he said.

She muttered under her breath, but he didn't hear her. What he did hear was the click as she switched the kettle on, and the opening of the kitchen cupboard door. She pulled out a mug and a box of tea bags and put them on the slab by the kettle, and waited for it to boil. 'Are you going to help me clean the bathroom, so it'll be done double quick, and then we can contact the social workers?' she asked.

'Will we both fit in the bathroom?' he asked. Sadly, she realised that was a reasonable question. She couldn't remember when they had been in the bathroom together, even when it had been in use as a bathroom.

'I 'spect so,' she replied as the kettle came to the boil. Good kettle, that new one, boils very quickly, she thought as she popped a teabag into the mug, poured boiling water onto it, and stirred. She went back into the kitchen cupboard and pulled out the container with sugar in it, spooned three heaped spoons into the steaming mug and stirred that into the mixture, and then opened the fridge door, and took out the opened milk bottle. She poured enough milk into the mug to make it the right colour, and put the cap back on the bottle and put it back into the fridge. She stirred the tea one more time, and then fished out the teabag with the spoon. She took the mug to her husband, who hadn't moved.

He sniffed it, and then took a slurp.

'Ee, lass,' he said, as if he was trying to sound proper Yorkshire, and she doubted he had ever been there in his life. 'That hit the spot.'

Two hours of elbow grease had got the dust out of the bath. She thanked her lucky stars it was an old enamel bath. She would never have got the coal out of a plastic bath, not in a month of Sundays.

The floor was now clean and shiny too. Her husband got up and looked at it too. He deemed it to be perfect, and then they called social services to tell them that Shannen had gone missing. They were sitting down eating lunch like the happy domesticated couple that they were when the social worker arrived.

Chapter 30

'See you, Mrs Kowalski,' said Tom Clark, as the patient left his consulting room. An alert had come up on his screen that Sam Shivalkar wanted to talk to him when he had a moment. He pressed the button on the internal phone.

'Sam here,' came the reply.

'Tom here. You needed me?'

'Ah yes, Tom. Billy McGregor has found his way onto my list for today; can I pass him over to you? I noticed you had a gap.' *A gap? I've got a gap on my list for the first time since the millennium, and he wants to fill it?* Tom smiled. Old Billy McGregor, he thought.

'Yes, pass him over.' Tom got up from his desk and opened the door, to see Billy walking sheepishly down the corridor towards him.

'Billy,' he said. 'How did you get on to Dr Sam's list for today?'

'Dunno, doc, I guess these things happen.' Billy had looked tatty for as long as Tom had known him. His boots were solid and brown; at least half of the colour was earth. His jeans looked as if he had been gardening in them. He wore an old T-shirt with the slogan no longer legible, and an open hoodie with the hood up, covering his long salt-and-pepper hair. His beard was unkempt too, but it didn't hide the friendly smile that was a permanent feature of Billy's face. He had learned over the years that you were more likely to get what you wanted if you looked affable and friendly. Billy was a heroin addict, and they both knew it.

Tom tapped the computer keyboard and Billy's record came up. Yes, he was due his script today.

'Well, Billy, if I were to test your urine today, would I find anything that might surprise me?'

'No, doc,' he said, looking slightly offended. 'Anyway, I did this one for Dr Sam a few moments ago,' he went on, pulling out a sample bottle nearly full of bright yellow urine. Tom felt it. It seemed to be awfully cold. He poured a little of the urine into a small plastic gallipot and opened a testing pack. Holding the test plate away from him, the urine flowed up the strips into the test window. Yes, it all looked very innocent. Too innocent: it wasn't even positive for methadone, and Billy was being prescribed that.

'Sorry, Billy,' he said, amiably enough. 'Whose is this?'

'What do you mean?' said Billy, knowing he'd been rumbled.

'If I were to do a pregnancy test on this sample, it would be positive, wouldn't it?'

Billy smiled and said, 'How did you know that?'

'It's your daughter's sample, isn't it?'

'You got me, doc. There's just no fooling you today, is there?'

'So would I have found anything apart from methadone and benzos in yours?' he asked.

'Little bit of H,' he replied. 'I got my money yesterday, you know how it is.'

'Ah, your payday hit,' Tom replied.

''Fraid so.'

'How much?'

'A baggie. I've got to get my beans and stuff as well, and I was down at the supermarket, and the dealer was outside. I couldn't not do it now, could I?'

'Did you smoke it or inject it?'

'Injected it.'

'Have you got any sterile works left?' Tom asked. 'Works' meant needles, syringes, and skin cleaning kit.

'I'm running a bit low.'

'Oh Billy, Billy, Billy, whose were you sharing?'

'No, no, no, they were clean and new, what you gave me last time – it's just that that was my last one.'

Tom walked over to the steel trolley at the head of the examination couch and opened the drawer. He took out a handful of sterets; two-centimetre pads soaked in isopropyl alcohol, sealed in a plastic envelope. He also took out half a dozen syringes for injecting insulin, with a very fine built-in needle. He put them down on the desk and told Billy, 'Don't sell them, they're for your use only. If anybody else needs some works, send them along to their own doctor or to the clinic. How's your injection site?'

Billy looked at the doctor for a moment, and then dropped his trousers. There was a pit overlying his left groin, but it looked clean enough.

'May I?' asked Tom. He pushed beside the pit, and felt the pulsation of the femoral artery.

'Well, you're still on target, Billy, but this really is dangerous territory, isn't it?'

'Yes, doc.'

'I would hate for you to make a mistake, Billy.'

'Me too, doc.' They locked eyes for a moment. Tom thought silently, as he looked at Billy, that he had already been far luckier than he had any right to be. Heroin addicts don't usually make old bones. And Billy hadn't caught any of the blood-borne viruses either, had he? Was that why he had come in in the afternoon, because he knew they wouldn't be able to do a blood test?

'When did we last do a hepatitis C test, Billy?'

'Oh, I don't know, doc. Can we not do it today? I need to prepare myself for that sort of thing.'

Tom went back to the drawer, pulled out a plastic envelope, and tipped its contents out on his desk. It had a form, a steret, a disposable pricking device and a card, folded over, covering a piece of what looked like blotting paper, with five circles on it.

'It just takes a finger prick,' he said, 'that's all. Give me your left index finger.'

Billy stuck out his finger, as Tom was pulling on a pair of rubber gloves. Tom pricked Billy's finger, producing a bleb of blood. He wiped it onto one of the circles on the card, and squeezed the finger slightly. Within a few moments he had filled all five circles, and he left it on the side to dry, while he filled in the form.

'We should have the results back when you come in for your next script,' he said, 'and make sure you make an appointment to see *me*. I'm the one who understands these reports.'

Billy looked at him. 'And my script, doc?' He suddenly looked worried that Tom might be about to drop his script.

'Aside from your payday present, is it holding you all right?' Tom asked.

'Yes, just about.'

'And you're on fifty millilitres a day, and you pick up three times a week from the chemist?'

'Yes, doc.'

'The system works,' said Tom drily, and pulled out a blue prescription pad. He pulled off the top sheet and fed it into the printer. He pressed a button on his keyboard. The machine whirred for a moment, and then spat out the prescription. Tom looked at it and then signed it. He passed it over to Billy, who started to look decidedly uncomfortable.

'Is there anything else, Billy?' he asked.

'Umm, doc?' Billy said, fidgeting.

'Yes, Billy?'

'Doc, it's like this.' He looked even more uncomfortable.

'Yes?' Tom's voice went up a semitone. What was worrying the man? He had known Billy for the best part of ten years, and they had never had a non-conversation like this before. Billy had tried the usual tricks to get extra drugs, but he had never looked awkward like this before.

'What is it, Billy?'

'Yeah, well, it's like this. I was told to tell you, by this geezer I know...'

'Yes?'

'Well, he said that I had to tell you to watch out – or else.'

Tom looked at Billy, thunderstruck. In all the time he had known him, he had never known Billy to threaten him.

'Who said that?' he asked.

'Oh, doc, you know I can't tell you that. But he did say to keep away from Sean James or else.'

'Who's Sean James?'

'I don't know, doc, but this geezer – well, you know, I wouldn't piss about with him, and he told me to tell you that, so I've done it. See you in a fortnight, I hope. Bye.' Billy stood up and shot out of the room as if a lit missile was attached to the seat of his pants, leaving a thunderstruck Tom Clark wondering what that had all been about.

The only Sean James he had ever heard of, he had heard about from Sam Shivalkar before they started surgery that morning. And that particular Sean James had died the previous night ... of a drug overdose. Tom's mind was beginning to work overtime. Was the threat actually aimed at Sam, and was that why Billy had booked in to see Sam this morning, instead of him?

Chapter 31

The pathologist looked at the boy's body. *Well at least this one doesn't have a fractured skull or anything. What is the matter with Peterborough?* passed through his mind. He looked at the pill on the table. His assistant had left it there as a reminder that this was what he might find inside the body. If the victim had taken enough of the stuff to kill him, he thought, then it wasn't likely that there would still be any recognisable pills left in his stomach. The staff always did that, nevertheless.

'George,' he called. He knew his technician anglicised his name when he was being talked to by native Brits. He had also heard him introducing himself as 'Yertsey', or even 'Yurek', when he was talking in Polish on the phone. The pathologist was traditionally British, however Latin he looked, and insisted on only speaking English.

'Guv?' the Pole replied from just outside the door.

'Did they send any of these pills up to chemistry to be analysed?' he asked.

'I'm sure they did,' came the reply. 'Do you want me to hurry them up?'

'It would help. There's a docket from the police suggesting that they need to know the cause of death of this one PDQ. If he did die of an overdose of these pink pills, we need to know what they were. If it's a rogue batch out there in clubland, we may be looking at an epidemic of dead kids.'

'I'm on it right away,' Jerzy told the pathologist, who was picking up a scalpel and looking at the body on the slab. Jerzy left the mortuary and headed straight to his phone.

The second call Jerzy made was one that would have interested the pathologist – if he had known anything about it.

'Uncle Lev, I think you have a problem.'

'Is that a threat or a statement?'

'Can you imagine me making threats to you?' the technician asked. 'Do you know anything about some little round pink pills that came in here yesterday?'

'How did pills get into your path lab?'

'They came in with a dead body from Orton yesterday evening. Apparently the victim took them. They're analysing them to see what they contain. Maybe I shouldn't be asking you this, but are they yours?'

'And if they are?'

'Then I would get rid of them quick. The kid who was killed wasn't a known long-term addict. The police are worried that there may be a rogue batch of drugs out there that might kill a few more kids. It would be bad for their image if a whole lot of nice posh kids ended up dead after a party. I think they'll be out hunting for them.'

'I get the message, Jerzy, leave it with me. I'll see if any of my boys know anything about it.'

'Look after yourself, Uncle Lev.'

'You too, Jerzy; and thank you for telling me all about this. Can you keep me informed about what might crop up? I might need to sort out a supplier.'

Uncle Lev put the phone down. Adelina was looking concernedly at him. He beckoned her over, and she sat down on the arm of the sofa. He put his hand on the smooth skin of her left thigh, and rubbed it for a moment with his thumb.

'Do you know where Yuri is?' he asked her.

'Not off the top of my head,' she replied, 'but I can find him for you.'

He looked into her huge eyes for a moment. When she opened them that wide, she looked like a girl in a Manga comic. She must have been very young when she had learned that trick. She had used it when she first met Uncle Lev, and he had become her protector on the spot.

'Does anybody else put their hand on your leg like this?' he asked.

'No, Uncle Lev, they wouldn't dare.' She gave him a smile that someone as young as she was shouldn't know how to make.

'Good,' he said. 'Remind me of that, in case I ever forget.'

'I don't think that for a moment you would ever forget,' she said, giving him another facial expression that he was certainly unlikely to forget while he was still in full command of his faculties.

He patted her thigh absently, and then told her to go and find Yuri for him, as he needed to have a word with him. There were moments when he really regretted being impotent. Yes, he would really like to enjoy that girl and everything she had to offer. He wondered whether she knew instinctively about his impotence. He had certainly never told her about it. Meanwhile, all he had to offer her was the ability to make sure that nobody else got there first – until he really needed her as a payment, or a favour, that is.

Yuri soon walked in through the back door, followed by Adelina. Uncle Lev and Adelina exchanged glances, then she disappeared back through the door.

'Yuri,' he said. 'Pink pills?'

'Yes?' replied Yuri curiously. 'What of them?'

'They have accompanied a corpse into the mortuary this morning, and there's a bit of a hue and cry about them. Anything I should know?'

'Do we know who the corpse is?' he asked.

'My man on the inside says it was someone called Sean James from Orton.'

'Oh!' said Yuri. Yes, he did know him – rather well. 'So what happened?'

'Well, we don't know the details, but they found him dead and the pink pills in the same place, and they're analysing the pink pills. So, if the police can trace them back to you, may I suggest that you do something about any others that may be out there, fast. I don't want to be wasting valuable merchandise like Adelina there bribing some copper to keep him quiet about a foul-up that you're responsible for.'

'I'm on it, boss.' He turned on his heel and left the room. He glanced at Adelina on the way past, wondering how on earth Uncle Lev could bribe a copper with her. The police – he would never understand them. Nor, come to think of it, would he ever fully understand Uncle Lev. He went and found a car.

He knew where he would find the people he was looking for. As usual, they were always where he expected to find them. He was amazed that they never got caught; they were so bloody obvious. Maybe the police knew who they were and were hoping they would catch someone further up the food chain, like himself perhaps. He was watchful, however. He pulled into the car park, and before he knew it he had Winston sitting in the passenger seat.

'Those pink pills,' he said. 'Have you passed them on yet?'

'Nah, man, y'only got them to me yesterday. I've not even tried one myself yet.'

'Well, don't,' said Yuri forcefully. 'Somebody did, and they aren't going to see tomorrow.'

'You mean they was poisoned, man?'

'I don't know what they were. The old man's got someone looking into them at the moment.'

'You mean you're getting them analysed?'

'Yeah, so don't take one until I get back to you.'

'So that leaves me out of pocket, man, if I can't sell them on.'

'I appreciate that, and if I have to take them back off you, I'll replace them with really good stuff in return. If it turns out it wasn't the pills that killed him, then I'll let you know they're all right. Twenty-four, maybe forty-eight, hours, and I'll get back to you and let you know. All right till then?'

'No sweat, man – thanks for telling me,' said Winston, and got out of the car. That was the good thing about getting your stuff from Yuri; you always knew exactly where you were. Yuri looked after his men on the street.

Yuri had a number of similar conversations that day in different places about town. Police in uniform, he saw in the distance, but never saw anyone remotely resembling a plod anywhere nearby.

As far as he knew, he had made sure that none of those pink things got out, but you never knew with dealers. What he didn't want to do was to frighten any of them too much. If any of them knew for sure there was killer gear out there, then it was possible that they might become weapons in a gang war, and Uncle Lev would know exactly where that started. It was sad about Sean, though. He had liked him, and he had trusted him, that was why he delivered the new stuff to him first. The moral of the story was, if you've got some new stuff to pass on, try it out on someone you don't much care about to start with.

Chapter 32

'Ow,' said Steff as she tried to move. 'That hurt.' *Where am I? There's a lot of light in here. Am I in here or is this an outside I don't understand?*

'I think she's waking up again,' said a voice near her right ear. Then, 'How are you feeling?' That sounded more as if the voice was speaking to her directly. Steff tried to look to her right, but moving her neck that far required her body to follow her, and any movement of her trunk hurt like hell.

A face appeared in her eye line. It seemed friendly, and looked as if it belonged to a nurse wearing a white tunic with dark blue epaulettes.

'Hello,' said the nurse. 'How are you feeling?'

'Where am I?' Steff asked, and then added, 'My tummy hurts like hell, and it's also really raw down between my legs. What's happened to me?'

'You've had an accident, and you're in hospital,' said the friendly nurse.

'Am I going to be all right?' Steff asked, suddenly alarmed.

'Yes, but it might take a little while. Are you planning on going anywhere in the immediate future?'

'Lunch?' the girl replied quizzically. Well, that was something, thought the sister, if she could already make a joke out of it. Then the girl asked, 'Why am I in so much pain?'

'You had to have some surgery to stop the bleeding,' the sister replied.

'Oh,' Steff said, but didn't ask any further questions.

'Do you want any pain killers?' asked the sister.

'Yes please, if it isn't too much trouble.'

'May I have a quick listen to your tummy?' the sister asked, taking out a stethoscope, and laying the diaphragm on Steff's abdomen. She listened carefully, in three or four places. She could hear no bowel sounds yet, so she decided Steff should remain 'nil by mouth'. The nurse walked over to her desk, picked up a key, and opened the locked white-painted metal cupboard on the wall behind her head. She took out an ampoule from a box, and tapped it to make sure all its contents were in the bottom. She then broke off the glass top, and put the top into the yellow plastic burn bin. She took out a syringe and needle, drew up the contents of the ampoule into the syringe, and then pushed the air out of it. She put the plastic needle guard back over the needle, put the syringe into a kidney dish with a steret prep pad, and went back to the girl.

'Your tummy's not quite ready to take any tablets yet, so I'm going to give you a little pain relief in the drip,' she said, and wiped the rubber access point on the giving set. She pushed the needle into the rubber, and injected the contents of the syringe into the giving set. She then ran a little saline through the drip, and the girl's eyelids closed.

'Simple as that,' remarked the sister drily to no one in particular.

'Will she be awake again soon?' asked the policewoman.

'Oh, yes, I think so, probably very soon. There was definitely a twinge of humour there for a few moments. It probably won't be very long before you can wreck it all by telling her she's under arrest.' The sister walked back to her station and started writing in the notes, logging out the ampoule, and allocating its batch number to Steff's notes. Once that was all complete, she then put the rest of the ampoule, with the needle and syringe into the yellow burn bin on the desk.

***

In a consulting room on the other side of town, a GP's internal phone line rang in the middle of a consultation, breaking his concentration.

'Hello,' he said crossly. 'Clark here. I am in the middle of a consultation, you know.'

'Hello, Dr Tom,' said one of his receptionists. 'It's Dr Klastru, wanting to talk to you for a moment. Will you take it?'

Tom looked at the patient in front of him. 'Quickly,' he said. 'As I said, I'm in the middle of a consultation...'

'I did tell him,' apologised the receptionist, 'but he insisted.'

Dr Klastru was a GP in a practice in the town centre. Tom found him a tedious and unnecessarily assertive man, and didn't like him that much. However, if he thought about it carefully, he didn't care for any of the GPs unduly – apart from his partners. He wondered whether that was simply because he had actually made the effort to get to know them.

'Yes?' he asked.

'Tom,' said Dr Klastru after the receptionist put him through. 'You're down to do Saturday night's overnight shift for the co-op. Would you mind doing tonight's instead?'

'And somebody else will do my Saturday night shift instead?' said Tom, flicking through his desk diary. He had a rehearsal with Jenny on Saturday evening, so changing shifts would be very handy, as he then wouldn't have to race back to Peterborough down the A14 afterwards to be at the co-op on time.

'Of course,' replied the GP on the other end.

'I can do that,' replied Tom. 'Are you going to tell them, or do you need me to?'

'No, I'm in the co-op office right now, so I can tell everybody who needs to know. Thank you.' The line went dead. Does Dr Klastru ever spend any time with patients, Tom wondered, as he looked at his patient. Probably safer for everybody that he doesn't, he started to think, before mentally slapping himself on the wrist and telling himself to behave.

'I'm so sorry about that,' he said.

'Not a problem, doctor,' replied the patient and they continued the discussion that Dr Klastru had interrupted.

After his surgery was over, Tom went down to the office to grab his wad of repeat prescriptions to sign.

'How's this afternoon's surgery looking, and tomorrow morning's?' he asked the receptionist.

'We've got some holes at the moment,' she replied.

'Well, Dr Klastru's telephone call was about me doing tonight's graveyard shift, and I wondered if we had room to shift people about. What time is my last booked slot tonight?'

'We've got Sue Baker booked in at ten past five this evening. I think that one's just a pill check, and then we've got empty slots up till six. Don't worry, we'll fill them!'

'Please don't,' said Tom. 'That way I can leave and get my head down for about twenty-seven winks, before getting up again at midnight to do the shift.'

'Blocked off as we speak,' said the receptionist, her fingers dancing on the computer.

'How's tomorrow morning looking?'

The receptionist looked at the screen. 'Hmm, moderately busy, actually. I take it you want to go to bed tomorrow morning?'

'I'd rather,' he replied. 'Just to catch up on my sleep.'

'Hmm, well, there are a couple there who I know would be just as happy to see Dr Cross tomorrow morning, and there's a couple who won't mind seeing Dr Sam. The rest I'll book in to see you tomorrow afternoon. Tomorrow afternoon will be busy, though.'

'Don't mind being busy when I'm awake; it would just be so embarrassing if I fell asleep in the middle of a consultation. Know what I mean?'

Chapter 33

Nick Fowler was a shabby man. He wasn't sure if he had always been shabby, or if there was anybody left he could ask – if he really wanted to know the answer. He had arrived in Peterborough as a mere stripling, on his way south to Fleet Street where he was sure a prizewinning career in investigative journalism was waiting for him.

'I stopped off for a pie and a pint,' he would say to anyone who would listen, 'and got this job in the local rag to restock my wallet, and get a little experience.' He had then met a good Yorkshire girl, also on her way south to the land of milk and honey. They got married, and then divorced, and she carried on with her southward journey, while he stayed behind in Peterborough at his job in the local paper. Nick was still there, as far away from the life he had dreamed of in Fleet Street as he had ever been. Even the local paper wasn't local any more, although you wouldn't know it to look at it. It had 'Peterborough news' written all over the masthead. Or, as one of his erstwhile friends had christened it, just to rattle his cage, the *Peterborough Nuisance*. He wondered what had happened to that old friend. Got married and settled down, he supposed, just like he had for a time. And once you had a wife and a home, you tended to spend all your time with your wife at home, and forget your old friends. And when the old ball and chain dumps you and wanders off, your old mates aren't around any more, he thought sadly.

He was still a staff reporter for the paper, but there wasn't a buzzing office any more. There was a front desk, which was mostly used by advertising staff so the public could drop in with adverts for the personal column. He supposed he could take his copy there, but why should he? He could just as easily type it up on his laptop in the little terraced house in Old Fletton on which he and his wife had taken out a mortgage, and which he had taken over when she left. It had a perfect mezzanine room, halfway up the stairs to his bedroom. Sadly, he usually only used the bedroom to sleep in nowadays, but if he ever did get lucky, that mezzanine room would be on show to impress.

He took publication day off, and often drowned the tedium of his existence in his local, drinking some locally brewed ale. It was sometimes so good that it could have been brewed by an ex-pat Yorkshireman. He was working on an article, and was trying to work out how he could get the next gig at the local blues club into it. The club never seemed to feature in the 'what's on this weekend' column in advance. Occasionally in a news column there was a 'You'll never believe who came to Peterborough last weekend' article about some great bluesman's son, like Muddy Waters or Elmore James, who had played a ShakeDown, but that was no damn use to anyone. The musician had landed, played, invariably a 'storming evening's blues which reminded everyone present of his great father', and had moved on to pastures new, all before anyone reading the paper had found out about the event.

He usually gave himself time to scrub the cobwebs out from the inside of his skull, and flushed his system through with large mugs of hot tea, like any good Yorkshireman, at the beginning of his week, which started on a Thursday around midday. He may well have spent considerably more than half his life in Peterborough, but he was still a Yorkshireman at heart. He had never met anybody who would admit to being a Peterborean, unless they really didn't have anywhere else to come from.

Unlike in most journalism-based television dramas, there was no press room in Thorpe Wood. In fact, if you ever found a reporter in there, the chances were he, or she, was under arrest. Not only were members of the press strongly discouraged to be anywhere near the police station, but members of the police were also strongly discouraged from talking to the press. After all, there may well be snippets of information about an investigation that the police did not want to be in the public eye. Anybody knowing that snippet may well be involved in the crime, and if it was made public, then the value of that piece of information would be lost forever.

Nick Fowler knew all that, and for the most part appreciated the point, but he also knew Dommie Odembe. Moreover, Dommie also knew that Nick would never drop him in it, whatever the 'it' of the week might be. Nick and Dommie both appreciated that, while Nick might be in the possession of an embargoed piece of information, he could be trusted not to release it until the embargo was lifted. The advantage of that to the pair of them was that Nick had the scoop he required, and he knew that no other reporter would be ahead of him, and Dommie knew that when he wanted to get a piece of information out into the public domain, all he had to do was press Nick's button, and there it was, launched.

So far, this system had worked well for both of them. They also knew that the flow of information could be a two-way thing, and there were times that Nick was in a position to tell Dommie things that he didn't already know.

They had a few favourite places to meet, where – as Dommie was usually in plain clothes – he didn't stand out as a policeman. They used to meet most Thursdays around lunchtime. Nick's hangover had usually cleared by then, and on this day they had chosen to meet at the pub round the corner from where Nick lived in Old Fletton. It wasn't far from the football ground, where you might also find representatives of big London dailies who had come up to cover the match, if the Posh's opponents were a famous team on their way back up the league, or occasionally racing past the Posh on the way down. On another occasion, the Fourth Estate might convene if the local NHS Hospital Trust was having financial difficulties, perhaps, but unless there was some financial jiggery-pokery going on at the same time, or some other form of corruption in the story, he doubted that anyone from London would bother to make the hundred-mile journey north. Anyway, Nick had a far better source: his mate DCI Schmidt of the fraud squad, another blues fan, who could also be trusted to drop him the nod quietly over some music and a pint, with the usual embargo rules applied.

'There you are, Nick,' said a dark chocolate voice behind him. Nick was nursing his second pint, and was concerned that he would end up drunk again, and Dommie would be telling him secret things about the state of the realm, and he wouldn't remember a damn thing when he got home to write them down. He knew DS Odembe's voice well. They had discussed many cases over the years. He had always found Dommie Odembe a reliable source. If only the copper liked the blues as well, they might get together on a more regular basis. Dommie might even introduce him to one of those female PCs he had dreamed about, like that girl in *Doctor Who* with the impossible legs. Nick had always had a soft spot for a woman in uniform.

'Hi Dommie,' he said. 'What's new?'

'I don't know where to start,' he replied.

'Is there something new?' Nick asked, and Dommie just nodded at him slowly.

'Coffee or a coke, or something?' suggested Nick. He knew Dommie didn't drink tea; he wasn't a Yorkshireman. Now, if they were working in a Yorkshire town, Dommie would be a Yorkshireman and drink tea, no matter where in the world he had started life. He also knew that in the middle of a working day, Dommie wouldn't let alcohol pass his lips.

Under the embargo, Dommie told him all about the murder of the Pakistani boy by the railway tracks the night before last. He also told him as much as he knew about Sean James's death – though he thought there wasn't really a lot of point in telling the local hack about that one. By the time that story had got into print in the weekly paper, it would either have been superseded by the follow-up story of a mass slaughter in clubland over the coming weekend, or it wouldn't, in which case the story wouldn't be hot. Still, Nick might be able to get it across to a newsman from a Fleet Street daily – or wherever they were based nowadays – so that it would at least make punters keep their eyes open when they were out and about over the weekend, and hopefully the message, 'Don't take the pink ones' would get about.

Nick, however, was much more interested in the Pakistani murder, which was an active crime, rather than an accidental overdose. If he could actually turn it into a race hate incident, and he wrote it right, it might yet catch the attention of some London press baron looking to fill a vacancy. He might yet get to escape this monochrome town with its unintelligible ghettoes.

On the other hand, although it was not a case he was deeply involved in, Dommie Odembe was far more interested in the drugs case, since unravelling it might actually save some lives, but Nick was more interested in getting out of Peterborough, any way he could.

Once they had drunk their fill and talked about this and that, Odembe explained that he needed to return to Thorpe Wood. Dommie left the pub and climbed back into his unmarked car. Within ten minutes, he was back in the incident room. DI Drake was waiting for him.

'May I ask where you've been?' the DI asked acidly.

'I was briefing a member of the press about the pink pills,' came the reply. This threw DI Drake, who didn't know anything about last night's incident.

'Last night a kid died of an overdose of pink pills,' explained Odembe. 'The pathologist thinks it was accidental, and may have been a rogue batch.'

'And what has this to do with Operation Riverbank?'

'Absolutely nothing, as far as I know.'

'So why are you telling me about it?'

'Because you asked.' And at that point the conversation died and they glared at each other. After a while Odembe started again. 'Of course, there may only be a couple of degrees of separation between the cases, I don't know.' He then wished he hadn't tried to be funny. That never worked with Drake, and it certainly didn't now.

'Explain.'

'Well, there may have been someone who knew the victim of this case, and also knew Stephanie Flack. They were the same age and lived in the same part of Orton.' He stopped there, and hoped Drake would too.

'Any evidence that they knew each other?'

'None whatsoever.'

'Well, you've now got two choices. Either look for a link between the two cases, like Stephanie Flack selling both dead boys your pink pills, or,' he paused for a moment, 'or you definitely exclude any links between them. Think you can do that?'

'I can try,' Odembe replied.

'You do,' replied Drake, working up to a Drake-ism, 'often … my patience.'

Odembe replied with a polite chuckle, in the hope that that would satisfy the DI. It appeared to do its job, as Drake just grunted and left the room. Odembe knew a couple of policemen who might be at a loose end that afternoon, and would value the opportunity to work with him. He called DC Rivers on his walkie-talkie.

'Danny, are you and Susie doing anything special this afternoon?'

'Go on,' replied the DC, waiting to see what he was going to be asked to do.

'Can you two go and dig around the Sean James case, and see if there's a link between him and Stephanie Flack? DI Drake's got his knickers in a twist about it. I'll go round and see the pathologist if you like; we know each other quite well.'

'Will do. Susie's got to go round sometime this afternoon to see the Shadeeds again. She's their liaison officer, and she needs to show them that we're still interested.'

'We are still interested, and the senior officer in charge is trying to link everything else in to the case as well.'

'Huh?' was Danny's reply, but it was to dead air, as Odembe had already disconnected.

Chapter 34

Tom looked through the list of visits that morning. That was funny; Mrs Whilden was listed. She was perfectly capable of getting down to the surgery, so why the house call? He put her notes in his box anyway. He had seen her yesterday at Steff's bedside in the ITU, so at least he knew what was going on in that family. He finished signing his brick of prescriptions, which he was sure he had read. The problem was that he didn't actually know a lot of the patients whose scripts he had signed. At a practice meeting a while back they had done a small exercise among themselves. They had each written down the names of a hundred patients they knew off the top of their heads. All four partners had written down a hundred names and given their lists to the practice manager. The manager came back to them a few days later, and told them that they had named one hundred and twenty-five patients in all. Basically the patients they knew were, for one reason or another, all the same people. Yes, they all knew the names of the difficult people, the people who were seriously ill, and the people with funny names. The lion's share of the practice list who didn't bother anybody didn't figure in the clinicians' memories.

'You're doing your "special" clinic this afternoon, aren't you?' Sam Shivalkar asked him, making inverted commas round 'special' with his index and middle fingers. Tom wondered why he found it so difficult to use the word 'addiction'.

'That's me,' he agreed. 'Anyone who's been avoiding me that you want me to bring up?' There were a few addicts who thought that Sam would be a softer touch than Tom. Neither of them could imagine why. Sam's reply, knowing Tom and his training was in the building, was simply, 'Go and see Dr Clark; he understands all that stuff.'

'Can't think of anybody you don't know already,' he replied, 'See you tomorrow.'

Tom wandered out of the back door of the surgery to the car park. He threw his box on the back seat, and climbed in. He looked at the sleek lines of Dr Shivalkar's big Merc, and vaguely wondered how he could afford to buy or run a car like that. But then he remembered he hadn't got an expensive record collection to maintain – and add to. The advantage of Tom's little Peugeot was that he could get it down the roads in Orton, many of which were cluttered with parked cars, wrecked prams, kids' tricycles and other assorted rubbish. Sam must have to park his Panzer right at the mouth of some of these streets and walk down to the darkest bowels of some of them, to get to the house he was visiting.

There was a police car parked outside the front of the Whildens' house, which worried Tom slightly. He hoped that Steff's condition hadn't worsened, and no one had told him yet. He knocked on the door.

The ruddy, and faintly paint-spattered, face of Mr Whilden appeared from behind the door. 'Oh, hello, doc, she's in the front room, come on in.' He followed him through.

There was a policewoman in uniform in the room with her. She looked somehow familiar. The dark hair, the fringe, the big eyes, the trim figure. *I know that woman; it's Volffy's new girl-friend Shuv. So that's what she does for a living. It figures.*

'Morning,' he said.

She smiled at him. 'Well, if it isn't Dr Clark,' she said. Well, if she felt she could be flippant, then at least the news wasn't disastrous. He acknowledged her.

'Morning,' he said again uncomfortably, suddenly realising that not only had he not known she was a policewoman, but also he had no idea of her surname, and it may be inappropriate to call her 'Shuv'. He smiled faintly and turned his attention to Mrs Whilden.

'What can I do for you?' he asked. 'What's happened?'

'It's Steff's boyfriend,' she said. 'He died last night. He was such a nice boy – or at least we thought he was. He died of a drug overdose at home. We're beginning to think we're perched on the edge of an abyss.'

'Before we go any further, can I ask how Steff is?'

'She's stable, no change, but certainly not getting any worse. She's had moments of consciousness, but she's still in a great deal of pain, so they have to keep knocking her out with pain-killers.' Without missing a beat, she changed the subject back to Steff's boyfriend. 'But when Sean's mum phoned me and told me what had happened, I had to go and see her. Apparently when she got home last night she found him in their living room, pills everywhere. They've had the police in there all night, and they weren't gentle like Constable Flynn here' – *Oh, so that's what her surname is* – 'who's our family support officer, but it was all drug squad and detectives and everyone. I don't know why someone like him would take drugs. He was such a nice sensible boy. He would come round here just to talk to Steff, and they'd play computer games and things. I don't think they'd even kissed each other yet. It wasn't that sort of grown-up relationship.'

'So his death was an accident, then?'

'Oh, they think so, they don't think it was suicide.' She suddenly looked at her doctor in alarm, an idea hitting her mind like a sledgehammer. 'Steff didn't take drugs, did she? You would have known if she did, you being a drugs doctor and all. We never found any, or anything, but when we heard, Craig here did go and look through her room, in case she'd got any hidden away.'

'I didn't find nothing,' her uncle chipped in. Tom was watching Shuv during this conversation, but she wasn't giving anything away.

Tom felt it was appropriate to tell the family that, as far as he knew, Steff didn't take drugs. He kept it to himself that her name had never come up in any of the conversations he had had with those who did.

At this moment Mrs Whilden broke down into floods of tears. Her husband put his arm around her shoulder; the helpless gesture of a man who didn't really know what to do.

'She's been like this all night, doc,' he said. 'That's why I called you. I didn't know what to do.'

Tom was interested that the death of this boy seemed to have upset Mrs Whilden more than what had happened to her niece the day before. But it may have been the accumulation of disasters that broke the camel's back rather than any single episode.

The sobbing became hyperventilation, and she was finding it increasingly difficult to catch her breath.

'Calm down, love,' said her husband to her, patting her arm ineffectually. 'You'll do yourself a mischief. Yes, it gets like this,' he said turning to the doctor, 'and then she loses consciousness for a while, and I don't know what to do next.'

Tom opened his box and took out a brown paper bag. He blew it open like a mask and held it over Mrs Whilden's nose and mouth.

'Breathe,' he told her, 'just gently. In and out, that's it, easy does it.' And Mrs Whilden calmed down again.

Shuv's eyes had opened even wider. She could tell immediately that Tom knew what he was doing, and that if he needed her help, he would ask for it. Afterwards, Mrs Whilden said, 'Sorry, I don't know what came over me.'

Tom fished around in his box and pulled out another couple of brown paper bags and put them on the coffee table.

'I hope you won't need those, but if you do, just hold it gently on her face and make sure she breathes the air in and out of the bag. Make sure she blows the bag right up, and then collapses it right down again.'

'But what exactly happened there, doc?' asked Mr Whilden.

'It was what is called a hyperventilation attack. What happens in respiration is that you breathe in oxygen and breathe out carbon dioxide as a waste product. Now, not a lot of people know this, but under normal circumstances, it is in fact the amount of carbon dioxide you've got in your blood that drives respiration. When you start over-breathing, like she did just now, you blow off carbon dioxide, and the level of the stuff in your blood drops, which then confuses the system, and you lose consciousness, so it can sort itself out again. What you do with the brown paper bag is help her breathe carbon dioxide back in again, so her blood level never drops, and it settles down without the loss of consciousness. Only ever use a paper

178

bag for that, though; never use a polythene one, as you might suffocate her.'

Tom wondered who this boyfriend actually was. The name Sean James only rang one bell – it was the name Billy McGregor had warned him about this morning. *What is this all about?*

So Sean James wasn't registered with his practice? That wasn't particularly surprising. There were several other practices that covered the townships, where Sean may have been registered. Tom was interested that the name didn't figure in his mental database from the 'special' clinic either. He stood up, as Mrs Whilden appeared to have recovered. He felt he had earned some lunch before he got to the clinic building near the town centre by two. He was letting himself out through the door, when he realised that Shuv was following him out.

'There isn't going to be a problem, us working on this case together, is there?' she asked as she pulled the door to, without actually clicking the latch and locking herself out.

He looked at her. 'Is it likely to be?' he asked. 'I was quite looking forward to finding out how Volffy's new girlfriend ticked without working it out in front of him. I didn't even know you were in the police till just now.'

'The rest of the force hasn't put me and Volffy together yet either,' she said, 'and for the time being, I think we'd like to keep it that way.'

'Fair enough. You'll be Constable Flynn when you're in uniform, and Shuv when you're not,' he replied. 'There is a question I would like to ask if I may, though.'

'Anything you like, within reason,' she added.

'If I need to discuss this case with you, when do I have permission to do so?'

'Only when I'm in uniform,' she replied. 'Volffy and I are trying to invoke a no-shop rule at home.' Interesting, thought Tom, she's already referring to Volffy's place as 'home'.

'No-shop?' he asked.

'We don't talk shop.'

'I'm sure you have much better things to talk about,' he replied, and then caught himself. 'With all that music round, and you giving him cooking lessons and all.'

179

'I think I'm going to have to be a little watchful around you, Dr Clark,' she grinned. And she added in a slightly louder voice as she pushed the front door open again, 'Thanks for that, doctor; no doubt we'll touch base again soon.'

As another police car drew in behind them, they looked at each other with an 'I wonder who that can be' expression. Shuv nodded at Tom and said, 'See you,' and walked purposefully towards the new arrival.

Chapter 35

The office manager acknowledged DS Odembe for the first time. She had completely ignored Odembe and DI Drake's presence a few moments ago as if they simply weren't there. What? Somebody talking? Surely not. She might, of course, have heard their conversation, and, if so, its content might even have sunk in, but who was to know?

'I'm going back to the path lab to see if those pills have been analysed yet.'

'Pills?'

'Different case, but I think DI Drake wants to include it in ours.'

'When did they find those pills you're talking about?' she asked.

'Yesterday evening.'

'I wouldn't think they'll have any sort of report back yet.'

'I'm inclined to agree, but one has to show willing, and if I actually go round there then they'll realise I actually want those results. That should ensure the pills get analysed. You'll never believe how many tests don't even get done because they think we're not that bothered.'

'And you'll be out of the way in case DI Drake wants you to do something else that you consider to be a cock-eyed idea.'

'There is that.'

'I'll let anyone who needs to know that you're out working.' She grinned at him.

It would be enough to make the hospital building paranoid. There were probably more police in the corridors of the hospital than there were in Thorpe Wood that day, although, not being in uniform, to the casual observer DS Odembe didn't look much like a policeman. However, if you looked at him more carefully, and thought about it a bit, what else could he be? He had the straight back, the watchful eyes, and the assertive jaw of a policeman.

The door to the lab was partly glass, and Odembe looked through the window before he walked in. The expression that looked back at him couldn't have been misinterpreted, however much he might try later. *What the fuck is he doing here?* was written all over the other man's face. The detective smiled back, as amiably as possible, and walked through the swing doors.

'Dommie!' erupted out of the middle of the room at him.

'Phil!' he replied, somewhat less explosively.

Various platitudes filled the decreasing space between them. They had known each other for what seemed like forever.

'What can I do you for?' Phil asked, knowing that Odembe wouldn't be there without a very good reason.

The detective took a breath, looking past the pathologist's wild hair, which surely hadn't seen a brush or a comb that day. There was, however, the point of a pencil appearing from within the bird's nest, which he found slightly distracting.

'Did the duty officers bring in some pink pills from an incident in Orton last night?' he asked.

'An incident in Orton,' Phil mimicked. And then slowly he replied, his voice slowly going up a semitone as he said it. 'Yes…'

'Well, I've been asked to get a warning out to the clubbers this weekend if it's particularly dangerous.'

'Well, I wouldn't take it,' Phil replied.

'You wouldn't take a paracetamol for a headache,' the detective replied drily, 'but that doesn't tell me anything about what those things actually are.'

'Well, if they're what I think they are, and I'm still doing a couple of tests to be absolutely sure, I think they're PMA tablets.'

'And that is?'

'Para-methoxy-amphetamine is its chemical name, hence PMA.' He waited to see if Odembe's eyebrows went up, and as he couldn't be sure one way or the other, he continued, 'They're also known as Doctor Death, Red Mitsubishis, or Pink McDonald's to the fool on the street.'

182

'Go on.' Odembe took out a notepad, and started scribbling away in his own brand of shorthand. He would need to make proper notes when he got back to the incident room, in his official notebook.

'Well, I understand it finds its way onto the street when MDMA is in short supply.'

'MDMA.' He'd heard of that one. 'That's the chemical acronym for Ecstasy, isn't it?'

'Spot on: 3,4,methylenedioxy-N-methylamphetamine, to be absolutely accurate.'

'You can understand why they use the acronym. Even if your lungs are in good enough condition for you not to have to take a breath in the middle of it, the other person in the conversation would still be at risk of getting bombarded with loosened teeth, or at the very least a mouthful of spittle in the face, every time the drug was mentioned by name.'

'The problem with PMA,' the pathologist continued, totally ignoring Odembe's feeble attempt at humour, 'is that it doesn't really have much of the positive effect that Ecstasy has. The effects that it does have are much slower-onset, and its toxicity levels are much higher.'

'So somebody expecting their new pink pills to work like an E will wait a while, and nothing will happen, and after a while they'll wonder whether the pills are just a weaker mix than they're used to, so they'll swallow a few more to get an effect, and that's when they'll get into trouble?'

Phil looked at Odembe and nodded. 'Got it in one,' he said.

'So why would dealers sell the stuff if it doesn't make the punters happy?'

'Because they can. Look at it another way; it's no *more* illegal than Ecstasy, and the dealers have to have something they can sell, because they're dealers. But unlike Ecstasy, it doesn't work, and it's a lot more dangerous. However, if you're a dealer, and you've got pills to sell, you're probably not that bothered if they work or not. There isn't any quality control department keeping an eye on what goes out. By making the drugs illegal, the government has cut out the safety checks. They won't declare something illegal, and then say, "But if you're going to break the law, then this is what you do to make sure you don't get hurt", will they? As a complete aside, have you heard that amoxicillin capsules are changing hands in the school playground for a pound a pop? My kid bought one with his lunch money once, and then decided not to take it, thank God, and brought it home and showed it to me. He's allergic to penicillin, my kid is.'

'Oh dear God,' Odembe said automatically. 'What happened then?'

'I had a very strong word in the kid's dad's ear. She certainly hasn't tried to sell my kid any more pills. What the little trollop is doing now, I really have no idea; hopefully all her dealing time's now spent learning German strong verbs.'

'Sounds like I need to get word out about this stuff. If it's going to be sold in clubland then potentially it's going to be dangerous.'

'Depends on the quantities people are going to buy them in, I guess. If you've just bought a couple of pills, probably all you're going to get is pissed off, as they won't have very much effect. It's the people who buy a fortnight's supply at once who will be in danger.'

'How do they kill people?'

'The serotonin syndrome,' Phil replied. 'Blood pressure and heart rate goes up, the body temperature goes up and they sweat; the victim becomes more and more agitated, and then they start to twitch. They may become nauseated and vomit, and may get simultaneous diarrhoea. This leads on to confusion, fits, coma and, as I said, it can be fatal.'

'So how do you find out whether someone's going to get serotonin syndrome? Does it run in families or something?'

'No, not at all. It's dose-related, not an idiosyncratic thing.'

'Huh?' Odembe looked at him quizzically.

'It's not a quirk that some individuals get and others don't. You take the right amount of the drug; you get it. Especially if you take the drug plus something else, like alcohol.'

'So how do you know if someone's got it?'

'You ask someone near them if they've taken anything that might cause it. The problem with that is that Joe Average

184

doesn't know what to look out for with the side-effects of individual drugs. Because of their illegality, the pills don't come in nice colourful boxes with the pills on push-out cards inside wrapped in sheets of paper with instructions on. Now, if they did, and on that instruction sheet there was a big friendly black box saying "Warning! This is what to look out for if you're running into trouble", a few lives might be saved. The government doesn't seem to care about that. Mind you, if Joe Scrote did know all about that, most people's temperatures still go up a bit in a club, as it's hot and sweaty in there with everybody bouncing around. I guess you might notice if your friend has suddenly become very stroppy, and if that's out of character you might take a bit of notice. By the time they're actually shaking and throwing up, or both, they're in trouble.'

'So if I've got somebody with me I think might have serotonin syndrome, what do I do?

'Dial 999, and get them to Casualty. Go with them, and if possible take one of the tablets your mate hasn't taken yet with you. Give them to the nurse in charge and don't worry about getting your mate into trouble. He's better off alive and in trouble than the other way around.'

'And that's what you think these things are?'

'And that's what I think these things are.'

'Phil, let's hope that we can get this out into clubland by the weekend. You might just have saved a few lives.'

'I suppose it's the point of what I do,' he replied thoughtfully. 'Please don't quote me by name about my views about the legality of drugs; the bollocracy upstairs would probably sack me on the spot.'

'I wouldn't dream of it,' the policeman replied, 'you're far too useful to us still in place. I'm not even sure I'll even mention that. I think the message I need to get out there is: Don't take the pink pills; they'll kill you. Nice and simple.'

'I don't know which one of us is the more cynical, you or me.'

Odembe raised an eyebrow. From the quick rant he'd just been on the receiving end of, Dommie doubted that anyone in the world was as cynical as the pathologist. But, the more he

185

thought about what he had just heard, the more he agreed with Phil's sentiments. Was that a piece of information he wanted to filter back to his superiors back at the police station? He didn't think so.

Chapter 36

Sergeant Warwick pulled up in front of the Victorian terraced house.

'Is this it?' he asked the woman sitting in the passenger seat.

'Yes,' she said.

'Well, let's do this,' he said and they got out.

Sergeant Warwick rang the bell and then stood back to let Mrs Patterson take the lead. A woman popped her head out of the front door.

'Mrs Patterson,' she said, 'you came.' And then she added in some dismay, 'Who's he? What's he doing here?'

'This is Sergeant Warwick from the Children's and Young Persons' Unit. You've reported a missing, er, young person.'

'Oh, right,' she said, brightening up. 'Come on in, both of you.' She stood back to let them in. 'Come into the parlour,' she said, and they walked down the narrow hall corridor into the back room. In the parlour there was a circular table with a plastic tablecloth with a vase of flowers on top of it, and four chairs round it. Seated in one of the chairs was a big bluff man, nursing a mug of tea.

'This is my husband, Mr Griffin. Albert, you know Mrs Patterson, and she's brought Sergeant ... er ... Worcester ...'

'Warwick,' interjected the policeman.

'Well, I remembered it was a town somewhere out west. He's from the kids' unit.'

'Pleased to meet you,' said Albert Griffin, half standing. 'Would you like some tea?'

'Well, that would be nice,' said Mrs Patterson.

'Dearest, while you're up, put the kettle on for everybody,' he continued, speaking to his wife. 'Please sit down. As you can see, there are four chairs, one each for me and the missus, one for our son Jervis, who's at work, and one for Shannen, only she's not here.'

'That's why we're here,' said Sergeant Warwick. 'Tell us, in your own words, exactly what happened.'

'Well, it appears Shannen just took off,' said Mr Griffin awkwardly.

'When did you last see her?'

'Yesterday morning at breakfast, before me and our boy Jervis went off to work, and Shannen went off to school.'

'Do you usually come home for lunch?' Sergeant Warwick nodded at the two sets of dirty plates on the table.

'Not usually, no, but the missus was so upset about Shannen that I came home.'

'You can get away from work that easily?'

'Self-employed chippie, me, I can get away when I want. I just don't get paid when I do,' he replied. 'I'll go back when this is all sorted, if I may.'

Mrs Griffin appeared with three mugs of boiling water with a teabag floating in each, and a teaspoon in each mug as well. She went back into the kitchen and got a glass milk bottle, and a bowl with granulated sugar in it. There were small clumps in the sugar bowl, suggesting that someone had already dipped a wet spoon in it.

'Help yourselves to milk and sugar as you like,' she said. 'The milk's semi-skimmed, and it was delivered fresh this morning.'

'You get fresh milk delivered still?' asked Mrs Patterson.

'Oh yes,' she said. 'That way we ensure there's always fresh milk for the kids' cereal at breakfast. You can't have kids going off to school without a hearty breakfast, can you?'

'Or me,' her husband chipped in.

'So what happened yesterday?' continued Sergeant Warwick.

'Well, Shannen phoned us last night, and told us she was having a sleepover.'

'She has her own phone?'

'Oh yes – mind you, doesn't every kid nowadays? But we always wanted her to be able to contact us whenever she needed to.'

'And you pay for this?' asked Mrs Patterson, 'and its bills?'

'Of course,' Mrs Griffin replied. 'Out of what you pay us, of course.'

'And she goes to sleepovers on a regular basis?' asked Sergeant Warwick.

'Not at all,' replied Mrs Griffin. 'It was her first time, but I took it as something positive.'

'How do you mean?'

'Well, she'd never brought a school friend home ever, and we were beginning to worry that she wasn't – you know, popular, or anything. So if someone had invited her round for a sleepover that made me think that I needn't worry about that stuff.'

'Did she tell you who she was staying with?'

'Well, yes, she did. She said she was staying at her boyfriend's place.'

'Her boyfriend?' asked Sergeant Warwick, suddenly considerably more alarmed.

'Well, yes, that worried me a bit too, but they're only kids, and the mum was there, so what harm could they get up to, really? And it did mean she'd got, you know, friends.'

'Have you met this boy?'

'Not yet, but I'm sure I will when she brings him round,' Albert Griffin cut in, and the social worker and the policeman looked at him.

'Have you met him, Mrs Griffin?' Warwick asked looking directly at the foster mother.

'No, like he said, but we will when she brings him round, like she promised to do when he brought her home, er, this morning.'

'And then he didn't?'

'And then he didn't, and so I sent her a text. She didn't reply to the text, so I called her to ask her where she was, and did she want Albert to come and pick her up if she was stuck somewhere. She didn't pick up. Well, I thought, that was okay. I mean, they're not allowed to have their phones on in class, are they? So I thought she had gone straight from her sleepover back to school.' Mrs Griffin paused to catch her breath and to order her thoughts.

'And?' Mrs Patterson wasn't going to let her stop here.

'Well, I thought she would probably put her phone back on at lunchtime, so that she could talk to her friends.'

'You mean she wasn't with school friends last night?'

'No, no, no. That's not what I mean at all. You know how kids are – they talk to each other on the phone all the time. Why get up and walk across the school playground when you can just pick up the phone? Anyway, there was still no reply when I called her at lunchtime, and so I phoned the school. I mean, had they confiscated her phone or something, if she had been caught playing a game on it in class? Anyway, they hadn't done anything like that, and she hadn't been in school all morning, and they were about to phone me to see if she was sick or something.'

'So you phoned us?'

'At that point, I thought something was wrong, and so, yes, Mrs Patterson, I phoned you.'

'So, at this point in time,' said Sergeant Warwick, 'neither of you has any idea where Shannen actually is?' There was a lot of question and a fair amount of exasperation in his voice.

'But we will, when she finally gets home,' said Mr Griffin cheerfully enough.

'You know she's coming home, do you? How do you know she's coming home?' Sergeant Warwick was leaning on the Griffins hard.

'Well, she will, won't she?' said Albert Griffin. 'Stands to reason, doesn't it? I mean, where else would she go?'

'That's the million-dollar question, isn't it? Where else would she go? Well, she could have run away. She could have been abducted. Maybe her father found her, and has taken her off to Spain or Majorca. She could have been kidnapped and sold into slavery.'

'Oh, that only happens on the telly; it doesn't happen in a quiet place like Peterborough,' said Mr Griffin.

'You reckon?' Sergeant Warwick's eyebrows went up.

'Isn't her father still in prison?' Mrs Griffin asked Mrs Patterson. 'Surely you would have told us if he'd been let out.'

'What I'm trying to say is that you don't know where she is, and we need to find her,' said Sergeant Warwick. 'Now, we're going to see if we can find her. If she comes back in the meantime, give me a call – at any time – on this number.' He tossed a visiting card from his wallet to both foster parents. 'You, Mr Griffin, go back to work; you can do less damage there. Meanwhile, we'll be back later. Mrs Griffin, don't leave the house, and keep your fingers tightly crossed that Shannen comes home. Quickly.'

Chapter 37

Siobhan Flynn watched Tom's car and the police car miss each other by inches in the narrow street. The policewoman who got out of the passenger side didn't seem unduly worried by the close shave.

'Susie,' said Shuv. 'What are you doing here? Do you think it's entirely appropriate that you are?'

'What do you mean?' Susie asked, nonplussed for the moment.

'Well, you are the Shadeeds' family liaison officer, and this is very much Stephanie Flack's territory.'

'I see what you mean, but we wanted to talk to you.'

Danny looked equally unflustered as he got out of the driver's seat, and tried to explain what they were doing there: about the drugs, Sean and DI Drake's instructions.

'Well, Danny, you can come in for a moment, if you have any questions you want to ask, but Susie, I think you ought to turn the car round and wait for Danny out here, don't you?'

There were moments like that when Siobhan was being small and cute with her glittering eyes that Susie couldn't help wondering why she didn't really hate her colleague, especially when Shuv was telling her what to do. All she said was, 'Good idea,' and walked round to the driver's side, and called 'key,' to Danny. She caught the key one-handed, climbed into the car and adjusted the seat slightly.

Danny followed Siobhan through the front door, while Susie started up and did a reasonable five-point turn in the square. It would have been a lot easier if cars had been parked in a sensible way rather than abandoned any old how in the square. When she had finished the car was pointing out of the square and ready to leave. After a couple of minutes she turned the ignition off and waited for Danny to reappear. She didn't have to wait long.

Danny climbed in to the passenger side.

'Where to?' she asked and he told her.

'And?' she asked, trying to read Danny's face, before she set off.

'Dommie was right,' he said. 'They were very close, Sean and Stephanie. Our next stop is Sean's mother, in the next street along.'

They drove back onto Goldhay Way. The Development Corporation townships were designed on a wiggling road that led from one end to the other. One end of Goldhay Way started at the city bypass on the Fletton Parkway and meandered to the Orton Centre, where there were shops and a secondary school. Off the Goldhay Way were a number of branches off which houses sat. Nobody had an address directly on the feeder road itself; everybody lived on one of those spigots. One of the problems of many of those branches was that once you had driven deep into them, there was no sign as to how to get out of them again, and some of those branches had a very large number of close-packed houses. Danny was also aware that the newer the street, the more complicated the framework. He had become very confused trying to get out of the latest township, Hampton Vale.

They parked outside the house where Sean James had died the previous evening, and rang the bell. It was answered by an incident scene officer in uniform: Constable Borlotti – nicknamed, obviously enough, Beano. He recognised Danny and Susie immediately.

'Hi guys, what's up?'

'Anybody home apart from the law?' Danny asked.

'The vic's mum,' Beano replied, affecting a drawl and trying to sound like a cop from an American TV show.

'Lead on,' Susie chipped in, and he led them through to the living room.

'Mrs James,' said Beano, 'these are two of my colleagues, and they have some questions they want to ask you.'

The woman looked up at them sadly, and nodded at the settee across from her, indicating that they should sit. Once they were in her eye line, and she didn't have to look up at them, she nodded at them both and said, 'What can I do for you?'

'I'm PC Susie Green, and this is DC Danny Rivers,' Susie began, jerking a thumb in the direction of the policeman in mufti. 'We're investigating a completely different case, but we understand that one of the people involved also knew Sean quite well, and we wondered if you knew her too.'

'Oh, who's that? By the way, I'm not Mrs James, I'm Miss. Sean's father and I never married.'

'Ms James,' said Danny, 'does the name Stephanie Flack mean anything to you?'

'Little Steff? Oh yes, she and Sean were such good friends. Her aunt told me that she's in hospital.' She looked up, alarmed. 'Don't tell me she's died too! Has she?'

'Not as far as I know,' replied Susie. 'The last I heard, she's coming round, though I haven't seen her myself today.'

'Oh, that's a relief. Her aunt was very worried about her when I saw her earlier this morning. Poor soul, Mrs Whilden I mean, I think she came round to commiserate about Sean, but all she could talk about was Steff.'

'So they were boyfriend and girlfriend then,' said Susie, leaning forward.

'Who, Sean and Steff? No, of course not, they were friends; you know, bosom pals, chums.'

'Sorry, I don't follow.'

Ms James looked at them. 'Sean was gay. He didn't have girlfriends.'

'Oh.' Susie looked confused.

'Sean was gay. He hadn't come out or anything, but a mother knows these things. And his friend Steff was a tomboy. They were pals together. So what did they get up to? Well, they tinkered on that bike of Sean's, told jokes, and they played computer games. I know Sean used to go out on dates, but when he wasn't doing, er, whatever it was he did, he and Steff would get together and behave like a couple of eleven-year-old boys together.'

'Tell us about Stephanie.'

'Well, you've seen her: short fair hair, rather boyish. Naturally rather nice-looking, but she didn't think that was her fault. She never enhanced her looks in any way. Didn't wear any make-up, and I never saw her in a frock or a dress of any sort. T-shirts and jeans were what she wore, and when she was in school uniform, she always wore trousers; I never saw her in a skirt. Now she's in sixth form, school uniform isn't an issue, but she doesn't dress girly, if you see what I mean.'

'I understand. So how did she and Sean get together?'

'I think once Sean realised what his inclinations were, he probably found it quite reassuring to have a female friend. There was no pressure on him. He could talk to her. Sean loved clothes and things like that, and Steff was a girl who really wasn't interested in them at all, so they weren't competitive in any way. But they were both quite bright and could talk for hours about politics or history and stuff. I must admit I wasn't looking forward to the day when Steff's hormones kicked in and she started getting interested in boys – or girls. I think Sean was worried about that too. I have a feeling that Sean would suddenly feel very alone when Steff started getting,' she thought about the word a moment, 'urges. She made him feel safe, you see. I think he was quite scared about what might happen every time he went out. I don't think he enjoyed being gay very much, but it was just how he was.'

'You mean Steff didn't have a boyfriend or anything?'

'She really wasn't interested in that sort of thing.'

'What did she think of Sean having a boyfriend?'

'I don't think it bothered her unduly, as long as she could still have some Sean time of her own, to tinker with that bike of his, and play computer games.'

'Did she ever meet Sean's boyfriend?'

'I don't think Sean had a single boyfriend as such. I suppose he was looking to find a boy who would also accept his having a close friend who was a girl. You must have had best friends when you were younger? You know, you did everything together, went to the football, played trains, told jokes, but you didn't have sex together; that would have been yucky. Well, that was Sean and Steff.'

'So who did Steff date?' asked Susie.

'Well, I don't know that she did. I know her aunt told me about what was supposed to have happened the night before last, but that just didn't seem right to me.'

'How do you mean?'

'Well, Steff being found half naked, with a boy on top of her, and that she'd killed him with an iron bar? That just wasn't anything like the Steff I knew.'

'You know Stephanie wasn't a virgin?'

Ms James looked up at them, wide-eyed, her mouth forming a large O.

'Really? You surprise me. If I were to use one word to describe Steff it would be innocent. I can't picture her having sex with anybody.'

Susie looked at her. 'Do you usually go around picturing people having sex together?'

Ms James looked at them both for a moment. 'Well, you two, for instance, yes, in a heartbeat. The chemistry between you is electric.'

Danny glared at her angrily. 'What on earth do you mean by that?'

'Well, you both keep looking at each other out of the corners of your eyes, and when you spot that the other is looking at you, you look away in a hurry. As Sean used to say, "Get a room".'

'I'm sorry about that,' said Danny to Susie, flustered, and then looked back at Ms James, 'You've got it all wrong, you know.'

Ms James said, 'If you say so,' and then, looking at the worried expressions on both their faces, she let out a cackle of laughter. 'Oh gor blimey,' she said in a forced Cockney accent, 'have I put my foot in it or what? You mean you didn't know? You know something? You two going to have so much fun finding out about each other. Now I wouldn't mind being a fly on the wall when you do.'

Looking away from Danny, Susie coughed and said very starchily, 'I think we need to get back to discussing your son and Miss Flack.'

'Sure, what else do you want to know?'

The two police officers remained silent. They couldn't think of anything else they wanted to ask Sean's mum. In fact, they couldn't think of anything they wanted to say at all. They felt uncomfortable, and excited; there were places they wanted to be which wasn't where they were at the moment, and there were things they wanted to say to each other, which they couldn't say there.

'I can't think of anything else, actually,' said Susie, standing up. 'But if we do, we'll be back.'

'I'm sure you will,' she said grinning at them, 'even if it's only to say thank you.'

Danny and Susie let themselves out of the front door, and walked towards their car.

'Are you going to drive?' he asked her, and looked at her.

'If you like,' she replied, and locked eyes with him. They laughed, and laughed, and were still laughing when Susie engaged the gear and drove out onto Goldhay Way. Susie was watching where she was going, and Danny was watching Susie.

Chapter 38

Danny walked round the car and slid into the driving seat.

'Give me a call if you want picking up,' he said, 'otherwise I'll see you this evening.' Once again his and Susie's eyes met over the top of the police car that was parked outside the house in West Town. It told them that, in all probability, Virender was there already.

Danny didn't adjust the seat, although he was slightly taller than Susie. It somehow mattered that they were her settings, and he was suddenly so excited that they had just made a breakthrough in their relationship. He almost felt like whistling, and Danny never whistled.

He pulled up in the police car park at Thorpe Wood, and went up to the incident room. A light buzz of conversation met him as he walked through the door, which stopped as soon as they realised who had walked in.

Siobhan and Dommie said, almost simultaneously, 'How did it go?' but he thought they were asking about different situations. Siobhan's question was almost certainly about the investigating that they had done at the James's house; but in Dommie's case it was likely to be about his pairing up of the two coppers who obviously liked each other, probably more than they knew themselves.

His reply to both of them was, 'Very interesting.'

They both then asked him, 'So?' and he decided to answer Siobhan's question.

'Well, there was a very close link between Sean James and Stephanie Flack; they were best friends, in fact.'

'So he was her boyfriend, then,' said Siobhan.

'No, that's not what came over. He was her best friend, and she was his, but they weren't romantically linked. They fiddled with his bike together, or they played computer games together, but they weren't romantically linked. Steff's a tomboy, according to Ms James, and doesn't do any of that lovey-dovey stuff at all. And Sean? Well, Sean was gay. He hadn't officially come out yet, but his mother knew, as apparently all mothers do, and Steff probably knew too because she was his best friend. Sean's mum described them being like eleven-year-old boys together: does that make sense?'

'It paints a picture, all right,' said Odembe, 'but it doesn't fit the evidence. Miss Flack was not a virgin.'

'And that completely threw Ms James. She didn't see Steff doing that sort of thing at all. There is suddenly an important piece of evidence missing from the crime scene: her trousers.'

'And how do you know they're missing?'

'Cos she never wore anything else. She didn't wear skirts or shorts. She never dressed for effect. Shuv, does she have any pretty girly clothes in her room? Because as far as Ms James knows, she's never worn any of them.'

Siobhan Flynn thought for a moment. She had looked in Steff's wardrobe once, and Danny was right – she hadn't been impressed with the clothing in there at all. She certainly couldn't remember any party dresses or ball gowns in there.

'I'll have a closer look when I go back.'

'The bottom line is, there weren't any trousers at the scene when you and Susie got there, and she would have been wearing trousers at the start of that day. That tells me that either the little old man who found them walked off with the trousers, or someone else discovered the scene before him, but didn't report it, and walked off with the trousers as a souvenir.'

'You know, you're a very strange young man, DC Rivers,' said DI Drake drily from behind them. No one had heard him come into the room, but he was standing right behind them.

'There is a third option,' Rivers continued stoically, acknowledging the arrival of his superior. 'Good afternoon, sir. Perhaps there were more people at the scene when the crime was committed, and one of them walked off with the trousers. After all, it was unlikely that any girl in general, and this girl in particular, would have gone to a public place out of doors, just wearing a shirt and knickers, whatever she was going to get up to later.'

200

'Hmm,' Drake mused, 'it's not quite as cut and dried as we thought, is it? Is there any way you can see us being able to pin the killing of the Asian boy onto Sean?'

'How do you mean?' Danny asked.

'Well, Sean comes along, sees the Asian boy doing the business with his chum, and hits him. Whether killing him was accidental or on purpose, we don't know, but kill him he did. He then panics, and, thinking his chum is dead too, pins it all on her, and,' he added, 'walks off with the trousers. How does that look?'

'Well, aside from the fact that there's no evidence of Sean ever having been there, what would he do with the trousers, and why?' replied Dommie drily.

They all looked at each other, and Siobhan said, 'Quite.'

'Any information about the drugs?' asked Drake, changing the subject.

'Sean's mother knew he occasionally indulged in Ecstasy,' Danny replied, 'but as far as she knew, that was a part of his life he didn't share with Stephanie directly.'

'Certainly Stephanie's aunt didn't think Stephanie had anything to do with drugs,' added Siobhan, 'but then, I'm not sure that we should expect her to know anything much about Stephanie. As far as she was concerned, Sean was her boyfriend; and if we told Steff's aunt that Steff had been having sexual relations with anyone, then she would have sworn blind that the other person involved would have been Sean.'

'Do we know when she started having sex?' Drake asked.

'I don't, but I could ask the gynaecologist if he could put an estimate on it,' Odembe suggested. 'I don't know if he could tell us that, mind you.'

'We could always wait until she wakes up, and then ask the girl herself,' suggested Siobhan. 'I gather she is waking up, and she has a very good chance of making a full recovery.'

'There is that,' Drake agreed.

'She might even tell us who she was doing it with,' Siobhan added. 'It may not be anything that she feels she needs to keep secret.'

'She's still underage, so she might not let on, just to protect the boy,' replied Drake.

'Hmm,' Siobhan acknowledged, 'but that is a bridge we can cross if we come to it.'

'Was there any evidence that she had an ongoing relationship with the Shadeed boy?' Drake asked Siobhan next.

'Auntie didn't know anything about him, but, as I said, I don't think she can be considered a reliable witness.'

'I'll ask Susie when I next get to see her, if there's any evidence from the Shadeed family's point of view,' said Danny. 'She may, of course, come back in here before she knocks off, and then anyone still in here can ask her.'

'In the meantime, Constable Flynn,' said Drake, 'would you mind going over to the ITU to relieve Constable Watson, who's watching over the suspect?'

'We can't arrest her when she wakes up,' Siobhan said. 'She's only fifteen.'

'I know that,' he replied tersely, 'but she might say something while in that twilight state between being asleep and awake.'

'It won't be admissible in evidence.'

'No,' said Drake, becoming a little irritated by the Irishwoman, 'but it might be informative, and you've all been driving a coach and horses through my case.'

Chapter 39

Tom drove back to the surgery with his bag of KFC and chips sitting quietly on the passenger seat, wondering what Sam had been given as a packed lunch by his devoted wife.

He parked the car on the rough ground behind the surgery, walked in through the back door, and walked down to the meeting room. Sam was already there, as was the practice nurse, a receptionist, and the practice manager.

'There you are Tom,' said the practice manager. 'One more and we're ready for off.' Tom cast an envious eye at the crisp samosas that Sam was tucking into, and the fresh salad on the plate beside them. He pulled out the box of coated chicken pieces and the chips and emptied them out onto his plate. He would get his hands greasy; well, that at least made sure it wasn't him who was the one to take notes.

'Until Judy arrives,' said Tom to the practice manager, 'can I pop one other thing onto today's agenda? I'm doing the graveyard shift tonight, so I've pruned today's afternoon and tomorrow morning's appointment list.'

'Oh,' said Sam. 'That's a bit short notice, isn't it?'

'Couldn't be helped. Dr Klastru only phoned me during this morning's surgery to ask me to change shifts.'

'You could have always said no.'

'Well, I could, but what answer would I have got if I ever needed a favour from the system? And I really wasn't doing anything tonight so it wasn't a problem for me.'

'Oh, don't talk to me about Dr Klastru,' came a voice from the door. It was Judy Cross, armed with a thermos and a mug dangling from one hand. She poured a thick steaming green liquid from the thermos into her mug. 'It claims to be asparagus,' she said, and then went on, 'Someone else got a Dr Klastru story for this meeting?'

'I was just telling everyone that he called me in the middle of this morning's surgery to ask me if I would do tonight's grave-yard shift, and that I had said yes,' replied Tom.

'A bit short notice, wasn't it?' asked Judy.

'That's just what I said,' Sam added.

'I'm sorry,' said Tom. 'I was only thinking of myself. Guilty as charged. I was booked in for tomorrow night, but I've now got a play rehearsal booked with my daughter tomorrow even-ing, so I would have had to rush back to Peterborough after the rehearsal, do a lightning-quick change and go straight on to the out-of-hours centre, so I saw this as a reduction in personal stress. Sorry, I'll call him and tell him it can't be done.'

'No, no, don't do that yet, what else has it changed?' Judy asked.

'Well, I've trimmed all the empty slots from my list this afternoon, so I can knock off early, and I won't be here tomor-row morning.'

'I've transferred Mr and Mrs Robinson across to your list tomorrow morning, Dr Cross; I didn't think you'd mind,' added the receptionist.

'Not especially,' said Judy and grinned at Sam. 'Is this really inconvenient for you, Sam?' she asked.

Sam backpedalled. 'No, not at all, it just took me by surprise, that's all, and you know what I'm like with surprises.'

Tom took that as an okay and quickly rubber-stamped it. 'Thanks Sam, and you know that if you ever need me to do you a favour...' He turned to Judy. 'Have you got a Klastru story too?' he asked.

'Yes,' she said, 'silly idiot says we referred too many patients to the gynaecologists last month.'

'What?' said Tom and Sam together.

'Well, he and the bureaucrats got together with our num-bers, and he said we were way over our quota of gynaecology referrals last month.'

'You mean there really is a quota?' said Sam.

'Oh yes, and last month we were way outside it. Reasons, chaps?'

Tom wasn't sure whether to take her seriously or not, and looked at the secretary for help.

'Well,' said the secretary, 'we did send a lot of two-week waits to them last month,' she said awkwardly.

'Surely they don't count two-week waits in our quotas, do they?'

'It appears they do,' said Judy. 'What were yours, Tom?'

'Well, there was one patient with postmenopausal bleeding, and I asked Mr Ahmed to see her. It turns out she has uterine cancer.'

'And I had two positive cervical smears,' added the practice nurse.

'And I referred Mrs Radetsky for her ovarian cancer last month,' said Sam.

'I sent a patient in with what looked like ovarian CA as well,' said Judy. 'They all mount up.'

'Two ovarian cancers in the same month?' said Tom. 'When did that last happen?'

'Then of course the gynaecologists also saw those two women last month we'd referred way back with uterine prolapses, so they got counted too,' said Judy.

'So it was a busy month for us in the gynae department,' said Tom. 'So?'

'So, the silly wee pillock wants me to present him with a plan that will ensure we don't overheat our contract in another month.'

'What?' said Sam.

'Well, I suppose we could put all our patients with cancer on a waiting list to go on to the NHS waiting list,' suggested Tom. 'After all, they're not serious, they've only got cancer.'

'I trust that was you being flippant, Tom,' said the practice manager, looking concerned for a moment.

'What do you think?' Tom replied drily, biting crossly into a piece of chicken. 'The thing that really amazes me about all this is that Klastru is a doctor, he's not a trained bureaucrat in whose nature it is to talk bollocks; he's a trained GP. I thought that was the whole point of putting GPs on the boards, so they would talk sense to the economists.'

'Just shows what you know, Tom,' said Judy. 'I'm sure we have something else to talk about.'

'So what are you going to tell him?' asked Sam, before the conversation moved on.

'I'm going to tell him that we couldn't come up with a coherent plan, and bounce it back into his court. I'll tell him that I told you all not to be such clever clinicians, but that none of you were particularly willing to dumb your games down. What do you think?'

'Shall we have a vote on that?' asked the practice manager. Needless to say the vote was unanimous and included the nurse, secretary, receptionist and the practice manager himself.

'Right, what else have we got on the agenda?' asked Judy.

Chapter 40

DI Drake walked in through the café door. He was expecting others to feel the anxiety his arrival always brought to any atmosphere, and each time this feeling of power gave him a little frisson of pleasure. Uncle Lev jumped up from his seat as he saw him arrive.

'Superintendent!' he said loudly and cheerfully. It was part of his act, or maybe charm, to promote a person in authority at least two ranks above his actual rank, or at least one above his level of competence.

Yuri, sitting by the door, did the usual business with the 'closed' sign and the blind, and sat down again. He stirred his tea.

'What can I do for you, superintendent?' asked Uncle Lev, laying on the grease with a trowel.

'I need to talk to you, Lev,' Drake replied tersely, pulling out a chair next to a wall so he could see the room, but no one could get behind him. He sat down.

'Certainly,' said Lev. 'Tea?'

'That would be nice.'

'Adelina,' Lev called. 'Two cups of the best Assam tea, if you would.'

'Yes, Uncle Lev,' said the girl behind the counter. 'Biscuits?' she added.

'How about some Battenberg cake?' suggested Lev.

'Oh, Battenberg cake if you've got some,' said Drake. He was a sucker for marzipan, and Lev knew that.

'Well, superintendent, what's the problem?'

'Does there need to be a problem for me to drop in on my old friend?' Drake replied.

'I don't know,' Lev replied. 'It just seems that the only times you drop in, you seem to be having a problem.'

'Well, I'm sure my problems don't always involve you directly, but it's funny that, when I do have a problem, talking it over with my old friend Lev always seems to help me sort it out.'

'Always happy to help. Tell me all about it. Is it a case?'

'Certainly is. There was a killing the night before last, down by the Nene Valley railway, and it all seemed cut and dried – until one of my officers drove a horse and cart through the case a few minutes ago.'

'Oh?'

'Well, we found two people at the scene, and it looked so elegant: they had killed each other. But there's a problem. One of them wasn't wearing any trousers, and we never found the trousers at the scene. It appears that that victim never wore anything but trousers, and my boys wondered whether that suggested that there had been anybody else at the scene.'

'A witness, you mean?' said Lev as a rattle of tea cups announced Adelina's arrival with a tray full of tea things. 'Adelina, dear, will you pour?'

'Yes, Uncle Lev,' she said, and set out the cups and plates. She poured milk into the cups from a small china jug, and then stirred the tea in the pot. She picked up a silver strainer, and poured Lev's first.

'Is that strong enough?' she asked.

Lev looked across at DI Drake, who was looking at the girl, very impressed. 'Oh yes,' he replied, and so Adelina poured his too. She then cut a hunk of cake off the Battenberg on the plate still on the tray, and picked it up with serving tongs and put it on Drake's plate. She put the knife and the server down on the plate and backed off, Drake's gaze following her all the way.

'Beautiful child, isn't she?' said Lev, telling her not to run away, he might need her again.

'Who is she?' Drake asked.

'She's my niece,' Lev replied. He caught the expression of disbelief in Drake's eye, and corrected himself. 'Great-niece, if you want to get pernickety about it.'

'Some very interesting genes between you and her,' the policeman chuckled.

'Her mother was a great beauty too,' Lev said. 'Very tragic story,' he added, and Drake knew he was not going to hear it this time. 'Tell me about the trousers,' Lev went on, and the conversation continued, but Lev was aware that the policeman was continuing to look at Adelina, who stood at the end of the counter with one slender leg poking out from behind it. She knew he was looking at her, and Yuri was monitoring the conversation very carefully as well. Drake, however, had no idea how much potential danger he was in, or what might happen to him if he made a wrong move when he was in that café.

Once their chat had reached its logical conclusion, and the tea, and a second slice of Battenberg had been consumed, Drake stood up.

'I'll ask my boys if they know anything, superintendent,' said Lev, 'and I'll get back in touch if I hear anything.'

'Please do that,' the policeman replied and, looking across the room at Adelina he said, 'Wonderful cup of tea, my dear, I shall recommend the café to all my colleagues.'

'Er,' said Lev, 'would you mind terribly not doing that? It would do the image of my little place no good at all if it became known that half the clientele was cops. You know how it is. I'm sure I'm more use to you if this little place remained – how you say? Under cover, so to speak.'

Drake chuckled at Lev and said, 'Your wish is my command. It was still a marvellous cup of tea.' Giving Adelina one final glance, he made his way to the door, which Yuri was holding open for him.

Once Drake had left the building, Yuri relocked the door and went to sit down with Lev at the table. He emptied the cup which he had been stirring, but not drinking from, into Drake's cup, and poured himself the dregs from the pot.

'Well,' said Lev. 'What did you make of that?' He turned to Adelina, and said, 'You can tidy the tea things away young lady.' Adelina walked over and picked up the tray, without Yuri's cup. As she turned away, Lev patted her bottom, but she didn't flinch.

'You made a bit of a hit with the policeman, didn't you?' said Lev.

Adelina knew, and the thought had terrified her, all the time she was showing her leg behind the counter. She was showing a little flesh, just to distract the policeman, like she had been taught, and so he wouldn't take a lot of notice of Yuri, so that if a balloon were to go up, then Drake would be caught off guard. Somehow she knew that he had taken rather more notice of her than she had intended.

'Do you know where the trousers he was talking about might be?' Lev asked Yuri.

'No, but I'll bet I know who does. It'll be one of Ruke's little gang, probably that lumbering pervert Mo.'

'Will you sort it out for me?' replied Lev.

'Of course. In fact, we may just use him to sort out that nosey doctor over the pills too. That would be killing two birds with one stone.'

'Literally?'

'If you like; that can be arranged,' said Yuri. 'What do you think of Drake?'

'I don't think we can go about killing him,' replied Lev. 'We may need to sort him out in an altogether different way. Can you arrange a passport for Adelina that makes her only fourteen? How young do you think would be credible?'

'Well, she could be a very tall twelve-year-old,' Yuri said, grinning amiably at the girl in question, who was walking back towards them.

'What are you talking about?' she asked cheerfully, though Yuri noticed a slight tremor in her voice. She knew that she might be the price they needed to control the policeman, and she didn't like that idea one bit.

'Just wondering how young you would pass for,' said Yuri.

'We could always dress you up in a school uniform,' grinned Lev. 'We could probably get you down to eight if we did that. You know, with white socks up to the knees, and brown sandals with brass buckles.' She looked aghast at the men. 'Just teasing.' She walked away with Yuri's tea cup, and replaced it with a half-full one he could take back to his place by the door.

Lev nodded at the pair of them. 'I think we're open for business again, don't you?'

Yuri walked back to his post, flicked the sign to 'open', and released the blind on the door.

Chapter 41

Steff opened an eye, and came face to face with the uniformed policewoman sitting by her bedside. She closed her eye again for a moment, and then opened it again. The policewoman was still there. Her stomach was sore, but that was tolerable. What was a policewoman doing sitting beside her bed, she wondered. She felt herself breaking wind, which was also slightly painful, and one that caught the policewoman's attention.

'Did you have to do that?' asked the policewoman.

'I think I probably did,' Steff replied. She was amazed when the policewoman started waving her hands in the air. Then came the sound of someone in clogs walking towards her back. She attempted to turn over to look at where the person was coming from, but she appeared to be tied down by pipes and pieces of wire and things. Then a different face appeared in her eye line.

'Stephanie?' the face asked.

'Yes?' she replied, also making it sound like a question.

'Have you just broken wind?' the face asked.

What an extraordinary way for someone I've never seen before to address me for the first time, thought Steff.

'Of course I have,' she replied. 'You don't think I always smell like this, do you?' The face roared with laughter, and so did the policewoman behind her.

'Oh Stephanie, you *are* getting better,' said the face. 'I'm Sister Bartram. You've had a bit of an accident, and you're on the intensive care unit in Peterborough City Hospital.'

'Oh,' said Stephanie non-committally.

'May I listen to your tummy?' asked Sister Bartram.

'Yes,' said Stephanie.

The sister drew back the sheet and, having warmed a stethoscope by rubbing it on her hand, placed it on Steff's abdomen. She moved it around and listened in a couple of places. She

211

then stood back and pulled the sheet back down, and smiled at Steff.

'That's great,' she said. 'Your bowel's started working again. Are you thirsty?'

'A bit,' she replied.

'Pain?'

'The bottom of my tummy's a bit sore, but I can cope with it at the moment. Why is there a policewoman behind you?'

'I'm Siobhan Flynn,' said the policewoman in a gentle Irish brogue. 'I'm your family liaison officer.'

'What's that?' she asked. 'Why have we got one of those?'

'Well, you had,' Shuv paused, 'an accident.'

'What sort of accident?' Steff asked.

'What do you last remember?' the policewoman asked.

Steff thought for a moment. 'Well, the last thing I can remember is sitting in the library doing some work. Did I have an accident in the library? Was I hit by a falling book? Did it hit me in the tummy? Ow!' she said. Moving was not such a good idea.

'N-no,' said the policewoman slowly. 'You'd already left the library when it happened.'

'I don't remember that,' said Steff thoughtfully.

'It was two days ago,' Shuv added.

Steff's eyes opened wide. 'Two days ago?'

'You've been a very poorly girl,' said Sister Bartram, returning with a glass of water with ice cubes in it. 'Shall we see if we can get you more comfortable, and give you a bit of a drink?' Another nurse appeared, and the policewoman stood back and let them move Steff. Movement was not good, thought Steff; it hurt.

'Let us do the moving,' said the sister, 'don't try to do anything yourself.' And with a bit of gentle help, Steff found herself almost in a sitting position. The nurse then picked up a beaker and put it to her mouth, and she swirled the soothing water round it.

'What has been nesting in my mouth?' Steff asked after a moment, and then she added, 'What happened to my tummy? It's very sore.'

'You had an emergency operation,' said Sister Bartram slowly, waiting to see whether Steff would ask for further details. She didn't, but she would; that would only be a matter of time.

'Can I have some painkillers?' Steff asked. 'Moving me around has really wound up my tummy, and it's hurting now, big-time.'

'Well, as your bowel is now working again, I'll get you some painkillers,' said the sister, who left her bedside again.

'So why are you here again?' Steff asked Shuv.

'We've always had someone here, in case you said anything that might lead us further in the case.'

'The case?' she asked. 'You mean, it wasn't an accident?'

'Not exactly,' said Shuv. 'You were attacked.'

Steff's eyes opened wider again before a wave of pain racked her. 'Did you save my life?' she asked.

'I was there,' said the policewoman.

In a very soft voice Steff said, 'Thank you.'

The sister came back with a small beaker with some clear liquid in it, and held it up to Steff's lips. She swallowed the contents, and then the sister gave her a mouthful of water to wash it down. Steff said 'Thank you' again to the sister, but that didn't mean as much as she had meant her first 'thank you' to Shuv, who was still tingling because of it.

The girl sank back onto her pillows and shut her eyes for a moment, and a few moments after that she was properly asleep again.

'Can I do anything?' Shuv asked the sister when it was obvious that Steff would be out of it for a while now.

'You're really in the wrong place to be asking questions like that. This is an intensive care unit, and even the nurses have got more degrees than a thermometer,' the sister replied. 'The only thing you're qualified to do here is to sit beside her and listen. She might say something interesting while she's still asleep.'

'She didn't remember being attacked,' said Shuv.

'And long may that continue,' replied the nurse. 'Can you think what remembering what actually happened will do to the poor thing?'

'When do you think she will remember the incident?'

'With a bit of luck, never. Post-traumatic amnesia is nature at its kindest.'

'She's got PTSD?' asked Shuv, aghast. 'How can you tell?'

'That wasn't what I said. What I said was that she's got post-traumatic amnesia. She's forgotten the incident – that's all that means. I didn't say anything about post-traumatic stress disorder. The only thing they have in common is that they both happen after episodes of trauma, hence the "post-traumatic". Does that make sense?'

'I'll probably have to look it up again when I get home,' grinned the policewoman, 'but I think I understand what you're saying at the moment. Then my boss will ask me to explain it to him, and I'll lose the plot completely.'

'Bosses are like that,' said Sister Bartram.

'Yours can't be as bad as mine.'

'The trick with bosses is always to know far more than they do about the subject. Just don't tell them that they know Jack, then they'll start looking for traps.'

Shuv moved as if to shake Sister Bartram by the hand, and realised that the sister still wore blue plastic gloves.

'You'd be amazed at the number of these things we get through in a working day,' she said, and smiled at the police-woman. 'Call me if she needs anything.'

Siobhan Flynn went back to the chair by Stephanie Flack's bedside, and sat down and looked at her sleeping face. She couldn't believe that face was guilty of anything – let alone murder.

Chapter 42

Adelina sat in the room at the back of the café. She was anxious, but then that was how she always felt when Yuri wasn't in the building. She felt safe when Yuri was around. She knew that he wasn't interested in her, not like that, and as far as she knew, he was the only person she knew who didn't want to have sex with her, apart from her flatmates of course – and even with them, she realised, her relationship was all about sex. She didn't want to have sex with any of them, any of them at all. She thought about it for a while. She hadn't had sex with anyone yet. She had never even really had a boyfriend – one or two boys who were friends, maybe, like Yuri. After school she had had to rush home on her bicycle, however cold it was to be out in a short-sleeved shirt. She had to work up a sweat, to get home to help her mother, who had taken such a terribly long time to die. Then, once her mother had died and she was on her own, her uncle – her mother's brother – didn't want a niece cluttering up his place, so he packed her off to a friend of his in England who had a job for her. She had thought she would be a paid professional carer; she was good at that, after all. She never worked out how her uncle and the man she now knew as Uncle Lev actually knew each other, but there were still so many things she didn't understand. Like, for instance, there was a girl in her flat called Jameela. Adelina couldn't help looking at Jameela's legs. She couldn't really avoid it; it was one of her jobs to be Jameela's dresser, and part of that was to help with her make-up. Jameela's legs bowed outwards, so you could put both fists between her knees when she stood up, even though her heels were firmly together. Jameela had a lot more meat on her legs than Adelina too. Jameela had also admired Adelina's legs, which were perfectly straight, and when she stood upright with her heels together, her knees were together too. Jameela told her that once she had put the

215

right amount of meat onto them, they would be really beautiful. One of the other girls had said there were dietary reasons for Jameela's legs being bowed, but Adelina didn't understand that. Sometimes back home Adelina's diet had consisted of nothing but bread and dripping, and she remembered she had often been really hungry for weeks on end.

'Were you ever hungry?' she had asked Jameela, who had shaken her head in reply. Adelina didn't understand how the different shapes of their legs could have been dietary.

'Vitamin D,' said Jameela.

'Vitamin D?' asked Adelina. 'What's that?' She had never heard of it.

'When you were out and about, were you exposed to the sun?'

Adelina thought about her school shirt, and the sun on her face as she cycled home every day from school. Sometimes they even played football at school, because there were more kids than there were classrooms to accommodate them. 'Yes,' she said.

'Well, there you are then.'

'Oh,' she replied, still not understanding.

One thing Adelina did understand was how Jameela had come to be a working girl. Jameela had told her all about that. Jameela had had a boyfriend, and the boyfriend was from a lower caste than Jameela. That was all right, she said, provided nobody found out. You couldn't tell his caste just by looking at him. The trouble was, somebody did find out, and it was her father, and that was what made it a problem, as he and the family then disowned her.

'But then that was all right, couldn't you go and be with your boyfriend?' Adelina had asked innocently.

'Ah well, because I had been thrown out by my parents, that meant that I hadn't got a caste any more, and therefore I was now of lower caste than my boyfriend, and his family wouldn't let him have anything to do with me.'

'So what happened to him?'

'He stayed with his family, went to university, married who they told him to, and he's probably now a doctor somewhere.'

216

For a moment Jameela looked wistful, and then grinned at Adelina and said, 'Come on then, things to see, people to do.'

Adelina had talked about sex with Jameela and one or two of the others. Jameela had had sex with her boyfriend, until her father had caught them at it. She told Adelina it had already stopped hurting, had become fun and was giving her a buzz when she climaxed. In fact, that may have been what had attracted the attention of her father. She may have been a little noisy about it. Ajit had been very gentle with her to start with. It had been his first time too, and he didn't want her to tell him they weren't going to do that painful thing again.

'What it needs is for you to get your insides into training,' Jameela went on, 'and to learn how to relax your pelvic muscles. Not too much, cos if you relax too much, then he won't know he's inside you and that doesn't work. Blokes like to feel appreciated, you know, that's what they're paying for.'

What were the chances of her first time being with someone who cared enough to only hurt her a little? Adelina knew that her virginity was being held back by Uncle Lev as a payment or a bribe for someone important, and important people don't do things nicely with girls whose virginity is the prize. Maybe she should have just rolled over and taken it back home, and got it over and done with with one of those boys.

'Did Uncle Lev ever tell any of your johns you were still a virgin?' she asked Jameela one day.

'Not for long,' she had chuckled. 'Somebody guessed I had been turning tricks for a while, and complained that he was being charged too much. So now I'm an exotic Brahmin Princess instead. I suppose that's not entirely untrue, though it does mean I have to do all this ridiculous make-up stuff. You want to smell the room where I work; the smell of joss sticks is extreme.' She looked at the girl she considered to be her protégée. She was still teaching her the art of make-up, and one day Adelina was going to be an expensive exotic something or other, and not just a cheap tart – that Jameela had promised herself.

Adelina picked at her knee for a moment. She understood that Uncle Lev would look after her, and would probably care for her for a while, but soon she would begin to look older, and he would care about her less. He had offered her some of his 'magic mixture' already – some sort of drugs, she had assumed – but she'd always declined, sweetly of course, and Uncle Lev had said 'of course' and 'one day' and other things while gently patting her thigh.

Once he had sold her virginity, of course, then there would be many men, and that might well be when she'd need to take drugs to take the pain and shame away. At the moment, she had a room of her own in a nice flat, which she shared with a couple of Lev's upmarket working girls, which included Jameela. It told her that he valued her. The flat overlooked the river, and she had some nice clothes to wear, and a job that wasn't too taxing – waiting on tables at Lev's café, and helping her flatmates get ready for work. The other girls understood she would soon be in training, but, apart from learning how to put on make-up, her real training would come from the girls after her virginity had been sold. Uncle Lev wanted the sale of her virginity to appear to be genuine, at least for the first few times.

She thought she needed to talk to Yuri about her problem. Of all the people she knew, surely he was the one who would help her with her virginity. However, Yuri was not so sure.

'You know I'm gay,' he said.

'It's not as if we would be doing this for fun,' she said. 'Perhaps it's because I know you're gay that I thought you were the right person to talk to.' But she knew that wasn't right either.

'You were saying you wanted me to train your pelvic muscles how to relax so it wouldn't hurt when you did it for real. How would I know whether I was going to hurt you? I've never had sex with a woman, any woman.'

'Oh.'

'And I'm not boasting when I say that my tool is bigger than any other man's that I've been with. I know they always say that size doesn't matter, but I think under these circumstances it probably does.'

'Oh.'

'So, sweet Adelina, I don't think I'm the right person to help you out with this problem, but I promise I will look out for someone who is. Does that help?'

Adelina nodded, disappointed, but went back to what she was supposed to be doing.

'Hello,' said a voice behind her. It was the girl that Ruke had brought in that morning, Shannen. She had changed from her jeans and a sloppy Joe into a short spandex skirt, a very tight T-shirt which showed her nipples, and a pair of very high heels, on which she looked quite unsteady. Her hair was now piled up on the top of her head, and her make-up reminded Adelina of the warpaint worn by the Indians in the cowboy films she had watched to help her to learn English back in the day.

'How do I look?' Shannen asked.

One of the first things Adelina had learned was tact, and thus she had to think of a word that worked. 'Spectacular' sprang to mind from the English dictionary she carried in her head.

'You think?' was Shannen's reply.

'Yes, people will certainly look at you. Do you work for Uncle Lev?'

'I do now,' she replied. 'I've just done my first job.' Which explained to Adelina why her warpaint looked a bit smudged. 'So I'm having a tea break. Is there any tea available?'

'Of course,' said Adelina and put the kettle on. 'Was the first time you had sex the first time you did it working for Uncle Lev?' she asked Shannen while she waited for the kettle to come to the boil. 'Or had you done it before?'

'I've got a boyfriend,' said Shannen. 'We do it lots.'

'And he does it nicely?'

'Well, he's certainly much younger than the old bloke I've just done it with. He kept going floppy in me, so he didn't hurt me. I think he must have hurt himself more trying to make it stand up again.'

'So who's your boyfriend?'

'Ruke,' she said, while Adelina put a tea bag into the mug, and poured boiling water on top of it. 'You know, the bloke I came in with this morning.'

'And he's gentle?'

'Yeah. Ruke's nice.' *Nice?* Adelina asked herself. *He brings his girlfriend into Uncle Lev's café, and within four hours she's already dressed up like one of the cheap tarts and has bonked some old bloke who can't do the business. And he's nice?*

That wasn't Adelina's idea of a boyfriend, but she had noticed that when she had seen him, Ruke had looked her up and down appreciatively, and Shannen had said he was gentle. That might be just the boy that Adelina was looking for to get her insides into training. She left the kitchen and went out to look for Yuri.

Chapter 43

Yuri walked up to the front door and pushed the bell. It rang for a moment and then was answered by a gruff voice from within. 'Who that?'

'Is Ruke in? Tell him it's Yuri.'

'I don't know, I'll go and have a look,' came back through the door, which remained shut, and the feet disappeared into the distance. Two minutes later a different set of footsteps approached the door and it flew open.

'Yuri! Good to see you, old friend,' came a very nervous greeting. 'What brings you all the way over here?'

'You don't need to creep,' said Yuri. 'You're in enough trouble already leaving me on the fucking doorstep, without making me sick by sticking your nose up my arse crack.'

'I'm so sorry, that was Mo. He has no idea how these things get done.' He called back into the bowels of the house, 'Mo, come and meet Yuri. He works for the boss.'

A large awkward youth walked through to the hall. 'Uh, sorry,' he said, looking at his feet.

'I shall be watching you,' said Yuri, carefully. 'I've heard of you already, and now I know what you look like. You're going to be watching your step from now on, or you'll get hurt. What will you get?'

'Hurt,' replied Mo uncomfortably.

'Hurt as in, if you're lucky, you'll only be in hospital hurt, like that girl you broke the other night.'

'What girl?'

'Don't bullshit me. You know exactly what I'm talking about. Now fuck off, and let me talk to Ruke.' And that's exactly what Mo did, disappearing into the bowels of the building.

'So what can I do for you?' asked Ruke, still all smiles, trying to encourage Yuri over the threshold and into the sitting room.

'I have a project for you, something I think you're perfectly equipped for,' said Yuri, beckoning to his car outside the front door. Adelina got out of the passenger side and walked up to the front door to join them. Ruke knew exactly who the slender girl was, and was most uncomfortable that she had crossed his threshold.

'What do you want me to do with her?' he spluttered.

'What do you think? We want you to train her.'

'Train her to do what?' he asked, increasingly desperately.

'Train her to turn tricks, what do you think?'

'Does Uncle Lev know anything about this?' he asked.

'Not a bit of it,' Yuri replied, shutting the door behind him.

'But Uncle Lev would kill me if he knew I was doing anything like this with her.'

'Only if you tell him. We won't mention it if you do it right, will we, Adelina?'

Adelina shook her head.

'But why don't you train her? You speak the same language and everything.'

'I consider Adelina to be a sort of little sister, and in Russia we don't fuck our sisters. I also have the disadvantage of having a very large prick, and as nobody's been in there before, we consider it might hurt her, and we really don't want to hurt her. Now on the other hand, you have a reputation for being quite gentle. What we want is for you to train her to feel like a virgin, but for it not to hurt her. Do you think you can do that?'

'But she's so little – she's much too young for this.'

'I'm nearly eighteen,' the girl replied crossly. 'I just look young.'

'She's much older than that girl you brought in this morning, and she's telling everybody that you've been in her knickers.'

'Suppose I just say no?'

'In which case I'll tell Uncle Lev that you did anyway, and who's he going to believe, you or me?

'Why not get Mo to do it?'

'Mo breaks people, and we really don't want to break this one now, do we?'

Meanwhile, Adelina fixed Ruke with an expression that most men would find difficult to resist. 'So what do you want me to do now?' he said, giving in to the combined pressure from Eastern Europe.

'This first time, all we want you to do is to take her virginity, very gently and nicely. I must insist that you don't hurt her, because if you do, I will hurt you, and if you hurt her badly, I will hurt you very badly indeed.' Yuri pulled a sheath knife out of his pocket, and popped the strap around the handle. He drew the blade part out of the sheath and looked at it as it glinted in the artificial light. He then put it back in the sheath, secured the popper, and put it back in his pocket. 'Capisce?' Yuri put his hand into his pocket and pulled out a condom. 'You will wear that, and you will not give her any of your nasty diseases. Are you happy with the arrangement, Adelina?'

The girl nodded silently.

'Where would you be doing her training? I assume you have a room in this house.'

'This is my house; of course I have a room.'

'Good, then lead on. We're following.'

Ruke led the way up the stairs and turned left up to his room. It was a male room, with a few centrefold pinups, making a sharp contrast to the Arabic symbols around the mirror. There was a double bed. The sheets were rumpled. Adelina sat on it and bounced up and down on it for a moment.

'It feels quite comfortable,' she said.

'I think you can get on with it now,' said Yuri.

Ruke looked at him desperately. 'I can't do it with you looking on. I wouldn't be able to get a hard on or anything. You're just too fucking scary, man.'

Yuri looked at him, and then at Adelina. 'If I take a chair and park it on the other side of that door, I will hear if you hurt her, and if you do, it will be the last time you hurt anyone.' He looked at the girl. 'That okay with you?' he asked, and Adelina nodded anxiously.

Yuri dragged the chair out through the door and pulled the door to. He then sat on the chair outside like a guard. He heard heavy steps walking up the stairs, it was Mo.

'Ruke in there?' he asked.

'Yes,' replied Yuri.

'I need to see him,' said Mo, putting his hand to the door handle.

'Don't even think about it,' said Yuri, his voice dripping threat. 'He's busy.'

'Just for a moment.'

'No. Go away, very quickly indeed. Oh, wait a minute, you're that Mo, aren't you?' Yuri's expression softened, and he broke into a smile.

'Depends,' said Mo awkwardly.

'Girl-splitter Mo, who breaks people,' Yuri continued, still smiling.

Mo grinned back. 'Could be.'

'Once the business in there is completed, and I've taken our client back to where she needs to go, I shall come back. I think you and I have some business to do together. You will still be here, won't you?'

'Could be.'

'Well, if you're not, you'll probably need to be heading for a province in Afghanistan where they don't find Europeans. Because if you're not here when I come back, and I find you later, you're going to really, really wish you had stayed here. Has that sunk in?'

'Yes.'

'Good. Now go, so I don't think about practising on you.'

Yuri looked as if he was about to get up. Mo thought that discretion was probably the better part of valour and went rapidly downstairs again. In the background Yuri could hear the bed squeak gently, and Adelina take a sharp breath, but there was no cry of pain. Yuri listened carefully. He didn't get too close to the door, as he felt that would be inappropriate – and, besides, this was a girl having sex, maybe his little sister having sex, and he really wasn't into that at all.

It didn't take very long before the door opened again. Adelina came through the door first.

'How was it?' he asked.

'Not as bad as I was afraid it might be,' she replied. 'He was a good choice.'

'Good, well done Ruke. We'll be back tomorrow after work, that's shortly after five. Be here, and be ready to perform.'

Ruke acknowledged the command, and walked out, doing up the belt of his trousers. 'Yeah,' he said, 'right.'

Adelina and Yuri walked down the stairs, passing Mo in the hall.

'I think he'll see you now,' Yuri tossed at him, and he shot up the stairs like a rocket with the blue touch paper well alight. Meanwhile, the Europeans left the building, and went back to the car. Yuri looked at the clock. Fifteen minutes. That would do.

'How do you feel?' he asked her.

'A little sad,' she said, 'but I suppose that will pass.'

'Once you get used to it,' Yuri replied.

'I had always hoped that this time would be with someone very special, not just as part of some training programme. Still, it would have been really bad if it had been with someone middle-aged who had paid for it. Ruke was certainly trying to be gentle.'

'I am so glad to hear it,' said Yuri.

'Did you have an orgasm?' he asked after a moment.

'I don't know,' she replied. 'What's one of those?'

'You'd know if you'd had one. We need to make sure you're having those by the time your training with Ruke has finished.' And with that he pulled onto Bourges Boulevard and headed south towards Adelina's flat in Viersen Platz.

Chapter 44

Andrzej followed his brother through the front door of the house where they were staying, and they went upstairs with the packed supper Sid had given them. Sid had taken the envelope, that the farmer's wife had given them following their day's work, off them before they had even opened it and, in exchange, he had given them their packed supper.

'We must open the envelope tomorrow, before he gets here, just to see what's in it,' said Sergei as he sat down on his bed to open the packed supper. In each bag there was also a screw-capped bottle of beer. It wasn't cold, but it was beer. They both twisted the caps off eagerly and the bottles opened with a welcome hiss. They wrapped their lips round the bottle necks to ensure that none of the precious liquid was lost.

Andrzej sighed in pleasure.

'That hit the spot,' he said. 'I wonder what's in the rest of the bag.' He tipped out its contents on his bed. A hunk of fairly fresh dark bread, a smoked sausage, some smoked pork, and a tub of mixed vegetable salad in mayonnaise rolled out. They were all labelled in Polish.

They looked at each other and shrugged.

'Can't Sid tell the difference between Polish and Lithuanian?' Sergei asked his brother.

'Does it matter to him who we are, as long as we work?' came back the dry reply. 'A pity about that coin; I'd have kept it from him just to make our point.'

'I did,' said Sergei.

'You did what?' his brother asked.

'I kept my coin.'

'You mean you found another one?'

Sergei dug into his pocket and pulled out the coin he'd dropped in there, and tossed it at his brother.

'Why didn't you tell me about this before?'

'The farmer came straight over as soon as we had found the other one. I was sure we were under some sort of surveillance, so I didn't mention it.'

'We were right in the middle of a field. How could we have been under any sort of surveillance out there?'

'I don't know, but I was sure they were watching us somehow.'

'So why don't you think they're watching us in here?'

'I checked the room over carefully yesterday evening and I found nothing. If they're watching us in some way I didn't find, then we'll find out soon enough, won't we? All it has cost us to do so is another coin.'

They toasted each other with their bottles of beer. 'Cheers!'

**

Shannen had been allocated a room off Alma Road, which she found disappointing. She had hoped that, at the end of a day's work, she would be taken back to Ruke's house, but they told her that he was 'busy' tonight. How could Ruke be 'busy'? He was her boyfriend, wasn't he? He would be expecting her, surely? No, he wasn't around tonight, they told her, so she needed to stay in the room and get some sleep so she could go to work tomorrow. Did she want some supper? Yes, but only if it was Ruke's homemade curry. Curry they could arrange, but they couldn't guarantee that Ruke had made it himself. In which case she wasn't interested. Had they got any of Ruke's coke for grown-ups? That they could arrange. Well, that would do. And would she make sure she had had a bath before she went to bed, and another when she got up in the morning. They wanted her to smell nice for work tomorrow.

**

Steff's aunt was back home, and explained to Craig that Steff was now awake, and she'd talked to her this evening. She didn't think that Steff fully understood the extent of her injuries yet, but she seemed cheerful enough.

'So what's she going to be able to do when she gets home?' asked Craig.

'Not you, for a start,' came back the dry reply. 'She'll be able to go back to school, and study, and get her A-levels and go to university, but I don't know about sex. She's been badly hurt.'

'Well, I hope you realise what that means, girl?' he replied evilly.

'What?'

'You're going to have to start making the beast with two backs yourself again now. I suppose you can count yourself lucky: you got away with not having to do it for the last two years since Steff has been here, but if she can't do it any more, I'm afraid it's going to be your job again.'

'Isn't there anyone else you can think of? Why don't you buy someone off the street?'

'I can't afford that on a regular basis. I'm only a glorified handyman, for fuck's sake. Now get your kecks off, girl, I've got the urge coming on me. I fancy a bit of pussy.'

***

Siobhan Flynn sat on the edge of the bed looking at Volffy. 'You'll never guess who I met today,' she said running her fingers through the silver mane of the man she found so attractive.

'Who?' he asked.

'I ran into your mate Rock-a-Doc. I was doing a bit of family support on the Flack family, and in he walked. He's their GP. Isn't that a thing? I'd never met him before yesterday evening and, within twenty-four hours, I'd met him again in a completely different set of circumstances. I don't think he recognised me at all at first.'

'I don't suppose he expected to see you in uniform,' he grinned. 'I don't see you in uniform very often either for that matter.' He thought for a moment. 'Probably more than I want to, though.' He unbuttoned her blue shirt and threw it across the room. 'See,' he said, 'no uniform.'

***

After he had delivered Adelina to her flat, Yuri had turned round and driven straight back to Ruke's house. Mo was still there, looking fairly anxious, and Yuri took him through into the front room and sat him down. He explained the plans for the evening. Mo knew exactly where he was to go, and at what time, and what he was to do there. After the job was done, Yuri would pick him up, and they would go and dispose of Steff's trousers – which the stupid idiot should never have pocketed in the first place.

After his trip to Ruke's house, Yuri drove out to one of the more exclusive parts of Werrington Village, and parked at the end of the drive of one of the houses. He walked quietly up the drive. To the right of the door the living room curtains were drawn, but there was light behind them, and there appeared to be movement. A television was on. He pulled the envelope out of his pocket. He pushed the metal flap on the letterbox open with his fingers and, as he held it open, he silently dropped a letter in. He then eased the flap silently closed again. He walked back down the drive to his car and drove back to the car park at the back of the tea shop.

He looked round the car pound, and was pleased to see that the little grey Peugeot 1007 was there. That was the car he would need later on that evening. It was a slightly quirky car, which suited his needs to a tee. The doors didn't open outwards; they were electrically powered and slid backwards on runners. The car itself wasn't particularly powerful, but enough for what he needed – and anyway, in a town, who needed raw power?

He went round to the shed and took out the folding bicycle with the broken front wheel, and threw it on to the back seat of the Peugeot. He rubbed his hands, then entered the back door of the café and made himself a cup of coffee. It was going to be a long night.

Chapter 45

She adjusted her dress. 'You bastard,' she said. 'You unspeakable bastard.'

'What you getting your knickers in a twist for, girl? That's what wives are for, and you are still my wife, whether you like it or not.'

'That wasn't how you used to do it when we got married, you were nice and funny and gentle. You didn't just screw me, you made love to me.'

'Yeah, well that was when I thought we was going to have babbies and stuff. After a while when I realised you wasn't going to do that, you know, like your sister did for her husband, I thought, what's the point?'

'Are you sure it's not you that's got the problem with having babbies?' she asked. 'Mebbe it's your bollocks that don't work properly.'

'Have you ever had a babby?' he asked. 'One that I don't know about?' He raised a fist and made to look like he was going to hit her.

'No,' she replied, but she wasn't frightened of him. What could he do to her that was more unpleasant than what he had already done that day? 'Have you?'

'That Sharon McKillop swears that one of her boys is mine,' he replied.

'There must be at least thirty blokes that slut Sharon McKillop is getting money off for those four rascal kids of hers. You never did get tested did you?' She looked at him drily.

'I don't suppose you fucking did either,' he snapped back.

'I did actually, and I'm normal, so there.'

'That's a matter of opinion,' he replied, 'You? Fucking normal? In a pig's eye!'

And the conversation went on downhill from there until he stormed out. She heard the tyres squealing as he drove off into the night. And she sat down on the chair and cried. After a while she got up and went into the kitchen to do the washing up.

About an hour later he was back, drunk, stroppy and demanding more sex.

'You haven't driven back in that state have you?' she screamed at him. 'You could have killed somebody driving that pissed.'

'Course I haven't, Pete brought me back. Now get them kecks down, I want a fuck.'

'Haven't you had enough for tonight?' she said, backing away.

'Nope, I wanna nutha fuck.' He said starting to unzip his trousers, releasing an apology for an erection, but he wasn't to notice. 'Come 'ere, woman.'

She had backed up against the chest freezer in the corner.

'Come along, girly, come to papa, Mister Wiggly wants his doings.'

She lifted the lid of the freezer and put her hand in, her fingers closing around the tail of a frozen salmon. As he put his fist on her chest and pushed her, she swung the salmon, making contact with the side of his head. 'Oh fuck,' he shouted. He spun on his heel and staggered out into the living room where he collapsed on to the coffee table, which, in its turn, collapsed under his weight. His head then crashed into the mantelpiece. Still holding the salmon, she followed him out and looked at the prostrate form.

She walked back to the kitchen table and put the salmon on it, and closed the freezer lid. After a minute's thought, she went back to the living room, and watched him for a moment as he breathed unevenly and stertorously. His breathing slowly stopped. She went back and took the fish kettle down from the top of the kitchen cupboard where it lived. She wiped it clean and then filled it up with water, and put it on the hob to bring it to the boil. While it was coming to the boil, she chopped a couple of onions and put them into the kettle and some herbs from the rack. Into the kettle she then put the salmon.

She went back to her husband and checked his breath with a mirror like she had seen on the telly, and there was no fogging. She felt like dancing. How could she have once loved that pig, she asked herself, and went back into the kitchen, and closed the door. She needed to make a Hollandaise sauce.

It takes some time and concentration to make a Hollandaise sauce, but she wasn't in any hurry. It wasn't the sort of thing that someone as proud of her cooking as she was would ever get out of a jar.

By the time the sauce was done, she checked the salmon, and it was simmering gently. She stuck a skewer through it, and it was no longer frozen in the middle. She turned it down to simmer gently for a while and put the kettle on to make a cup of tea.

It was after she had finished the cuppa that she poked the salmon again, and thought, yes it's about time. She walked through the living room, being careful not to tread on the corpse lying there, picked up the phone and dialled.

Chapter 46

'Tom, we've got a call out,' said Bob. 'Are you free?'

'No,' replied Tom, 'but I'm not very expensive.' It was an old joke, but at two in the morning it would have to do. They climbed into the on-call car and set off. There were moments when Tom thought the car looked too much like a police car. It was only when the lights on the roof flashed that you could tell the difference. The lights on the top of the car flashed green, and gave the medical car absolutely no rights whatever. However, they did tell the world at large that there was a doctor heading to an emergency in that vehicle, and *one day it might be heading to you*. If you were in a paramedic car, however, provided by the Ambulance Trust, the lights on the top would flash blue, with all the legal rights they possessed. That was another twist that amused Tom, when he was thinking about things bureaucratic.

The visit was to see a Mrs Bi, in Millfield. The call wasn't clear, but the bottom line was that she wasn't very well, but the history given over the phone didn't suggest that she was having a heart attack, or anything else that would require a blue light ambulance to rush her to hospital. At the same time, she was unwell enough to need to see a doctor in the middle of the night to assess the situation, rather than to wait until morning surgery, or when she could next get an appointment, whichever was sooner. Tom would decide on the spot whether she did actually need to go to hospital, or whether she would cope at home until the morning, when her doctor, who presumably knew all about her, would take over responsibility for her care.

The address was a terraced house in Millfield, and the satnav took them straight there. There didn't seem to be many people about, but then it was the middle of the night and it was drizzling and miserable. Why would anybody be about at that time in the morning?

Bob pulled up outside the front door, and Tom got out. He picked up his black bag from the back seat, and took an orange box out of the boot. The orange box, locked with a padlock, to which all the doctors knew the combination, was owned by the co-operative, as were the drugs and the kit inside. Tom again thought that, as there were well over a hundred GPs in Peterborough who shared the on-call rota, that was a fairly large number of people to know a code number. However, the actual quantity of any particular drug in any box was relatively small. Once a box had been opened, and the seal was broken, the box was returned to the centre, with the doctor involved signing out what they had used and for whom, and the box would be restocked with the drug or piece of kit in question and resealed for the next night. The other box was Tom's own, and all the kit in that was his – his own stethoscope, lights, and other medical equipment he needed to hand.

The door opened almost immediately, and a big Asian man, who Tom guessed to be in his early twenties, looked out.

'Doctor Clark,' Tom introduced himself. 'I've come to see Sanyat Bi.' He checked the docket he was carrying. Well, that was what it said.

'Come in,' said the man. 'Follow me.'

He led Tom through the living room, in which sat three other men, all holding mugs. None of them looked at him. At the back of the living room was a door, which opened inwards, and behind the door was a staircase. 'Follow me,' said the man again, and they went up the stairs. At the top of the stairs there was a small landing, with three doors off it. The man opened the door on the left, and walked through. On the other side of the door was a corridor. The house was much larger on the first floor than it was on the ground floor. Obviously the terrace had been converted, and the upper floor was effectively all one building. They walked along the corridor and then turned right to another door, which had a landing behind it. The doors off the landing all had numbers screwed onto the doors, and the man tapped on number four. There was a mumbled response from within, and the man behind him said, 'Go in.' Tom turned the door handle and stepped through the door. For a moment the room appeared dark, and then suddenly he was blinded with light. He stepped backwards in surprise, straight into the man who had led him there.

'Come in, Dr Clark,' said a male voice from behind the light.

Tom, completely thrown by what was going on, assumed there had been a communication failure. 'Sanyat Bi?' he asked.

'If you like,' said the voice. 'Come in anyway. Sit down.'

Tom found himself being manhandled from behind, and led to a dining chair without arms. He also felt a hand in his pocket removing the phone, and his boxes being taken from both hands.

'What the hell is going on?' he asked. 'I've come to see Sanyat Bi. I understand she's not very well, and she needs to be seen.'

'Sanyat Bi,' said the voice which appeared to think for a moment. 'You can take it from me that she's fine; however, you may not be soon, so I think we need to talk about that. Don't you?'

Tom was, quite simply, terrified. Never during his career had he ever been hijacked, and that appeared to be what was happening.

'What do you want?' he asked. He still couldn't see who was talking to him. The voice appeared to come from behind the light that was shining in Tom's face. The speaker had an Asian accent, which he supposed was something to think about.

'You were warned about Sean James today,' said the voice. 'Then immediately after you were given that warning, you went directly to a house to which he was connected. Now, either you were being very stupid, or you were ignoring the warning. Which do you think might have been the case?'

'Sean James? I didn't go to Sean James's house.'

'No, but Sean James had connections with the Whilden house, and you did go there, no more than a couple of hours after you were told to keep away from Sean James! I think you were being either very stupid or very disobedient. Which was it, Dr Clark?'

'I don't know what you're talking about. The Whildens are patients of mine, and Mrs Whilden needed a visit.'

'And why was that?'

'You know very well I can't tell you that; Mrs Whilden has the right to privacy.'

'And there was a policeman there: did you know anything about that?'

'Not until after I had got there.'

'And what was the policeman doing there?'

'I have no idea, I didn't ask her.'

'Her? Oh, so it was a policewoman then?'

'Yes,' said Tom. Was he breaching Shuv's confidentiality now? Did Shuv, when she was in uniform, have a right of confidentiality? he wondered.

'So what was *she* doing there, then?'

'I told you – I didn't ask her what she was doing there.'

'We're not getting anywhere, are we?' said the voice, a great deal of menace in it. Tom suddenly found his arms being grabbed from behind, and a pair of cuffs being closed on his wrists. The cuffs felt like metal, and were too small to be comfortable, even if they were part of a game.

'What are we going to do next, I wonder?' said the voice. 'If I ask Mo behind you to hit you, I am sure he will do it, and probably enjoy every moment of it. But I have to ask myself what the point of that would be. You would be damaged, and probably not a lot of use to Peterborough for the rest of the night. Am I right?'

Tom mumbled for a moment, probably in agreement.

'Yes, I'm right,' said the voice. 'Have you got that iPad?' he asked, presumably of the man standing behind Tom.

An iPad appeared from behind Tom's shoulder. And it suddenly came alive. An eye filled the whole screen. It had a blue iris. Mo's hand then pinched the picture so it revealed the face of the person who owned the eye. Tom was first filled with recognition and relief. He knew that short blonde haircut; his daughter Jenny had had her hair cut just like that the previous week to play the part of the boy in the piece they were rehearsing. In fact, Tom was rather proud his daughter had done that for the play, and at the same time he thought it made her look rather fetchingly gamine. Then he became alarmed. The picture did not simply have his daughter's haircut, it was his daughter's face, wearing a gentle innocent smile. Where had they got his daughter's photograph?

'Where did you get that?' he asked

The man behind him silently pinched the picture again, and the scale got smaller still. Tom realised to his horror that Jenny was naked, certainly from the waist upwards. He had not seen Jenny with her top off since she was a child, and he found the experience of looking at his daughter's breasts, which were looking straight back at him, alarming. There was a bruise on her left forearm. Had somebody grabbed her arm to force her to do the picture? So why was she smiling like that? Was that an injection site that had gone wrong, and was that why she was smiling?

It was when Mo pinched the picture again that Tom realised what he was really looking at. She was completely naked, sitting astride a male torso. At least, he assumed it was male: the head was balding, and the trunk was fairly portly, but there were no male genitalia on view. Her thighs were either side of his pelvis, and there was only one place that the man's hidden erection could be. The innocent smile Jenny was wearing was completely inappropriate. Tom tried to free his hands to knock the iPad away, to knock away that image. He tried to stand up, but as he tensed his thighs, he realised that the cuffs were anchored to the floor, and pulled him back down hard onto the chair.

'I take it you recognise that face,' continued the voice behind the light.

'You bastard, how did you get her to do that?' snarled Tom. 'Where did you get her to do that? When? Who is that?'

'Oh, I think that worked. You can put the iPad away now,' said the voice. 'We've got your attention now, haven't we, Dr Clark? I think we can at least assume you have an appropriate parental relationship when a man doesn't recognise his daughter's tits when she's got them out. I think we're going to have to do something about that, don't you?'

'You bastards, what do you want from me?'

'Well, that's the question, isn't it? What do we want from you? In a word, silence. As you can see, we have open access to your daughter, as well as yourself. I cannot imagine either of you would want that photograph being made public, or indeed the movie it was taken from.'

Tom groaned. They had a sex tape of Jenny. *She's still a child, for God's sake. Who are these bastards?* Who was that man in the picture she was doing it with? Was that the man who played Gregory in the play, the victim in *Murder at the Grange?* He was thinning on top. Was that why she was into amateur dramatics, for the middle-aged men?

'Have I still got your attention, Dr Clark?'

'Yes,' he said sadly, knowing that his world would never be the same again. Suddenly he felt the chair being pulled backwards. If whoever was holding the chair behind him actually let go, he would crash backwards onto the floor. He tried to retain his balance by waving his hands, but they remained restrained. The chair remained stable at half tilt. Then the voice behind him said, 'Got them.' The chair was then moved back into a vertical position again.

'Good,' said the voice behind the camera.

'What was that all about? What just happened there?' asked Tom.

'We just took your picture,' replied the voice. 'To be exact, we took a picture of the top of your head.'

'What for?'

'Well, remember the man Jenny was doing it with in the picture?'

'Yes.'

'Well, we'll Photoshop the photo we've just taken of you into that picture, to replace the rather boring man there at the moment. Your wife would like that, don't you think? I think it would show her exactly what her ex-husband and her daughter get up to when they tell her that they're out doing amateur theatricals.'

'But that is what we do – we don't do *that*.'

'The camera never lies, though, does it?'

'What do you want from me?' groaned the defeated Tom.

'You will never talk to anyone about Sean James – ever. If you do, the pictures and the movie will go viral. We will

240

make sure Jenny's mother gets an autographed copy just to be absolutely sure. You know we've got the pictures, and we will always have them.'

'So what do I have to do to get them from you?'

'Nothing. You have absolutely no chance of ever getting those pictures back. We will always have them to hold over you. That will ensure your continuing co-operation, won't it? Do you understand that? Moreover, the very fact that we have the original surely shows you we can get to your daughter any time we like. Have you got that, doctor? Oh, one other thing; you're going to have to think up some excuse about the patient you came here to see, aren't you? Do you think you can do that? It would be an awful waste of your daughter if you couldn't even get that right.'

Tom closed his eyes. Was it his eyes closing that shut out the light, or did the lights actually go out? He opened his eyes again and saw nothing. He moved his hands and realised the cuffs had been removed.

'Follow me,' said the voice behind him. 'Pick up your bags.' The door behind him opened into the landing, and he followed the big man out of the room. He went back down the corridor, down the stairs and out.

The co-op car was still waiting outside.

'That didn't take very long,' said Bob. 'I take it she was all right. You didn't call me to get you an ambulance.'

'My phone…' said Tom. 'I think I left my phone in there.' He patted his trousers. *No, hang on, there it was.* 'How long was I in there?' he asked.

'About ten minutes.'

'Is that all?' Tom's nightmare felt as though it had lasted an age. Sadly, he said, 'No, there wasn't a lot wrong with her, so where are we off to next?'

'Back to the centre. We can grab a coffee and wait for the next one. Did you open the orange box?'

'No, it can stay in the car.'

Chapter 47

Yuri watched the medical car drive away from his seat in the little Peugeot. When it had turned the corner, he got out and knocked on the door.

Mo looked through the spyhole. Seeing it was Yuri, he opened up. Yuri walked in and put his hand in his pocket. He pulled out a screw-capped bottle of juice and tossed it at Mo.

'What's this?' asked Mo, at the exact same time as Yuri asked, 'Got the trousers?'

Yuri looked at him hard. Mo broke first.

'Yeah,' he said, 'I got the trousers. In the pocket of my coat.'

'Good,' said Yuri, and nodded at the bottle Mo was looking at sceptically. 'That's a light stim, so if the police catch us on a stop and search, between here and where we're going, we don't seem so daft that we get taken apart. We really don't want them to find those trousers on us.'

'Caffeine?' Mo asked.

'Yeah, something like that,' said Yuri, pulling another bottle out of his pocket and drinking its contents. It didn't open with a *fft* as Mo would have expected either, so he was less concerned that his hadn't. Yuri had already told him that the juice had some extra additives, hadn't he? Mo drank too. 'How did tonight go?' Yuri asked.

'That was one very scared and confused doctor,' said Mo. 'I don't think we'll get a lot more trouble out of him.'

'Good,' said Yuri. 'Onwards and upwards. Trousers?'

Mo pulled a bit of cloth out of the pocket of his hoodie, then followed Yuri out of the front door.

Yuri clicked his key fob, and both the doors of the Peugeot slid back.

'Why on earth are we driving about in this crap little box?' Mo asked.

'Because I like it, and it doesn't look like a gangster's car.'

'No, it's more like a little old lady's car.'

'Exactly. Now get in.'

Mo got into the passenger seat, and looked around for the seat belt. He pulled on the handle of the door behind his left shoulder, but he was at the wrong angle to reach it.

'Hang on for that,' said Yuri, starting the engine. He then pushed two buttons on the right side of the dashboard, and both doors slid shut.

'Clever, that,' said Mo, a little more impressed with the car now.

'Very handy in supermarket car parks. People can park really close to your driver's door, and you can still get in.' He pulled out into the street.

'Why would you go to supermarkets?'

'A man needs to maintain his independence.'

'Isn't that what women are for?' asked Mo. Yuri looked at him out of the corner of his eye, and realised that Mo really believed what he had just said. Ah well, he thought, there's going to be one fewer Mo soon.

They headed south through Stanground and then headed out east to Whittlesey. Yuri wondered idly where the police cars were going as they stormed past in the opposite direction with blue flashing lights on their roofs. At least they weren't sounding their sirens as well. People were trying to sleep.

'Where are we going?' asked Mo after a while, and then added, 'I feel a bit rough.'

'You'll see,' replied Yuri, feeling slightly relieved by Mo's subsequent statement. He was beginning to worry that it wasn't going to work. Two-thirds of the way through Whittlesey, he turned left up Delph East towards the Dog in the Doublet riverside pub. When he crossed the bridge over the river he turned left onto the North Bank, noting with pleasure that the pub looked as if it had reopened for business: there were a number of cars parked in the forecourt again. There were no obvious lights on, but then it was the middle of the night. He turned into the forecourt, where he had been taught by his driving instructor how to do a hill start, and had tested cars new to him, to see how they behaved under such circumstances. There weren't many hills on which to test hill starts round Peterborough. He pulled back onto North Bank, and looked at the river.

The River Nene, along whose north bank the road ran, looked much higher than usual, even downstream from the sluice, where he was sitting. From here to where it drained into the sea near King's Lynn, the river was tidal, and the flow could be in either direction, at least partly due to the activity of the sluice. The sluice had been built in the thirties to prevent the persistent flooding of parts of Woodston and Old Fletton when a high tide, flowing upstream, met a high flow, flowing downstream following bad weather in Northampton, or parts between. For the most part the sluice had been a resounding success, both for the people of Peterborough and the Dog in the Doublet pub. To begin with, the landlord had run the lock gate on the north side, built so that boats could make their way past the sluice. The boat skipper needed to moor up on whichever side of the sluice he was, and go and knock on the door of the pub. Invariably food, ale and cash used to change hands long before lock gate fees were paid, and the boat made its – probably wobbly – way in the planned direction.

There were no lights on in the house on his left by the sluice, so it looked like all its residents had gone to bed too. Beside him, Mo was snoring and intermittently twitching, like a dog dreaming about chasing cats. Yuri drove slowly back along the little road and parked on the bridge looking back the way he had come.

He pressed the buttons on the dashboard and opened both doors of the car. You couldn't do that while you were still moving, but the car would drive with the doors open if you could stand the infuriating electronic *meep-meep* noise it made. He unbuckled Mo's seat belt and prodded him. Mo didn't stir. Whether he could be defined as asleep or unconscious didn't really matter to Yuri; he just wasn't rousable. He got out of his side of the car and, using the railing of the bridge as a lever, lifted Mo from his seat. He thought he made rather a quiet splash, considering his size, as he tipped him into the river. At that point Yuri looked around, just to reassure himself that no one was watching. It all appeared to be quiet.

He looked back down over the railing and watched the body slowly sink, followed by a trail of bubbles. Mo made no attempt to move on his own.

Yuri got back into the car. Turning the engine on, he closed the doors and drove back down to Whittlesey. Opposite the petrol station there was a pull-off in front of a few houses. He turned the car round there and drove back out one further time up towards the Dog in the Doublet. As he reached the bridge he slowed, looking for any activity around the bridge. There was none. He set off down the North Bank road, driving sensibly and slowly like all young men with a sense of self-preservation.

Just ahead was a bend in the road, where the powers that be had erected a crash barrier; presumably in the hope that its presence might stop the little hooligans who used the North Bank as a speedway from ending up in the river when they forgot to take the corner.

He drove the final hundred yards along the North Bank, and stopped where the cycle bridge crossed the river. There, he thought about the second half of his plan; the bicycle. He decided not to bother throwing it in the river. As and when they finally found Mo, there would be no obvious reason how he had got into the river. He left the bicycle on the back seat of the car. When they pulled Mo out of the river, and found Steff's trousers in his hoodie's pocket, it would not take a major flight of fancy to suggest he was pilled out of his mind when he had fallen in the water, especially when his autopsy showed positive for drugs. That was, always assuming they found him fairly soon. Nobody much walked along the stretch of river between the Dog in the Doublet and the small village of Guyhirn about ten miles downstream, apart from the odd farmer whose fields bordered the water. All kinds of flotsam and jetsam washed up in Guyhirn.

Yuri checked the clock in the car. It had been ten minutes exactly since he had turned round in the Dog in the Doublet car park.

Chapter 48

Mrs Whilden was waiting for the doorbell to ring, and while she was waiting she was inhaling the smell of fish, tarragon and garlic; somehow it relieved her. The doorbell rang, and she walked from the kitchen, through the detritus that was the living room and out to the front door. A large sergeant, with three stripes on his epaulettes, and a smaller policewoman stood there. Neither of them she recognised from before, but then that nice Constable Flynn needed to get some sleep at some point, didn't she?

'Mrs Whilden?' said the sergeant.

'Yes,' she said flatly.

'I'm Sergeant Molinari, and this is Constable Watson.'

'Come in,' she said, leading the way to the mess that they had once called a living room. She pointed at her husband's body lying in the wreckage of the coffee table.

'You know he's dead?' asked the constable.

'I think so.'

'Did you touch the body?' asked Molinari.

'Only when I tried to revive him. I tried to shake him a bit.'

'How did you realise he was dead?'

'I held the mirror up to his face – that one,' she said pointing to the hand mirror on the mantelpiece.

'Tell me, in your own words, what happened.'

'Can we go into the kitchen, please? I don't like being in here with him. I mean, he's not going anywhere, is he?'

'Of course,' said the sergeant and they all walked through to the kitchen. She lifted the lid on the fish kettle, just to see how it was doing, letting the aroma into the room. 'Tea?' she asked. 'Coffee?'

'No thanks,' replied the sergeant, not allowing Constable Watson to get a word in. 'As I was asking, in your own words.'

He stopped, and jerked a thumb at the fish kettle. 'It's a strange hour to be cooking fish, isn't it?' he asked.

'It's something about us Smithfield girls; in moments of stress we do stuff. Smithfield's my maiden name, you see. My late sister, bless her, she used to clean. You could always tell when my sister was upset, cos her house would be shiny like a new pin. Me, I cook.'

'As I was saying, in your own words.'

'We had a row, much earlier in the evening. I had come back from the hospital from seeing Steff – you know, our niece, who's in hospital.' She stopped and looked at the police, and said, 'Why should you know?'

She was about to go on when Constable Watson chipped in, 'We all know about Stephanie Flack.' Molinari glared at her and the constable shut up again.

'Well, as I was saying, I got in, a bit later than I would have liked – public transport's a bit all over the place in the evening, you know, and my husband was sitting in here twiddling his thumbs, and seething, waiting for his tea. Well, I got him his tea, all right, sausages, carrots and mash, his favourite – goes very well with his beer. But the atmosphere was still, you know, stormy. It wasn't long afterwards, when the football was on, and I started talking about Steff and how she's, you know, getting better. It was all my fault, I know, I shouldn't talk when the football is on, but I did, and he blew up, and stormed off to the pub. Well, I was so upset I started cooking.'

'Sorry, but that doesn't explain how he ended up down there in the living room,' said Sergeant Molinari, hoping to speed up the narrative.

'I'm getting to that. Anyway, he must have been down the pub awhile, cos I heard him come back and he was swearing, and sounded very drunk, and there was a crash, and then it all went quiet.'

'When was that?'

She looked at her watch. 'Ooh, at least a couple of hours ago, I would reckon.'

'And you only thought to tell us just now?' Molinari sounded exasperated.

'Well, I was busy in the kitchen, and I'd just started the Hollandaise sauce, and you know, you've got to keep beating the Hollandaise sauce, don't you, dear?' she added, trying to bring Constable Watson back into the conversation. Constable Watson had no idea how to make a Hollandaise sauce; she probably didn't even know what one was. 'And, anyway, this wasn't the first time he had come home drunk and passed out on the sofa. And generally it's better just to let him sleep. If you wake him up and he's still drunk, there's hell to pay. I just leave him there overnight, and he wakes up in the morning, right as nine pence, and goes off to work.'

'Go on.'

'Well, I finally finished the Hollandaise sauce, and I had a cup of tea, and then I went to put a rug over him, like you do, and then I found him. He was like that – you know, how he is.'

'And you shook him?'

'Well, he wasn't snoring. He always snores when he's like that; actually, he always snores, even when he's not drunk, but I wondered why he wasn't snoring. Then I saw his chest wasn't moving and I thought, oh dear, he's done himself a mischief, and got the mirror down and held it up to his mouth, like they do on the telly in *Casualty*, you know. It didn't fog at all, and I thought ooh Gawd, I think he's dead. So I shook him, and pushed his chest a bit, but I haven't got one of those electric shock things they've got on the telly, and as he still wouldn't fog the mirror, I called you.'

'Why didn't you call an ambulance?' asked Constable Watson.

'Well, I tried, but the girl down the other end of the phone said that as I was sure he was dead already, I didn't want a medic, it was the police I wanted. Anyway, here you are.' She lifted the top off the fish kettle and poked the contents with a fork. 'Hmm, looks done. Do you want some?'

'What?' said Constable Watson.

'Well, it's done, and it'll probably all go to waste if we don't eat it now. I mean, when I have one of my cooking attacks then I tend to give food to the neighbours and the old people, but as there's been police round here all the time over the last couple of days, then I don't suppose any of them would want anything I've cooked now, would they? Stands to reason, I suppose.' She got three plates out of the cupboard, took the fish out of the fish kettle and put it on a wooden chopping board. She cut a hunk of salmon and put it on a plate and then poured some Hollandaise sauce over it from the bowl in the bain-marie. She repeated the performance twice and passed a plate and a fork to both police officers. And then when they both looked at her, but didn't start eating, she said, 'Oh, silly me,' and tasted the fish herself. 'Not bad, though I say so myself.'

Molinari and Watson also dug into the fish, and tasted it.

'Oh, very nice, Mrs Whilden, very nice indeed. Can you cook like that, Constable Watson?'

'No, sarge.'

'I don't think even my mum can cook fish like that,' said Molinari, licking his lips. He picked up his walkie-talkie and spoke into it. 'Hello there, can you send down a blood wagon to Orton Goldhay?' There was a pause and then he continued, 'Yes we've got a body here, seems to have come home drunk and crowned himself on the mantelpiece.' Another pause, and then he added, 'And if they're really quick about it, there's some amazing fish on offer here, and if they don't hurry up, Watson and I will have eaten it all ourselves.'

'So when you're stressed you cook?' asked Molinari again. 'A good way of getting over stress, I expect.' He wished he hadn't started that line of conversation, especially when Constable Watson chipped in, 'Isn't teaching him good behaviour, is it? I mean, every time he pisses you off, he gets fed like this. If I was going to get fed like this every time I annoyed my boyfriend, he'd be so pissed off with me, he'd have kicked me out years ago.'

'Was that an entirely necessary picture, constable?' asked Molinari.

'I can understand what she's saying, though,' said Mrs Whilden. 'I'd never really looked at it that way. A bit more fish?'

'Oh yes, please,' the officers said in unison.

'We'll make sure there's enough left over for your friends in the, what did you call it, blood wagon?'

'You know, it's okay to cry if you want,' said Constable Watson.

'What about?'

'Your husband.'

Doris Whilden thought about it for a moment. 'I probably will when it actually sinks in. I'm still, how do you say it, numb?'

'Quite.' The room was silent for a while apart from the sound of eating.

After a while there was a ring on the doorbell, and Constable Watson got up and answered it. She ushered in two men in dark suits. They had a collapsible trolley and a scoop, like those found in the back of a paramedic ambulance.

'Fish?' asked the constable.

'Shall we just get him loaded up first, and then we'll come back and have a mouthful?' said one of them cheerily. 'Thank you so much, Mrs Whilden; you really didn't have to, you know.'

'I probably did,' she replied, 'but do whatever you have to do, and then come and join us in the kitchen.' She went back into the kitchen and sat back down with her back to the living room, preferring not to watch what was going on.

Five minutes later, the men were back in the living room. 'I'm Mr Gurney – kind of appropriate, considering what I do,' said one.

'I'm Mr Knight; not so much,' said the other.

Mrs Whilden had pulled the spine out of the fish and was now cutting the pink meat off the skin from the other side. She had got two more plates out of the cupboard, and was piling them up with hunks of fish, and pouring more sauce from the bowl.

'Oh, this is nice isn't it, Mr Knight?'

'Very nice, Mr Gurney,' his colleague agreed. 'We don't often get served fish as good as this when we get called out at night, do we?'

'We certainly don't, Mr Knight. Thank you, Mrs Whilden. It is much appreciated.'

'Please have some more,' she said. 'It'll only go to waste.'

And they all did. By the time they had finished, all that was left of the salmon was the head, the bones and the tail.

Chapter 49

Sergeant Odembe walked into the incident room. A glazed-looking Molinari was still in there waiting to hand over to him.

'Hi Lou, quiet night?'

'Not really,' replied the policeman in uniform. 'Your Operation Riverbank's gained an interesting new wrinkle during the night.'

'Oh?'

'Stephanie Flack's uncle died during the early hours.'

'Oh shit! How?'

'He seems to have had a skinful following a row with his wife, and cracked his head on the fireplace when he came home. By the time she found him, he was dead.'

'Poor little Stephanie, she's really had a rough ride hasn't she? You heard she's waking up?'

'Yes, Mrs Whilden is hanging on to that as a positive bit of news. You know, she's one hell of a cook, that Mrs Whilden.'

'Really?' and Lou Molinari told Dommie all about the salmon the night before. After Lou had finished, Dommie replied, possibly with a tinge of jealousy, 'Bit risky eating food on the premises cooked by the number-one suspect.'

'How do you make that one out?'

'When a man is murdered, the wife is always the number-one suspect to begin with.'

'He wasn't murdered; it was an accident.'

'You sure of that?'

'Well, she hasn't done me any harm. I'm just a bit sleepy, that's all, and that was nothing to do with her.'

'It's easy for you to say that now,' said Odembe, and then changed the subject. 'So what happened to the body?'

'Well, Gurney and Knight picked him up.'

'So he'll be in the mortuary, and they'll do a post mortem on him?'

'I guess. Anyway, I'm going off to bed. See you.'

Lou Molinari and Siobhan Flynn squeezed past each other in the doorway, Molinari muttering, 'Loser,' as he walked out.

'Top of the morning to the colleen from the bogs,' said Odembe, not sounding in the slightest like an Irishman.

'And good morning to the Prince of Darkness – what rattled his cage?' she said, jerking a thumb at the now closed door.

Odembe told her about Molinari's midnight feast at the Whilden house and what brought it on.

'You mean Craig Whilden's dead?' she asked.

'That's what he said. You knew him, didn't you?'

'I'd met him, yeah.'

'What was he like?'

'To be honest, I found him a little creepy. You know, like his eyes had zip fasteners attached. You know the phrase 'he undressed me with his eyes'? Well, that was how Craig Whilden looked at me.'

'Half the men in this building look at you like that, and one or two of the women as well, come to think of it,' replied Odembe, 'and that doesn't usually seem to worry you, so what was it about *him*?'

Shuv giggled. 'Oh you!' Then she thought about it for a moment, and replied, 'I'm not bothered by the blokes in this building, because I'm damn sure that none of you would ever do anything about it. Somehow I wasn't so sure about Craig Whilden. I certainly wouldn't want to have been alone with him in a dark alley at night. Do you know what I mean?'

'Did he seem violent?'

'No, not really, just like I said – creepy.'

'Evidence?'

'None whatsoever. It was just a feeling I had in my water, you know? Tell you something,' Shuv added, 'it would be funny if you were right, and the salmon was the murder weapon. I can't imagine how it would work, mind you. I'm just picturing Drake's face when he found out that the murder weapon was eaten by the first on scene!'

'What was that?' said DI Drake as he walked through the door. 'Somebody taking my name in vain?'

254

They looked round. 'No sir,' replied Flynn, responding quick as a flash. 'Stephanie Flack's uncle died during the night, and I was just commenting that it would be a shame if your case died of natural causes before it ever got to court.' She looked at Odembe for a moment, and he caught her glance. The poached salmon was not going to be mentioned again.

'You have a nasty flippant mind, Constable Flynn.' Drake cleared his throat. 'Natural causes, you say?'

'The uncle hit his head on a mantelpiece when he came home drunk last night.'

'And he's in the mortuary?'

'Yes sir,' replied Sergeant Odembe.

'Awaiting a post mortem?'

'Oh, yes sir.' Odembe made a mental note to make sure that a post mortem actually did get done, just in case DI Drake asked about it.

'I suppose I had better go and see the grieving widow,' said Shuv. Visiting Doris Whilden hadn't really been top of her 'things to do' list this morning, but the incident last night had changed all that.

The arrival of the incident room manager made less impact on the two men than Siobhan Flynn's departure almost immediately afterwards.

'Annoying girl,' muttered Drake after she had gone.

'Oh, do you think so? I always find her quite amusing.' Aware suddenly of being the target of Drake's glare, he rapidly changed the subject. 'Anyway, does Mr Whilden's death have any impact on the case?'

'Not that I can think of, provided the death was accidental and he wasn't hit over the head by a Shadeed in revenge for the boy's killing.'

'You mean, like a sort of Montague and Capulet thing? For God's sake, we'd never live that one down with Cambridge, they're the ones with the rights to arty stuff.'

'This isn't an arty killing; this is just a messy one, like all the rest. And anyway, who is this Montague?' he said, riffling through the papers on the desk. 'Can't see him listed here, nor the other bloke you mentioned.'

Odembe rolled his eyes. 'It's part of your literary tradition, not mine,' he replied.

'Literary tradition? What are you on about, man? It's too early in the morning for that sort of stuff.'

'Shakespeare, you know Romeo and Juliet? Juliet was a Capulet and Romeo was a Montague – or the other way round, I can never remember. Anyway, their families were at war, but the two kids fell in love, and it all ended in tears.'

'Oh right,' said Drake, obviously not giving a tinker's cuss for any of that nonsense. 'So,' he said, 'where do we go from here?'

'I'll go down to the mortuary to make sure that the autopsy on last night's corpse is prioritised, and Flynn's gone off to see Mrs Whilden, so we'll have to wait until any other evidence comes our way. There didn't seem to be any remarkable new information that came out of the school the kids were both at. Sergeant Warwick didn't have much to add there. Anything you've got yourself?'

Drake shook his head. 'I've spoken to a few of the terriers I know to see if they can dig anything out from under any loose stones, but I don't have a lot of hope there, either. '

Forty-eight hours after the start of a case, it was ever thus. It went quiet, and there was nothing apparent to do while the police waited for something – anything – to break. When it did, it usually came from somewhere quite unexpected.

Chapter 50

Andrzej looked up at the gloomy sky as he climbed out of the van. So this was the famous English weather. They ate breakfast quickly and then they were out in the rain. They hadn't been out in the field very long before they knew it had been raining all night. The earth stuck to their boots, and the barrow's wheel sank into the soil, even though they were wheeling it down the furrow to where they had stopped the previous evening.

'Got to get the tatties out before they start to rot,' said the farmer's wife, but they didn't understand what she meant. One day, Andrzej felt, at least one of them should learn a smattering of English.

Sergei took the first turn with the fork, turning over the earth and releasing the potatoes from the muddy ground. Andrzej picked them up and put them in the barrow. A barrow full of potatoes was a lot heavier than an empty one, and sank even deeper into the furrow when he wheeled it back to the farm. Once he had got it into the farmyard, he handed over the barrow to the foreman. Looking around the yard, he noticed a barrow with a ball instead of a wheel at the front. It was propped up against a wall, and nobody seemed to be using it. He walked over to it, and tried it. Yes, it rolled okay. He wheeled it over to the foreman and, with a mixture of gesticulations and grunting, he managed to get across the idea that he wanted to try the ball-barrow that morning. The foreman said that was all right. It was almost with gaiety that he wheeled the barrow down to where Sergei was forking the mud.

'That's clever,' said Sergei, tossing potatoes into the new barrow.

'Certainly was easier pushing it this way than it was pushing the full barrow the other way,' agreed Andrzej. 'Any coins?' he asked softly, looking away from the farmhouse in case some-one was lip-reading their Lithuanian through a telescope from one of the upstairs windows. There was nobody out the other way, just the river at the bottom of the field.

Sergei looked at the river while he tossed potatoes into the barrow.

'Not a single one today. Maybe we'll find more when we get back up to where we found the last lot.'

'Maybe,' said Andrzej, also looking towards the river while picking up potatoes and putting them in the barrow.

It was Andrzej's turn to fork the earth while Sergei picked up the potatoes. Slowly, but surely, they progressed to the bottom of the field by the river's edge. They agreed that the ball-barrow had been a good idea on the sodden ground, and Sergei had to defend his ownership of it back in the farmyard from a Pole who had also found his wheelbarrow was hard work in the mud. The foreman, however, stood by Sergei, and appeared to honour the 'finder's keepers' rule among the workers. The Pole took it with bad grace, and waved his fist at Sergei as he stumped off with his barrow back to whence he had come. Sergei realised there would be a race for ownership of the ball-barrow the following morning.

Sergei got back to where Andrzej was forking the soil. He had reached the water's edge, and had turned round and was coming back the other way, hoping to reach where they had found the gold coins. When Sergei joined him, he stopped forking for a moment, and pointed at the river.

'Here, what do you think that is?' he said, pointing at the stream, which was flowing rapidly.

Sergei looked at where his brother was pointing. It looked like a large dark bag, slowly rotating in the middle of the stream. It wasn't moving as quickly as the water appeared to be, and there were moments when both men thought it was floating upstream. Surely that wasn't possible.

Suddenly, about two feet away from the bag, something else broke the surface, and there was no doubt what that was; it was the heel of a shoe. Immediately they realised what they were looking at.

'Oh shit,' said Sergei. 'That's a body.' He looked at his brother. 'What the hell do we do now?'

Andrzej looked at the body. It wasn't going anywhere. It was caught in an eddy. It was rotating gently, but it wasn't moving downstream, where it could disappear and become somebody else's problem.

'We have to tell someone, we can't just ignore it.' He tossed more potatoes into the ball-barrow.

'I'll tell the foreman when I go up with the next load of potatoes. One thing,' he added, looking out beyond the body, 'we need to do is keep people away from where we found the gold pieces. If there are any more, we want them.'

And Sergei, also tossing potatoes into the barrow, agreed.

When he wheeled the barrow back to the farmyard, the foreman was talking to someone else. He unloaded Andrzej's barrow without actually looking at him. It was only when Andrzej didn't just take his barrow and leave, like the brothers had done every time that day, that the foreman took any notice of him. It took a further moment for Andrzej to properly catch his eye, and when he did, he mimed what he wanted to say. His 'dead man' was for a moment amusing, with his right hand round his throat, and his tongue hanging out, with his left arm swinging loosely. Then he made a *splosh* noise and a rippling movement with his hand to imply the river. The men looked at him as if he had lost the plot, so he repeated the performance, and they understood this time.

Sergei, busy with the fork, realised that Andrzej had got his message across, as two other men were following him back to the field. Sergei kept forking until they got close; he didn't want to get into trouble for slacking.

They pointed at the body rotating gently in the eddy.

The foreman looked at the other man.

'Oh fuck,' he said. 'You know what that is, don't you? That's a body, that's what that is. We've got to call the police, cos just look at it, that body isn't going anywhere, and it'll be on the edge of our land for a good while yet.' He paused and looked worriedly at the man he was talking to, then he continued, 'Now if old Mr Giles, who owns the bit on the other side of the river, comes down and sees us working here, and we haven't reported that body, there'll be shit to pay. He's got taters in that field over there too, so he'll be harvesting them soon. He should be harvesting the buggers today, but he's not. Probably afeard of the rain, I shouldn't wonder.' The foreman turned back to the two Lithuanian men and gave them a thumbs-up to say thank you. He then pointed to himself and mimed dialling a telephone, and then pointed to them and mimed digging. They translated the sign language to mean 'Well done, lads. I'll go and phone someone, you get on with your work.' Andrzej and Sergei also gave him a thumbs-up and, just as instructed, they carried on forking up potatoes, aware that in a few hours' time, they'd be back in the area which seemed to grow gold coins as well.

They had got halfway back to the coin field when the foreman reappeared, followed by two uniformed police. Neither brother had seen a policeman close to since they had been in Britain, but a policeman always looks like a policeman wherever you are and however they are dressed. Both of them were amazed that these police didn't carry any obvious firearms. Back in Lithuania, they had seen policemen who appeared to be carrying howitzers on their belts. The foreman pointed at the body and there was a buzz of conversation. Then the foreman pointed at the brothers, and the police walked carefully through the mud towards them, and addressed them.

Andrzej had no idea what they said, but mimed forking the potatoes, and then looking out with a flat hand, palm pointing downwards, as he looked out over the body and beyond.

The policeman spoke to him again, and this time Andrzej just shrugged, pointed to his ear and shook his head.

The policeman turned back to the foreman.

'What's he saying? Is he deaf, or does he just not understand English?'

'Doesn't speak English.'

'Constable, you speak Polish, try that.'

'Shouldn't do that, sir,' said the foreman. 'These boys are Lithuanians; they won't speak Polish.'

'Won't or don't?'

'Probably both, sarge. There's no love lost between the Poles and the Lithuanians.'

'What's that all about then?'

'I haven't the faintest idea. I just know to keep them apart if we've got both on the farm, like we have at the moment. Both groups on their own are great workers. I just gotta keep them apart or they stop working and start fighting. Blood and giblets everywhere. Nasty!' and he shuddered.

'Do you speak Lithuanian, constable?' asked the sergeant.

'No sir,' replied the constable.

The sergeant changed tack. 'How deep is the river out there?' he asked the foreman, pointing at the body.

'Oh, about nine, ten feet, maybe more, I reckon. Over your head, anyway.'

'We're going to need to get a boat, aren't we?'

'I imagine so, sergeant,' replied the foreman.

'Have you got a boat?' asked the sergeant.

'No, sarge,' replied the foreman. 'Back in the day, there was a big kerfuffle when him on the other side of the river accused us of going over the river at the dead of night and digging up his tatties, and bringing them back over here and selling them. So our farmer had to show him that he hadn't got a boat to cross the river in.'

'How would you go about showing someone that you haven't got a boat?' asked the sergeant.

'You show him all over your farm, anywhere he wants to go, and no boat.'

'So where had he hidden it?' asked the sergeant with a grin.

'Oh, there's no flies on you is there, sarge?' the foreman grinned. 'We'd chopped it up for firewood before he got here.'

The sergeant spoke into his walkie-talkie and asked for a boat to be sent down from the Dog in the Doublet sluice to where they were, to fish the body out of the Nene.

'You stay down here and keep an eye on the scene, constable. I'm going back up to the farm to get a couple of statements.'

'Yeah, right,' muttered the constable, 'and get in out of the rain, and get a mug of hot tea into you.'

'Just think, constable, one day it'll be you being me. All you have to do is pass your exams, and then we'll have a sergeant who speaks Polish.'

261

The constable grunted and parked himself on the riverbank, looking upstream. To the Lithuanian boys digging potatoes, and slowly moving away from him, he began to look more and more like a statue. They hadn't got much further to go before they reached the gold field, when they heard the distinctive chug of a small marine diesel from upstream. There appeared round the bend in the river a small motor-boat, bearing down on the floating corpse, two policemen standing on one side holding boat hooks. They fished the corpse out of the water and it landed on the bottom of the boat with an unpleasant thud.

There was an exchange of English between the policeman on the riverbank and the police in the boat, and the boat then puttered over to the riverbank, and they helped the constable on board. He turned to the Lithuanians in the field and shouted something incomprehensible at them, then the boat disappeared again upstream.

They were in the patch of field they considered most likely to find more coins, when the sergeant reappeared from the farmhouse. It had just about stopped raining, but the mud underfoot was no less glutinous, as he struggled down to where they were working.

Andrzej mimed that a boat had come down from upstream, that it had loaded the body, and then the constable had got on the boat and it had gone back upstream again. The sergeant obviously understood the mime, but it didn't seem to improve his mood at all. He wandered off shouting to no one in particular – as of course the Lithuanians didn't understand what he was saying: 'What does the fucking idiot think he's doing? He's got the fucking car keys in his fucking pocket!'

They just kept on digging up potatoes and looking for gold.

Chapter 51

Steff was already awake when Shuv put her head round the ITU door. The Irish policewoman had decided to pop in to see how the girl was doing before going down to see Mrs Whilden, who she assumed would be an emotional mess.

'I remember you,' said the girl in the bed. 'I've seen you before.'

'Yes, I was here yesterday afternoon when you were awake,' Shuv replied.

'Ah, that explains it.' She was propped up on pillows, slowly eating a bowl of cereal. The drips looked increasingly redundant, as did the electronic wizardry making graphs and bleeping noises on the wall behind.

'So how are you feeling?'

'Better.' The girl nodded, and went on, 'I really get it, what they did or why. The doc's coming back shortly. And I'll see if I can get it this time.'

Shuv decided not to jump the gun, at least partly because she would have no idea how to answer if Steff asked her a tricky question. She resolved to stay, and hear what the surgeon had to say, if she could.

'Not so much pain, then?'

The girl smiled. 'Not so much now. I'm still aware of it but I can cope.'

Shuv drew in a breath. 'I have some bad news for you, I'm afraid,' she said. May as well get this one over and done with while she's still on a monitor, she thought drily. 'I'm afraid your uncle died last night,' she said. She didn't expect Steff's reaction.

'Really?' said the girl, raising another spoonful of cereal to her mouth. She chewed a few times and then swallowed. She looked at Shuv and then said, 'Well, there's a thing.'

'Aren't you upset?' Shuv asked.

Steff thought, then replied, 'Well, I know I ought to be. Maybe I will be later.' She paused and then added, 'Put it down to the drugs, if you like.'

'What drugs?' asked Shuv, not following.

'The drugs they're giving me to keep me quiet. You know, the painkillers and stuff.'

'They're not giving you any drugs to keep you quiet.'

'Aren't they? Well, there's a thing.'

'Have you any message for your aunt? I'm going to see her shortly.'

Steff thought again. 'No, not really. Tell her to keep her pecker up, and that I'll be home soon.' She was quiet for a moment, and then asked, 'What happened to him?'

'I gather he came home drunk, fell over in the living room and bashed his head on the mantelpiece.'

'Figures,' said the girl non-committally.

At that point they found themselves being surrounded by an entourage of staff led to the bed by Sister Bartram. The sister presented the case: 'This is Stephanie Flack, who was admitted via Casualty three nights ago, and was seen by Mr Ahmed on admission, who took her straight to theatre.'

The tall silver-haired man who was obviously the star of the show looked at the file Sister Bartram handed him. He perused the paper, and then looked at Steff, and then at Shuv. It was to Shuv he spoke first. 'You're wearing a uniform of some sort, but I don't actually recognise it. Are you a naval commando or something?' he asked.

'No,' she replied. 'I'm with the police.'

'Ah,' he said, and appearing to think no more about it, addressed himself to Steff, 'It looks like you had a pretty rough ride, young lady. How much do you understand what happened?'

'Not much,' she replied. 'I seem to remember having moments when people were talking to me, like I remember this policewoman here, but I can't remember anything anyone has said.'

'Fair enough,' said the consultant. 'You may not remember everything I'm going to tell you either, but that's okay. You'll remember it, won't you, officer?' He tossed the last sentence at Shuv, who opened her eyes wider.

'I'll try,' she said.

'You were attacked three nights ago,' said the consultant. 'We're not sure what happened – that's probably where this policewoman comes in. However, you had severe damage to the blood vessels of your womb. Our team here had to operate on you to save your life, and I'm glad to say, they were successful. There was, however, a price. They had to remove your womb to stop the bleeding.' He stopped and looked at her. 'Do you understand that?'

'They had to take out my womb, yes.' Steff still remained remarkably calm.

'That means you will be unable to have any children of your own,' continued the consultant resolutely, expecting the truth to dawn on Steff and there to be tears and an emotional outburst. Nothing happened so far.

'So from the moment I was attacked, I was never going to be able to have kids of my own,' she said. 'I was either going to die hanging on to my womb, or you were going to save my life by taking it out?'

The consultant looked at her, amazed at her response. 'That's about the long and short of it, yes,' he said, thrown by the calm of this girl who was little more than a child.

Steff looked at Shuv, and said, 'You *are* going to catch these people who have prevented me from becoming a mother, aren't you?'

Shuv jutted her chin out. 'I'm going to do my damnedest,' she replied, meaning every word of it.

'Thank you, sir, for saving my life, you and your team. I hope one day I can do the same for you.' Steff looked at the silver-haired consultant and smiled softly.

The consultant nodded at her. Turning away, he muttered into the Egyptian's ear, 'A psychological assessment might be interesting.' He turned on his heel and his entourage followed him out, all except the young Egyptian, who stayed behind talking to Sister Bartram. He introduced himself to Steff as Mr Ahmed and asked her if he could look at her tummy. Steff

265

passed the bowl of cereal over to Shuv and lay back passively. The Egyptian gently put his hands on her abdomen, and the sister peeled back the dressing over her wound. It was nice and clean. He pushed gently near the incision, and Steff took a sharp intake of breath. The Egyptian immediately apologised, and took his stethoscope out of his pocket and listened to her tummy. He then stood back, just avoiding treading on Shuv behind him, and said, 'I'm the surgeon who actually did the operation.'

'Thank you,' Steff replied.

He smiled at her. 'I don't think you need to be on the ITU any longer, but we would like you to stay in hospital for another few days, just so we can keep an eye on you. There's two places we can put you, and I suppose you can have the choice. We can either put you on a children's surgical ward, or we can transfer you to a gynaecological ward.'

'Which would you recommend?' she asked.

'Well, I think that the nurses on the gynae ward are more experienced in looking after people who have had the sort of operation that you've had,' he said.

'And you're more likely to be around on the gynae ward?' she asked.

'Yes, I will,' he replied.

'I think that's answered your question. Do you allow the police on your gynae ward?' she asked, looking behind him at Shuv.

Mr Ahmed grinned at her. 'I don't think we can stop them,' he said, and added, 'but only if they're women.'

Steff grinned at him. 'That's definitely sorted then. Will you tell my aunt which ward they're sending me to, and how to get there?' she asked Shuv.

'Can I take the details before I go?' Shuv asked the sister.

And the conversation became a discussion of logistics. Shuv was still stunned by how calmly the girl was taking everything. Maybe she wouldn't remember anything that had been said to her when she next saw her on the gynae ward.

Chapter 52

Siobhan was thoughtful as she drove down Goldhay Way then turned into the street where the Whildens lived. Yes, it was good to see Stephanie recovering so well, but she was rather alarmed by her reaction to the news about her uncle. She pulled up outside the door and pushed the bell. After a moment the door opened, and there, covered in flour, was Doris Whilden.

'Come in girl, come in.' She was quite effusive.

There was a wonderful aroma of baking coming out of the kitchen.

'I'm making cinnamon buns,' she said. 'Do you like cinnamon buns?' she asked. Before Shuv had a chance to answer that, Doris came back with, 'Would you like a cuppa?'

'Er, yes,' she replied. 'Tea would be lovely.' And then she added, 'I'm so sorry for your loss.'

'Don't be, dearie,' she said. 'I'm not – well, not yet anyway. It might all come and hit me between the eyes, sometime, but at the moment I'm just cooking.'

'Yes, I heard about the salmon you made for Sergeant Molinari and Constable Watson. Lou was all over it at handover this morning.'

'Liked it, did he?' she asked, turning on the kettle and taking down a couple of mugs from the shelf.

'Just a bit,' Shuv replied, as Doris popped a tea bag into each mug.

'I've just come from Stephanie in the ITU,' she went on.

'How is she doing?'

'So well, they're moving her into the gynae ward later on today.'

'That's good. Won't be long before she's home, then?'

'I guess not. I suppose you'll be glad of the company after last night.' Siobhan was fishing for Doris's response to the death of her husband.

'I suppose. Does Steff know about her uncle?'

'Yes, I told her on the ward this morning.'

'How did she take it?'

'Well, I'm glad you asked that, because I was totally thrown by her response. She wasn't in the slightest bit upset. Does that surprise you?'

'Stephanie? No, not really – she doesn't show any emotions at all, that girl. Bright as a searchlight, certainly, but hasn't got an emotion in her body. When her parents died, she just got on with it, kept studying for her exams, of course, and got loads of them.'

'Are you worried about that?'

'Me? No, not really. She's not a girl who's going to suffer much in life, is she?'

'She didn't seem to be upset about being unable to have children either.' Siobhan thought about that for a moment. Neither she nor Doris appeared to have any particular urge to have babies either. Before she left home, she was often nagged by her mam not to leave it too late.

'You never hear the clock ticking till it stops,' she would say, tediously often, which was no doubt partly why Siobhan got on the boat to Holyhead all those years ago. It appeared to be far more important to her mam to have grandchildren than a son-in-law. Well, Siobhan had siblings who had given her both of those. Her mam probably forgot all about her once she stopped going home on holiday. She wondered what her family would think when she turned up with her current consort. She stopped that line of thought, and pulled her thoughts back to the present.

'You have to remember that she's only fifteen. She wouldn't be wanting to be a mother now. In all probability, most girls of her age would probably be relieved they couldn't get pregnant.'

Mrs Whilden shrugged and said, 'Well, there is that of course.'

Siobhan continued, 'That's a thought. Talking about sex, do you know if anyone has told her what happened to Sean? I know I didn't bring it up when I was talking to her this morning, and I don't think she would remember anything from our conversation last night.'

'I haven't mentioned it. Why did you say "talking about sex"?' she asked.

'Well, you said Sean was her boyfriend, and the surgeons said she had been sexually active before she was assaulted.'

'Oh!' said Doris. 'Well, I suppose they must have been then. They were obviously very good at covering that sort of activity up. Mind you, she was on the pill to control her periods. She had dreadful period pain before her doctor put her on the pill. The pill would have stopped her getting pregnant, wouldn't it?'

Siobhan thought back to her mid-teens, and a boy called Liam in the sunshine and straw. She thought she had been damned lucky to get away with what they had done. She certainly never had the excuse of 'period pains' and wouldn't have managed to get on the pill even if she had.

'I suppose so, yes. You can't think of anyone else she might have had sex with?' asked the policewoman, well aware of Sean's sexual orientation, even if Mrs Whilden wasn't.

'Not that I'm aware of.' She paused. 'Why would you ask that?'

'Well, Sean's mum told someone that Sean batted left-handed, so to speak. He was great buds with Steff and all, but wasn't interested in that sort of thing with her.'

'You mean he was one of those, what Craig would have called, poofs?'

'In a word, yes.'

'Well, there's something else I didn't know. He didn't act gay, or anything. I always thought you could tell. So she went round there, and he came round here just to be matey and stuff, and that was it?'

'So it appears.' One thing Siobhan had noticed was that Doris Whilden had forgotten the cinnamon buns, and they were now beginning to burn. There was rather acrid smoke coming from the oven.

269

'Shall I get that for you?' she asked, opening the oven. Grabbing a clean dishcloth, she pulled out the tray with the buns and put them on the steel draining board behind her.

'Oh dear,' said Mrs Whilden, despairing, 'it looks as though they've all been quite burned.'

'Yes,' agreed Siobhan, 'they're probably not edible now.'

Mrs Whilden opened a drawer in the kitchen table, picked out a very sharp knife, and hefted it for a moment. Shuv became watchful. *She's not about to attack me, is she?* Then Mrs Whilden picked up a tea cloth and one of the blackened buns, and slit it down the middle. They looked into the middle of the bun.

'There,' she said thoughtfully, 'buggered. Going to have to start them again from scratch. It's not often that I get so distracted that I burn things. That didn't happen last night; the fish was perfect. Oh, I'm so sorry, you were looking forward to one of them buns, weren't you?'

'No, it's not a problem. It's just a shame they were ruined.'

'You could always come back later, I'll have made some more by then and I'll remember to leave some on the side for you, to take to that young man of yours.'

Funny, the policewoman thought, I can't ever remember mentioning Volffy in here, and she doubted that she would have mentioned his age even if she had. She wondered if Rock-a-Doc had brought the subject up. She'd be a bit cross if he had. She would have a word with him when they next met.

Chapter 53

The back door opened in a hurry, and a bedraggled form rushed in.

'Get the kettle on, mate, it's pissing down out there.' Even in a coat and under an umbrella, Shannen's knees looked blue. Adelina filled the kettle, put it back on its plinth and turned it on. The blue light came on.

Shannen threw off her sodden raincoat and left it on the floor. Her hair hung in rat's tails off her head.

'Don't tell me – I look like I just lost a wet T-shirt competition.' The girls grinned at each other.

'How's it been?' asked Adelina, as Shannen looked for a towel to dry her hair on.

'Oh, it's been a busy morning. You wouldn't have thought so in this weather, but it seems that johns will do practically anything to get in out of the rain, even take their trousers and pants off. I've had three already this morning. Tell you something; one of them was just huge.'

'Oh?'

'He was so big, like a baby's arm almost. I thought, you're never going to get that into little me. But he was kinda gentle, and we used a bit of jelly, and we got it in.'

'Oh?'

'And oh, I must tell you, I had the most monumental orgasm, fucking brilliant.' She shuddered for a moment. 'Sorry about that; still getting aftershocks.'

Adelina looked at the younger girl intently. 'Tell me about it. What was it like?'

'What do you mean? Have you never had an orgasm?'

Adelina looked at her shyly and a little sadly. 'No, I don't think so.'

'Oh wow, you have missed something, girl. Mind you, until this morning I'm not sure that I ever had an orgasm – certainly

271

not like that one.' Another shudder racked her. 'More after-shocks; pay no attention.' She thought about it. 'Well, have you ever had any of that grown-up's coke that you sniff up your nose?'

'No. Uncle Lev did offer me some once, but I didn't want it.'

'Oh, well, anyway an orgasm is like that, only more so, and it starts round your front bottom like electricity, and then spreads all through your body, and makes you want to scream and shout. No, that's not right.' She shuddered again. 'More aftershocks. Babes, you've gotta have one to understand.'

'And it was this really big bloke who did it for you?'

'No, he wasn't particularly big – just his, you know, thing.'

'And he didn't hurt you or anything?'

'I thought he was going to, when I saw it, but no. I felt a bit, you know, full, but when the orgasm came on, whoa.'

'What did he say?'

'Oh, something like "You liked that, did you?" Yeah, something like that.'

The kettle boiled. Adelina put a teabag into a mug and poured in the water while Shannen rubbed her hair with a towel. The phone went off, and Adelina said, 'Sorry about this, must answer it.' She pulled the phone out of the charger, and listened to it.

'Yes,' she said, 'he's in the other room, I'll take the phone through to him.' She walked through into the tea shop itself where Uncle Lev was sitting, deep in conversation with Yuri.

'It's Jerzy from the path lab. He wants to talk to you, Uncle Lev.'

Uncle Lev took the proffered phone from Adelina and gave her a slightly quizzical look as she walked back through into the kitchen.

'Hello,' he said. 'Lev here.'

'Jerzy here, from the path lab.'

'Hello Jerzy, what can I do for you?'

'Ah, Uncle Lev,' said Jerzy. 'Got some information for you. Can't stop long, they're coming in so fast it looks like even the corpses are dying just to get in out of the rain.'

'Get on with it, then.'

'Well, that boy who came in a couple of nights ago. Well, he'd not had sex with the girl. The blood on his todger was only on the top side, and not on the ball side at all, so it appears that he had lain with his knob up against her, but he hadn't put it in. There was also no semen in his urethra, so he had had at least a few pees since he last ejaculated. They don't think he did the damage they said he did to her. That's all I've learned about him since we last spoke, but one of the other two things I've got to tell you is that they brought Steff's uncle in during the night. Died of a head injury.'

'Did they say how he got it?'

'Haven't heard. You might be interested in the other one they've just brought in, though. Big Paki lad they fished out of the river. Two things about him. Huge schlong that could certainly have done any sort of damage to anybody if they weren't watching, and he had a pair of trousers in the pocket of his hoodie, which were slit down the outside of both legs so you could just pull them away. The police took them away in a plastic bag, but I did see them before they went. Just thought you'd want to know.'

'Yes, thank you, Jerzy, that's very interesting. I'll ask around and see if we're missing anybody.' He disconnected and called out, 'Adelina!' while waving the phone at the kitchen door. The girl walked through and collected the phone from him.

'Put that back on charge, girl,' he said.

'Yes, Uncle Lev.'

He took a hold of the back of Adelina's thigh for a moment, hard enough to stop her in her tracks.

'You look different this morning, girl,' he said. 'Is there anything you want to tell me?'

'No, Uncle Lev.' She felt very lucky that she had never been one to blush. She had also learned, for the entertainment of her dying mother, how to make interesting and amusing expressions with her face. She drew out her 'surprised innocence' expression and opened her eyes, which already dominated her heart-shaped face, just that little bit wider. 'What, Uncle Lev?'

'You look a little, shall we say, post-coital this morning. Want to tell me about that?'

'Me, Uncle Lev? What's that mean, Uncle Lev?'

'It means how you look the morning after a damn good shagging, especially if you haven't done it before.'

'Not me, Uncle Lev – Shannen was just telling me about some of her adventures, that may have been it.'

'You've got Shannen in there with you? What the fucking hell is she doing in there?' Uncle Lev leaped up and went storming through into the kitchen, Adelina following in his wake, trying to calm him down.

'What the fucking hell do you think you're doing in here, girl?' he shouted at Shannen angrily.

Shannen smiled with the insolence and insouciance of a girl who has just had the orgasm of her life and replied, 'I'm having a nice cup of tea.'

'But why are you in here instead of at work?' the old man shouted at her.

'Listen, I've spent the whole morning doing "man in girl" work, and as it's tipping it down out there, I thought I'd come in here and have a nice cuppa and dry off with my bestie Addie, who makes the best cup of Rosie ever. We've been having a little girl on girl gossip about men. I think I've earned it.'

'So you've been working this morning?'

'Three,' she replied, still rubbing her hair with the towel, and Uncle Lev deflated.

'Well, don't be too long about it,' he harrumphed and walked back into the shop.

'God, he can be difficult. You've been around him a while – is he always like this?'

'He's particularly scratchy today, I don't know why,' said Adelina slowly.

Shannen drank the rest of her tea and walked over to where she had thrown her raincoat. She picked it up and shook it. It was still drenched, which wasn't really surprising, as neither of them had made any attempt to pick it up and let it dry off. The rain was easing a little, they noticed, as they looked out of the window. Maybe she would give it a few minutes. Her knees had lost the blue tinge they had had when she came in, and any shivers she now had were aftershocks, and had nothing to do with being cold.

Adelina washed the mug and put it back on the rack. She sat on the stool, deep in thought. So a big one was no more painful than a little one once you got used to it, she thought. She felt encouraged by that. Maybe it wasn't going to be completely awful, then.

'Adelina,' came through the kitchen door. 'We need you to work out here.'

'Must go,' she said to Shannen. 'See you. Don't be a stranger.'

'I won't,' giggled the younger girl, realising probably for the first time in her life what it was like to have a real friend. 'Laters,' she added.

Adelina walked through the door into the tea shop, a cloth over her arm and a pad in her hand. It was only Yuri and Uncle Lev sitting there, but she played along. 'Yes, gentlemen,' she said. 'What can I get you?'

'Yuri here would like a mug of the tea that your friend speaks so highly of,' said Uncle Lev, loading the 'friend' with subtext. 'I would like a glass of my special vodka.'

'At this time in the morning?' she enquired, turning on her heel and getting out of the way before he grabbed her leg as he had done a few minutes earlier.

'Yes, I would like a vodka now,' he said testily. 'Who do you think you are, my wife? To be able to nag me like that, there are a number of other duties you will have to do for me as well.' Adelina shuddered and got the bottle out of the freezer under the counter. She poured it into the glass, and then went through out into the kitchen to make Yuri's tea. Shannen had gone, and so had her soggy raincoat.

In a moment the kettle had boiled, and the tea was made in a pot. She walked out with the tea things on a tray. Picking up Uncle Lev's vodka, she took them to the table. 'Cakes or biscuits?' she asked.

'No thanks,' said Yuri.

'Listen,' said Uncle Lev. 'You don't want to take any notice of what that girl has to say. She's a strange girl, not like us.'

'Oh, I wasn't taking any notice,' she replied. 'I was just listening. She's quite entertaining with her stories about a working girl's life.'

Yuri's expression said, 'Don't, just don't.'

Uncle Lev looked at Yuri as soon as he had tossed the cold vodka down his throat, and had his hand round Adelina's leg before she had thought to get out of the way this time.

'It looks like they found Mo pretty quickly,' he said.

'It looks like they did,' Yuri replied, 'but that was always possible. I don't think it matters very much. The important thing is that they found the girl's trousers. Let's just hope that they realise what and whose they are, and blame the whole sorry mess on Mo, which, as he's dead, will hopefully be the end of it. That was the point of rivering him.'

'Yes, I suppose so. What do you think, pretty thing?' he asked Adelina.

'About what, Uncle Lev?' she said, switching on her quizzical face.

'Good answer,' he replied, and patted her bottom. 'Now bugger off. Yuri and I have got man things to talk about.'

'Yes, Uncle Lev,' she said and cast a further glance at Yuri, who met her glance with one that read, *Not now*. She walked back into the kitchen and made herself a cup of coffee, which she felt she had earned.

Chapter 54

Tom tossed and turned, but sleep eluded him. He wished he was still on speaking terms with those drug company reps who used to leave samples about. He could really use a sleeping pill to knock him out just for a few hours. But did they ever leave samples of hypnotics? They didn't usually leave drugs that a doctor might take himself. He supposed that they were for a doctor to give to a patient for a few days just to see if they got any benefit from their new advanced product, which was still on patent, and therefore made more money for the drug company in question. Perhaps it might be an overnight supply for his box, given out waiting for a chemist to open in the morning – antibiotics or a painkiller perhaps. If that was the logic, then surely a sleeping pill was ideal. Patient phones up: 'Doctor, I can't sleep.' The doctor would pop out, give her a sample box and tell her to come round to the surgery in the morning and tell him how it went. That might have been the marketing logic. Who knows? He only saw reps from a distance nowadays, and they knew he wouldn't see them professionally, so they didn't bother him. There were a couple of reps who were his registered patients, but they were professional enough not to pitch to him during a consultation. He had no idea what either of them were selling now, or indeed which company they worked for. Certainly neither of them had commented on the old mug on his desk which he kept his pens in, which also served as a reminder to him of the dangers of listening to reps. It was a promotional mug for a drug that had been suddenly withdrawn from the market, following the unexpected deaths of a few patients who had taken it. Tom knew it was more by luck than judgement that he had never prescribed the drug himself. Maybe he had disliked the rep in question, he really couldn't remember, but he had hidden the mug in his drawer and forgotten about it, while the reps and their managers had come round en masse asking for all their promotional material back when the drug was withdrawn. A couple of years or so later he had found the mug in the bottom drawer, and it had found a role on his desk as a penholder – and a warning.

The bottom line was that he hadn't got any sleepers. In the end he got up and made a mug of cocoa, in the hope that a hot milky drink might do the trick. He had only four hours before he had to get up anyway to do his afternoon surgery, and then he was off to the rehearsal with his daughter, which, under normal circumstances, he would have been looking forward to. He was not looking forward to this occasion one bit. He had no idea what he was going to say to her.

He stirred the mug and sat by the kitchen table. At least the smell from the mug was comforting. He thought for a while. This was what he advised punters to have if they complained they couldn't get to sleep: a hot milky drink just before bedtime. The French, he thought, often drank this stuff for breakfast. When he was on holiday in France he was often offered it. He had always preferred the caffeine hit of a strong milky coffee as a breakfast accompaniment. The kids would tease him: 'You've had at least two cups, haven't you, Dad? We don't want you falling asleep behind the wheel.' As if! The Jenny he thought of at that moment wasn't as tall as she was today, and her hair was still long. The Jenny he had seen in those pictures last night was a completely different person now. It wasn't just the short hair; it was the bare breasts and the sexual activity. He knew she would have that short hair when he saw her in the evening, so with that hair he would imagine the rest of the new Jenny, and it was a Jenny he didn't much care for. He was desperate for a return to the old days when he was Dad, and they were 'the kids'. He wondered whether he was also wishing his wife was still in that daydream too. Well, certainly if the kids were still young and innocent, she would have to be there too.

He finished the cocoa. He couldn't be bothered to read the paper, but he realised he wasn't going to get to sleep. The images that haunted him were still there. He decided to take a shower and then come back down and make himself a proper breakfast.

He went back upstairs, and grabbed a towel off the towel rail, and sat down on the side of the bed for a moment, before having his shower.

He woke up three and a half hours later, entangled in the towel.

He looked at his watch. Oh hell, he was already late! He leaped into the shower and gave himself more of a lick and a promise than a real shower. He rapidly towelled himself off and threw his work clothes on. He was down the stairs and out of the front door in a jiffy. He climbed into his little car and headed off to Hampton, to the McDonald's drive-thru. He ordered a couple of quarter pounders and a large paper cup of coffee, then drove to the practice.

He walked into the staff common room. Having put his burger bag on the table, he found a china mug to pour the coffee into. The mug had a logo on it, which he didn't immediately recognise, but he assumed it was a drug company mug.

'Oh hello, doctor,' said a voice from the door. 'We didn't expect you in so early, so we haven't booked you anything till three.'

His mouth full of burger, Tom munched, but after swallowing, without choking, he asked, 'Are there any visits that need doing?'

'There were only two that came in this morning, and Dr Cross and Dr Shivalkar took one each,' said the receptionist, sitting down and opening her Tupperware box, revealing a healthy tuna fish salad. 'So there really isn't anything you need to do.'

'Prescriptions?' he asked.

'All done.'

'Incoming mail?'

'You can do that if you like, but there isn't a lot.'

He took another bite out of his hamburger, and quietly chewed.

'Good night last night?' she asked.

He thought for a moment about how best to reply to that one. Medically it had been a relatively easy night with relatively few sick people, but for Tom himself…

He thought about it and gave her the medical answer. 'Not bad. But you know how it is when you're lying around waiting for something to happen – you don't sleep even if it never does.'

'Quite,' she said, probably not understanding at all.

'What I'll do is finish these burgers, and read the mail, then I might go out again, and I'll be back in for three, if that's okay with you.'

The receptionist nodded.

Tom had decided to visit the Whildens, in the hope that Shuv was there. He had to tell somebody what happened last night, or he'd burst.

Chapter 55

Susie Green was feeling very contented with her life when she pulled up outside the house in West Town. She knocked on the door and Yasmin opened up for her. She was led through to the sitting room in the back, where Saeeda waved at her politely, smiled and grunted before carrying on sewing. She accepted the offer of tea, and sat down. Interestingly, Yasmin sat down too, so there was obviously someone else to make the tea.

Sorayya came out, resplendent in a dark blue and green iridescent sari with a matching headdress. She carried a tray with three mugs on. She was not intending to go to school dressed like that, surely? She would dazzle the rest of the class.

'I am having a couple of days off because of my brother,' she said. 'My teacher told my father that she thought it would be a good idea. I haven't put any sugar in the tea.'

'Thank you,' said Susie. 'I don't take sugar.'

'Well, you might want to, as I have made our traditional spiced tea and I think a bit of sugar helps the flavour.'

Susie sniffed at the tea; it certainly smelled different. She took a quick sip. There were other flavours in there as well as the tea. She could recognise cardamom and cinnamon. There was more too. It didn't contain a kick as such, so there weren't any chillies in the infusion, she thought, relieved, but it did taste quite sharp; yes, maybe a spoonful of sugar might help. After adding a spoonful of sugar and giving it a good stir, she tried it again. It didn't taste anything like the tea she was used to, but she was thrilled. It was absolutely delicious, and she said so.

'You must let me know how you make it like this,' she said. 'My mother would adore this, and even my father might like it, and he doesn't usually like anything…' she paused, 'so different.' She had just stopped herself saying 'foreign' in time.

Sorayya smiled and burst into a cloud of Punjabi at her mother, who was sewing, who replied equally incomprehensibly. Sorayya then turned back to Susie.

'My mother says she'll tell you later; she's busy at the moment.'

Susie wondered whether Sorayya had made the tea from a kit that her mother had prepared in advance, or whether it was reheated. It didn't taste like the tea that her aunt had reheated in the microwave, but then absolutely nothing tasted like that.

'So how are you doing?' she asked.

'All right, I suppose,' came the reply, as she sipped tea. 'How is that girl?' Sorayya looked Susie straight in the eyes.

'Which girl?'

'The girl who killed my brother – that girl.'

Susie thought for a moment. 'Still very poorly,' she replied, not giving anything away.

'Good,' she replied. 'I hope she dies too.' The venom that came out with that line was so totally opposite to the way Sorayya looked that it shook Susie to the core.

'Why do you say that?'

'She killed my brother, so she deserves to die too, especially as she was my brother's friend.'

'She was your brother's friend? How do you know that?'

'Because every day he came home from school he talked about the nice blonde English girl he sat next to. He said she was his multicultural friend, and he liked her a lot. Then his multicultural friend goes and kills him. Is that the sort of thing a friend does? Tell me that.' There was a fractured sob in the girl's voice.

'Not on purpose, no,' agreed Susie. 'Do you know how close they were? Did they do things together out of school?'

'I doubt it. Father would have had a fit if Az was going around with Q'fir girls after school. No, he came home on time every day and did his homework. He was a good boy, was Aziz. But he did talk to me about her.'

'What sort of things?'

'Well, he wanted to know how girls thought about things, and I kept trying to tell him that I had no idea how that sort of girl thought about anything. I'm a Muslim girl, and I don't think the way that Q'fir girls think. I don't think about sex and drugs and make-up and alcohol and stuff like that.'

'Why do you think Stephanie thinks like that?'

'Well, she would; that's who she is. White girls with their short skirts and their teasing ways – I could see the effect she had on my brother.'

'Did you ever meet her?'

'I didn't have to meet her to know who she was. Do you wear short skirts still when you're not in uniform, or are you married?'

'No, I'm not married.'

'Why not? Didn't your family want you to have children or anything?'

'I wanted a career first, to make something of my life before I settled down. Besides, I don't know whether I've met the right man yet.' She grinned at the girl, who scowled back.

'What has that got to do with anything? You will meet the right man when your family finds him for you. You don't have to worry about looking for one yourself. What are you going to know about choosing a man when you're only eighteen? You have no experience at all with men, apart from your brothers.'

'Huh?'

'Now, when you are as old as Mum here, then you will have enough experience of men, and you will be able to pick the right man for your daughter to marry, and you will persuade your husband which is the one you have chosen and why.'

'You know your parents will pick the right man for you?'

'Of course. They're my parents – why would they pick me a man that was no good?'

Susie thought for a moment. The idea of marrying a boy who had been selected by her parents appalled her. Even her drone sisters, as she called them, who had been baby factories since their late teens, had at least picked their children's fathers themselves. Admittedly Cheryl hadn't been very successful with her picking, at least as a long-term project, and her two children had been sired by different men. However, she had selected them both herself, as she would no doubt pick the unfortunate fool who would be the father of her third child – when she found one that took her fancy. Susie was beginning to understand some of Sorayya's life view, or at least the view she had been taught to believe. At least, she would have understood that view until yesterday afternoon, when Ms James had suggested that she and Danny were already an item. *Oh, Danny, to think that we might never have noticed what the other was thinking.* Maybe that was what Az and Steff thought of each other too. Maybe Az was Steff's secret love that nobody knew about. If she loved him, then why would she kill him?

'Do you know who they've picked for you?'

'Why would they have done that now? I'm only fourteen, and I've got a lot of growing up to do before I think about getting married and having kids of my own. I have to learn how to make my own variety of special spiced tea, to start off with. There are other things I have to learn how to do in the kitchen too. And that doesn't even begin to touch on what I'm learning at school. Maybe what I'm learning at school will help me to pick husbands and wives for my children in my turn.'

It is all rather confusing, isn't it? Susie thought to herself.

Chapter 56

Tom stopped outside the Whildens' little terraced house, disappointed. There was no police car in sight. He nearly turned round and left. He certainly thought about it. After all, he hadn't been asked to do a visit. In the end, however, he opened the car door and got out. He rang the doorbell.

'Oh, Dr Clark, fancy seeing you too today. Come on in.' Mrs Whilden hadn't had time to look through the spyhole and open the door on the chain. The door had just flown open. The smell of baking hit him as soon as he walked through the door.

'I'm so sorry for your loss,' he said.

'Thank you. But at least Steff's getting better,' she replied.

'Oh, how is she?' The latest bulletin from the ITU hadn't got to Tom's practice yet.

'Oh, she's fully come round and will be moved to a women's ward later on today. She's not in any danger now.'

'You've been up there this morning?'

'No, that nice Constable Flynn was here earlier on today, and she'd seen Steff before she got here. What a nice girl Constable Flynn is; I'm so glad she's our family liaison officer. Mind you, there's not much of a family left now really, is there? Do you want a cuppa? I've got some very nice buns to go with it, even though I do say it myself.' She proceeded to give him the rigmarole about cooking to relieve stress, and sharing what she had made adding to the stress relief.

The second batch of buns was flawless. It, and a cup of traditional tea, strong enough to please a builder, but without the sugar, was just what Tom needed too. He wouldn't share his stresses with his patient, but helping her relieve hers would do him good too. Munching happily on the bun, he asked, 'Are you likely to see Constable Flynn again today?'

'If I do, may I tell her you asked after her?' Mrs Whilden smiled gently at her doctor. She knew, as did most of his patients, that his wife had divorced him, and he had yet to find a replacement to fill his life. There was a sort of cabal in the Ortons of middle-aged women whose project was to find Dr Clark another companion.

Whether Tom was aware of the cabal was uncertain, but he didn't want to send Shuv his regards as a person; he wanted to see her as a police officer.

'Can you tell her I would like to discuss a legal issue with her?' It was after he had said this that he realised how what he had said might be taken, and he stuttered that it was nothing about Steff, or Craig for that matter, but that he really didn't know any police officers well, and she was the one he had met most recently.

'Of course, doctor, I'll tell her as soon as I see her.'

'Thank you for that.' He changed the subject back to Craig. 'So what happened?'

She trotted out the official story of the drunken return from pub, his fall, and how he had cracked his head on the mantelpiece. Tom drew in his breath and said 'How awful,' and 'You poor thing,' in all the right places. He then asked her whether she was all right.

'At the moment, I'm fine,' she said. 'The police are expecting me to break down in floods of tears or something, but that hasn't happened yet.' She looked at Tom. 'Good therapy, is cooking.'

'I must remember to put that on a prescription,' said Tom. 'Gastronomo-therapy: take once, three times a day. Probably cheaper for the NHS too.' He then stood up, drinking the last of his mug of tea. 'I must away, I've a surgery to start in a few minutes, but if you need anything, particularly if things get so stressful that cookery can't help, just give one of us a call. Whatever happens, you don't need to suffer – remember that.'

'Thank you, doctor, I will, and thank you for all your help, especially what you're doing for poor Steff. And,' she added, 'what you will be doing for her in the future, bearing in mind she won't be having any babies or anything. I don't suppose that will be much of a blow for her at the moment, but in the future it probably will.'

'As long as Steff is registered with the practice, she can count on our support.'

'And if she's not?'

'I suppose that depends on why she's not. If she's left the practice because she's getting a better service at a different practice, then I don't suppose she'll want us still being involved in her life.'

'But if she's moved away to go to university or something, and just comes back to stay for the weekend with her old aunt?'

'Then of course we'll see her if she needs to; that's not a problem.'

'Good to know. I'll let Constable Flynn know that you want to see her too.'

'If you would, that would be appreciated.' Tom let himself out of the front door and walked to his car. He climbed in thoughtfully and set off back to the surgery. He was very uncertain about Doris's mood, which seemed almost fey. That could be the sign that something unpleasant was going to happen. She was showing no sign whatsoever of distress at her loss, though whether kitchen therapy was an appropriate treatment, he had no idea. One thing he did feel was that somebody should be keeping a close eye on her. Whether it was appropriate that that person should be Shuv Flynn, he was uncertain. Certainly Doris liked her, but then Shuv was very likable. Whether, however, she was up to doing the surveillance job he had in mind for her, and whether he had any right to do so anyway, was less certain. She was a policewoman, after all; not a social worker, or a district nurse. Would she be able to spot if things were about to go up in flames, and if she did, would she know what to do?

He pulled up in the car park behind the surgery and let himself in through the back door. Sam followed him in.

'You know your Mr Whilden bought the farm last night?' Sam asked.

'Yes, I've just been round with his widow. Very strange; a total absence of grief reaction.'

'That'll come,' said Sam. 'That'll come. I'll let the nurses know, as I'm heading down to the office. The later the reaction, usually the louder the bang, and sod's law states that when the balloon goes up, nobody will have any idea where you are.'

Chapter 57

Sergei looked carefully around. Their last pass through the gold field had revealed nothing, and they were approaching it again on their next pass down the field towards the river. The rain had stopped and the sun was just about visible from behind a cloud. The ground was still very muddy, and they reckoned their clothes, caked in mud as they were, weighed at least half as much again as they usually did. The ball-barrow was still in their possession, and was doing sterling work ferrying potatoes back to the farm.

'I think if we find nothing on this pass, that's probably it,' said Sergei. 'They must have been here a very long time, and most of them will already have been picked up over the years.'

'At least since this area was reclaimed.'

'What do you mean?'

'Well, I was talking to this chap in the bar the other night and he was saying that the fens were under water until about three hundred and fifty years ago, and they were drained by an earlier generation of imported labour into Britain. They may have been paid with those coins.'

'That explains why the river looks more like a canal. Rivers don't usually run in straight lines. I wonder who those people were.'

'He said they were Flemish. They'd just finished reclaiming the land in Holland, and they needed something to do, so the English king invited them over to reclaim the fens too. Not a bad idea – at least they didn't go to war instead. Usually what happens when a group of men finishes a job, if there's nothing else for them to do, they go off and thump someone.'

'You talk to a lot of strange people in bars,' remarked Andrzej drily.

'Well, we were off to our new lives in the fens the following day, so it was a good opportunity to have one last drink with the lads before we left.'

'So they knew all about the gold?'

'I doubt they had the slightest idea about that, otherwise there would have been coachloads coming with us. But he did know a bit about the history of the fens.'

They were both picking up potatoes and putting them into the barrow, when Andrzej said, very quietly, 'There.' Sergei noticed what he was looking at and nonchalantly picked it up, along with the potato that was lying next to it. The potato went into the barrow, and the coin went into his pocket all in one movement.

'Sharp eyes, that man,' he said. 'We'll clean it up when we get home. We're going to have to wash these clothes anyway; they won't be fit for anything tomorrow.'

The barrow filled with potatoes, but they didn't see any more gold pieces. But that meant that they had found three so far. That surely meant that there must be more. One Flemish labourer couldn't have lost just three of them. Sergei wondered, as he picked up the handles of the barrow, whether they were going to find the remains of the Flemish labourer himself. That would at least be an explanation. He pushed the barrow up the furrow while his brother turned over more of the field with the fork.

Sergei reached the farmyard with his barrow load, and the supervisor said, 'Good, good.' Sergei noticed that the police car had finally gone, and there was no longer an annoyed sergeant stamping round the farmyard, glaring at everybody.

'Aha,' said a voice behind him. 'The barrow is back: we take this now.' Two strong Polish boys were standing behind him with a wheelbarrow full of carrots. One of them already had his hand on the ball-barrow as the supervisor passed it back empty.

'We take this one,' said the Pole.

'No, that's mine,' protested Sergei. Without any warning, the Pole pulled back his fist and punched Sergei squarely on the jaw. Sergei staggered backwards, bells ringing in his ears, to be caught under the arms by the man behind him. Unbalanced, when the man behind him withdrew his support from under Sergei's arms, he dropped to the ground. Instinctively expecting a kicking, Sergei rolled up into a ball. That wasn't what happened. The two Poles dropped on top of him, and in the next moment all three of them were kicking and punching and gouging at each other.

'What's this?' asked a voice behind him, pulling something from Sergei's pocket. He had found the coin. Sergei looked up at the supervisor for support, but he had already turned and was walking away. He was having nothing to do with a gang of brawling labourers. They could sort themselves out.

'This,' said the Pole, 'we take, and the ball-barrow we also take. In exchange you take our wheelbarrow, and we let you, at least for the time being, hang on to your life.'

Whether Sergei understood exactly what he said or not was uncertain, but he certainly got the gist of it. He was still lying on his side when the ball-barrow was wheeled away through the opposite end of the farmyard. He slowly, and painfully, climbed up the drainpipe that was next to him until he was on his feet. He picked up the handles of the Poles' wheelbarrow and limped back towards his brother.

Whether it was Sergei's limp or the wheel at the front end of the barrow that Andrzej spotted first, he wasn't sure, but when he did, he left the fork standing wobbling in the mud, and ran up the field towards his brother.

'What happened?' he asked. 'You weren't attacked by that policeman, were you?'

'The Poles,' said Sergei, spitting out a tooth. 'And they took the new gold coin.'

'So what did the supervisor say?'

'The bastard just walked off. I think all that going down was a little too much for his stomach.'

'So we've now lost another gold coin.'

'And the ball-barrow,' said Sergei, picking up a potato and tossing it angrily into the barrow. They swore at each other in Lithuanian until it became ridiculous and they finally laughed.

Andrzej looked at his brother's swelling left eye and remarked that it was going to look sensational tomorrow.

They filled the barrow with potatoes, but they didn't find another gold coin – and, much to their relief, they didn't find the coins' previous owner.

It was Andrzej's turn to wheel the next barrow load up to the farmyard. The supervisor was back, but would not meet the Lithuanian's eye. The Poles were nowhere to be seen. He didn't even make his 'good, good' comment as Andrzej emptied the barrow onto the scales. He just emptied it and passed the handles back to Andrzej, and made a gesture that could only be read one way: 'Go.'

Andrzej wheeled the barrow back to his brother.

'Found another one?' he asked.

'No.'

'We've got to keep looking, then.'

Sergei just grunted and, picking up a potato, tossed it into the barrow.

Chapter 58

Shannen heard someone shouting her name from outside.

'What?' she shouted back.

The pimp's head appeared round the door. 'Put on something less obvious,' he said. 'The boss wants to see you.' He shut the door. She opened the cupboard in the corner. She hadn't looked in there before, and like old Mother Hubbard's it was empty. She opened the bedroom door and shouted, 'Are there any less obvious clothes?'

The door to the room on the other side of the hall opened, and the pimp, who was called Dubya, reappeared, zipping up his fly.

'I hope that's another bog,' she said drily. He walked silently and crossly into her room, and threw open the cupboard door. He was momentarily thrown by the fact that it was empty. He walked over to the wooden chest in the bay window, and opened it. He pulled out a pair of jeans and a pullover, and threw them on the bed.

'There,' he said, 'they'll do. Get changed.'

Again he left the room, not apparently looking at her, though she could feel his eyes boring through her clothes despite his apparent lack of interest.

She took off the tiny piece of elasticated cloth that covered her midriff to the upper part of her thighs, and replaced it with the jeans. Were they her old ones? You could never tell with jeans. These fitted just like her old ones, but they looked a bit newer. Maybe they'd just been washed. She put on the pullover, and looked in the mirror for a moment. This was a changed look indeed. It took her back three days, to before she met Ruke.

Oh Ruke, where are you? When will I see you again? she thought sadly, looking out of the window. The weather was clearing up. The rain had stopped, which perhaps explained why the steady trickle of men coming through her door had also stopped. Opening the door, she shouted, 'Ready' as if she were a kid playing hide and seek.

Dubya reappeared from the other room, appropriately dressed, and said, 'Follow me.' They walked out of the front door, and set off in the same direction as she had about three hours before, when she had gone round to have a cup of tea with Adelina. He walked quickly, with her almost trotting in his wake; he had a much longer stride than she did, and obviously he was doing something he didn't want to be doing.

They walked in through the back entrance of the café, and went into the kitchen where Adelina was sitting looking at something on her phone, half an ear open for a summons from the café. Dubya eyed Adelina with a certain amount of approval, thinking, perhaps, that there was a girl he would have little difficulty selling, and wondered when he was going to get the opportunity.

'Hello, mate,' said Shannen to her. 'Be a love and put the kettle on.' The pimp looked at Shannen with a little more respect. This girl knew Uncle Lev's future prize? Well, well, well. He walked into the café.

'Back again?' asked Adelina. 'Who's he? That isn't your boyfriend, is it?'

'What, him? No, he's just the pimp.'

'Pimp? What's that?'

'I think he's supposed to protect us if one of the johns starts getting difficult. Dunno what happens to the other girls in the house when he gets summoned to see Uncle Lev.'

A voice came from the other room. 'Adelina, will you bring Shannen through? Don't bother making her a cup of tea; she hasn't got time for that.'

Adelina looked at Shannen and shrugged. 'Looks like Uncle Lev wants to see you straight away. This way,' she said, and led her through to the public half of the café. Yuri was sitting by the door, which had its blinds pulled down.

'Come in Shannen,' said Uncle Lev. 'I keep hearing good things about you – well done, girl, well done.'

Shannen smiled and wondered whether he would expect a curtsey. As she wasn't exactly sure how to do one, she just looked awkward instead.

'One problem with people with the very high work ethic that you have, my dear, is that you're at a greater risk of getting pregnant, and we can't be having that now, can we?'

'No, Uncle Lev,' she agreed. 'Does it really happen that easily?' she asked after a moment.

'Can do, my dear, can do. We never know how easily you might get pregnant until after it's actually happened – if you see what I mean.'

Shannen shrugged, and looked at Adelina, who also shrugged almost imperceptibly, after making sure that Uncle Lev wasn't looking at her.

'So what we are going to do is make sure that doesn't happen,' Lev continued. 'You're going up to the surgery to get an implant fitted.'

'A what?' she asked.

'A contraceptive implant.'

'What's that?'

'The doctor will inject, just under the skin, a contraceptive implant, which will stop you getting pregnant.'

'When's he going to do that?'

'Now, as soon as you can get there.'

'Won't that hurt?'

'Not at all – he'll use a little local anaesthetic, my dear, and you won't feel a thing.'

'So where is he going to do that?'

'In his surgery, or in your arm, depending on which answer you were looking for. Dubya, can you take her up there now? The doctor's waiting.'

Dubya looked at the girl and then Uncle Lev. 'Can I borrow a car?' he asked.

Uncle Lev tossed him a set of keys from the table in front of him. 'It's the little Peugeot with the sliding doors. It's out the back,' he said.

'What? The little-old-lady-mobile? Can't I have anything racier?'

'No. If you want a racy car, then you work hard and pay for it just like everybody else. And where did you get that stupid name Dubya?' Uncle Lev looked over the top of his glasses like a cross schoolmaster. Dubya knew only too well that you didn't make Uncle Lev cross if you wanted to avoid suffering a considerable amount of pain.

'You gave it to me,' he said, 'when you first took me on?'

'And why would I do a thing like that?'

'Cos you said that I looked as stupid as that American president, and so I might as well have his name.'

'Oh, yes, I remember.' Uncle Lev chuckled. Adelina and Shannen were deep in conversation.

'You want to come?' Shannen asked.

Adelina looked at Uncle Lev. 'Can I go with her?' she asked.

'Why on earth would you want to do that? You're in the middle of your working day here. Of course you can't, whatever are you thinking?' He looked at Shannen and the pimp. 'Now go, the doctor's waiting, and he won't wait forever. If you're too late, you'll have me to answer to, so get on with it.' With that, Dubya rushed through the door into the kitchen, Shannen in his wake, shrugging at Adelina as she left.

The car was out the back and the remote control opened the doors as they approached.

'Get in,' said Dubya. Shannen hadn't seen anything quite like the 1007 before, and belted herself into the passenger seat. She was even more amazed when the door shut all around her.

'How on earth did it do that?' she asked the pimp as he pressed buttons on the dashboard.

'Car's got magic buttons,' he said drily as he pulled out into the street.

They pulled up in the car park at the surgery, and as they got out of the little car, he said, 'Follow me,' and they walked through the entrance to the reception. 'Shannen McGinley here's got an appointment with Dr Klastru. He's waiting for her.'

'Take a seat,' said the receptionist without looking at them.

'He said to send us straight down when we arrived.' He locked eyes with the receptionist, who, for a moment looked straight back. Then her courage failed her, and she picked up the phone and pressed a button.

'Dr Klastru, I've got a couple of young people up here who said you were expecting them straight away.'

'Is it a girl for a Nexplanon?' he asked.

'Are you here for a Nexplanon?' the receptionist asked Shannen, who looked at her, bewildered.

'What's one of those?' she asked.

'Is that a contraceptive implant?' asked Dubya quietly.

The receptionist asked the same question down the phone, and then came back with one word: 'yes'. She told them to make their way down to Room 5, where Dr Klastru was waiting for them.

'Come in,' said Dr Klastru, 'and make yourself comfortable on the bed.'

'Do you want me to get undressed?' asked Shannen, feeling that this was an opening line she was expected to come up with all the time nowadays.

'No, not particularly,' replied the doctor. 'Are you right- or left-handed?' he asked.

'Right-handed,' replied the girl.

'In which case, it's going in your left arm,' he said. 'Are you allergic to anything: iodine, local anaesthetic, plasters or anything else?' he asked.

She shook her head. 'No, nothing that I know of.'

'So what we need is to take your left arm out of that pullover and lie down on that couch, with your left hand, palm up, under your head.' He wheeled a steel trolley to the side of the bed, pulled up a chair and sat down beside her. He looked at the pimp, and said, 'If you want to stand on the other side of her and hold her hand, then she probably won't jump.' He rubbed the inside of her upper arm with something cold, and then said, 'You'll just feel a little scratch.'

It felt like a wasp sting when he injected a local anaesthetic into her skin. 'Ow,' she said.

'You won't feel any more,' he said while he changed the needle on the syringe. He put a much longer needle on, and injected the inside of her upper arm, which was now completely numb.

The needle went up under the skin, and he withdrew it, injecting all the way. 'How does that feel?' he asked.

'Strange,' she replied.

'Good; that means the anaesthetic's working. Now, you may feel a little pulling, but that's all. If there's anything more, then tell me.' She felt him pinch the skin of her arm, and heard a click or two, and then he let go of her arm, and there was a soft clang as he put something on the trolley. She looked at her arm. He was holding a cotton wool ball on her arm, while securing it with a couple of strips of plaster. 'All finished,' he said, rubbing the skin just above the cotton wool ball. 'Feels in the right place. There, you feel it.'

She rubbed the skin where he was feeling, and she could feel a slender rod about the size of a ballpoint refill, just under the skin.

'Is that it?' she asked.

'That's the implant,' he replied. 'I'm afraid that, with these new implants, we don't get one outside the injector that I can show you. You should be able to feel that at any time while it is on board. Do check to see if you can still feel it from time to time, and if you can't feel it at any time, then come back and I'll check it over for you. It will need changing after three years, as you'll see on the card I'm giving you.' He gave her a small plastic card the size of a credit card. 'If you try to use it as a credit card, you'll be disappointed – it doesn't work, I've tried.' He chuckled gently. 'If you want to get pregnant, then make an appointment to come and get it taken out. If you want another one in three years' time, then you'll need an appointment to get another one fitted and have this one taken out at the same time.'

'Why will I need the old one taken out?'

'To be honest, because the manufacturers have no idea what will happen to one that has been left in for twenty years and forgotten about. Therefore when a new one is put in, then the old one that probably won't work for much longer is taken out. It's not a problem; it's the work of five minutes to take out an implant that has been put in by a trained operator like me.'

'What happens if I get pregnant?'

'You won't – that's the point of the whole thing.'

'But if I do?'

'Then we'll have a party, as you'll be the first person who has with one of those things.' The doctor chuckled again. 'If there are any other problems,' he said, looking at Dubya, 'bring her straight back.'

'Come along, Shanns,' he said. 'Time to go.' And they walked out of the room.

They were crossing the reception area heading for the door when they heard a voice say, 'Shannen McGinley? Is that you?'

Shannen stopped and turned.

'It's Mrs Patterson,' she said to Dubya, who had just grabbed her left arm. 'She's my social worker.' She didn't need to shake his hand off. He let go with an, 'Oh shit!'

'It is you, Shannen, where have you been? We've been looking all over for you. And what are you doing here? This isn't your doctor's practice.'

'Oh, I've just been having a nexpla-thingummy fitted,' she said.

'You've what?'

Shannen looked around for Dubya to ask him what the name of the device was, but he was gone. Looking out into the car park, she saw the little Peugeot pulling out and driving off.

Chapter 59

Siobhan walked back through the doors into the incident room.

'Oh, it's you,' said DI Drake. 'Haven't you got anything to do, Constable Flynn?'

'I'm reporting back, so that the records are up to date,' replied the constable, a little mortified.

'Constable Green's already using that excuse,' said Drake testily, waving a hand at Susie, who was busy at a laptop in one corner. 'Want to try again?'

'No sir,' she replied, 'but I'll put the kettle on and wait till she has finished. Would you like a cup of something?'

Damnable girl, he thought. She always has an answer for everything, and doesn't get flustered either.

'Tea,' he said. 'Strong and sweet.'

'Your wish is my command.' She paused. 'Sir.' She looked over to where Susie Green was sitting. 'Susie?'

'Huh?'

'Tea? I'm making a pot.'

'Yes, please.'

The room reverted to silence, apart from the sound of the kettle. In the end the silence got too much for DI Drake.

'All right, all right, tell me what you've found.' Siobhan had taken a deep breath in order to reply when the telephone rang. Drake picked it up.

'Yes?' he asked. Siobhan gently let the breath go.

'Dr Walsh here, divisional surgeon. I'm down in the path lab with Doctor Waterhouse, and we're going over Mr Whilden, who arrived during the night. Any reason why there might be fish scales in his hair round his head wound? There are also one or two in his clothing. Don't know which breed of fish they come from, yet, but we're suspicious.'

Drake put his hand over the mouthpiece. 'Flynn, were you going to say something about a fish at the Whildens, by any chance?'

Siobhan looked at him, surprised; this was the first time she could ever remember Drake making an inspired guess.

'A salmon, perhaps?' she replied.

Drake spoke again. 'Would they be from a salmon?'

There was a small buzz of conversation at the other end of the phone, and then Dr Walsh came back. 'Yes that would fit; anything else you would like to tell me?'

'Why don't you talk to Constable Flynn directly? It seems that she has all the answers – as always.' He passed the phone to Siobhan, and added, 'Dr Walsh.'

'Hello, sir,' Siobhan said. 'The salmon?' She added the last as a sort of prompt to kick off the conversation.

'Tell me about the fish,' Dr Walsh said.

'Well, Mrs Whilden said she was preparing and cooking the salmon when Mr Whilden came back from the pub, drunk. Apparently he fell into the mantelpiece. She didn't respond immediately; apparently being drunk is not uncommon for Mr Whilden, especially after they had had a disagreement. When she finally left the kitchen, and went to see her husband, she realised that he was not at all well, and tried to revive him. She obviously had fish scales on her hands and they were transferred to the victim while she was trying to revive him.'

'And where is this salmon now?'

'It's a cooked fish, sir; it's been eaten.'

'What? You mean Mrs Whilden has eaten a whole salmon since last night? They're not small fish, salmon, you know.'

'I'll take your word for it, sir, but she did have some help.'

'What do you mean?'

'Well, Sergeant Molinari had some fish, and Constable Watson. Then of course when the undertakers came to collect the body, they had some fish, and I'm sure Mrs Whilden had some fish too. When I got round there this morning, there wasn't any salmon left, so I wasn't offered any.'

'All right,' said Dr Walsh. 'I get the picture. Thank you, Constable Flynn.'

'Any time I can be of service, sir,' she replied, and passed the phone back to Inspector Drake.

'Well?' said Drake.

'Well, at a cursory glance, that would fit the picture. At least it's an explanation,' he said. 'Leave it with us, and we'll see if that all fits together.'

'Thanks, speak to you soon.' Drake disconnected, and watched Siobhan make a pot of tea. He was pleased that her first action had been to warm the pot by swirling boiling water round in it before pouring it away down the sink. She then put a good many teabags into the pot while re-boiling the kettle, and then poured the water into the pot on top. She stirred the mixture with a dessert spoon that was sitting on the table.

'Did you believe all that guff you came out with just now?' he asked.

'It all fitted what she had said. Mrs Whilden is very upset and she's just about managing to hold it all together. The girl to whom she is legal guardian is in intensive care, and her husband is dead. Life hasn't been very kind to her in the last few days. Her solution to being stressed is to cook.'

'And yet, you, her favourite policewoman, didn't get anything that she had cooked. Didn't you find that curious?'

'Bearing in mind I came after Sergeant Molinari, who has a rapacious appetite, no sir, not really. I had a cinnamon bun she had just made. Delicious.'

'So if I were to go round to Mrs Whilden's house, she would have something tasty for me to eat?'

'I imagine so, sir; do you want me to take you round and introduce you, sir?'

'No, don't be ridiculous, girl. I was merely positing a concept. I will not have my officers walking around to a victim's family's house and using it as a canteen. That is to stop as of this instant, do you hear?'

'Yes, sir.'

'So what else did you find out since you were last here?'

'Well, that was most of it, but Steff is continuing to improve, and will soon be transferred out of the ITU into the gynae ward, for further observation and nursing.'

'Is she under arrest?'

'No sir, of course not, sir, she's under sixteen. And she isn't going anywhere anyway, sir; she may be conscious, but she's not at all well, and I can't see her escaping anytime soon.'

Drake grunted. 'Fair enough.' As far as he was concerned, Constable Flynn was now just a machine to make tea for him, which he felt he richly deserved. Within the next five minutes the tea was in a mug in front of him, the sugar bowl beside it and the dessert spoon sticking out of the bowl.

Susie's mug was beside her, and she was told she could go and raid the sugar bowl when she had finished doing whatever she was doing, and vacated the chair so Siobhan could use the laptop. Susie grinned at her and said, 'Won't be a moment, promise.'

Chapter 60

Dubya took one look at Shannen and the middle-aged woman chatting and thought, *Oh shit! Time I wasn't here.* He let go of Shannen's arm and hustled out of the waiting room door. Within moments he was in the little Peugeot and was off out of the gate and down the road.

A few minutes later, he had parked in the car park behind the shop, and he was facing a growling Uncle Lev, trying to explain why he had abandoned Shannen in the waiting room.

'She was recognised by someone,' he said. 'What do you think the odds were of that happening?'

'Fairly high,' Uncle Lev replied. 'What puzzles me was that I didn't have a bet on you behaving like a complete twat! It was very simple: you just should have said, now come along, you haven't got time to stop here chatting to people, and pulled her out of there. Instead, in all probability, you've lost her. Who do you think this middle-aged woman is, hmm?'

'Dunno, but she knew Shannen, and seeing her stopped Shannen in her tracks.'

'Well, she could have been another doctor, or it could have been a nurse, only they tend to wear uniforms. Health visitors don't. Or it could have been somebody who knew Shannen, like a teacher from her school. It might have been a plain-clothes cop even. Did anyone think to check whether Shannen has a record? It's part of your job to keep people away from the merchandise when they haven't paid for it, or have no apparent intention to do so. Pillock! What do you think we ought to do with him, Yuri? Adelina? He's lost your friend – what do you think I should do to him?'

Adelina said nothing, and shook her head. She had never seen a situation like this before. Uncle Lev was as furious as she'd ever seen him. She wasn't going to come up with any suggestion herself. She was far more worried about what Yuri might suggest. Might his solution be a lot more frightening than anything she thought possible?

Yuri's suggestion was fairly simple. 'Don't you think he ought to go back to the house and make sure the other girls are all right? We can sort out what to do with him later.'

'Yes, I think that's right. Now, you had just better pray that those girls are all right, and they haven't run away, or someone hasn't gone in and abducted them.'

'Where would they run away to?' asked Dubya desperately. 'They've got nowhere to go. That's the whole point.'

'You'd better hope you're right,' said Lev. 'Now get the fuck out of here and we'll see you later when we've made a decision.'

The pimp disappeared out of the back, leaving the car keys on the table.

'I need a vodka,' Uncle Lev announced to Adelina, who was too scared to consider giving him any back-chat. She went and pulled the bottle out of the freezer.

Uncle Lev turned to Yuri. 'Do you think that woman was anything to do with Ruke?' he asked.

'Last time I was round Ruke's place, there weren't any middle-aged women there, and if there had been they would surely have been dressed in a sari. Dubya didn't mention a sari, but I can go and ask him. If she's gone back to Ruke's, I could go and get her and bring her back here.'

Adelina put the tray with the glass on the table beside Uncle Lev's right hand. He picked up the glass and poured the contents down his throat in one shot. He then slammed the glass back on the tray, which the girl picked up and stood back one pace.

'Another?' she offered.

Uncle Lev looked at her for a moment, and then softened slightly. 'What a good idea, girl. I don't mind if I do.'

Adelina hurried off behind the counter, and disappeared from view. The best vodka was kept in a bottle which nestled between various tubs of ice cream, which Adelina could never remember serving to anyone. They were, however, there if anybody official came to pay a visit.

'I think that's a good idea,' said Uncle Lev to Yuri, looking back at the Russian. 'But let's let it all play out first. If she is one of Ruke's scouts, then she may not have got Shannen back to Ruke yet, and if you turn up too soon, it will warn him.'

'You're sure Ruke isn't loyal to you?' Yuri asked.

'Ruke is loyal to Ruke,' Lev replied. 'If he was loyal to me, he would have been round already this morning to let me know that his sidekick Mo had gone missing. Have you seen him this morning?'

'No.'

'And nor have I. Tell you what,' he paused as Adelina put the tray down by his hand again. He swallowed another shot of vodka, put the glass back down on the tray, looked the girl in the eye, and said, 'Before you ask, no, thank you. A third would be unnecessarily self-indulgent, don't you think?'

'Yes, Uncle Lev,' said the girl, and walked off with the tray. Uncle Lev watched her depart, then turned back to Yuri and continued where he had left off. 'Tell you what, why don't you go round to see Ruke when you're taking Adelina home? That would give everything time to settle.'

'Yes, Uncle Lev,' he said. 'I could do that.' He thought for a moment and added, 'Thank you for giving him the Peugeot to use.'

'No problem,' replied Uncle Lev, and then looked slightly quizzically at Yuri. 'What do you mean, thank you?'

'Well, after dumping Mo in the river my prints would have been all over it, now it'll be his and Shannen's. There aren't that many of those sliding door Peugeots about, they never really caught on, and if someone had spotted it either in the surgery, or by the sluice, they might remember it.'

'Do you think I ought to dump it?' Uncle Lev asked.

'Either that or give it to Dubya as his permanent runabout. Is your name on the registration papers?'

'As if I would do a silly thing like that.' The old man chuckled. 'I don't even think it's on the log-book.'

'We could always arrange for its previous owner to pass it over to the little twerp so that it really is registered in his name.'

'Don't you think he would be a little suspicious?' asked Adelina, reminding the two men that she was still in the room, 'if you gave him a car for losing Shannen?'

The men looked at her. 'You know something, Yuri, that girl's not just pretty, she's rather bright. I might just hang on to her, to pass the business over to her to run it when I'm past it. Could you work for Adelina, Yuri?'

'I would think so,' he said, a gentle smile crossing his face. 'That would, of course, depend on what having that sort of power did to her head. Absolute power affects different people in different ways.'

'Would absolute power turn your head, Adelina?' asked the old man.

'I've no idea, Uncle Lev. I've never had any power so I've never found out.'

The old man chuckled to himself. He liked this girl; she was very special.

Chapter 61

'Where have you been, girl? Everybody's been looking for you all over the place.'

Shannen looked at Mrs Patterson, trying to gauge the mood underneath her anxiety and failing completely. 'Oh, I've been about.'

'And why have you been having a Nexplanon fitted?'

'That's easy,' the girl replied carelessly. 'To stop me getting pregnant, of course.'

The social worker put her arm round her shoulder and said, 'Ssh, not so loud. Come with me.'

'Where?'

'Shall we go and sit down and talk about this?'

'I've got to go.' Shannen was beginning to feel uncomfortable, especially when Mrs Patterson replied, fairly fiercely, that she hadn't *got* to go anywhere at all, but she did have to follow her and have a chat. 'Follow me now, child.' The use of the word 'child' cleared up any lingering doubts; Mrs Patterson was pissed off.

Shannen thought about trying to run, but decided against it. An attempt to run the length of the waiting room with Mrs Patterson shouting, 'Stop that girl!' wouldn't work. If she managed to get out of the entrance, where would that leave her? In the car park, that's where. And where would she go from there? She hadn't the faintest idea. She had been brought to the surgery by Dubya, and while they were driving here, she hadn't taken any notice of where they were. She had assumed Dubya would take her back to the tea shop when it was all over.

She followed Mrs Patterson through into the bowels of the surgery. Mrs Patterson opened a door into a small room with a desk and a few moulded plastic chairs with metal legs in a stack. There was a window that looked out onto a small tiled courtyard, with nothing in it apart from a couple more stacking chairs that looked as if they had been thrown out there when there had last been a boisterous party in the surgery. The legs had started to go rusty, and the colour had started to fade.

'Sit,' said Mrs Patterson, pointing to a chair.

Shannen did as she was told.

'Right,' said Mrs Patterson. 'You've just had a contraceptive implant fitted?'

'Yeah.'

'And this was to stop you getting pregnant if you have sex?'

'That's the idea.'

'You know that it's illegal for you to have sex?'

Shannen looked up, a little surprised. 'Sex? Illegal? How are babies made if it's not by having sex? My mum must have had sex for me to be here, and so must your mum. Are all our parents criminals then? Is it illegal for you to have sex?' she asked.

'No, but then I'm considerably older than you. It's illegal to have sex until you're sixteen.'

Shannen repeated the word 'considerably' under her breath, but Mrs Patterson heard her and glowered at her.

'Have you had sex already?' she asked.

'What if I have? What are you going to do about it?'

'Who have you had sex with? Have you got a boyfriend?'

'Yes.' Shannen stuck her jaw out defiantly. 'Who else would I have sex with?' I hope she doesn't answer that one, she thought. This woman's tricky.

'Who is this boy?' Mrs Patterson asked. 'Was it that boy you were with a moment ago?'

'Him?' Shannen asked, amazed. 'I don't think so! He'd just got the wheels to drive me here.'

'So you didn't have sex with him?'

'Of course not. I already told you, I've got a boyfriend.'

'So why didn't your boyfriend bring you here?'

A good question, thought Shannen. Why didn't Ruke bring me?

'He's at work,' she replied hopefully.

'So he's old enough to have a job?' asked Mrs Patterson.

'Yeah, he's cool and grown-up, is my Ruke,' grinned Shannen.

'Ruke? That's his name?'

'Yeah.'

'How long have you known him?'

'A few days.'

'And you've had sex with him?'

'Once or twice, yeah.'

Mrs Patterson stood up and paced around the room. 'Are you registered here?' she asked, looking at the girl.

'Registered? What's that?'

'Is this your doctor's practice?'

'No, I don't even know where this place is. The bloke with the car brought me here, and the doctor was waiting to do me.'

'The doctor was waiting to *do* you?' Mrs Patterson's eyes grew wider and rounder and her eyebrows almost disappeared under her fringe. 'I hope you got that wrong.'

'You know – fit the thingy in my arm.'

Mrs Patterson looked relieved. 'I misunderstand you; whew.'

'What?' Shannen giggled. 'You thought I was saying that that doctor had sex with me? As if!'

'Had you ever met that doctor before?'

'No,' Shannen grinned suddenly. 'There's a first time for everything.' She liked that phrase, and she was sure she would use it again.

'So you came here, never having met that doctor before, and he fitted a Nexplanon into your arm?'

Shannen thought. Another cliché came to her, so she used that one too. 'That's the long and the short of it, yeah.'

'So how did you know to come here?'

'Well, my uncle arranged it all.'

'Your uncle?'

'Well, he could hardly be Ruke's uncle, could he? Ruke being Asian and all.'

'I didn't know you had an uncle,' the social worker said, slowly trying to picture Shannen's file. She couldn't picture any names on the close relatives column, and someone as close as an uncle would certainly feature in there.

'What sort of uncle is he?' she asked. 'Is he your mother's brother or your father's brother?'

Shannen gave her a bewildered look. 'What? Or is he a monkey's uncle?' Mrs Patterson did not respond with the faintest inkling of a smile. Uncomfortably, Shannen continued, 'No he's not anybody's brother. He's an old bloke that we all call uncle, that's all.'

'Uncle? Uncle who?'

'Gawd, I don't know, just Uncle I guess.'

'Who else calls him uncle?'

'Well, Ruke, of course, and Addie.'

'Addie?'

'She's a girl who works in Uncle's shop. She's my friend.' She said the last three words very proudly.

Mrs Patterson was beginning to get a picture in her mind that she wasn't liking at all. 'This Addie, does she have sex with you?'

'Don't be silly; Addie's a girl. She's my friend. She's not my girlfriend.'

'No, I didn't mean did you have sex together, I meant in the same place.'

'No, Addie doesn't have sex, not yet. That's why she's been asking me all about it.'

Mrs Patterson felt somewhat relieved, she had obviously got that wrong after all. 'So where does this Addie live?'

'I don't know. All I know is she works in Uncle's shop.'

'And where is your uncle's shop?'

Shannen was beginning to realise she was being pumped for information and she was beginning not to like it. She was afraid she was going to get Adelina into trouble, without really understanding why, and that wasn't going to happen. 'In Peterborough somewhere,' she said vaguely.

'Where in Peterborough?'

Shannen looked sourly at Mrs Patterson. 'Listen,' she said. 'I haven't the faintest idea where we are at the moment, so how could I get you anywhere else from here?'

There was a knock at the door, and Mrs Patterson said doubtfully, 'Come in.' In walked Dr Klastru.

'Is there a problem in here?' he asked. 'The receptionist said you had brought this girl back into your office, and you were almost dragging her by the ear.'

'Yes,' said Mrs Patterson. 'This girl's in care, and had gone missing. It was by complete accident I saw her in your waiting room.'

Dr Klastru looked uncomfortable, and Mrs Patterson continued, 'You know this girl's under age.'

'What do you mean? She's seventeen.'

'She's not going to be seventeen for at least a couple of years,' said Mrs Patterson drily, 'so anyone having sex with her is guilty of statutory rape, and anyone colluding with that act could also be in serious trouble.'

'Are you threatening me, Mrs Patterson?' asked the doctor. 'If indeed she is under age, and indulging in sexual intercourse, then making sure she is adequately protected contraceptive-wise is paramount. If she is too young to have sex, she's certainly too young to be a mother.'

'You mean you're condoning this?'

'I'm not putting my own value judgements on any of this. It is not my place to judge other people's wishes; my job is to facilitate them so that they don't all end up in tears.'

'An interesting position to take, Dr Klastru. May I ask exactly where you would draw a line?' Fortunately, at this moment Shannen had an uncontrollable urge to cough, and the conversation stopped immediately.

'Come, Shannen, I think we need to go and see your foster parents, don't we?'

'Yes, Mrs Patterson,' said Shannen, and turned to the doctor and said, 'Thank you, Dr Klastru.' She trotted off after Mrs Patterson.

Dr Klastru walked back to his consulting room, uncertain whether to laugh or punch the wall. He picked up the phone and dialled.

'Hello, can you put me through to Uncle Lev please?' There was a pause, and then a voice spoke into the earpiece.

'Lev here.'

'Hello, Klastru here. I think we have a little problem. The implant went fine, so there's no worry there; however, the girl ran into her social worker in the waiting room, and they recognised each other. It appears, Uncle Lev, that the girl was younger than you told me. Two years younger, to be exact.'

'Oh well, you're getting paid so what are you worried about?'

'I'm not getting paid enough to wreck my career,' replied the doctor testily. 'I hope you bear that in mind.'

'Don't worry, it will all go away. What's more important, what happened to the girl, Shannen?'

'She went off with the social worker.'

'Do you know where they went?'

'They were going to Shannen's foster parents' house.'

'Fine, doctor, leave it with me, we'll take it from here. Thank you for calling, and once again, don't worry about getting into trouble. It's all under complete control.'

'Is that a promise? It doesn't seem to be anywhere near under control from where I'm sitting. Don't be in the least bit surprised if you hear that I've had words with the powers that be, to make sure you're under the proper control.'

'I wouldn't rattle the man's cage if I were you,' replied Lev. 'Take it from me, he doesn't take kindly being disturbed in the middle of a council meeting.'

Uncle Lev's calmness was having no effect on Dr Klastru's temper. 'As if I would bother to take any further advice from you,' he snapped and slammed the phone down. He swore, and thumped the desk with his fist. He then picked up the phone and started to dial again.

Chapter 62

Uncle Lev popped his fingers and Yuri looked up from his permanently cold, half-drunk cup of tea. Lev tapped his watch.

'I think it's time for you two to go,' he said.

Yuri walked through into the kitchen and tapped Adelina on the shoulder.

'Do you want to go through and kiss your uncle goodnight?' he asked. Her expression said 'not really,' but she walked through to the shop, and then reappeared at the door a few moments later.

'Let's go,' she said. They walked out of the kitchen to the car park, and got into the car that Lev always called Yuri's car, although Yuri had never claimed it as his own.

'So,' she asked, 'what's the plan?'

'Well, I think we go round to Ruke's first,' he said. 'If he's on his own, you can do a little training – that's if you want to, of course. If Shannen's in there with him, I think it might be more tactful not to mention your training tonight, don't you think?'

'I suppose so,' she said, doing up her seat belt.

Yuri pulled out of the car park and turned into the street. It took no more than ten minutes to drive to Ruke's house. As soon as he turned into Ruke's street, he pulled into the nearest parking slot and turned the engine off. There was a lot of police activity up ahead. There were at least two marked police cars parked carelessly, their roof lights flashing, blocking the street. There were three uniformed police officers in the street too, two talking to each other, the third having an animated conversation with someone on a walkie-talkie.

Yuri tried to work out which house was the cause of their interest. It soon became obvious when a door opened and Ruke was marched out in handcuffs, another uniformed policeman behind him. A couple of bystanders seemed to be taking photographs. Yuri vaguely recognised the shabbier of the two paparazzi. Ruke was pushed into one of the police cars abandoned in the middle of the road, and it promptly drove off, the other one in hot pursuit, leaving the rest of the police standing by the open front door, deep in conversation.

Yuri started the engine and drove up to the shabby man with the camera.

'It's Nick, isn't it?' he asked.

The man turned round and looked into the open window.

'It's my man Yuri,' the man replied. 'How's it hanging?'

'Can't complain. What's all this then?' he said waving his hand at the police. Yuri wondered what the appropriate collective noun for policemen was: a posse? No, surely not – that conjured up an image of deputies on horseback shouting 'yee-haw' and spitting. He had watched too many Westerns as a schoolboy, in order to learn English, to forget that image.

'I gather they've grabbed a slaver,' he said, and looked across at Adelina's coltish form strapped in the passenger seat. 'You're not a slaver too, are you, mate?'

'What, her? No, she's my sister's kid, I'm taking her home from work.' They grinned at each other and Adelina put on an amused expression.

'How did you know they were going to make an arrest this evening?'

'Got a tip-off, didn't we? Sort of "teddy bears picnic" type of invite.'

'Huh?'

'If you go down to the woods today, you're going to get a surprise. Except they told us the address to park outside and wait – and, yes, cameras were permitted, cos they were going to take down a child abuser and slaver. And it would probably be the one chance we'd get to take usable pictures of him before the bastard "lawyers up".'

'You mean you got an invitation from the police to the takedown?'

'That's the long and short of it, yes.'

'What happens if he isn't a paedophile and a slaver?'

'We've got it all on film, so they must be pretty fucking sure of their facts.'

'They sure must. Anyway, I'll see you, Nick. My sister will be getting twitchy.'

'Yeah, see you.'

Yuri squeezed the accelerator and drove to the far end of the road, where he turned left. 'Well, that's the end of that,' he said. 'I doubt you'll see your chum again, I'm afraid.'

'Why? What will happen to her?'

'Well, she'll probably go back to her foster parents, or some different foster parents, somewhere else altogether. They'll probably get someone to take out her implant, and kind of change her back to being a kid again.'

'Will she accept that?'

'Christ, I don't know. You tell me; you know her as well as anybody.'

'I've no idea,' she said after a moment's thought. After a while, she spoke up again. 'So what happens now with my training? Have you got a condom on you?'

'Of course I have – I'm a man who has sex with men, remember.'

'So will you do my training with me, please?'

Yuri slowed down and looked across at her, surprised.

'Me? Have you taken leave of your senses, girl? I don't do that sort of thing, you know that.'

'This isn't a pleasure thing,' she replied, quick as a flash, 'you know that. It's a thing to train my bits to be ready to receive anyone that Uncle Lev wants to pleasure with them.'

'I don't do it with girls, remember.'

'You don't do it, for pleasure, with girls; I do know that. I'm not doing it for pleasure either, just remember that. I think you would be gentle with me, and wouldn't break me, like that brute Mo did with that poor girl down on the riverbank.'

'How the hell did you know about that?' asked Yuri, amazed.

'I listen to conversations. I may be the shop eye candy, but I'm not deaf, you know.'

'I think we'd better be careful when we talk around you, hadn't we?' said Yuri with a grin.

'So,' she said, 'are we going to do it then?'

She wasn't giving up, was she? Yuri thought.

317

'Look,' he said. 'I've got a very big knob, and I don't know how it would fit you. You're not a very big girl. And,' he paused, 'you've done it more times with a member of the opposite sex than I have.'

'I've done it precisely once, yesterday evening.'

'As I was saying, more times than I have.'

'What?' she said, surprised. 'You've never done it with a woman?'

'Nope.'

'So why haven't you? You're fairly gorgeous in your own way, you know.' She looked at him.

'And that comes from someone who knows about the problems of being gorgeous herself,' he replied drily.

'Anyway,' she said, 'you were saying?'

'I was at school, and we had communal showers after sport, and I played a lot of football. Quite good at it, I was. Anyway, another boy spotted me. He was quite impressed.'

'And?' she asked, as Yuri had stopped, and did not appear to want to go any further. He didn't reply, so she said it again.

'And?'

'Well, we did stuff together, and I rather liked it.'

'And?'

'Apparently he did it with one or two other boys too, and one day he got caught and arrested. I heard that they were rounding up all the other lads he had been doing it with, so I made myself scarce, and here I am.'

'You mean, that's why you're here, as in Peterborough here?'

'Uncle Lev is a lot more open-minded than the bigots back home, you know.'

'But it's a very long way to have come to get away from your past.'

'But for whatever reason, we both ended up in Uncle Lev's café. Homosexuality is still frowned upon in Russia. Didn't you hear all about the demos that were held before the Sochi Winter Olympics?'

'Didn't come to anything though, did they?'

'I don't know. All the gay athletes were able to compete without fear of arrest. That was a positive result of the demos.'

'Hmm,' she said thoughtfully. Then she looked at him cheerfully. 'So are we going to do it, then?'

'You never give up, do you?'

Adelina grinned at him. 'Nope,' she replied. 'Are we going to do it, then? We can do it in my room; I don't think the girls will object. They'll know it's just for training purposes.'

'And how will they know we're just doing it for training purposes?'

'Because I'll tell them, of course. I also trust them not to grass us up to Uncle Lev.'

Yuri looked at her as he pulled up in the car park in front of the block of flats in Viersen Platz, just across the river from Charters pub, and a few yards downstream from where Steff had been so brutally assaulted three days before.

She was looking at him expectantly, but not in any way flirtatiously. She was not trying to seduce him: that, he could have resisted. She looked like a friend who needed his help, and that was really unscrupulous.

'Come on, then,' he said, and got out of the car. 'Just remember,' he added as he locked the car door, 'I have no idea what I'm doing, so you're going to have to tell me if I'm doing anything wrong.'

Chapter 63

Tom drove up to the rehearsal hall and went in. He couldn't remember the last time he had less looked forward to a rehearsal. His ex-wife had already dropped Jenny off – there she was, deep in conversation with two of the middle-aged men in the company, the chap who she was 'chums' with in the play and the man who played Gregory, the victim – who, up until last night anyway, Tom had always found to be a very likable chap. In the play Gregory played the funniest stage corpse Tom had ever seen. The script called for the murder to take place in view of the audience, and the corpse was examined and pulled about on a number of occasions 'post mortem' by various characters. The cast of the play outside the melodrama, so to speak, was instructed to leave Gregory in as uncomfortable a position as possible, and the corpse was to try to make himself more comfortable, and at the same time the actor playing the corpse was really beginning to lose his temper. It was a very funny bit of acting, but right now, Tom was no longer amused.

He walked over to them and looked down onto the top of Gregory's head. He was wondering whether Gregory's head was really the one in the photograph. He couldn't be sure. There were so many other balding middle-aged men in Cambridge. If it was him in that photograph, he would kill him soon enough anyway.

'Hello, Dad,' called Jenny cheerfully as she spotted him walking across the room. It was a simple rehearsal room. There was no stage, and indeed no real room for an audience, just chalk marks on the floor. Tom still remembered the director calling to him once: *Tom, Tom, love, you've just fallen off the stage! You're still supposed to be sober at that moment.* When he looked down, he was standing well on the wrong side of the chalk marks.

There were moments when Tom wondered when they would actually get pieces of set to interact with. Part of the comedy was the cast's interaction with an over-built set, and its destruction.

He walked over to Jenny, who looked up at him, welcoming him into her conversation. She was typical Jenny, bubbly and exuberant. She had always managed to relate to adults as adults, but she had mastered this when she was very young. She had learned, when her younger brother had been little and very cute, that in order to compete with him she had to become a very grown-up and rather severe seven-year-old. Her brother was now fourteen, and already taller than she was. He was well-enough muscled to get a bouncer to rear up off the middle of the pitch against a cricket team at least two years older than he was.

'Hello Dad, Bill brought me direct from school,' she said cheerily. Yes, that would be right, thought Tom. Most of the men in the company were either school teachers or parents of the youngsters, which was, of course, where he fitted in.

'Well, at least I can take you home again, I'm not doing an all-nighter tonight after all. I did that last night.'

'How are you feeling?' she asked, concerned. 'Did you get any sleep today?'

'A bit,' he said. 'I'm okay,' but he really wasn't. However, it was nothing to do with a lack of sleep that was making him feel so ropy.

In the end, he could stand the tension no longer. He took hold of Jenny's left wrist, and pushed the sleeve of her pullover up past the elbow. The skin of the inside of her lower left arm was pristine. There was no bruising, no needle marks, nothing. He looked at it for a moment, not understanding. Then he got it: his daughter had very even features, maybe the photo had been switched. You would never tell if it was a mirror image or not. He dropped her left arm, grabbed her right wrist, and pushed the sleeve up.

Jenny pulled her arm away crossly. 'Dad, what do you think you're doing?'

Tom was looking at an equally unbruised right arm. He didn't understand what was going on.

'Uh, nothing,' he said.

'I'm afraid that's not good enough, Dad,' she said. 'I know what you do for a living. I know what you're looking for. What I want to know is why.'

The sight of Jenny losing her temper with her father caught everyone's attention. She had both sleeves of her pullover rolled up beyond the elbows, and with her balled fists planted on her hips, in her blue top she gave the perfect impression of a Wedgwood sugar bowl. Everyone was watching, wondering what would happen next. She was staring straight at her father, who was looking at his feet.

'Why do you think I've been taking drugs?' she asked furiously. 'That's what you're checking for, isn't it? I want to know who has been telling you what and when.'

It was just the wrong person who tried to stand between them to make peace. Gregory told them to calm down, sounding even more ineffectual than Michael Winner in the TV advertisements. If he had called them both 'dear', which is not unheard of in theatrical circles, Tom would have hit him on the spot – well, on the jaw. He stood up and faced Gregory down. Gregory stepped back a couple of paces. Tom followed, maintaining their nose-to-nose position.

'Dad! What is the matter?' Jenny asked from behind him. Tom stopped and sagged into the nearest chair. He couldn't get it out of his head that he had seen Gregory in that photo, copulating with his daughter – and, probably more distressing, Jenny had seemed to be enjoying the experience. But then in the photo Jenny had a large injection site bruise on her left arm, and his daughter had no such injury. The girls had identical faces and haircuts, and Tom knew his daughter did not have an identical twin. His daughter's hair had been shoulder length when he saw her a week ago, and he only knew about her haircut because she had sent him a selfie. The logic was bewildering. Even if the photo had been taken ten minutes after her hair appointment, that bruise wouldn't have faded between then and now. The logic was inescapable: the girl in the photo was not his daughter. Somebody had been photo-shopping the image.

He looked up at Jenny, who was rolling her sleeves down.

'Sorry,' he mumbled. 'I'll try to explain later, when I've worked it out properly. Meanwhile, shall we get on with the rehearsal?' The second sentence was aimed at the others.

'It's not quite that simple,' said Gregory. 'That was tanta-mount to an assault that you did there. Even if she has been injecting drugs, she is entitled to some privacy, and you had no right to expose that to the rest of the company.'

'But she hasn't,' said Tom, and then realised what that meant; he himself understood that now. It wasn't Jenny in the picture. He had come very close to exploding at Gregory, but just managed to remain silent and not say what was on the tip of his tongue, about Gregory's right to screw his daughter. He doubted his daughter would ever have forgiven him for that.

'Settle down, everybody,' said the increasingly anxious director, trying to silence the cast. 'Mrs Griffin, are you organ-ised for tonight?' he asked a grey-haired woman in a tweed skirt and sensible brogues who had been present at the previ-ous three rehearsals, but as far as Tom could remember, hadn't uttered a single word.

'Yes,' she replied.

'Everybody, this is Mrs Griffin, and she's the prompter. Today, she'll be working you all quite hard, as we're going to do this rehearsal off-book.' Sooner or later, every play had to be rehearsed without the cast holding their scripts in front of them. They all knew that the time had come for rehearsals to get serious. Tom was willing to give it a go, and he knew Jenny had been 'off-book' for the past fortnight, but he knew some members of the cast were still some way from knowing their lines.

'Is Mrs Griffin going to play the part of the prompter where it is scripted?' asked the stage manager, who had read the prompter's part up to then. Bill, who played the part of Jenny's chum, would also be interested in knowing that, Tom mused. After all, part of the business of his part, and thus Jenny's part, was concerning the actor he played mishearing a prompt, and cutting out a sizeable part of the play as a result.

'I suppose that depends on how the next few off-book rehearsals go,' he replied thoughtfully. 'You're just going to have to be a not-very-amateurish amateur dramatic society, aren't you?'

Tom breathed easily. Bryn, the director, had seized the tension in the room, without understanding anything about it, and had changed it to be about the play and the rehearsal: very clever.

Chapter 64

Yuri walked from the kitchen to the café. Uncle Lev was still there, scratching numbers on a piece of paper.

'You took your time about it,' the old man snapped. 'Excuse?'

'Well, sort of. Ruke's in custody.'

'Nasty little shit deserves to be behind bars.' The old man stopped and looked at his henchman. 'All right, tell me what happened.'

'Well, I dropped Adelina off first at her flat down by the river, and then drove up to Ruke's place in Walton. The place was surrounded by coppers – loads of uniformed coppers were there with police cars and lights flashing all over the place. They were making a huge song and dance about making this arrest. It was very public indeed; there was nothing discreet about it at all.'

'Did you recognise anyone there, like Drake?'

'No, I didn't recognise any of the pigs, but my mate the newspaper man, Nick Fowler, was there waving a camera. That's where I got the gen from.'

'Looks like that little Shannen's a write-off, then. I'm going to bash that Dubya when I next see him. We lost two promising kids this week.'

'Huh?'

'That Shannen, she seemed to get off on being sold for sex, I don't think we'll see her again, and that girl they picked up after school and then Mo split in half. We won't see her again either.'

'We never actually saw her at all, Uncle,' Yuri replied drily.

The phone beside Uncle Lev rang suddenly. He picked it up and immediately switched into obsequious mode. 'Yes, councillor, anything I can do for you, councillor.'

'I need a girl, tonight. I've got a man flying in and he'll need some company. If he decides to bring his business to

Peterborough, it will mean a lot of jobs and a lot of money coming into our fair city.'

'Yes, councillor, so how can I help?' Lev's piggy little eyes were already adding up the extra money he would make, turning the children of these new workers into drug addicts.

'This man has a taste for young flesh. Can you help us out?'

'Ooh – bit difficult, that. Our best little worker got picked up by her social worker this afternoon, and another girl I had high hopes for is … unavailable. I've not got anyone else you'd call young. He wouldn't like to spend time with a genuine Brahmin Indian princess, would he? Very pretty, and a very skilled entertainer, I am assured.'

'From what I understand, he's a bit of a racist pig about his sexual encounters. Good thing he doesn't actually employ his workforce; he has menials to do that. How about that girl in your café, the skinny Slovakian girl? I bet he'd just love a crack at her.'

'Oh, she's … er … not really trained for any of this yet.'

'All the better. If she's really raw, he'll just love it all the more. Course, if you really can't help, I'll take my ten grand elsewhere.'

'Your how much?'

'The council's got a lot riding on this business coming home, and I've got a free hand, no questions asked, to make it happen.'

'Yuri,' Lev said, his hand over the mouthpiece, 'go and get Adelina and make her dress up young – you know, that flowery summer dress, white ankle socks, sandals – and bring her back here. Chop chop.'

'What are you doing, Uncle Lev?'

'It's happened – we've got her a contract, now go.' He reverted to talking on the phone again. 'My man, he's gone to get her. Poor little thing, she'll be in bed now, so he's going to have to get her up. She should be here in fifteen minutes.' He shouted, 'Fifteen minutes' after the vanishing Yuri.

'So, tell me about the business we are all contributing our little bit to.'

'I think, Uncle Lev, this is one of those occasions when careless talk costs lives. I've put my client up in the Bishop's suite in my town centre hotel, and in half an hour you will deliver the merchandise to him. Once he has had his fill, he will release the merchandise back into your care, and the following day you will get your money. She will not ask the client for money, though if he offers her some, she can take it. That will not reduce what I will pay you in any way. There may even be a bonus for you if we land the contract. How does that sound?'

'So how will we know she was satisfactory?'

'I'll phone you tomorrow after I've seen him again. I can read this man like a book, and I'll know whether or not he had a good night. And, talking of good nights, you remember which room I told you to take her to?'

'Yes. The Bishop's Suite. Incidentally, is that really your hotel?'

'You'd be surprised.'

'And the Bishop's Suite? The old boy would be rolling in his grave if he know what was going on in there now.'

'Why do you think the Bishop needed a suite in a luxury hotel? What do you think the old bugger got up to, with all those dear little choirboys? Anyway, goodnight then.' A click came from the telephone. Lev sat silently in his room, alone. *Oh, shit,* he thought. *It's happened; an offer I couldn't refuse.* He tried to think up all sorts of apologies to Adelina but, dammit, that was what she was there for. It wasn't her fault that she had got under his skin so badly. Serves me bloody well right for feeling so bad about this, he thought. A businessman should never get emotionally tied to his merchandise. It hasn't happened often, and it certainly won't happen again.

Ten minutes later she appeared. All the make-up had been scrubbed off her face, and she was looking endearingly child-like in a summery floral frock with white ankle socks and sandals. She looked at him with ill-disguised contempt – and if it was ill-disguised, then she meant to look like that. The one thing she had learned, even before she had arrived in England, was her skill in facial expression. 'I suppose you're making a lot of money out of this deal,' she said.

'What do you think?' he replied, and turned to Yuri, after theatrically looking her up and down once. 'Very nice. Deliver her to the Bishop's Suite at the town centre four-star. Can you hang around there, and take her home when he's finished with her?'

'Yes, Uncle Lev.'

'And, Adelina, my dear, as you're working tonight, you don't have to come in to work here tomorrow. Catch up on your beauty sleep. Now go, the pair of you.' And the enforcer and the victim shuffled out.

As Adelina settled in the car, she said, 'Well, this was what my training was all about wasn't it. Thank you, by the way, for this evening.'

'You sure I didn't hurt you?'

'Honest, you didn't. Let's hope that this john doesn't either.'

'Fingers crossed.'

'Oh, and if Lev thinks I'm not coming in tomorrow morning, he's got another think coming. I'm coming in just to show the old bastard what he's done to me.'

They pulled in through the back entrance to the Bull. He gave her the room number, and told her he would be in the bar, waiting. She grinned at him, but it was a brave grin, the grin of a Christian walking into the Coliseum expecting to be greeted by lions.

'See you later,' she said, and she was up the stairs and gone.

Yuri walked into the bar. Why didn't she raise a ruckus? he wondered. She could easily have jumped up and down, especially dressed like that, and said 'this man is delivering me to be screwed by a fat plutocrat staying in this hotel – help me!' One or two of the women sitting in the bar, and it was obvious why they were there, would gladly have thrown her out – after all, she was unfair competition. He ordered a cup of coffee and sat down at a table that was visible from the door. The waitress delivered the coffee, and asked for his room number.

'I'm not resident. I'm a driver, and my client has asked me to stay available until he tells me I can go. He said he would refund my coffee bills in the morning.' He paid the bill with cash from his wallet. She looked at him sympathetically. There were far more people working in a hotel than met the eye. He glanced at the hookers sitting by the bar. They weren't as young as they looked, and to be honest, they didn't look that young.

He had another three coffees, and was beginning to tingle, when Adelina reappeared, two and a half hours later. She looked as if she had been crying. He put his arm round her shoulder, and led her towards the back door.

'Is she all right?' said a voice behind them.

Yuri turned round. The maître d' was looking at them.

'Yes,' he replied. 'She's just had some really bad news, and I'm taking her home to her mum. Today was to be such a great day, and it's now all turned to ash.'

'Oh, I'm so sorry, hope you get home safely, dear.'

And with those platitudes ringing in her ears, they made their way to the car.

'How was it?' asked Yuri. 'What was he like?'

'I hope for your sake you never know,' she replied. 'He was East Asian, Chinese or Korean or something, middle-aged and paunchy. You were so nice and caring – even Ruke was nice enough. But this bastard didn't care a fuck about me; he just cared about having his thing stimulated. Nobody even considered teaching me about oral sex! Do you know what that stuff tastes like?'

Yuri looked at her awkwardly as he drove out of the car park. 'Well, yes I do, actually – man who has sex with men, remember?'

That got a whisper of a smile out of her. 'So he didn't have penetrative sex with you?'

'Oh, he did that too, both ends, and I think he may have discovered a few other holes I wasn't aware I had before tonight. He'd already stuck that thing up my arse before he made me suck it. Can you imagine what it tasted like?'

'Oh my God, honey, I'm so sorry.' He paused. 'Hang on, wasn't he wearing a condom?'

'It wasn't still on when it reached my mouth – I think it may still be up my bum.'

'Do you want me to have a look when we get in?'

'You know, it's funny, but no thanks. I felt really quite proud of how I looked when you saw me earlier this evening. I'm really not so much now. I think I'll have a quick look with a mirror on my own. It'll all come out when I take a dump anyway.'

'Oh Adelina, you have no idea how sorry I am.'

'It's not your fault; it's not even Uncle Lev's fault, really. It's the business he took me on for, and he managed to keep me away from it for quite a long time. I can understand why it leads girls to want to take drugs to forget how disgusting they feel. I feel foul, and I'm going to have a hot bath when I get in. In fact, I may have three hot baths, one after the other.'

'Are you sure you want me to bring you in to work tomorrow?' he asked. 'You can just as easily stay at home and recuperate.'

'Listen, sunshine, if you're not here on the dot tomorrow morning, I'll know you're on his side. Incidentally, the john gave me a fistful of banknotes – what should I do with them?'

'I think you bring them in tomorrow and give them to Lev and see what he says. If you're in luck, he might tell you to keep them as a tip, as that was a contract hire.'

'What's that mean?'

'Someone bought your services as a payment or a bribe for the guy you just did it with. He wasn't supposed to pay for anything.'

'What a sick world we live in,' she muttered as they pulled up in the car park outside her flat. She leaned over and kissed him on the cheek. 'Thanks for everything,' she said. 'I'll see you in the morning, and I'll be dressed to work in the café.'

'Sleep well,' he said.

'Oh, I shall sleep the sleep of the just,' she said, 'and the sleep of the just after.' She forced a grin, but Yuri could tell that it was an act. She tapped the combination that released the door, and she ran up to her flat.

A baseball bat appeared from Jameela's room, followed by Jameela.

'Oh!' she said, relieved. 'It's you. You're very late in.'

'I've been at work.'

'This late?' Then Jameela saw how Adelina was dressed and the bags under her eyes. 'Oh, that sort of work.'

Adelina nodded. 'That sort of work. I think I've still got a condom stuck up my bum.'

'Oh, you poor love, do you want me to have a look?'

'Would you mind terribly?'

'Come on,' and they both went into Adelina's room.

Adelina removed her clothes and bent over the chair.

'You know something,' said Jameela, 'put a tail here and you would look like a thoroughbred racehorse from this angle.' Adelina felt her buttocks being eased apart. 'Yes, here it is.' She felt something being pulled out.

'How does it look?' she asked.

'A little red and sore, but no major damage. How does it feel?'

'A little sore, and undignified. That's about it.'

'We're going to have to do some different training, aren't we?' said Jameela, looking Adelina straight in the eyes.

'What do you mean?'

'Well, you've learned the mechanics. What you now need to learn is the skill of becoming a high-class escort. You don't want to be a cheap tramp turning tricks and that's that. You've got the natural skills, I've known that all along, and whether you like it or not, you've got the looks to appeal to the paedophile line of the market. Now what we need to do is teach you the social skills to go along with that.'

Jameela thought for a moment and then left the room. She was back in a moment with a camera.

'What's that for?'

'You're going to need a card to prove you're over eighteen for buying wine and stuff, especially if you're going to be made to look a lot younger.'

'But I'm not – I'm only seventeen.'

'Not a problem; this card will say you're nineteen. The john will probably be impressed anyway if he thinks you're really fourteen.' She pointed the camera at her and pressed the button twice.

'Oh thanks,' said Adelina crossly. 'I've not got anything on.'

'It's only going to be a mugshot. They won't see anything below the neck. I'll get these off to my mate, and he'll knock you up a fake driving licence tomorrow. Now, don't think a fake driving licence immediately turns you into a racing driver. You'll be no better at driving than you are now. The other thing it would be handy to learn is how to appear to be drinking more than you actually are. More than once, my john has drunk practically the whole bottle himself, and passed out on the bed before we've even got undressed. Now, I'll run you a nice hot bath, and we can talk about this more tomorrow. What do you say?'

Adelina burst into tears and threw her arms around Jameela's neck. 'Thank you,' she sobbed. 'Why are people being so nice to me?'

'Because, despite where you find yourself at the moment, underneath it all, you're a very nice girl, and don't you ever forget that.'

Chapter 65

'Sarge, look at this.' The constable turned round from the desk he was examining.

The sergeant was still testy with the constable since the constable had abandoned him at the farm with no means of getting home, earlier that day.

'Have you found a spare set of car keys?' he asked drily.

'No, sarge, but—'

'And have you found other evidence that this lout has been kidnapping kids with nefarious intent?'

'No, sarge.'

'Then why should I be interested?'

'Just look.' The constable was holding a large curved Arab dagger, a wicked edge on its concave side. 'What do you think of this?'

The sergeant became interested very rapidly. 'Let me see.' Holding it in his fingertips, wearing blue polythene gloves, the constable passed the weapon over to the sergeant. 'Nasty-looking thing that, isn't it? You could do someone a lot of harm with one of those – slit them open like a fish on a riverbank, couldn't you?' He glared at the constable, who missed the jibe.

'Beautiful handle and scabbard, though, isn't it? That's got to be lapis lazuli, don't you think?'

'What are you on about?'

'The dark blue on the scabbard?'

'If you say so. Bag it anyway. If it turns out it's nothing to do with the case, we can always return it when we apologise for arresting the bugger. A thing with a blade like that probably qualifies as an offensive weapon anyway.'

'Will do, sarge,' said the constable. He dropped the dagger into a large Ziploc bag and put it in the open case lying on the bed, which dominated the room. The knife came to rest on top of a laptop. 'Sarge, if you were a pervert, where would you hide the pictures you had taken of underage kids?'

The sergeant looked up again at the constable. 'Not being a pervert, I haven't the faintest idea,' he replied testily.

'No, I know, but just for a moment, say you were?'

The sergeant wondered whether this pipsqueak was actively trying to piss him off. If so, he was doing a damn good job of it. 'Where did you find the dagger?' he replied.

'Top shelf of the wardrobe, sarge.'

'Well, that just may be where he hides things, always assuming he was trying to hide the dagger. Have a closer look up there and see if there's a shoebox or something. That's where you would hide things, in a shoebox, isn't it, constable?'

'I don't hide things, sarge.'

'Quite,' replied the sergeant drily, rummaging through the large chest of drawers in the bedroom. He had hands full of socks, shirts and smalls, but nothing apart from clothing, and one or two condoms. There was a copy of the Qur'an in the bedside table – at least, he assumed it was a Qur'an. It was printed in a language he didn't understand, and on very thin 'bible' paper. He hadn't found any other books at all, not even a novel of any sort. There were no magazines either. He was vaguely disappointed not to have uncovered a copy of *Guns and Ammo* – that was the sort of magazine he expected to find in Ruke's house.

'Somehow I'm a little disappointed with all this,' he said. 'I'm going to try the other bedroom. Finish off here before you come through.' The sergeant went out. He saw a pair of size ten boots at the end of a pair of dark blue legs coming down the loft ladder.

'Anything up there, lad?' he asked.

'Bugger all except dust,' said the voice that followed the legs down. 'Don't think anybody's been up there in ages, even to service the water system, which is the only thing up there. That seems to be working okay.'

'Plumbing expert, are you, constable?'

'Had to be recently,' the constable replied. 'My mum's plumbing went funny the other week, and dumped a whole lot of water through the ceiling in the spare bedroom. She called a man in, and I went round there to make sure he fixed it properly and didn't rip her off. Got a few of his cards, incidentally, if anybody else needs a good plumber. I would recommend him, and I'd trust him in my house, even if I couldn't be there to supervise.'

'A trustworthy handyman in Peterborough?' muttered the sergeant. 'Whatever next?'

The constable slotted the hatch back down, and then pulled the ladder out. The hatch slotted back in place. The sergeant went into the other bedroom. There was little there apart from bedclothes in the built-in wardrobe. The bed was not made up, but had an uncovered duvet and pillows on top of a mattress. He walked back out onto the landing, and put his nose into the first bedroom.

'I'm going down,' he said. 'Bring the evidence case with you when you come.'

'Will do, sarge,' said the constable from inside the wardrobe.

The sergeant made his way downstairs and joined the others. He shrugged his shoulders. 'Nothing up there apart from a laptop, and a strange Arab dagger. Any joy downstairs?'

'Looks like he used this place to crash, and that's about it. There's food in here, standard groceries and stuff.'

'Any drugs?'

'Haven't found any, but I guess we can go round here again tomorrow with a sniffer dog. If he's tricky enough to be dealing in young flesh, he's not going to be stupid about where he hides his drugs. How else would he get to live alone in a house like this? Even if he rents it, he's got to get his money from somewhere. I can't find anything to suggest a job or anything. There aren't any bank statements, utilities bills, cheque books or anything that suggests that this guy actually exists as a human being, apart from food and clothes.'

'And an Arab dagger and a laptop.'

'Exactly. I wonder whether he's got another place somewhere else.'

'That had crossed my mind too,' said the sergeant. 'And he just uses this place to bring his victims to seduce them and

337

clean them up. Let's hope that there's some information about that on the laptop.' He shouted up the stairs. 'Come on, constable, we've gotta go, and bring that case with you.'

'Coming,' said a voice from upstairs. 'Don't go without me.'

'As if I would,' he called up, and then dropped his voice. 'I would, but he's got the evidence case, hasn't he?'

The constable came galumphing down the stairs with the case held out in front of him. 'Here's the case, sarge,' he said.

'Come on then,' said the sergeant. 'Lock the front door.' He took the case off the constable and put it in the boot of the police car. 'Now give me the key of the house,' he said. 'You don't think I'm going to trust you with a set of keys twice in one day, do you?' He put the keys to the house in his pocket and climbed into the front passenger seat of the car. The other police officers climbed into the back. That left one seat: the driver.

'I haven't got any car keys,' said the constable plaintively.

'I have,' said the sergeant, and tossed them on the driving seat. 'Now take us to Thorpe Wood, and don't break anything – even speed limits.'

Sergeant Warwick was waiting for them in the Children's and Young Persons' office. He passed the laptop straight to the evidence team to do their wizardry on. If there was anything hidden on there, their pet hacker would find his way into the nooks and crannies of the laptop. He had learned his craft on the other side of the legal tracks, and had only come over to work for the police because any other option would have involved a fairly long stretch behind bars.

The dagger interested Warwick. It was a beautiful thing, and he wondered why it was the sole personal possession of any note in the house, apart from the laptop and the large flat screen TV and DVD player in the sitting room. They hadn't even found any DVDs to play on it, apart from a copy of *Dirty Dancing*, which was still in a cellophane wrapper. They'd put it into a Ziploc bag anyway. Warwick put on a pair of lenses and looked closely at the blade. It had been recently sharpened, and not by a professional, he thought. The blade edge was, in one or two places, a little jagged. That's interesting, he thought, there's a little fibre caught there. With a pair of fine tweezers, he pulled the fibre off and put it into a tiny Ziploc bag.

'Take that down to the lab,' he said to the constable, 'now. We need to find out exactly what this bloke was up to – and where. His house seemed too good to be true, and the only evidence we have against him at all is Shannen McGinley's word. I'd like more than that. I don't think his lawyer will let us hang on to him at all with just that, even if he's only one selected by the court as a defence attorney. Somehow, I think a bigger, much more powerful, defence lawyer will pop up out of nowhere on his side.'

'Yes, sarge,' said the constable, and left with the little bag in his hand.

Chapter 66

It was evening and Steff was now able to sit in the chair beside her bed. She had a book open on her lap, and was reading by the light over her shoulder. The curtain was partly drawn, so as not to disturb the woman in the bed next to her, who had been asleep ever since Steff's arrival from the ITU.

'Do you need any painkillers?' asked a nurse who was wheeling a white trolley around the ward.

Steff thought about it. 'Not at the moment, no. Am I going to regret saying that in two hours' time when I'm in pain, and you and that trolley are nowhere to be seen?'

The nurse smiled at her kindly. 'No, don't worry, I'll note down you haven't had any now, so if you need some in two hours, you'll be quite entitled to have some then. There will always still be somebody here; all you have to do is press the button.'

'Thanks for that,' said Steff, who was feeling better by the hour.

***

Dr Waterhouse looked up from the microscope.

'Well, there's a thing!' he exclaimed.

'What?' asked the technician, who was busy packing up his things to go home for the night. He was concerned that whatever the old man had found would require him to stay on, and there was a football match he wanted to watch on the box that evening.

'This piece of thread that Sergeant Warwick just sent down to us...'

'Yes?'

'It matches the trousers we found in the pocket of that fellow they fished out of the river this morning.'

'So that links both cases?' asked the technician.

'And we already know that those trousers, before they were cut, were being worn by Stephanie Flack. And now we have found the knife that cut them.'

'DI Drake will be insufferable after all this, won't he?' remarked the technician drily.

'How do you mean?' The pathologist suddenly wasn't sure where this was all going.

'We've managed to pull all three major cases together under one umbrella: Operation Riverbank, the body in the river, and now the child abduction case. If he's not careful, he's going to get promoted, and then where will we all be with Chief Inspector Piddle-Snotty, trying to lord it over all of us?' Dr Waterhouse groaned. Heaven forbid, he thought, as he picked up the phone and called Sergeant Warwick. Warwick, however, was delighted.

'Great news. That means we not only have a good reason to hang on to Farooq Ahmed indefinitely, but also, I can pass him upwards to the homicide team, and I don't have to do loads of paperwork myself.'

Following the call from Dr Waterhouse, Sergeant Warwick leaped out of his chair and raced round to the Operation River-bank incident room, in case someone was still in there. He was in luck. There sat Sergeant Odembe, and he was talking to DI Drake himself.

'What are you doing in here?' asked Drake.

'I've got your villain downstairs in the lock-up,' Warwick said, grinning from ear to ear.

'What do you mean, our villain?'

'I think I've found your killer,' said Warwick and explained.

'And he's down in the lock-up?'

'He certainly is. I was looking for reasons to keep him, because in my case it was simply his word against my victim's. Suddenly we have all sorts of reasons to hang on to him, including his involvement in two homicides and a very serious grievous bodily assault. I don't think even Cherie Blair could talk him out of prison in the near future.'

'What's Cherie Blair got to do with it?'

342

'She's a Queen's Counsel, isn't she?'

'Oh, I see what you mean. I didn't know she defended killers.'

'I don't suppose she does, but that isn't the point. I thought QCs were supposed to be very influential.' Warwick was back-tracking and feeling uncomfortable all of a sudden.

'What did I tell you about trying to be funny with DI Drake?' said Odembe to his friend. 'I told you that you'd have to explain the joke, and a joke broken down into little pieces simply isn't that funny.'

'And what do you mean by that?' Drake rounded on the Nigerian.

'See what I mean? Not explaining any further, boss,' he said, and turned back to Warwick. 'But we'll take it from here, thanks.'

***

Sergei was lying on his bed in a towel. One thing he loved about Britain was the ease of having a hot bath. His bruises were going down. Because it had been a chilly wet day, there was a queue for the bathroom so he hadn't been able to take very long in the bath. He had yet to learn the old public school adage, 'He who baths first, baths fast.' He didn't suppose that people towards the back of the queue would get hot water in their bath, but at least he had and was now lying on his bed. Moreover, Sid hadn't taken their envelope that day either, but he had handed out a food bag as before, so they even had a little money as well as their sausages and bottles of beer. Life was getting better and better. Andrzej looked at the gold coin. 'Where do you think we could sell this?' he asked.

'Why do you want to sell it?'

'To make money, of course.'

'And where would we keep the money we make from selling it? And also, people would know we had money then, whereas the only people who know we have that coin, right now, is you and me. We're going to have to find a place to hide that coin. It's much easier to hide a piece of treasure that nobody knows about than a wad of money that everybody knows about. Am I right?'

Andrzej agreed he was right, unscrewed the cap from the top of his bottle of beer, and took a long pull.

***

The rehearsal had gone okay, especially for the Clarks. Tom hadn't fallen off the stage even once, and they had both remembered their lines. Various other members of the cast had a pretty rough time for their first experience off-book. Tom and Jenny were driving back to her house, when she asked him, 'What was that all about, Dad?'

'What, you mean looking for injection sites?'

'Yes.'

He thought about it, and then told her only what she needed to know.

'I was shown a picture earlier on today, of you, and you had injection sites on your arm.'

'But I haven't,' she said.

'I know that now, but it was of your head – and it was you with your new haircut, not the old style.'

'Okay…'

'So I suppose someone had Photoshopped a photo of your head onto a picture of somebody else's body. I had no idea that it was possible to do that sort of thing so well, so I believed it was a genuine picture.'

'But where would someone get a picture of me from?'

'Well, you sent me a picture of you with your new hairdo, didn't you?'

'Well, that was a selfie, just from my phone to yours.'

'And God knows how many other phones besides. You must have heard all about the *News of the World* phone hacking enquiry?'

'Well, yes, but that's a big thing. Surely nobody would bother hacking the phones of a small-town GP and his school-girl daughter! Be reasonable, Dad.'

'You're probably right,' he agreed, 'but then who knows what people's motives are? You have to be careful, Jenny, and you really shouldn't be sending selfies – you have no idea where they'll end up.'

'Yes, Dad.'

***

'Right,' said Siobhan, clearing away the dishes. 'I'll put these in the dishwasher, and tidy up down here. Volffy, you go on upstairs and scrub yourself down in preparation for whatever is going to happen next.'

Shuv heard Volffy climbing the stairs, and she breathed out slowly. She sat down on a kitchen chair and took her boots off, then her socks, tucking one in each boot. Usually she changed out of her uniform before sitting down to supper, but tonight she had been late in and was famished, so she just went for the food as soon as she got in. Of course, sitting eating across the table from him had meant her mind was on other things...

She wiggled her toes at herself and giggled quietly, and then stood up. She then unbuckled her belt and took off her trousers. That would save time when she got upstairs. She was about to start on her shirt buttons when she stopped. No, he could do that; he needed to do something to get his rewards.

She picked up the trousers and put them over her forearm, picked up her boots and started to climb the stairs, her tawny legs reflecting the moonlight that shone through the upstairs landing window.

Chapter 67

Uncle Lev stared gloomily at the newspaper. He really wasn't interested in anything in it. He had no idea why they even published that one; the only news it ever carried concerned the sexual antics of footballers, politicians and WAGs. Why politicians' nocturnal activities were considered more important than their policies defeated him even further. Maybe he would have to go and order himself a proper newspaper, as well as the cheap ones he ordered for the café.

'Morning, Yuri,' he said as Yuri walked in from the kitchen.

'Morning, Uncle Lev, have you been here all night?'

'Pretty much,' said the old man. 'I couldn't sleep much. Did you sleep okay? And what's more important, how did last night go from your point of view? How's Adelina?'

'Why don't you ask her yourself?' Yuri replied.

'How? She's not come in after last night, has she?'

'Why should I not be here?' said a familiar Slovakian voice from the kitchen door.

'Adelina!' exclaimed Uncle Lev, leaping to his feet, wearing the largest smile she had ever seen on his face. 'How are you? How did it go? Why are you here today? I gave you the day off.'

She looked at him sourly, not showing any of the excitement that the old man appeared to be feeling. 'I work here,' she replied. 'Of course I should turn up for work.'

He looked her up and down. Her hair was as immaculate as ever, her make-up, a light touch, no more than she usually wore, was perfect. Her clothes, however, were unkempt, and her tights were laddered. She was making an obvious statement. 'Come here, girl,' he said. She walked over as Uncle Lev sat back down. 'Why have you come to work looking like that?' he asked, putting his right hand round her thigh. 'You look like you were at it all last night, and then came straight here, and I know that wasn't the case.'

She slapped the wrist holding her leg, and pulled it away.

'I don't think you have a right to touch me there any more,' she snapped.

'I think you'll find that I can touch you anywhere I damn well please, young lady. I still own you. That's what last night was all about.' He made no further attempt to get hold of her physically again, though.

'In which case, this is yours,' she snapped, and threw a handful of banknotes at him from the purse on the belt at her waist.

'What's all this?' he asked her, picking up the money.

'It was what the Korean gave me last night.'

'He gave you all this?' said Uncle Lev, wide-eyed.

'Where else would I have got it from?' she asked.

'It's yours, girl – you earned that. Put it all back in your bag and put it somewhere safe. Don't get it mixed up with the takings from the café.'

'You mean you don't want it?'

'Of course I want it; it's money, isn't it? It's not mine, though. It's yours; you earned it. I'll let you into something, though; that Jameela at the flat where you stay has access to a cash savings scheme, which I can recommend. Tell her I pointed you in her direction.'

The phone rang and Adelina picked it up. She listened to it for a moment and then passed it to Uncle Lev.

'It's for you,' she said.

'Hello,' said the old man down the phone. 'Oh hello, Signore… Yes, that was she… Oh, really? … Well, thank you, Signore, I'll tell her straight away. Thank you… Oh, I'm sorry to hear that… Yes, I've got one here.' He picked up a pad and noted down what looked like a telephone number. 'Well, thank you very much, Signore, I'll make sure they all know. See you soon.' Uncle Lev looked at Adelina and Yuri.

'Well, my children,' he said. 'I understand you did well last night.'

'*You* might think so,' said Adelina sadly.

'No, really – the Korean signed the contract first thing this morning, and gave the entertainment the councillor set up last night as one of the main reasons for his choosing Peterborough. He would never put that in writing, of course, but he did say that he would like to see you again, my dear.'

Adelina groaned and rolled her eyes.

'And moreover,' Uncle Lev continued, 'he wants to put a monopoly on your services.'

'What does that mean?' the girl asked, still cross.

'He's happy to pay for you not to work on the street. He wants your services – exclusively. He hopes you will be able to show him some of the other delights of Peterborough when he is next in town.'

'I still don't understand.'

'He wants you to be his professional escort when he's in Peterborough, and he wants you to be his entertainments director as well. Think you can do that?'

'Oh, joy unbounded,' she said glumly. 'So you're going to sell me to him?'

'Not at all, my dear. You're still going to work for me, and you're still going to look after Jameela and the girls; you're just not going to do anything like you did last night with anyone else.'

'Do I have to do it with him? I hated every moment of it, you know.'

'In which case, you're going to have to train him to treat you how you would like to be treated, aren't you?'

'Oh yes? And how do I do that?'

'Well, you've already started at escort school, haven't you?'

'What exactly do you mean by that?' she said, her voice dripping acid.

'Don't go all coy on me; you know exactly what I mean. I wouldn't have put you through last night if you were still a virgin; you do know that, don't you?'

Adelina whirled round and glared at Yuri. 'You told him?'

'No, he didn't,' said Uncle Lev. 'There is *nothing* that goes on round here that I don't know about. And Yuri, don't worry, I'm not going to expect you to do that sort of business with either sex for me. That's not the job of an enforcer, is it? Mind you, if you want to help this young poppet out with her studies, I won't object.' Yuri looked at his feet. 'Oh come on, cheer up you two – this is a great opportunity for the pair of you.'

'How come?' Adelina was still boot-faced.

'Over the weeks to come, you've got to go and find your way round all the nightspots and restaurants in Peterborough. You've got to learn which restaurant is the best, and find out about their wine lists. If it turns out he has a taste for sweet white wine, then you'll need to know where you can get it. If he has a taste for Thai food *and* sweet white wine, you may have to become known by a Thai restaurateur so that you can get them to order some Sauternes or a German Beerenauslese in specially for him. If it turns out he's into claret, then you'll have to find out which one he particularly likes. Maybe he will be entertaining other people for his business. He will expect you to make him look brilliant – think you can do that? We will make sure that his contract prevents him from selling you to anyone else. With a bit of luck, you'll learn how to get him so drunk, he won't be able to diddle you even if he wants to.'

'So how am I going to be able to afford to do all this flash dining?'

'As I said, I have money, and you are still my employee. Yuri, you're going to have to take her out to dinner tonight. If I get a bill from McDonald's, or Burger King, I'll be cross. I'll get you a credit card too, my dear, and you can have a clothes allowance too.'

'And how will I pay you back for all this?'

'My dear girl, you already have. You gave the performance of a lifetime last night, and right now, because of you, my business is thriving. What I need you to do is keep the Korean happy, and occasionally titillate the odd police inspector who puts his nose in here. You don't have to do anything with the plod, just look nice, as you do. And while you're about it, you must go and get out of those dreadful stockings. There's a new pair in the kitchen. Go and put them on now, and wipe that sour expression off your puss. You haven't just been raped, that was hours ago, and you have no idea how sorry I am about that.'

'How do I avoid getting pregnant or getting an STI from the Korean?' she asked.

'You will be well-equipped with condoms, and if you like, we'll arrange for a contraceptive implant to be put in, like your friend Shannen had. It's not going to be fitted by the same doctor that fitted Shannen's, I'm afraid. I understand he had a car accident in the early hours of this morning on the A47. However, we appear to have access to a different doctor, who I'm assured is at least as good as that unfortunate fellow. Would you like that?'

'I'd feel safer,' she said.

'You can also do your "homework" without getting up the duff too,' said Uncle Lev drily. 'We could hardly go telling the Korean that you were being saved for only him, when there you are with a little pot-belly. I imagine with that tiny little body of yours, you'd probably start showing after eight weeks or so.'

Adelina didn't blush, but if she ever had the tendency to blush, that would have been the moment it would have happened.

'Phone,' said Uncle Lev, holding out his hand. Adelina passed it to him. He dialled the number he had written down on the piece of paper.

'Hello,' he said. 'Is Dr Clark there? I understand he's expecting a phone call from me.'

About the author

Following a highly successful career as a GP, R.M. Cartmel returned to his first love, and took up writing again. He is now the author of five novels, with a sixth coming out in Spring 2019.

He writes two very different series. The first, The Inspector Truchaud Mystery Series, features a French policeman based in Paris but closely involved in the family vineyard in Burgundy. Cartmel, a lifelong wine buff, introduces fascinating details of viticulture and wine-making alongside his well-plotted, charming crime cosies.

The first three novels in the Truchaud series are set in the small Burgundy village of Nuits-Saint-Georges. The fourth takes the French Inspector to the Rhineland vineyards of Boppard, to investigate the murder of a colleague.

The second of R.M. Cartmel's series, North Sea Noir, is a long way from Truchaud's 'wine and crime', both in tone and geographically. The first book in the North Sea Noir mystery series is *50 Miles from Anywhere* (first published under the name Michael Cayzer), which describes in harrowing detail the dark underbelly of contemporary Peterborough over the course of four days. *North Sea Rising* is the second in the series.

Books by R.M. Cartmel

The Richebourg Affair (2014)
The Charlemagne Connection (2015)
The Romanée Vintage (2017)

50 Miles from Anywhere (2017)
North Sea Rising (2018)

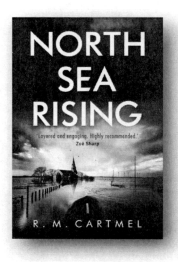

North Sea Rising

by R.M. Cartmel

North Sea Noir mystery series 2

Set forty years in the future, the landscape of the Great Britain, both political and geographical, is very different from the one we know today. The United Kingdom is united no more, and the rising sea level has drowned whole communities on the East coast.

When an eminent novelist is found dead on the eve of her much-acclaimed book launch, Steff Flack, a private eye, and Siobhan Flynn, the local chief of police, combine forces to solve the murder, and find themselves faced with some deadly criminals who will stop at nothing to turn a profit - even if that profit is soaked in blood.